CHRISTMAS IN Carling

A Tale of Two Seasons.

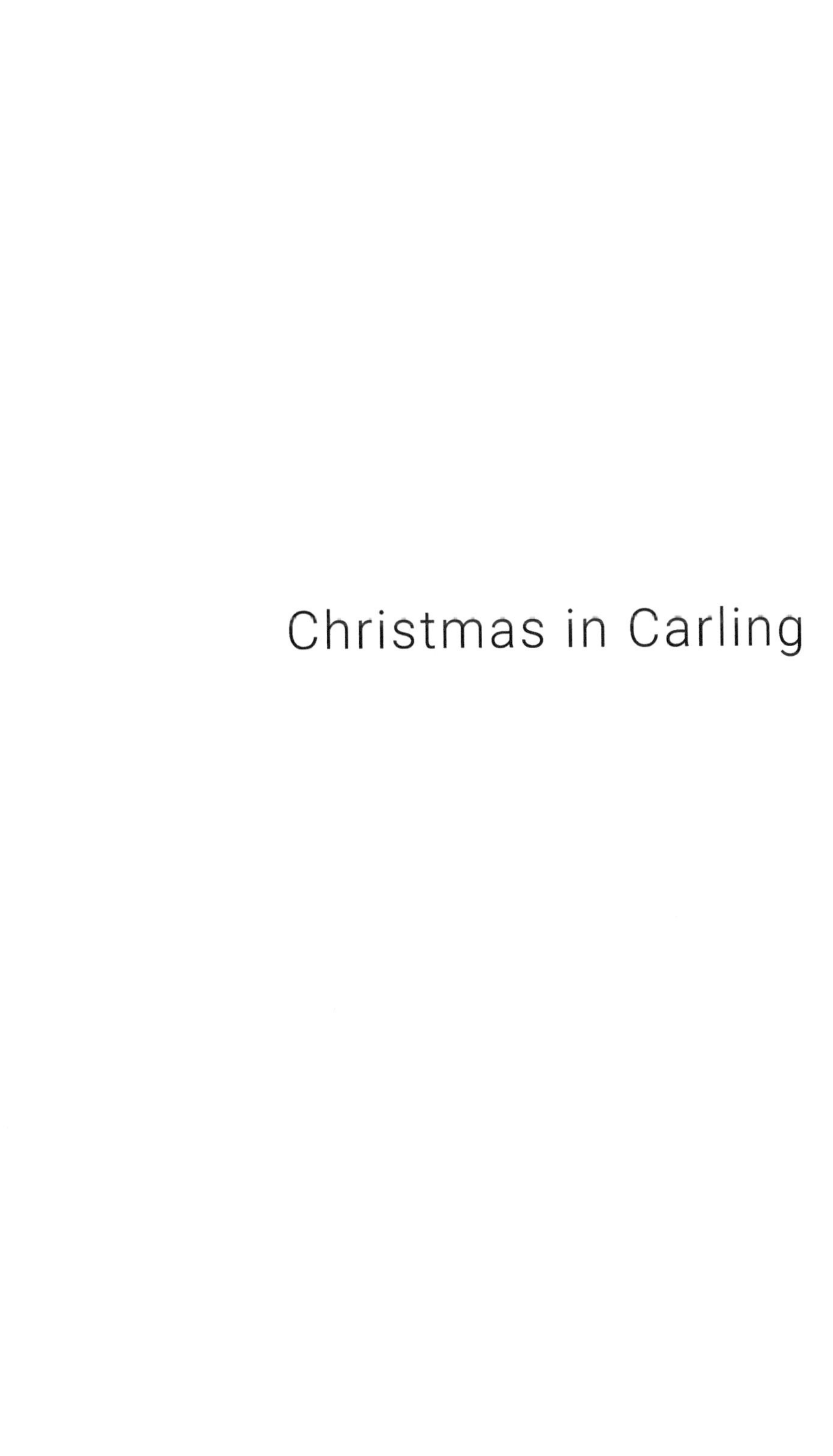

Christmas in Carling

Christmas in Carling

E.A. STARK

BURCH Publishing

Dedicated to those missing loved ones around the holiday season.

Visit the

book page at EAStarkBooks.com to

1

December 19th

City of Toronto

"Grief changes shape, but it never ends," Julia Mariani recalled while packing the last of their luggage in the SUV. "The wise man who said that was so right."

Their street was quiet for the middle of the day. Hearing the hum of traffic in the distance, she peered down at the green grass, showing through a light dusting of snow. It immediately sparked a series of memories.

"Five years," she murmured, her voice catching. "It's been five years to the day."

Before returning inside the house to check on her daughter, she scanned the many festively decorated homes on their street. Sadly, the exquisite wreaths adorning front doors and strings of lights on all the trees and shrubs didn't emit an ounce of Christmas spirit. Despite all the beauty surrounding them, Julia knew none of it felt like home. All the parties, events, and festivities in the city over the past few weeks could never compare to spending a Christmas in Carling.

Fondly thinking about the sleepy little town with an undocumented population, she could hardly wait to arrive at the luxurious lakeside retreat. The Carling Resort Hotel was Julia's best-kept secret. A hidden gem in a remote northern area.

Set amidst many scenic lakes and rivers coated by a unique rocky landscape and dense forests, the region boasted a reputation for high-end real estate, the most beautiful water views, unparalleled sunsets, and, of course, epic social gatherings. But this bustling summer tourist mecca eventually transformed into a frozen icy haven. Not exactly the Caribbean beach getaway most gravitated to when wanting to escape the cold. That is why Julia loved it so much. It was secluded, peaceful, and filled with memories. Both good and bad. After living through and surviving the unthinkable, it was the only place they wanted to be this time of year.

A brisk breeze unexpectedly hit Julia, breaking her from her deepest thoughts. Shivering, she reached up to press the SUV's rear tailgate button. When the door locked automatically behind her, the well-organized Mom with long blonde hair went back inside the house to make sure they had everything. Looking around the cold, starkly furnished space, lacking any feeling of warmth, let alone the Christmas spirit, she noticed her daughter had not made it downstairs yet.

Briefly hearing Sydney rumbling about in her room, she decided to light a bit of a fire underneath the nine-year-old by calmly bellowing up to the second story, "Hey, Syd? Are you all packed? We need to get going! I want to arrive at the hotel before the storm hits!"

A muffled reply came from her daughter's room. "Yes, Mom! I know! You've only mentioned that like a million times today!" Stuffing her favorite blanket into her backpack at the last minute, the girl replied cheekily, "I'm coming!"

Julia smirked at the sass in Sydney's tone but kept moving, double-checking everything she needed for her mobile office as she packed her briefcase. Zipping it closed and slipping the medium-sized tote on her right shoulder, she spotted her daughter bounding down the stairs.

Carefully setting the backpack on the foyer floor, the little girl put on her boots, coat, and hat. Cramming her scarf and warm mittens into the front pockets of her jacket, she happily produced a forced smile for her Mother before leaving the house and walking down the path, inserting her earbuds along the way to the truck.

Remotely unlocking the SUV just as she was about to pull the handle and get in, with her mind reeling through a mental checklist, Julia closed the front door while juggling her briefcase, tote, and cross-over bag. While standing in the doorway, there was only one thing left to say. Praying for God to bless their house in their absence, she locked up and loaded the baggage into the second row behind the driver's seat. All buckled up, ready to leave, she turned to Sydney, who had settled in beside her.

Hesitating a second, she adjusted the rearview mirror and caught her own reflection briefly. "Well? Are we all set then, Sweetie pie?"

"Yep, ready," Syd declared concretely, sitting with legs crossed and nodding with subdued excitement versus other years.

In an instant, her daughter was suddenly not so little anymore. Turning ten in a few months and developing an ever-expanding maturity level, Julia often wondered how Ben would have interacted with his younger sister in this phase of life - if they might have gotten along or possibly clashed as siblings often do. Ultimately, she would never know.

Breaking from that train of thought, she carefully backed out onto the crescent and shifted gears before slowly leaving their neighborhood. With a sigh of relief and a deep breath, she was happy to be on schedule. Attentively maneuvering the many city streets, they soon joined the main highway and headed north. Leaving the city limits, bound for the small town two hours away, Julia got comfortable behind the wheel and set the cruise control. Lacking conversation, thinking Sydney was listening to music, she looked over to find her fast asleep with her head resting against the window and buds still in her ears – a scene that had become the norm over the past while.

The hum of the tires against the road filled the quiet car, giving Julia space to let her thoughts drift. As the snow-dusted landscape blurred past, she couldn't help but reflect on how different the holidays had become since she'd lost her parents. An only child with no extended family to lean on, she'd once dreaded the emptiness of this season. But she'd vowed it would be different for Sydney.

Her hands tightened briefly on the steering wheel as she thought about the traditions they'd built together over the years. It all started as a way to survive those first agonizing holidays: one simple act of kindness each day, just to keep moving forward. Julia could still see Sydney's cautious excitement the first time they delivered cookies to the resort staff and gifted them handmade ornaments.

Those early efforts had grown into something more—*Sydney's Operation Christmas.* The name was her daughter's invention, and Julia smiled faintly at the memory of Sydney, barely six, declaring their "mission." Now, it was as much a part of their holiday as the snow on the ground or the lights in the trees. Sydney's list of creative, thoughtful gestures seemed to grow longer each year, and what had once been a distraction had become a joy neither of them could imagine the season without.

As she glanced at her little girl, fast asleep in the passenger seat, Julia felt a familiar swell of gratitude. The tasks weren't just about giving to others; they had become a way to anchor themselves in something positive and warm. Even in the face of their loss, they'd found a way to celebrate.

While easing into the next lane, her thoughts settled on the days ahead. Whatever this holiday brought, she knew they'd spend it creating memories that mattered—together.

2

December 19th

City of Boston

"Hey, Matt?" Ty Reynolds shouted to his assistant while on speaker-phone, standing in the middle of his walk-in closet, trying to decide what to pack. "Where did you book me this year? Remember, no crowds. I don't want to be surrounded by a mob of people!"

"Yes, I know, I know. That is what you keep telling me. I promise this year you will be alone for the holidays. I found this place called The Carling Resort Hotel. It is literally in the middle of nowhere, and they assured me that there are no bookings until December 30th, by which time you will be on a plane back to Boston."

"You'd better be right," Ty said sternly, still bitter about losing the AL Division Series to Houston a few weeks prior, knowing his head could be on the chopping block during the December Hot Stove trades.

"The car should be downstairs within an hour to pick you up, and your flight leaves at 5:50. I sent all the info via email. When you arrive in Toronto, the hotel is two hours north of the city. I've rented you a large SUV since it looks like they have some snow in the forecast. Are you sure you don't need a driver?"

"No, I'll be fine. What? You don't think I'll find the place?" Ty spouted with a hint of arrogance.

"No, that's not it. The resort is just really remote. You will need to follow the GPS precisely."

"Okay, okay. I get it." Hesitating a second, Ty sincerely muttered, "Hey, Matt... Merry Christmas, man. Have fun with your family."

Matt did not say a thing. Shocked to hear the great baseball player wanted to talk about something other than business for a change, he replied, "Thank you. Enjoy your stay at the Carling. I'll contact you if I hear anything from Michael."

Lowering his head, Ty went silent. Feeling a little jealous that Matt had a wife and two little boys under the age of five, he knew his Christmas would include an enormous amount of excitement.

"Hey, Ty? Are you still there?" Matt wondered if they got disconnected.

Speaking up, he mumbled, "Yeah, yeah. I'm here."

To reassure his friend and keep him in a positive frame of mind, Matt encouraged, "Everything will be fine. You'll see. Michael knows what he is doing. He always gets you what you want."

"I know. This month is always stressful for me. Not winning adds to all that." Pausing a second, Ty exhaled, "I'm kinda looking forward to the trip. You know, finally getting some rest and much-needed peace and quiet."

"Right..." Matt replied. "Umm, Ty, you know, you're always welcome at my home during the holidays." He knew the guy would never accept the invitation.

"Thanks. No offense, but I need to be alone."

Matt let it go because Ty's past haunted him every December.

"No offense taken. Well, Merry Christmas then. We'll talk soon. Text, email, or call if you need anything. I'll contact you if Michael hears any important news on the wire."

With dead air left between them, Ty's mind went into overdrive.

Being around the veteran athlete for the past eight years, his friend knew what he was thinking. "I know you have a big decision to make. Everything will be fine; you'll see."

"Yeah... It'll be fine. Always is," Ty mumbled. "Merry Christmas."

"Merry Christmas, Ty."

Ending the call, he closed his suitcase and wheeled it to the front door, setting the duffle bag down on the left side of it. Not long after, he received a call from the concierge saying his car had arrived. Leaving the condo near Boston Common for the two-week vacation, the Red Sox first baseman jumped into the chauffeur-driven SUV at 2:30 pm and headed to Logan International to catch his flight just as a few lazy snowflakes drifted into the city.

3

December 19th

The Carling Hotel

An hour-and-a-half into the trip, Julia noticed Sydney stirring. Waking up, she rubbed her eyes and slowly scanned her surroundings to see where they were.

With the last town in their rear-view mirror, her Mother said, "Hello, sleepy head."

"Are we almost there?" the young girl asked, noticing it becoming more and more remote.

"Yes. We are on the home stretch now."

Julia merged off the main highway and paid close attention while driving on the snow-covered roads leading to the secluded hotel. Enjoying the water views while passing countless partially open lakes and rivers, this part of the journey was, by far, their favorite. Moving through tiny hamlets, crossing over one bridge after another, the landscape soon became quite rocky and tightly forested. Something very unique and picturesque. The profound beauty captivated them no matter how often they'd seen it. Soon, they were rounding the corner at the base of a hill. Sydney looked out the window to her right and spotted the Carling shining brightly on the mountaintop. Accented by thin ribbons of mid-afternoon sun, a sprinkle of snow sparkled as it fell.

"We're here!" she shouted with excitement. "Doesn't it look magical, Mom?"

"Yes," Julia confirmed, slowing down to enjoy the view. "It certainly does." Wholeheartedly believing her troubles would disappear upon arrival like snow melting in the spring, she could hardly wait to walk inside and feel at home.

"I'm so happy," Sydney gushed, clapping her hands with an enormous smile. Almost jumping out of her seat, the little girl in her finally made a brief appearance.

With the Carling sign coming into view, the Marianis turned right and ventured up the winding road to the hotel perched upon the highest point in that area. As they got closer, they saw a multitude of shuttles and private airline SUVs waiting to take guests to the airport. Patiently stopping on an incline close to the circular driveway, a few shuttles departed, opening up space for them. Julia carefully maneuvered their vehicle under the grand entrance to park, check in, and unload. Seeing the snow increase, knowing the weather turned on a dime in that area, she was thankful they'd arrived before it got too bad.

Not wasting a minute, Sydney jumped out and went through the front doors. Ready to explore the newly renovated spaces, remembering that the owners started construction last January, she saw so many changes. The very first was the new light fixture in the lobby. Modernly crafted into the shape of a beehive with small suspended glowing gold lights all around symbolizing bees, Syd sat down to marvel at the beautiful piece of illuminated art. Seated under the chandelier, running her hands along the smooth, sculpted bench, she wondered if the creators fashioned the long, seamless structure from a single tree. Having changed the front desk and concierge to reflect a more contemporary look, Sydney and her Mom spotted the giant Christmas tree in the Lakes lounge, all decorated brilliantly in blue, silver, and gold. With the scent of burning logs lingering in the air, the two knew they were finally home for Christmas.

Surrounded by the hustle and bustle of guests preparing for departure, Julia approached the main counter, still amazed by the transformation.

Amidst the chaos, she heard someone cheerfully ask, "Good afternoon, Ma'am. Checking in?"

Turning in the direction of the voice, she found an older gentleman with snow-white hair and rosy cheeks, smartly dressed in a crisply pressed white shirt, a red plaid blazer, and a bow tie.

"Good afternoon. We have a reservation for Mariani," Julia confirmed, not recognizing the man's face. "Are you new here?"

"Yes, Ma'am. It's my second day. My name is Nick," he said, flashing a friendly smile while pulling up their reservation on the computer.

"It's very nice to meet you. I'm Julia, and that's my daughter Sydney standing over there admiring the Christmas tree."

"So lovely to meet you, Ms. Mariani. It looks like you will have a very quiet Christmas. Everyone else is checking out today."

"That is perfectly fine with us. It's just the way we like it. Peaceful and quiet."

"There is only one other guest booked for the next two weeks," he added, not missing a beat.

"Oh? Another family with no place to be over the holidays?" Julia questioned curiously, wondering if Sydney might have another child to play with during their stay.

"Sorry, Ma'am. I'm not supposed to give out that information." Apologizing, he squinted one eye and said under his breath, "But he is due to arrive very late tonight, so until then, you will have the hotel to yourselves."

"He? Meaning one person?" She was disappointed to hear the news.

"Sorry, can't say," Nick denied with a shrug of his shoulders. "But I have heard he intends to avoid Christmas festivities at all costs."

"Right..."

"A bit of a Bah Humbug, perhaps?" Nick prepared their access keys for room 1444, the same suite they reserved each year.

When he slid the cards across the counter, she took them and placed each safely in her jacket pocket. "Thank you so much for your help. It was nice meeting you. I'm sure we will see you during our stay."

"Yes, Ma'am. I will be here," he replied with an odd twinkle.

Nick's face looked vaguely familiar, but she couldn't pinpoint why.

Scanning the space to find Sydney, Julia located her standing a few feet away. Wanting to introduce her to Nick, she waved her daughter over and said, "Hey, Sydney, come over and meet…." In an instant, Julia stopped and looked left to right, but Nick was gone.

"Meet who?" Sydney scoured the check-in desk, a bit confused.

"Umm, the man…he was right there a second ago. He must have stepped away a moment. Perhaps you will see him later. Come on. Let's grab a cart and get unpacked."

Commandeering an empty trolley, glancing back at the desk, and not seeing Nick return, Julia walked through the main doors to their vehicle parked outside amidst the mass exodus. Thankful that everyone would soon be gone, she opened the back hatch of the SUV to unload their things. The two started stacking their bags on the cart when they noticed a joyful face on his way out to help them.

"Bryce!" Julia exclaimed with open arms. "Hi…" Her cheerful tone went solemn. With a sympathetic tilt of her head, she hugged the older man, now slightly hunched over. He seemed more frail than last year but still young at heart.

Stepping back to look at him, she said. "How are you doing? We've missed you."

Lowering his head, trying to keep himself from tearing up, Bryce replied, "Thank you, my dear. I am hanging in there."

Giving him another hug, she separated from their caring embrace. The grandfatherly man immediately found Sydney standing to the left of her.

"Oh, is this my little Sydie? My, how you've grown in the past six months." Glancing at Julia, he asked, "What are you feeding this girl?"

"She has grown a lot taller and is almost ten now."

Sydney squeezed him tightly. "Hi, Grandpa Bryce."

"Hello, my sweetness. Did you have a good trip?"

"Yep. It didn't seem long."

"That's because you slept almost the entire way," her Mother pointed out. Able to tell Bryce was not his jovial self, she said, "You have been in our thoughts and prayers. I hope you know that."

"Thank you for coming to the service. I received the cards and flowers you sent over the past while. That was so thoughtful. As you know, the first few months are the hardest, but then you realize life must go on. Bev would want me to be happy, so I keep working here to fill the time and, of course, to see my favorite guests." Arms out to welcome hugs from his girls, the two obliged without question.

"We love seeing you too," Julia revealed with the biggest smile. "All of you have become our family here, so there is no place we would rather be."

"I'm so glad to hear that. Now, let me help you with those bags," Bryce insisted.

Stacked to the brim, he maneuvered the trolley through the entrance doors and handed their car keys to the new Bellhop, Jason. "Here, J, please take care of our special guest's vehicle for me. Park it in the VIP lot."

"No problem, Sir," Jason said hastily.

Veering right towards the elevators, with Bryce allowing them to lead the way, Sydney pressed the button and impatiently waited for the doors to open.

"You will see many improvements throughout the hotel. I think you'll love it. The owners have been very busy," their old friend explained as the doors parted.

They stepped inside, parking the full luggage cart on the left.

Turning to Sydney, Julia smiled and said, "I'm sure we will. It's so exciting."

"Same floor?" he questioned.

"Yes, the usual. Fourth floor." Julia was so thankful to be back. She could feel her mind already beginning to relax.

When Bryce selected the top button, the doors slid closed. Placing his hand on Sydney's shoulder, he whispered, "They expanded the craft room to include a painting studio. Something I know you will make use of."

Showcasing great enthusiasm and bright eyes, she clasped her hands together in front of her face, almost like she had received her first present on Christmas morning.

Upon reaching the top floor, the three entered the beautiful upper hallway, which boasted gleaming natural hardwood, custom-made accent tables with aroma-infused festive pine arrangements, and wall art featuring local artists. Swinging left toward room 1444, Julia stopped outside their door, not far down the hall. Touching the card to the reader to gain access, she held the door open to make space for Bryce to thread the trolley through.

Unloading everything together, Julia passed Sydney her suitcase. She quickly rolled it into her bedroom and returned to grab her backpack. Resting the cooler bags filled with food on the kitchen counter, Bryce wheeled Julia's baggage over to her bedroom door while Sydney placed their toiletry tote in her Mother's bathroom.

"I guess that's it," Bryce said cheerfully. "So happy to have you both home for Christmas. I look forward to seeing you as often as possible."

"We will see you every day," Sydney promised, hugging the man she considered her grandfather.

Needing to start a headcount for dinner, Julia took out her notebook and asked, "I assume you are joining us for Christmas Eve?"

"Absolutely. I'll be here with bells on," Bryce confirmed with a smile to light the room.

"Wonderful! We have lots to do before then, right, Sydney?"

"Yes! We have so many surprises for all of you this year."

"Well, I can hardly wait." He maneuvered the trolley over to the entrance. "On that note, I think I should get back to work and let you settle in. Enjoy the rest of your afternoon."

Holding the door open for Bryce, Julia said, "Thank you for all your help."

She waved to him as he moved down the hallway. When he disappeared around the corner, Julia closed the room door, removed her coat, and hung it in the closet. Sydney did the same. Placing their boots on the tray, they began unloading the food and stocking the cupboards and fridge before organizing their rooms for their extended stay.

"I think this will be the best Christmas ever, Mom. I can feel it," the young girl said with abundant energy.

"I hope so, too," her Mother replied.

4

December 19th

Home for Christmas

They finished the rest of their unpacking duties in just under an hour. Julia looked around their suite calmly. Out of all the places on earth they've traveled, she felt the most at home here. It had this warmth that was hard to describe.

Sydney walked out of her bedroom. "So, can we see the changes they've made in the hotel?"

"Sure, if you'd like. Where do you want to go?" Julia hugged her little girl tightly, ready to let the festivities begin. She had a hunch about what she wanted to see first.

With hands clasped under her chin, fingers tightly intertwined, Sydney nodded. "I, like, really want to go to the new art studio."

"Okay then, that will be our first stop. Do you have your Operation Christmas notebook?"

Running into her room to grab the red patterned book from her backpack, she held it up while emerging from the room. "Yep, I've got it right here."

"Great. Let's go exploring. We can discuss our holiday plans during dinner. How does that sound?"

"Perfect."

Opening their room door, closing it tightly behind them, with card keys in hand, the two made their way down the hall to the elevators. It didn't take long for Sydney to reinstate the game she'd created when she was about four years old.

"I pick the door on the left," her daughter exclaimed, standing in front of the one she had chosen, believing it would open first.

Julia had no choice but to pick the other side. "Well, let's see who wins."

When Sydney's side opened, Julia accepted defeat.

"Point for me. I'm up one – nothing," her daughter revealed, eager to keep track.

Laughing, they walked inside the elevator. Sydney pressed M to take them to the mezzanine level. She was eager to see how they improved on the art space. Descending to the basement floor, they continued down the long hallway past the gym, spa, and indoor pool and made another right into a glass-enclosed corridor. Around the corner from the circular lookout room, Sydney pressed a second elevator button to take them to B2, yet another level below.

Once at the lowest point in the mountainside resort, the doors opened to the gaming room, with new pool tables, foosball, arcade games, and shuffleboard. Amazed by it all, Sydney suddenly spied a set of mahogany wood doors gracing the entrance to the studio with big windows flanking each side, making it look like an indoor storefront. The custom-made sign said *Creative Corner*. It even had shutters, a welcome mat, and cute awnings installed above the windows.

"Wow!" Sydney said with wonder. "This is beautiful." Slowly moving inside, she looked around, investigating every detail. With eyes dancing about, unsure where to start, she went over to the well-organized wall of built-in white shelves lined with every paint color imaginable, all placed in a rainbow sequence, with vertical tray holders for the palettes and stainless-steel buckets for the brushes. There were new easels, a canvas of every shape and size, and even a scrapbooking center with a wall of quality art papers, boxes of decals and clip art, pens, markers, and pastels. You name it, they thought of everything.

Watching her daughter with a tearful gaze, Julia was so happy that Syd loved to create as much as she did. It seemed like a piece of her had passed along to the next generation—sadly, the last one remaining.

Turning to her Mother, she asked, "After dinner, can I come back and explore a bit more?"

"Of course, you can. Maybe we can start the ornaments, then?"

In total agreement, Syd reluctantly left the studio, continuing to glance back as they walked away. "It's so perfect," she exclaimed with great sincerity, looking at her Mom with eyes sparkling.

In usual fashion, the two arrived on the main floor around 4:30. While strolling through the lobby toward the Cottages restaurant, Julia and Syd hoped to see some familiar faces along the way. Approaching the Lounge area, she noticed Bruno and Rebecca behind the bar. Waving to them both, Sydney skipped ahead to run into Rebecca's waiting arms while Bruno finished a phone call.

"Sydney!" the tall woman with long dark hair said excitedly. "Oh, how you've grown, my sweet girl. Step back. Let me take a good look at you."

With hands still linked together, Sydney backed away bashfully.

"Oh, you look so much like your Mom."

Reaching her arms to hug her friend, Julia greeted, "Hi, Rebecca. We've missed you so much."

"How are you both doing? Last we spoke, things seemed okay," the young woman stated with great concern. "How's the new house? Have you settled in yet?"

"The house is just that - a house. We are still taking one day at a time. It doesn't feel like home yet, you know. Can't believe it's been five years already," Julia revealed, lowering her head and tilting it to one side.

Bruno hung up the phone and joined the ladies on the opposite side of the bar. With open arms, he happily hugged Julia when she met him halfway.

"Hi, Bruno. How are you doing? How is Maria?"

"We are doing great," he admitted, raising his eyebrows, trying to contain some exciting news.

"What?" Julia pleaded, looking back and forth between him and Rebecca, not needing to pry it out of him. "What is it?"

"Maria and I are expecting a baby," he announced with a bit of nervousness. "She's four months along."

"Oh! What amazing news. I'm so happy for you both. That is fantastic."

Rebecca smiled, tapping his shoulder. "They will be great parents."

Nodding shyly, Bruno replied, "Thank you. We are so excited."

"Well, that's the best news I've heard all day. Congratulations. Will you and Maria be joining us on the 24th?"

"I'm so sorry, Julia, but we won't be able to attend this year. We are traveling to visit my in-laws, so I'm not working throughout the holidays. It will probably be our last visit with her family before the baby arrives. We leave in two days and won't be back until New Year's Day."

"That's wonderful. We completely understand. It will be a special visit for all of you. Make sure you wish Maria Merry Christmas for us and send our congratulations too."

"Will do, for sure."

The mass exodus of guests bellowing for service took Bruno away from their cheerful reunion. Many people still requested takeout orders before their shuttles arrived to drive them to the airport.

"Everyone here will be leaving just after five. Then, it will just be us," Rebecca assured Julia and Syd. "So excited to spend time with you guys. I am on shift until December 23rd but will be away to spend two days with my family in the city. Sorry, I won't be around for the festivities. I return the day after Boxing Day. We can celebrate then. I hope it's okay. Just FYI, I think they brought in a temp to cover for Bruno and me. Supposedly, he's just at the hotel for the holidays. Some Jack of all trades kind of guy? Hey? Did you bring the craft cart?"

"Sure did," Sydney interjected. "Mom and I fully stocked it before we left. I have some terrific ideas this year."

"I can hardly wait." Seeing so many impatient people bombarding Bruno, she said, "Look, I'd better get back to work. I promise we will chat later." Rebecca went to the kitchen to pick up a series of orders that had just popped up in the queue.

Bruno waved to the girls while preparing a drink for an older gentleman, hunched over the bar, with salt and pepper hair and modern, black-rimmed glasses.

Moving on, they arrived at the Cottages restaurant to find Lisa and an unfamiliar waiter swamped with guests. Passing by the hostess station, not seeing anyone there, Lisa suddenly spotted them before drifting into the kitchen.

"Hello, Marianis. So happy to see you two." The hostess with a blonde pixie cut looked around in a bit of a panic. "Sorry. We are pretty busy. I'm helping Jun right now. We need to get these people on their way, and then it'll calm down. Grab a seat in the far section, and I'll be with you shortly. Apologize..."

"Don't worry about us. We'll be fine. Do what you have to do," Julia replied, knowing the two of them were sadly being run off their feet by a few demanding people.

Happy to see their usual table by the window unoccupied, they settled in and watched the crowd diminish one by one. This chaotic departure took place every year at this time. Days before the Christmas holidays, guests took a break at the Carling before being converged upon by family back home.

Julia opened their menu. "So, what are you going to order tonight?"

"Not sure? Kinda feel like fish and chips, but the mini burgers are calling my name right about now."

Laughing at her response, Julia turned to the salad page.

"Wait! No salad. You need comfort food today. How about the Lobster Ravioli?" she suggested, remembering it was her Mother's favorite last year.

"Decision made. Thank you, Sydie," Julia said enthusiastically, almost forgetting how tasty that dish was.

"So, shall we talk about Operation Christmas now?" Sydney had already opened her notebook.

"Sure. What are your thoughts? I know we have three different types of cookies to make. I bought all the ingredients for those."

"Right. I've chosen three ornament styles this year, too. I have made samples for two of them, just not the third one. It's a button wreath. I hope I have enough buttons in the bulk bag I brought to make what I need. I may have to give out only two ornaments to each person and use all three styles to make it work."

"That's fine. What about the Christmas tree theme? Any thoughts?"

"Hmmm." Sydney paused. "I figured I might wing it."

"What? Really?"

"Last year, I tried to find the ornaments I needed at Clarence and LeeAnn's, but it didn't work out as well as I'd planned, so this time, I was just going to see what they have and spontaneously put something together."

"That would make it more fun. You might find something you least expect that way."

"Precisely."

While they were finalizing the details, Julia reminded Sydney, "Oh, by the way, I've booked an excursion in two days."

"What are we doing?"

"Since we've done the nature walk, dog sledding, snowshoeing, and snowmobiling, I figured we'd try something new. It's called ski-shoeing."

"Huh?"

"It's short, wide-plank skis that act like snowshoes seemingly, and we use poles to push us along on top of the snow. Kind of like a combination between snowshoeing and cross-country skiing. Want to give it a try?"

"Sure, I can do that."

Julia looked around the restaurant and out the window at the snow blowing past them. "So, are you happy to be back?"

"Are you kidding? You know I love it here."

Smiling, Julia watched her daughter record a few notes in her notebook.

"For whatever reason, I feel like something is different. Besides the renovations, that is. Not sure what. Maybe it's because I'm not as organized this year. Especially when it comes to the plan for the tree," Sydney analyzed with an abundance of careful thought.

"Maybe it's because you refuse to believe in Santa Claus," her Mother chuckled.

Syd shot her a look. "Mom, I'm too old for that now. Give it up, please. You just have to face facts."

Julia snickered. "Never know. Maybe you'll change your mind. Guess time will tell."

5

The customs area at Toronto Pearson International Airport hummed with weary conversations and the occasional scrape of luggage wheels. Even at eight o'clock in the evening, the line inched forward at a frustratingly slow pace.

Ty Reynolds shifted his weight from one foot to the other, his tired legs aching from the flight. Around him, a handful of passengers grumbled loudly, their irritation sharp enough to cut through the airport's white noise. Word of canceled flights and an impending snowstorm had left tempers frayed. With his head down, he clutched his passport as the line crept closer to the customs counter. The stern-looking agent behind the plexiglass called him forward with an abrupt nod, his expression softening the second he scanned the passport.

"Ty Reynolds," the man said, a flicker of recognition lighting his eyes. "Big fan. Tough break for Boston this year in the Series."

He produced a small smile, his fatigue momentarily giving way to pride—and regret. "Yeah, we gave it everything we had. Just wasn't enough this time."

The agent handed back his passport, looking at him knowingly. "Well, there's always next year."

"Yep."

The first baseman tucked the passport into his jacket after the brief exchange and walked past the counter into the bustling arrivals area, where he followed the steady stream of passengers toward the baggage claim. The fluorescent lights overhead buzzed faintly, casting a sterile glow on the polished floors.

A cluster of people huddled near his flight's carousel, which sat motionless, its conveyor belt empty. He could hear genuine concern as some checked the weather updates on their phones. Leaning against a nearby pillar, tired of airports, he rubbed a hand over his face. The faint flash of a camera made him glance up.

"Excuse me, Mr. Reynolds?" a young man ventured over.

Ty tried to look happy as the man took out a random piece of paper for him to sign. The ripple of recognition spread like wildfire, and soon, fans surrounded him, some angling for autographs while others held up their phones for selfies. He obliged with a strained smile, though his jaw tightened. He wasn't sure what stung more—the exhaustion in his body or the memory of falling short this season. After all, the team wasn't a World Series champion this year—a fact that gnawed at him more than he cared to admit.

Finally, spotting his bag sliding down the belt, he grabbed it quickly, grateful for the excuse to break away. As he adjusted the strap on his shoulder, the words: *There's always next year* kept repeating in his mind, making him wonder if he had enough left in him to give it one last try.

More than ready to get out of there, he left through the arrivals doors and scouted for signs leading to the car rental area. Locating the company kiosk Matt had booked him with, he got in line and patiently waited his turn.

When the guy behind the counter called, "Next!" Ty greeted him and presented his ID. "Hi. Reservation for Reynolds."

"Yes, Mr. Reynolds. Good evening," he said, referring to the name on his driver's license and typing it into the system to pull up the reservation. "You have a Premium SUV, and your credit card information is already on file."

Focusing on the snowy scene outside the window behind the desk, Ty confirmed what he said, hoping he'd make it quick so he could get on the road before the weather worsened. While the guy printed his paperwork, the snow started to fall at an alarming rate. It made him wonder if it was wise to carry on to his destination tonight.

"So?" Ty asked, wanting some advice."Are the roads supposed to get bad? I'm driving two hours north of the city. Is it wise to risk it tonight?"

"I can't technically answer that for you, Sir, but I can tell you that the weather network is calling for significant snowfall this evening. Upwards of ten to twenty centimeters."

"What's that in inches?" he asked, not knowing the equivalent conversion.

"I am not sure, but there is a weather warning in effect. Whatever decision you choose is up to you," he confirmed, denying any liability while sliding the rental agreement across the desk.

Scribbling his signature on the line at the bottom of the paper, he replied, "Right...."

"Here you go. Two sets of keys to your Chevy Tahoe. You will find it parked in spot A19." He circled the lot number on the card.

The guy handed Ty a copy of the paperwork in an envelope. He quickly slipped it into his jacket pocket along with the keys. "Great, thanks."

"Merry Christmas, Sir," the man cheerfully wished.

"Yeah, Merry Christmas, man," Ty said.

When he left the desk and passed the people still in line, he heard the guy shout unexpectedly, "Next!!"

Wheeling his suitcase out the doors, Ty looked at the sign directing patrons to the parking structure. While bundling up, the raw northwest wind hit him hard. With his chin tucked into his chest and jacket collar raised on end, he alternated his hands into each pocket to keep them warm. Easily locating the Tahoe parked in spot A19, his body started to show its age. It ached considerably, which had become a regular occurrence the past year, especially in the winter. Inevitably, that pain also reminded him of the decision he soon needed to make.

Upon clicking the button, the vehicle's side and interior lights turned on, illuminating the space around him. As the rear hatch lifted, he placed his suitcase in the back and shuffled to the driver's side to hop in. Tossing his leather duffle on the passenger seat, finding the push button start, he placed the keys in the cup holder and started the ignition. With heat blasting and the seat warming, he plugged in his phone charger and selected the GPS app. Entering the hotel address listed in the email from Matt, Ty waited for the route to calibrate. Within seconds, he discovered that it would take him over three hours to reach his destination. Factoring in weather and road conditions, Ty assessed the snow situation outside the parking structure as it seemed to have lightened up. Deciding to make a run for it and carry on in the dark, he was thankful not to be spending the night in the city. He had had his fill of that for now.

"I'll get there when I get there. No big deal," the athlete muttered to himself.

Pulling out of the parking lot, maneuvering through the many exits and ramps to the highway, Ty soon realized the trip would be slow going. Trusting the SUV to do its job, he turned on the radio.

"Really?" he said, changing the station from Christmas music to eighties rock. "Haven't people had enough of this? They've been playing holiday music for almost a month now. It's insane."

Signaling into the northbound lane, Ty noticed the snow getting heavier and heavier. In spots, the roads were entirely snow-covered. Not given a choice, he slowed his speed to a crawl. Leaning forward over the steering wheel, in almost zero visibility, driving for nearly an hour, Ty second-guessed his decision about traveling tonight. Seeing a rest stop show up on the GPS, he crawled along the off-ramp, hoping to grab a coffee and a small bite to eat before continuing on his way.

Almost deserted, there were only three other patrons in the entire restaurant. With a large hot coffee, bottle of water, and a bagged burger and fries in hand, Ty returned to his truck about fifteen minutes later. Frozen, he started the engine and turned on the wipers to rid the windshield of a thick layer of freshly fallen snow. Unwrapping the burger, taking bite after bite, he thought of his family, wondering what his sister might be doing at that very moment. He was sure she'd be wrapping his nephews' gifts or preparing for her husband's family to arrive in a couple of days. Her house during the holidays always had abundant laughter and happiness. She created her family traditions just like their Mother did. Feeling a hint of emotion creeping in, he quickly stopped himself from venturing down the self-pity route and straightened up in the seat. Swallowing the last bite of the burger, he propped up the fries in the cup holder to eat on the go. With hands firmly on the steering wheel before putting the truck in drive, ready to get back on the road, Ty took a deep breath.

Practicing patience, he figured he would use this time to decide what the future might hold. It was nice to think freely about it without all his advisors prodding him with suggestions and options. Realizing that his baseball career was about to end, he couldn't believe he was fortunate enough to play for as many years as he had.

"Seventeen years is a long time," he whispered, "and it went by in a blink."

6

December 19th

First Night at The Carling Hotel

After dinner, Julia and Sydney visited with as many staff members as they could find. Each of them was happy that they had returned for another holiday season. Knowing that many of these people played an instrumental role in helping them through their darkest hour many years before, Julia felt indebted to them for everything they'd done.

On their way to the elevators, Sydney asked, "Can we return to the art studio now? I want to paint the Merry Christmas sign."

"Okay. We have about an hour before bed," Julia said. "It has been a busy day. We should settle in early tonight. Lots to do tomorrow."

Sydney nodded in agreement. "No problem. I'll be fast."

Skipping ahead of her mother, using two sets of elevators, they soon reached the craft room.

Not wasting any time, the little girl started designing a festive sign to display on a small easel to welcome everyone the day of Christmas Eve.

With her off and running, Julia said, "And so another season begins."

Moments later, Rebecca joined them. As she walked through the mahogany doors, she said, "Hello, my friends."

Wanting to catch up with the family of two without interruption, Rebecca saw Sydney's face light up upon seeing her.

"Rebecca! You made it!" After showing her what she had painted thus far, she said, "I'm so glad you're here. Now you can keep Mom company while I work."

The woman laughed at the girl's sassy tone. "I will do my best."

Over the next hour, Julia told Rebecca everything that had happened in their lives in the past while. Rebecca did the same. Shedding fewer tears, like many Christmas holidays before, the ladies expelled every emotion bottled up inside.

Julia blotted her cheeks with a tissue. Checking the time, she said, "Syd, I think it's time to go. Are you finished?"

Stepping back from the easel, she looked at the painting and replied, "All done. What do you think?"

The ladies walked over to see the masterpiece the young artist had created. Surrounded by decorative holly, pine bows, ribbon, and stars, the calligraphy title stood front and center, beautifully balanced.

"It's perfect, Sweetie." Julia beamed.

Sydney took a bow. "Thank you. Thank you."

They cleaned the space and returned it to its original immaculate condition.

After turning off the lights, the three of them closed the door and made their way up the two levels to the lobby on the main floor.

"Good night, Rebecca," Julia said. "It was so nice to catch up. Guess we will see you tomorrow?"

"Yes, you will."

"Night night." Syd couldn't wave with full hands.

"Have a good night, you two. Enjoy the rest of your evening. Sweet dreams. I will see you in the morning," their friend said on her way to the staff room to grab her things.

Julia helped her daughter carefully transport the Christmas sign upstairs. While riding the elevator to the top, they waited for it to open. Both were starting to fade.

Minutes later, they were standing in front of their suite. Scanning the card key to gain access, she held the door open for her daughter.

Not entirely ready to go to bed yet, the young girl propped the painted sign against the wall. "I think I'm going to figure out the last ornament sample. I must determine if I have enough supplies to make at least fifty."

"Sure, I can help if you like," her mother offered.

Sydney pulled the craft cart beside the dining table. Both sat down and started to count out buttons. One by one, Sydney slid them on the pipe cleaner to create a structured wreath. Happy to have assembled the sample in record time, counting how many buttons it took to produce the ornament, Julia and Sydie began dividing the buttons into groups, surprised to have a handful left over in the end.

"Great. I have more than enough. Oh, I am so happy." Syd was relieved. "Now I can go to sleep and not worry about it." She was her mother's daughter. Always a worrier.

Looking at the time, noticing it was now ten o'clock, Julia said, "It's pretty late. I think you should go and get ready for bed."

"Fine. I'm kinda tired now anyway." Leaving the table, the young girl went to her room to change into her pajamas and brush her teeth.

When Julia checked on her, she found her snuggled under the duvet. "Goodnight, Sweetie," she said, tucking her in.

"Night, Mom. Have a good sleep."

"I will. You too."

Julia walked out and slowly closed the door, leaving it open a crack. Sliding her laptop from her briefcase, she set her heart on sourcing materials for a new project that had come across her desk a few days before. The fast paced landscape design world was a welcomed distraction anytime loneliness set in.

Immersing in her projects, allowing her creative side to run wild, to Julia, there was nothing more fun than creating dream boards for her clients to draw inspiration from. Bringing the computer to bed, she wanted to review the newest file and get a feel for their style.

While winding down, she changed into a white T-shirt, black leggings, and a warm, cozy sweater and found her favorite slippers in one of the bags. Outside, the wind whistled loudly, and ice pellets gently hit the windows, creating white noise. Despite the storm, the room was peaceful.

Sitting on the bed, she got comfortable and perused her notes, not fully knowing the direction she wanted the backyard to take. Jotting a few brainstorming ideas on paper, Julia doodled layout options and selected two that best enhanced the property and maximized the space. From there, everything spilled onto the page effortlessly. Perhaps it was the lack of hustle and bustle or the serene atmosphere that made it easy to concentrate. The projects she designed during their visits were always her best.

About five hours in, Julia continued designing on her tablet into the early morning. Thinking of her clients when designing the spaces was like creating a story. She imagined them having pool parties, al fresco dinners, bonfires with smores—even hot tubbing in the dead of winter with snow magically cascading around them. Every time she presented a finished backyard to her clients, it seemed their story ended. To Julia, it was like gifting them their happily ever after.

On a roll, she didn't want to break her flow. By finishing most of the work now, she knew it would free up more time to spend with Sydney throughout the day.

7

December 20th

Somewhere in Cottage Country

Barely able to see the signs above the highway with the snow blowing sideways across the northbound route, Ty brought his speed down to a crawl. It seemed he'd been driving forever - a lonely trip with few cars on the road. Eventually, finding the exit that would lead him to the town of Carling, looking at the GPS, he noticed that he had only twenty minutes to go.

Happy to almost be at his final destination, sprouting a hint of confidence, he said, "You can do this. Just a little while longer."

While following the directions to a tee, fatigue crept in as he pulled onto a snow-covered road with no tracks to follow.

"Great," he said, passing over a bridge while blazing a trail, unable to appreciate the beauty of his surroundings

Cloaked in darkness, unable to see a thing, Ty noticed a small sign guiding him ever closer to the Carling Resort. By this time, the snowstorm had turned into an outright blizzard. Afraid he would veer off into the ditch, Ty paid attention and hunched himself over the steering wheel so he could focus better. Inching along, he carefully maneuvered the winding roadway, hoping to see the resort sooner than later. With trees on either side, the GPS told him to turn onto a deserted road.

"This can't be right?"

Scanning his surroundings, he noticed a dimly lit boulder. Ty exhaled and stopped the vehicle to read the sign with large gold letters.

"The Carling Resort Hotel and Spa." With a smile and a sigh of relief, he knew he'd made it safe and sound.

8

December 20th

The Carling Hotel

All cozy and warm in room 1444, Julia was ready for bed. Going to grab a bottle of water from the fridge, thinking about her morning coffee, she saw no pods in the basket beside the Keurig. Now ten minutes to two, Julia thought about heading downstairs to grab a few pods until housekeeping could replenish her supply in the morning. Stiff from sitting so long, she figured taking a walk downstairs wouldn't be that bad. She loved the peacefulness of the hotel at night.

Soft instrumental Christmas music played at the Carling twenty-four-seven throughout the holidays. They also dimmed the hallway lights, allowing the Christmas trees to illuminate every corner.

Leaving a post-it note for Sydney in case she got up while she was gone, Julia quietly opened their door and snuck out of the room. Shuffling down the hall to the elevator in her slippers, she was thankful that the doors slid open the second she hit the button.

Emerging on the lobby level, she grabbed the edges of her sweater and wrapped it tightly around her, feeling a draft wafting through the grand foyer. Continuing to slide her slippers along the marble floor, she found Nick reading a newspaper at the front desk.

"Does this guy not sleep?" she questioned, realizing that he'd already been on duty at the desk for almost twelve hours. A few feet away from him, she whispered, "Excuse me, Nick?"

The older gentleman peered up from the paper and caught a glimmer of headlights pulling up the roadway. "Yes, Ma'am? What can I do for you?"

"Is it okay to grab a couple of coffee pods from the restaurant? I'm all out."

"Why are you whispering?" he laughed merrily. "There is nobody else here."

Pausing a minute, she shrugged her shoulders and raised her voice. With a chuckle, she replied bashfully, "I don't know. It's late. Being quiet is a force of habit, I guess."

"No need to worry, Ma'am. To answer your question, yes, please help yourself, no problem. Take however many you need."

"Thank you," she replied.

"Enjoy your evening." Seeing the black truck park under the entrance, he said while she was about to walk away, "Our mystery guest has finally arrived."

Julia looked out the front. Hearing the vehicle door shut, she moved along, not wanting the stranger to see her dressed the way she was.

Speedily heading toward the restaurant, she heard someone drag their suitcase inside the first set of doors and stomp their feet. Afraid to turn around, she continued past the first support column separating the grand foyer from the open corridor. Sadly, her curiosity got the best of her. Wanting a glimpse of the man Nick warned her about, she pivoted to her left just as he walked through the main doors. Slugging a brown leather duffle bag on one shoulder, dressed in a snow-covered dark overcoat, jeans, and Red Wing classic boots, he loosened the plaid scarf around his neck. Quickly brushing the snow from his hair, she had yet to see the tall man's face. In an instant, he looked up and immediately caught sight of her in the distance.

Frozen in his tracks, it seemed time stood still.

Julia's pace slowed to a crawl. She couldn't help but notice the kindness reflected in his dark brown eyes. Suddenly, the stressed expression on his face gave way to a bright smile that cast a warmth that spread through her from head to toe.

As he watched everything unfold before him, Nick perked up. His cheeks became rosy, and his eyes twinkled as he witnessed the makings of something extraordinary and rare.

In a panicked state, breaking away from the intensity between them, Julia felt embarrassed to be seen looking so disheveled. Mortified, she realized she was not wearing her contacts, just her black-framed glasses. They slid down the bridge of her nose slightly, making her push them back into place. To make matters worse, she was not wearing one stitch of makeup and could only imagine how ghostly her face seemed since her summer tan had faded. Picking up the pace while repositioning her glasses a second time, not watching where she was going, the pretty blonde-haired woman hit something. Having walked straight into the prickly branches of the hallway Christmas tree, the tinkling noise of the ornaments sloshing about echoed through the foyer.

"Damn it," she said under her breath. Her heart raced as a rush of heat spread past her neck into her cheeks.

Desperately grabbing hold of it, hoping it wouldn't fall over and smash, she steadied the tree and herself before stepping aside and bolting toward the restaurant. Behind her, she could hear the two men chuckling.

Hidden from sight, disappearing around the corner, Julia stopped at the Cottages restaurant, beyond rattled by what had just happened.

"What was that? Seriously? Oh my gosh. How embarrassing." She released an agonizing huff, "All you had to do was walk away. That's all. But nooo...."

The image of him smiling flashed through her mind, rekindling the warmth of his stare. This helped dissipate her overall humiliation, and in its place emerged a feeling of flattery.

"How is it that a man of that caliber would even bother to look my way?" she questioned, staring at her reflection in the window, displeased by her appearance.

Staying on task, she searched for the coffee pods. It wasn't long before a surge of disgrace flowed through her. Disappointed by her reaction, a battle of feelings gave way, pulling her in many directions. Thoughts of David drifted through her mind, making her silently ask for his forgiveness, wishing nothing would ever come between them.

"You are an adult. A mother at that," she told herself fiercely. "Now, act like one, for heaven's sake."

9

Early Hours of December 20th

Lobby

When Julia disappeared, Nick watched the man stand stoically, seemingly astonished by the scene that unfolded. Intent on breaking the guest from his trance, Nick said, "Excuse me, Sir? Welcome to the Carling. Are you checking in?"

Not at all listening, still stunned by the unexpected moment, the guest lowered his sights to the floor and broke out in a smitten smile.

Chuckling to himself, Nick repeated, "Excuse me? Sir? Checking in? Hello?"

Finally turning to acknowledge him, Ty replied in an exhausted tone, "Umm, yeah. Sorry."

"And the name, please, Sir?"

"Name? Umm, Reynolds. Ty Reynolds," he muttered, still quite distracted. While walking over to the desk, he kept looking in the direction where the woman had gone.

"Here we are. Mr. Reynolds, you have a one-bedroom Lakeview suite booked until December 30th. Is that correct?"

"Yes," Ty confirmed, desperately trying to concentrate on what he was saying while scanning the foyer for any sign of movement.

That gave Nick an idea.

10

Early Hours of December 20th

Scrooged

Stashing a selection of single-serve pods into a small brown manila takeaway bag and adding a few extra creamers and packets of sugar, Julia nervously prepared to walk back toward the lobby, hoping the gentleman had already gone to his room by the time she got there. Reminded of the promise she made long ago, she refocused with her head held high, knowing she'd never betray that trust.

Steps away from the Lakes lounge, gearing herself up, she cautiously peeked around the corner to find the guest hadn't completed his check-in yet. Taking a deep breath, she straightened both arms. Anxious beyond words, uncontrollably bouncing her feet off the floor, she built the courage to stroll past the men still talking. Nick had passed him his access cards and offered additional instructions. Leaving his car key behind for the valet to move his truck, the man picked up his duffle bag off the floor and slung it on his shoulder again.

Attempting to zip past them undetected, still upset to be seen looking quite unruly, Julia sped from the restaurant to the closest Christmas tree beside the pillar. Peering through the branches, she was thankful they hadn't noticed her. Realizing the next target point was across the vast open space of the main foyer, the designer focused on the next festive tree adjacent to the pillar about twenty feet away. Whatever happened next, she knew she needed to get to the elevators before he did. Worst case scenario, she would take the stairs.

With another deep breath, she darted across the hall. Almost there, a mere five feet away, Julia did not glance in the direction of the men. But that is when she heard it.

Out of nowhere, Nick shouted to get her attention. "Oh, Ms. Mariani! Excuse me, Ms. Mariani!"

Stopping dead in her tracks, she closed her eyes in disbelief, feeling her blood pressure rise exponentially. The pretty blonde-haired mom swiveled at a snail's pace in Nick's direction as both he and the handsome guest focused on her.

"Could you please show Mr. Reynolds the way to the elevators?" Nick asked.

Eyebrows raised, shocked by his request, Julia paused, knowing he'd put her on the spot. Not given a choice, she had to oblige. "Umm... Sure," Julia replied while her heart began beating erratically.

The handsome man offered a killer smile.

"The elevators are this way," she directed with a wave.

Prompted to follow, the guy bid Nick goodnight. Hearing his suitcase rolling along, Julia frantically moved on ahead to check her reflection on the shiny brass doors to make herself look presentable. Unable to fix her hair, she pressed the button and stepped into the elevator, holding the door, giving the man time to catch up.

"Thank you," he said, pulling his suitcase inside and readjusting the bag on his shoulder.

"What floor?" Julia demanded, briefly glancing over while clutching the bag of coffee supplies.

Mesmerized by her eyes hidden behind the dark-rimmed glasses, foolishly taken by their barely-there blue color, Ty mumbled, "Umm, floor? Ahh, I think the Nick guy said the fourth floor." Confirming the room number written on his card key envelope, he smiled upon seeing the button already illuminated. "I think we're going the same way."

Julia fretted upon hearing that. "I guess so."

Looking up at the speaker installed in the ceiling, he said, "Don't you hate listening to Christmas music twenty-four-seven this time of year? It's everywhere. You can't escape it."

Stunned by what he said, believing she heard him wrong, she asked, "Pardon me?"

"You know? I heard it the moment I walked through the door. Even my rental had the radio tuned to a holiday station. It's so annoying."

Afraid to argue with him, she wasn't in the mood for an altercation. "Some people like it."

"Not me," he paused. "And what's with a Christmas tree in every corner? One wasn't enough?"

Julia rolled her eyes. Within seconds of him talking, her opinion of him plummeted. "Well, I think they're pretty."

"You and everyone else."

Fuming, Julia stayed quiet because she knew she might regret it. Not muttering another word, she kept tabs on the floor numbers while they passed each level, believing the elevator had suddenly become sluggish. About four feet apart, anxiously wishing for this awkward ride to end, she prayed that his room was on the opposite wing of the hotel – somewhere far from them. Envisioning him turning right when she turned left after the doors opened, the elevator slowed to a stop.

When the doors parted, Julia mumbled, "Goodnight then," before shuffling left.

In the process, he faintly said, "Yeah, goodnight."

Listening intently for any evidence of the man following down the hall, unfortunately, the sound of his rolling suitcase in the distance soon got louder. Afraid to confirm her suspicions, she stopped in front of her suite and glimpsed back only to find the handsome guy checking the door numbers one by one. Tapping the card key on the locking mechanism and opening the door, she was about to walk into the room but hesitated. That is when he stopped and pointed at the number plate across the hall.

"Huh? Would you look at that? We're neighbors," he revealed.

Feeling like he'd invaded their privacy, she stammered, "I see that."

"Well, goodnight again," he said pleasantly.

"Yes, goodnight."

Entering her room, Julia set the coffee bag on the counter in the kitchen and just stood there. "I can't believe he's the holiday guest." A million things raced through her mind, knowing he would be there for at least ten days. "So much for a quiet family Christmas..." she whispered with great disappointment. Ready for bed, she checked in on Sydney, who was still sleeping soundly.

Experiencing a déjà vu while moving across the living room, remembering back five years to the day when she got the devastating phone call, Julia mumbled, "I can't believe we've made it this far." Taking a deep breath, she added, "I still miss you both every day... Love you."

Slipping under the covers minutes later, she closed her eyes, wishing this Christmas holiday would be a little better than the year before - healing them slowly while they soldiered through life on their own as a family of two. Calmly falling asleep, with thoughts of years past, she tried not to give the disgruntled guest across the hall a second thought.

11

Morning of December 20th

Rise and Shine

The following day, a milder southern blast blew in, bringing a series of anticipated winter squalls expected to cover the town of Carling and the Resort Hotel in over two and a half feet of fluffy, lake-effect snow. Something not unheard of in that area.

Waking later than usual, happy to sleep in for the first time in a long while, Julia got up and wrapped herself in a fluffy robe. Tying the belt around her waist, she wandered over to the window. Quietly sliding the drapes along the rod, not wanting to make any noise, the winter wonderland outside brought a smile to her face. The large trees were all covered with a heavy white layer. Almost pressing her nose against the window, she watched the lazy flakes fall inches away from her face. With a warm and fuzzy feeling enveloping her, making it feel more and more like Christmas, Julia anticipated Sydney's reaction to it all.

Slightly tired, she returned to bed and checked her phone for the latest news. Hearing her little mouse in the bathroom brushing her teeth, it didn't take long for her daughter to notice the weather outside.

"Good morning, Mom! Did you see the snow? Isn't it pretty?"

"Yes, I've been staring at it for at least ten minutes. What do you think? Does it feel like Christmastime yet?"

"Yes, much better now. When we left home, it was still kind of green." She noticed her Mom's laptop next to the bed. "So, did you work late?"

"No, not too bad. Probably went to sleep just after two o'clock." Julia stretched, unable to pull her attention away from the falling snow. It was mesmerizing.

"Really? That's early for you." Knowing her Mother's routine, she asked, "Since it's only eight-thirty, don't worry about me if you want to finish something."

Julia grabbed her computer from the nightstand. "Well, maybe I'll work a little bit longer," she said, "If that's okay?"

"Sure, no problem. I want to watch TV anyway. Tell me when you're done. Maybe we can play in the snow for a bit this morning? Or go for a walk?" Looking at her Mother, Sydney didn't know what she would say to that.

"Yes, absolutely, we should get some fresh air. Give me one hour, okay, Sweetie?" She sat up in bed.

Her daughter gave a double thumbs-up before disappearing and closing her room door behind her. She didn't want the sounds of the television to disturb her Mom.

Trying to get comfortable, shifting the pillows just right, Julia settled in and began to review the textures she'd used thus far. Immersed in the design she'd created, struggling with the work timeline, she grouped each task and inserted them step by step into the plan based on the equipment needed over the two-month project. Without warning, she thought about what had happened with the guy across the hall. Instantly, her embarrassment returned.

"How could you walk into a Christmas tree?" she whispered, leaning her head against the headboard. She was sure he was still laughing at her but hoped he'd eventually forget about the incident. Straightening up again, she said, "Come on, Julia. Just finish this last little bit, and you can go for breakfast." Despite trying to focus, her mind kept wandering. Giving up, she said, "Hey, Syd? Want to go for that walk now?"

Hearing that she had snuck out of her room and quietly poured a bowl of cereal, Sydney shouted from the kitchen, "Sure!"

Closing her laptop, Julia placed it gently on the nightstand. Inching off the bed, ready to experience the winter wonderland outside, she joined her little girl. Desperate for a coffee, she placed the pod in the machine and recalled the reason she was in the foyer in the first place.

Shaking her head, not wanting to ruin the day, she asked her daughter, "So, what's first? Breakfast or walk?"

"I kind of want to go outside while it is still snowing. If we go to breakfast first, I'm afraid it may stop."

"Okay, walk it is." She confirmed before adding, "You know, the snow looks like it might be suitable for making a snowman. Up for that?"

Excitement flashed across her face. "Yeah, sure am!"

"Afterward, we can go have breakfast and start making the ornaments. It'll be a lot of work but worth every second, right?" Julia emphasized with a heightened level of sentimentality.

Nodding in agreement while eating a spoonful of cereal, Sydney silently acknowledged her. Finished chewing, she revealed, "I was looking through the paints while you were working. Did you pack the shopping bag that was on the kitchen counter?"

"Shopping bag? Oh, no. The one with the gold and silver paint?"

"Yeah, that one."

"No, I don't think I did... Now, what are we going to do?"

Thinking briefly, Syd suggested, "Well, we can always use the paint from the studio downstairs."

"That's a good idea. I'm sure the hotel wouldn't mind. I can always leave them money to replace what we used."

The young girl rinsed out her empty cereal bowl in the sink. "We should probably get moving if we're going to finish all the ornaments on time."

"Don't worry. We have four full days until Christmas Eve," Julia pointed out calmly.

"Still. It always goes by fast," her daughter reminded. "I'm going to get dressed now."

"Meet you back here in five?"

With eager eyes, Sydney shouted from the other room, "Deal!"

After disappearing to change into cozy tights and warm sweaters, the two soon met at the front closet and gathered everything they needed from the outdoor bag, including their hats, mitts, boots, scarves, snow pants, and coats.

Bundled up, with their card key in hand, Julia zipped it in her pocket before walking out the door.

"Hurry up, Mom. Let's go!" Her little girl skipped down the hall.

"Hopefully, it's not too cold outside," Julia said while glancing at the room across from them. Remembering their awkward introduction last night, she cringed.

Perhaps we won't see much of him this week. With any luck, he will keep to himself and save us a lot of grief, she thought.

12

Morning of December 20th

Memories

Inside the cozy Lakeview suite, Ty woke to the sound of a door closing shut with a rubbing slide and a subtle click. Hearing people talking, not restraining their laughter, he listened and heard the sound of boots shuffling along the carpet, dissipating the further the guests got down the hall.

Grabbing his phone from the side table, seeing that it was almost ten o'clock, he rolled over in utter disbelief that he had slept that long. Attributing it to the heavenly sleeper mattress, he couldn't remember the last time he got an uninterrupted eight hours. Raising his head off the pillow, discovering a faint view through the sheers, focusing in, he spotted a partially open lake speckled by large snowflakes falling lazily past the window. Double-checking the date, he said, "Wonder what Mom would've been up to today?"

Fondly recalling the lead-up to Christmas in the Reynold's household years ago, he could still see his Mother standing in the kitchen tying her red Christmas apron around her waist. Not long after that, like clockwork, she would be sporting a smidge of flour on her cheeks and nose. Even now, he could still smell the heavenly aroma of freshly baked cookies. It was amazing how the sweet smell of gingerbread filled their house with the unique feeling of home. Sadly, reality sunk in, reminding

Ty that those memories were now a figment of his imagination. That made him miss the traditions beyond belief.

"Why didn't you appreciate it back then? Appreciate her more?" he said with anger, looking back in hindsight, now seeing twenty-twenty. "She often asked you to come home for Christmas, but you didn't. Why? Because of a grudge? So selfish. Stupidest decision ever..."

Trapped in that self-badgering cycle, Ty heard voices outside his window. Slipping both feet from under the covers and placing them firmly on the floor, he stood up and stretched before going over to see what all the commotion was about. Peering through the sheers and pulling them back slightly, he found a young girl playing in the snow with the beautiful woman from last night. His heart sunk at the sight of it, knowing she was probably married and had a family staying with her here. Feeling foolish for how he stared at her, embarrassed by what she must have thought of him, he watched for a few minutes, intrigued by how much fun the two were having.

Rolling a snowball, having a hard time pushing the massive base another inch, the two tried again and again with all their might to shove it forward. He couldn't help but chuckle when their feet slipped out from underneath them, causing both to fall flat on their stomachs and break into hysterics. Not giving up, they got on their feet, turned around, and rested their backs against the massive boulder, thinking they could get more traction that way. Unable to move it, the Mom and her daughter laughed nonstop. Legs giving out, they leaned against the snowball and fell to the ground in utter defeat.

Having no choice but to snicker at them, he saw the woman suddenly look up at the window. Backing off, letting go of the drape, he hoped she didn't think he was spying. Believing he should keep his distance now, sure he weirded her out, Ty scanned the empty room. "Well, you wanted to be alone. You got your wish, Reynolds."

With a pull of the sheets and a yank of the comforter, Ty made the bed and straightened the pillows. In the process, he could hear more laughter from outside. Still intrigued, wanting to see what they were up to, he resisted the temptation.

Happy that the room was tidy, the baseball player turned around to unzip the suitcase on the elevated luggage rack beside the bed. Quickly pulling out shorts, socks, and a t-shirt, ready to begin his usual morning off-season routine, the athlete grabbed his baseball hat and slid it on his head with one hand on the brim and the other positioning it just right from the back. Hesitating a second, knowing he was on vacation now, Ty suddenly turned the bill around backward, hoping to separate his headspace from any thought of work and the decisions he needed to make before the end of the year. Nervously checking his phone and refreshing the page a couple of times, sadly, no new emails popped up on the list. Pulling a swimsuit from the suitcase at the last minute, wondering if the pool was close to the gym, a part of him felt like doing some laps after his workout, believing it would clear his head.

Washing up, he left his room, not knowing where he was going.

While strolling down the quiet corridor, Ty figured he would get directions to the gym from whoever was at the front desk.

Reaching the main level, he exited the elevator and looked around. Not seeing another soul anywhere, he spotted a woman working behind the bar. She glanced up for a split second while he rounded the corner.

"Yes, complete seclusion," he whispered, wondering if staying there was the best decision.

Nick emerged from the office while Ty approached.

"Nick, my man. You're still here?"

"Yes, Sir, Mr. Reynolds. How can I help you this morning?"

"Can you direct me to the gym and pool?"

"Sure can. Go back to the elevator and press M. It will take you down one level. Exit and continue past the Spa. You will see the gym on your right and the pool straight ahead."

"Great! Thanks, man," Ty replied, slapping the desk with his flat hand before leaving.

"You're welcome, Sir."

Doing as instructed, the baseball player descended a level and followed the signs. Finding the glass doors of the gym, having it all to himself, he connected his phone to the Bluetooth speaker in the corner and listened to some music to pass the time.

During his workout, thoughts of his Mom surfaced again. He could still see her sitting at their dining table, weeks before Christmas, making handmade ornaments for every gift she purchased for friends and family - each one crafted with love - all one of a kind. Wondering whatever happened to those ornaments, never placing too much importance on their significance all these years, every ounce of him wished he still had them. Only now did he understand each possessed a piece of her. Maybe she wouldn't seem so far away if he had them.

Knowing his sister had sold their family home seven months ago, he assumed she had packed up his old room. Not having spoken to her in two years, he felt he didn't have a right to ask about his stuff, given she ended up solely handling all of their parent's affairs after they died. He wasn't involved in anything, not that she didn't ask.

Staring at himself in the mirror, he scolded, "In the off-season, you could have been the bigger man and gone home to help her. You also should have spent time with Mom each Christmas, but you didn't. Your beef with Dad made you selfishly not go back. Instead, you chose crowded beaches and warm climates. You chose Christmases surrounded by strangers. That was just plain stupid. Now you have nothing. No one..." he whispered, criticizing his past mistakes.

Disappointed with the reflection in front of him, lifting the dumbbell, letting it fall at his feet halfway down, he blurted out in frustration, "Well, you're about to start a new chapter of your life, and you got what you deserve - a lonely existence. Hope you're happy."

He glared in the mirror and sighed. All hunched over, his chin rested on his clenched fists.

Ending the workout early, deciding to check out the pool and hopefully decompress with a swim, Ty located the change rooms and put on his swimsuit. Showering before walking out, he placed his towel on the chair and walked over to the steps. Immersing his feet in the warm water, he looked around and realized the pool was an indoor/outdoor kind of thing. Descending the stairs, he waded to the large sliding door and ducked under the glass. The air was bitterly cold as the snow fell. Floating on his back, with steam rising all around him, he felt a few snowflakes hit his face. They melted within seconds. Amid his grief and loneliness, he found a little happiness in something simple and pure. Lifting his head above the waterline, he listened to the wind whistling through the trees. With his ears beginning to freeze, he headed back inside. Carefully ducking under the window and clearing his face of water droplets with one hand, he slowly opened his eyes and noticed people standing at the very end of the pool deck. Focusing on who was there, he found the woman and the little girl standing with their outdoor clothes still on.

With mittens in one hand, the girl dipped her fingers into the water to feel the temperature.

At the same time, startled, not expecting to see anyone there, her Mother locked eyes with him.

Raising a steady hand, he greeted, "Hi. Good morning."

Shocked to see him showcasing a chiseled physique, Julia panicked and covered her daughter's eyes. Quickly escorting her out the door, she said, "Come on, Sydney. We need to go."

Ty watched them leave in a hurry. "That didn't go well." He wasn't used to people avoiding him. Usually, it was the other way around. "I guess this is going to be one long, drawn-out holiday," he said before starting his laps.

13

December 20th

The Lonely Guy from Across the Hall

Looking straight ahead, hearing the pool door close behind them, Julia didn't turn around for fear that he was still watching. Within seconds, the two had shuffled down the hall, almost out of sight. While continuing in silence, Julia glimpsed at Sydney, hoping to avoid discussing what had just happened.

While passing the Spa, the girl asked, "Who was that man, Mom?"

"Nobody," she replied bluntly, feeling very uncomfortable.

"No, really? Who is he?" Sydney questioned again. Stopping, she placed her hands on her hips and stared at her Mother, expecting an answer. "He seemed to know you."

"Sydney..."

Intentionally blocking Julia's path, raising her eyebrows, and exuding a tween attitude, the girl asked one more time, "Mom?"

"Fine," she said, pausing a moment. "There isn't much to tell." Tilting her head, unable to believe she had to explain herself, Julia concluded, "Last night, I went downstairs to get coffee pods for the machine. That man arrived at the hotel when I was walking to the restaurant. On my way back upstairs, we shared the elevator. That's it. Turns out, his room is right across from ours. I guess management wanted their guests close together for housekeeping purposes."

"Did you not notice?"

"Notice what?"

"He seems kind of nice," her daughter smiled in a carefree way.

"No. No, I didn't." Passing by Sydney, Julia immediately changed the subject. "So, I suppose we should get on with our day."

Witnessing her Mom's strange behavior, Syd knew she needed to investigate this mystery guest. A gut feeling said there was more to her Mother's story than what she was letting on.

While they waited for the elevator, the doors soon parted. Julia walked inside and pressed the number four, but to her surprise, Syd stepped forward and selected the Lobby button.

"Wait? Where are you going?" her Mother asked.

"Umm, I'm just gonna see if Rebecca is around today. Go back to the room and change. I'll meet you in the restaurant."

"Okay, but remember, mind your manners. I'll be back shortly."

"Don't worry, I will," Sydney said, handing her Mother her coat with the hat and mitts stuffed into the sleeve just before the doors closed behind her.

Upon rounding the corner into the vast open space, Sydney's first stop was the front desk. Believing the man behind the counter could help her, the curious girl confidently walked over.

Hearing the shuffling of snow boots, Nick looked up and greeted her with a smile. "Hello, there. Ms. Sydney, I presume?"

"Yes, how did you know my name?" she questioned, a little suspicious.

"Your Mother pointed you out when you arrived yesterday. I believe you were admiring the Christmas tree at the time. That said, you are also the only young lady staying at the hotel."

Pointing his way, in a very Sherlock Holmes sort of manner, she slowly replied, "Right...."

"How are we this morning?" Nick sparked a general conversation, knowing the girl would soon ask him something. "Enjoying your stay?"

"Yes, very much. I love it here. It's like a second home. Our day started a little strangely, though," she stated very matter-of-factly.

"Oh? Why is that, Miss?"

Resting her elbows on the desk, holding up her chin, she sneakily inquired, "So, Nick? What do you know about the man staying across the hall?"

Aware it was against policy to divulge information on any guest, he subtly looked left and right to ensure nobody was within an earshot of them. Able to hear a pin drop in the place, the white-haired gentleman leaned forward while Sydney turned a listening ear. He whispered, "Mr. Reynolds is a baseball player from Boston."

With eyes bulging, mouth open wide, she queried further, "Like what? A professional baseball player?"

Reacting quickly to diffuse Sydney's reaction, Nick placed his finger over his lips. "Shhh...."

Swiftly covering her mouth, she realized she had spoken too loudly. Looking left and then right to see if anyone had heard what she said, the girl quietly asked, "What's he doing here?"

"From what he said, he's visiting for the holidays in search of some much-needed rest and seclusion, but you didn't hear that from me. If you know what I mean..." he offered stealthily with a wink, touching his pointer finger to the side of his nose.

"Got it. Not a word," Syd promised, "Thanks for the info."

"You are very welcome, my dear. Now, is there anything else I can do for you?" he asked, raising his voice to the usual standards.

"No, I think that's it for now. Thank you."

"Very well."

Making her way to the lounge to see Rebecca, Sydney turned to wave goodbye to Nick, but to her surprise, he was gone. Believing he had slipped into the office, Sydney shrugged her shoulders. Approaching the bar, she found Rebecca taking inventory.

"Hey, Rebecca. Morning," she greeted their friend before taking a seat in a bucket chair to remove her boots.

"Morning, monkey. How are you?" The young woman walked around the counter.

"I'm good," she said while removing her snow pants and slipping her boots back on her feet.

"So, how was your walk outside? I saw your snowman. It's a big one."

"Yes, it could have been even bigger, but we couldn't stay out any longer. My toes and fingers got cold. I feel like I'm just beginning to thaw out now," Sydney laughed, tucking the snow pants alongside the arm of the chair. "Mom just went upstairs to change, and then she'll be down for breakfast."

"So, what do you have planned today? Anything exciting?" Rebecca queried while getting comfortable in an adjacent chair.

"I guess we need to get started on the ornaments. If I could finish half of them today, that would be great."

"I'm sure you will. You are very organized, from what I recall."

"Suppose so." Seeing her Mother appear, she pointed and said, "There she is."

Julia strolled over to join the girls. "Good morning, Rebecca. How are you?"

"So far, the day is going well. I'm happy the hotel has quieted down."

"I guess so. Yesterday was pretty busy here."

"Yeah, you're not kidding. It never ceases to amaze me that after an exodus like that, within hours, I can shoot a cannon through the halls."

"Yesterday, we had to wait a few minutes for the shuttles to leave and make room for us to park. Now, with everyone gone, there's only one guest to contend with. He arrived late last night. Have you seen him?"

"Oh, yeah. I did earlier. Pretty sure the guy was wearing athletic wear. Guess he went down to use the gym." Rebecca gave her the eye. "He's handsome, don't you think?"

Julia knew what her friend was implying. "Oh, no, no, no. Please, not you, too?"

"What? I'm just saying?" the young woman chuckled.

To avoid a more embarrassing conversation, Julia turned to Sydney and placed her hand on her shoulder. "So, Syd? Ready for breakfast?"

"Yes, I'm so hungry."

"That's a good sign." Julia handed Sydney her notebook and pen. "I brought this with me just in case you wanted to double-check your lists."

"Oh, good. Thanks," Sydney said, getting up from the chair.

Walking alongside them, Rebecca veered behind the bar.

Julia noted, "Maybe we can meet up later? Syd and I will probably be in the craft room."

Taking hold of her clipboard resting on the counter, she replied, "Yes, that would be great. My shift ends at three o'clock today. I'll find you afterward."

"Perfect. See you this afternoon," Julia assured.

"Looking forward to it."

Walking toward the restaurant with her snow pants tucked under one arm and notebook in hand, Sydney toyed with how to phrase what she was about to say.

"Mom?" She couldn't look her in the eye.

"Yes."

"Umm... I was thinking. Since that man across the hall is here for the holidays and is all alone, shouldn't we put him on the list, too?" Sydney squinted her eyes, leaving them partially open, and waited for the lecture to ensue. Bracing for impact, she prepared for her Mother's reaction.

"Sweetie pie, I'm sure he wouldn't care about something like that."

"How do you know? You might be surprised." Laced by her Mom's firm facial expression, Sydney put her hands up between them to hold her back. "Just saying... You've always taught me that Christmas is about giving to others?"

Not willing to say another word, knowing her daughter was, in fact, right, they spotted their friend at the hostess podium.

"Morning, Lisa," Julia greeted.

"Hello, Marianis," she welcomed them with open arms.

"How are you?" Julia asked while offering a hug. "We missed talking to you yesterday because of how crazy it was."

"I'm sorry about that. It was busier than we anticipated. By the time I had a minute, you had left already. Thought I'd see you this morning."

"We woke up bright and early," Sydney revealed.

"How was your trip yesterday? I'm so glad you got here before the storm hit. I was praying you'd arrive safely."

"It started to snow the moment we pulled in," Julia confirmed while walking toward the large bank of windows at the back of the room.

"Well, you're here now. You can rest and relax." Arriving at their usual table, Lisa announced, "Here we are."

"Thank you so much. I love the view from here."

"It's a little obstructed right now. Hopefully, the storm will clear so you can see the lake better."

"Will you be joining us for Christmas Eve dinner?" Syd opened her book to record her answer.

"Oh, I wouldn't miss it. I am on the schedule to work over the holidays, so please, count me in," Lisa said happily. "Our new waiter, June, is also working. Is it okay if I ask him, too?"

"Yes, the more, the merrier," Julia said while Sydney wrote their names on the list.

The woman handed them their menus. Both declined, already knowing what they wanted.

"Wow, that didn't take long." Placing their orders, Lisa said, "Okay, I'll be back in a second with coffee and juice."

"Perfect. Thanks a bunch," Julia graciously said.

When Lisa left the table to pass the information to the kitchen, Syd and her Mom started discussing their plan for the day. Amidst their discussions on ornaments, cookies, and resort activities, the young girl added Jun and Lisa's names to the list and secretly added another at the very bottom – *The Lonely Guy from across the Hall.*

14

December 20th

Breakfast

Finishing his last lap of the pool, Ty climbed the steps and grabbed the towel from the chair, drying off as best he could. It was strange not to see another living soul around.

Putting on his running shoes and tucking in the laces, leaving them untied, he slipped on his t-shirt and gathered his shorts and socks before making his way back upstairs. Hungry after the workout, he looked forward to having a hardy breakfast.

Reaching his room on the fourth floor, not hearing anything coming from across the hall, he figured his neighbors were somewhere else in the hotel. Going through his suitcase, he changed into jeans and a fresh T-shirt. Deciding to wear a casual sweater versus a hoodie, the baseball player ran his fingers through his damp hair and inserted his earbuds while flipping through emails, frustrated to find nothing from his agent.

"Gotta be patient," he whispered on his way out the door. "You know how to play the contract game this time of year."

Walking down the hall, on the way to the elevator, Ty turned on some music to lighten the mood. Arriving in the lobby minutes later, he casually strolled past Rebecca, who was restocking the bar. Wondering what to eat, he smelt the welcome aroma of freshly brewed coffee while approaching the restaurant.

Lisa was at the podium and greeted the handsome guest with a smile.

Taking one earbud out of his right side, he heard her ask, "Good morning. Table for one?"

Sadly agreeing, he said, "Yes," and returned the bud to its rightful place.

With the hostess leading the way, he followed her into the large dining room and immediately spotted two people sitting by the window—the woman and her daughter from across the hall. Making eye contact with them while taking a seat two tables away, Sydney waved while Julia looked on with little emotion.

When handed a menu, Ty removed the earbuds and respectfully set them on top of his phone in the middle of the table.

At the same time, Lisa explained the a-la-carte offering since no buffet was available during the holidays. Leaving him to decide what he wanted to order, Ty saw the little girl glance over as her food arrived from the kitchen.

Curious about their choices, he followed the plates and inspected what was on them.

"You should order the blueberry buttermilk pancakes. They are pretty awesome," the little blue-eyed blonde girl blurted out.

"Sydney?" the woman said under her breath, not approving of her interaction with the man.

"It's not a problem. I appreciate the suggestion." In hopes of striking up a conversation, he said, "Do you mind me asking what you ordered?" He quickly noted the ring on the woman's left hand.

Put on the spot, Julia replied, "Me?"

"Yeah." Focusing on her plate, Ty respectfully questioned, "Looks like you got some kind of eggs benny there?"

Caught off guard, Julia stayed silent.

Quickly interjecting to speak for her Mom, Sydney replied, "Yes, it is. It's her favorite."

Right then, Lisa walked by to take his order. "So, what will it be? Have you decided?"

"Yes. I got some help from...." Hesitating a second, he looked at them and inquired, "I'm sorry. I don't know your names."

The young girl introduced herself without reservation. "I'm Sydney, and this is my Mom, Julia."

"Good to meet you both. My name is Ty."

"Nice to meet you, Ty," Sydney innocently replied as her Mom forced a grin.

Returning his attention to Lisa, the guy placed his order. "As I was about to say, I got some helpful advice from Sydney and Julia. I think I will start with the steel-cut oatmeal and have the Eggs Benny."

Turning to the little girl, he added, "I'm going to try the pancakes tomorrow if that's okay?"

Syd gave a thumbs-up.

Recording his order on her notepad, Lisa asked, "Coffee, tea, or juice to start?"

"I'll have orange juice and a coffee. Thanks."

"No problem. I'll be back shortly."

"Great."

Watching Lisa walk by with her back to the man, Julia and Sydney saw her eyebrows raise excitedly. She gave them an intriguing eye signal, mouthing the words ~ He's *cute.*

Seeing him pick up his phone with a look of disappointment while scrolling through it, Julia wondered if he was waiting for something important. At least, it seemed that way. Caught up in her thoughts, realizing she was staring, the words: *Look away. Look away* echoed through her mind just as Ty happened to lock eyes with her. Swiftly diverting her attention back to Sydney and the tasks they planned to tackle, Julia went about recapping their lists.

Ty unintentionally heard something about a Christmas tree farm. Eavesdropping on them, he heard Julia confirm that she'd arranged the tree-shopping excursion in two days. Trying not to seem obvious, he continued perusing the sports news while Julia glanced over from time to time, wondering if he'd listened in on their conversation.

Shifting his attention to the obstructed view outside, he thought, *Why haven't Mike or Matt contacted me with an update yet?* Feeling deflated, going down a negative path, he figured someone else would probably end up making this life-altering decision, not allowing him even to have a say.

When the two ladies finished their brunch, Ty spotted them getting up from the table and pushing in their chairs. Seeing each walk by, he took a sip of coffee and said, "Thanks again for the menu advice. I'm sure I will see you both later."

"Oh? Why's that?" Julia nervously asked with a slight attitude.

"Well, for one, we are the only guests at the hotel, and two, you're right across the hall, so..."

"Right," Julia responded bluntly, feeling entirely out of her element. "Umm... Enjoy your day."

"Thanks," he said, offering a charismatic smile.

Outside the Cottages Restaurant, Julia seemed flustered. Feeling that this guy was invading their Christmas holiday, knowing full well she selfishly didn't have a right to shut down the entire resort and keep it for themselves, Julia took a deep breath and thought, *Okay, you can do this. You can put up with him. It's only for ten days; then, he will be gone. Maybe he'll get bored before that and leave early.*

Picking up on her Mother's weird behavior, Sydney turned to her. "Ty is nice. We should invite him to Christmas dinner."

"What? No. I'm sure he doesn't want to spend Christmas with all of us."

"Shouldn't you let him decide? He will see everybody coming and going from our room with a plate of turkey and stuffing, mashed potatoes, and gravy, and we don't invite him? Seriously? Come on? What's wrong with you? You always include everybody. Even the new staff we've never met before. Why is this any different?"

"I don't know. It just is," Julia exclaimed.

The girl lowered her head and built up the courage to speak her mind. "I overheard Sarah's Mom talking about you with Michaela's Mom. They seem to think you should move on. Just want you to know I'm okay with that."

Stopping in her tracks, she looked at Syd, believing her to be way too mature for her age. "Is that what this is all about? Look, Sweetie, I'm not upset, you know. I'm just not ready for, umm, yeah, anything like that."

"But Mom?"

"Sydney...please. Can we get on with our day?"

Noticing tears developing in her eyes, the little girl knew she had gone too far. Realizing her Mother was still grieving and wasn't ready to meet anyone else, Sydney desperately wanted to retract what she had said.

When they returned to their room, Julia opened the door without saying a word. Needing to break the silence and change the subject, she asked, "So, what do you want to do first? Ornaments or Christmas baking?"

"Ornaments, I suppose." Syd shifted her attention to their fully stocked craft trolley. Waiting for a second, looking through the drawers, remembering again that they forgot the gold and silver metallic paint at home on the kitchen counter, she pointed out, "We will have to make the one style in the studio downstairs. I need gold and silver paint. I don't feel right bringing it up here to the room. You okay to go with me?"

Her Mother was deep in thought.

"Hello? Earth to Mom? What are we doing? Going downstairs or not?" Sydney waved her hand in front of her.

Julia broke from her thoughts and mumbled, "Yes. Sure." With her head reeling a mile a minute, she wondered if she should address the comment. *Why does everyone think I need to move on? She wondered.*

"Ready to go then?" Sydney rolled the craft trolley to the door and out into the hall.

"Yes, I'm ready. Let me just brush my teeth quickly." Going into her bathroom, she looked at herself in the mirror and exhaled. "Okay, pull yourself together," she said, intent on shaking off their uncomfortable conversation. "It'll be okay. Just go."

Walking out, expecting to find her daughter waiting for her, Julia said happily, "I'm ready!" While closing the door, she turned around and was surprised to see her speaking with the man across the hall.

"Hi again," he said with a warm smile.

"Hello," Julia replied, lowering her head a few times, unable to look him in the eye more than once.

"Ty was asking about the cart." The girl giggled. "He didn't know what it was."

"Wait, in my defense, if you ask anyone else in this hotel what this thing is, I bet they wouldn't know either," Ty argued, trying to save face.

"No, everyone here has been seeing this craft trolley every Christmas for years. It's just you," Syd settled factually.

Julia agreed. "Yes, she's right."

"Where are you going with that thing anyway?" There was a hint of humor in his tone.

"To the craft studio downstairs. We have some things we need to make," Sydney explained while her Mother gave her the eye.

"We should get going, Syd." Julia started pushing the cart along slowly.

"Well then, happy...crafting?" Ty offered while they walked down the hall. Opening his room door, he stepped inside. "Crafting? Huh. I wonder what they're making?"

Reaching the elevators, Julia was a bit annoyed. She wished their holiday could be like other years, quiet and secluded from any guests. Knowing she had to make the best of it, believing being rude wasn't the answer, she figured she should be pleasant to the guy and not ruin his vacation.

Intent on distracting her Mom, Syd swiftly started their game. "I pick left!" she quickly shouted.

With a bright smile, Julia pointed to the other side.

When the doors opened on the right, Julia snickered because of her competitive nature. She then walked into the elevator, whispering, "I win," and purposefully bumped Sydney's shoulder to lighten the mood.

"Don't worry. I'll get the next one," Syd challenged.

The two girls wheeled the trolley past the spa, gym, and pool area to the adjacent hallway that led to the other elevator on the Mezzanine level. Getting into the smaller people mover, they ended up again on the lowest level at the mountainside resort. Not seeing anyone, they arrived at the craft studio. Julia followed her daughter and maneuvered the trolley inside. Setting up everything on an empty table, spreading out a felt-backed tablecloth to protect it from the hot glue and paint, Sydney opened her notebook and showed her Mother the ornament styles she had selected this year. Organizing all the materials in the middle of the table, she grabbed her portable speaker and connected her phone. Soon, festive tunes filled the air around them.

Looking at the little girl across from her, seeing how grown up she'd gotten in the past few years, Julia felt like she'd missed a few milestones. Those feelings prompted her to ask, "Syd, are you happy?"

"Yeah, of course. Why wouldn't I be?" she said, slightly confused.

"Just wondering. I know that life has been pretty rough the past while."

"Mom, I'm fine. Look where we are and how far we've come. We're spending another Christmas in Carling. My absolute favorite place in the whole wide world, and it's snowing. It doesn't get any better than this," she added, pointing to the wintery weather outside the large bank of windows across the hall from the craft room. "On top of that, we are making ornaments for our Carling family in this new studio. What more could I ever want?"

The positive response was encouraging. Julia felt she was slowly healing from the loss they'd suffered. But for whatever reason, this year, the pain seemed less than the year before. Assembling the first ornament, she thought, *Guess that's why they say 'time heals all wounds.'* Still unsure if she would fully recover, Julia knew only time would tell.

"Umm, Syd?" Not knowing how to start the conversation they were about to have, Julia tried to think quickly on her feet and figure out how she would phrase the question.

Her daughter said casually, "Yeah?" while warming up the glue gun.

"Why did you say it is okay for me to move on?"

Sitting on the chair across from her Mom, Sydney looked at the floor. "Isn't it hard being alone?"

Tilting her head, Julia answered, "Alone? I'm not alone. I have you."

"You know what I mean. Eventually, I will finish high school and move out when I go to university, right?"

"I realize that."

"I don't want you to be lonely when I leave."

"I'll be okay. I know you need to find your place in this world. You never have to worry about me."

"Doesn't matter. I do anyway," Syd said sympathetically. "Look, I was young when all that happened. I remember bits and pieces. I miss them too, but the bottom line is, I know you are often sad, and I believe if you met someone, maybe that person could make you happy again."

"But what if I am not ready?"

"Then, you're not ready. I just wanted to tell you how I felt. You know, in case it made a difference."

Understanding her now, Julia tearfully said, "Well, thank you for thinking of me. For the time being, I'm still good with how things are."

"In the end, that's up to you. I can't push you one way or the other. All I can do is tell you I'm fine with it."

"When did you become so smart?" Julia snickered, surprised by their adult conversation.

Placing her hand on her hip, she dramatically mimicked a sassy teenager and offered in a saucy voice, "See... I have this great Mom who's, like, so cool. We do, like, everything together, and she's, like, the best Mom Ev-R!"

Laughing and giggling, Julia quickly got up and walked around the table to hug her. "I love you, Sydney Mariani."

"Love you too."

"Oh, my sweet girl."

Just then, in the midst of it all, Rebecca walked in. "Hey? What did I miss?"

15

December 20th

Bored

Sitting in his room, perusing a selection of television channels and movie rental options, bored out of his mind, Ty wasn't sure what to do. Walking over to the windows to check on the storm, he saw the snow falling a bit heavier than earlier that morning. Spotting the snowman the mother-daughter duo made, Ty wondered where this craft studio was. Desperate for human interaction, he was curious about what they were making. About to go and find them, he quickly opted against the idea for fear that it may give off a negative or creepy vibe.

Deciding to head down to the front desk to inquire about some of the excursions and activities, he hoped to book something challenging - anything to help pass the time. Riding an empty elevator that opened to the hallowed halls of the lobby below, Ty found none other than Nick at the Concierge Desk.

"Nick! My man. How's it goin'?"

"Mr. Reynolds. How are you enjoying your stay?"

"Not bad, not bad. Little bored. Have to say. I guess outdoor activities are limited with the snowstorm and all?"

"Yes, unfortunately, Sir. But rest assured. The storm should end in about five hours."

"Okay, so what do guests usually do for fun around here?"

Grabbing a handful of brochures, Nick quickly placed a row of options on the desk.

"Our most popular activities onsite are snowshoeing, ski shoeing, and fat bike riding."

Interested in those options, Ty nodded while Nick continued his spiel. "We have a ski-shoeing excursion scheduled for tomorrow. This sport is like snowshoeing but uses wide-plank, short skis that slide over the snow versus snowshoes that punch through it. A little easier to muster. Our guide takes you to the top of the Pointe, a lookout with a glamping tent, firepit, and, of course, an extraordinary view of the lake. Upon arrival, a picnic lunch is ready, and the staff packs everything up after you leave. It is quite fabulous. A must-do."

"Sounds interesting."

"If you are into more extreme sports, I suggest fat bike riding and ice climbing, but with so much snow, both activities will not be available until operators can assess the conditions. The trails need packed snow for the bikes to work effectively, so the groomer will go out and do that once the snow stops. As for the trek to the frozen waterfall along a series of scenic lakeside cliffs, it is usually dependent on the conditions as well, which are not ideal at the moment."

"Okay..."

"If you feel like doing something creative and more low-key, there is watercolor painting in the studio downstairs," Nick added.

Ty immediately shook his head at that idea, knowing the ladies were there.

Not receiving the response he'd hoped for, the older gentleman said, "We also have snowmobile rentals. You will need a guide for that as well. There is an hourly fee for them. I suggest you have proper winter attire to stay warm since the weather changes quickly here."

Leaning toward the ski-shoeing, he figured it would get him outside for some fresh air. "Okay, I guess the first thing is to go shopping and buy some warmer gear. I brought winter clothes, but it's probably not polar vortex-worthy. Any suggestions?"

"We have outdoor attire in the Resort Shop, but if you cannot find your size, I suggest you drive into town and visit the Liv Outside store. They can also help outfit you, but with the weather as it is right now, I wouldn't risk going out until the roads are clear."

"Right..." Ty contemplated things. "Okay, I'll go check out the resort shop. If I can't get what I need there, I'll head into town in the morning."

"Excellent, Sir. I think that would be wise."

Slapping his hand on the desk again, Ty said, "Perfect. I appreciate your help. Where can I find this store?"

Nick raised his hand. Veering it to the right, he said, "Go past the elevators and continue down the long hallway. It will be there on your left. You can't miss it."

"Thanks," the great baseball player said before walking back through the lobby. Continuing as directed, he found the long hallway and a series of window displays just ahead of him. When he went inside, he found a friendly guy behind the counter.

"Hello, Sir. How can I help you?"

Ty laughed and said, "They told me I can buy warm clothes here."

"Yes. Absolutely. What are you looking for?"

He snickered and said, "Everything."

16

December 20th

Operation Christmas

Within an hour, having purchased everything he needed to survive the cold, Ty hoped he'd be able to enjoy the activities without freezing. Confidently equipped with warm boots, an insulated hat and pair of mitts, base layers, snow pants, and a new ski jacket, Ty left the store toting three large bags. Returning to the Concierge Desk to sign up for the ski-shoeing activity, he felt confident about participating now. Rounding the corner into the lobby, he immediately noticed that Nick had gone and another man had taken his place.

"Hello, Sir. What can I do for you?" the white-haired gentleman questioned.

"Hi." Reading the name tag on his shirt, Ty said, "Bryce, is it?"

"Yes, Sir."

"I spoke to the guy at the front desk earlier about the ski shoeing activity tomorrow. Is it possible to book me for that?"

"Certainly, I can register you. Under what name?"

"Reynolds. Room 1445." Ty watched Bryce write his name below Julia and Sydney's on the sheet.

"Thank you, Mr. Reynolds. I have registered you for that excursion. Please meet the group and your guide here at exactly one o'clock."

"Sounds good. Thanks."

"No problem, Sir. Have a good rest of the day. Let me know if there is anything more we can do for you."

"Appreciate that. Thank you."

While walking away, Ty couldn't believe the ladies were participating in that activity. "Wow, what are the chances," he said, trying his best to juggle the bags on his way to the elevators. Pressing the button, he heard the one on the right arriving first and stepped to that side. To his surprise, he met Julia, Sydney, and their wheeled craft trolley when the doors parted. Hesitating, he shifted his shopping bags, making sure not to hit either of them. The girls squished further into the corner to make room.

"Sorry, Ladies," he sincerely apologized.

"Wow, I see you did a lot of shopping today." Julia couldn't help but point that out.

"Umm, yeah. I wanted to try a few outdoor activities but didn't have warm enough clothes, so I went to the resort shop and bought what I needed."

Sydney tried to look inside each one. "I think you're all set now."

"I think so, too." An awkward silence hung in the air between them. "Hey, how did your crafting thing go?"

Giving Sydney the eye, not wanting to let him in on what they are up to, Julia revealed, "It went well. We got half of the project done."

"That's good to hear. What kind of project?"

Not sure if she should share the details, Sydney suddenly spouted, "Handmade ornaments."

Believing he heard her wrong, he replied, "Wait. What?"

Unable to contain her excitement, Sydney spilled their secret in a flood of words. "It's all part of something we call *Operation Christmas*. We make special ornaments to hand out to all the staff. They are our Carling family. It's one of the many things Mom and I do every year."

Caught off guard, reminded of his Mother, Ty glanced over at Julia, who refused to look his way. "Is that so? I must say this is very kind of you."

"Well, it helps us get into the Christmas spirit when we arrive here and also helps pass the time," Julia divulged, still focused straight ahead.

As they rode the elevator upwards, the doors opened on the fourth floor. Ty held it for them and insisted, "Please, after you."

"Thank you," Sydney said, wheeling the cart into the hallway.

Happy to get a glimpse of his gentlemanly nature, Julia watched Ty lugging all his bags. Finally looking him in the eye, she offered some courtesy. "Can we give you a hand?"

Drawn to her blue eyes, making him delay his answer, the baseball player said, "Thanks, but no. I've got it. Appreciate the offer, though."

"No problem." Julia kept walking alongside Sydney. The two pushed the trolley along the carpeted corridor, careful not to tip it over.

Stopped outside their suites, a mere eight feet apart, Ty dropped his bags on either side of him and touched his card to the reader. Turning around, he watched Sydney enter their room and hold the door open for her Mother to guide the trolley inside.

Before departing, the young girl waved at him. "Bye. Maybe we will see you after."

"Possibly," he replied while Julia looked on, not saying anything more.

Hearing both doors slam shut, they noticed the time. It was almost half past four. Knowing they hadn't eaten anything in hours, Julia suggested they head down to the restaurant to grab some take-out and bring it back to the room to start the first batch of Christmas baking.

Wholeheartedly agreeing, her little girl washed her hands and changed out of her crafting clothes.

Julia also freshened up.

In minutes, both looked more presentable. The tween opened their room door, ready to leave, while her Mom grabbed their card key and followed. To her surprise, she found out their neighbor across the hall had the same idea.

"Hey?" he said, pulling his door shut behind him. "Are you guys going to get something to eat?"

"Yep," Syd quickly responded, skipping along to the elevators and leaving the adults behind.

Noticing the woman wasn't exactly happy to accompany him, he tried to break the unease. "So? Umm, this will be my first dinner here. Any suggestions?"

Not turning one iota to have a face-to-face conversation, she hesitated a second to think of what to say. "I like the lobster ravioli, but you might prefer a steak?"

"Normally, I suppose that is true. Since I'm on vacation, I believe I should live a little and venture outside the norm. So, anything goes."

"The Carling burger is quite good, but instead of regular fries, you may want to try the truffle ones. It comes with roasted garlic aioli to dip them in. I like that once and a while."

"Decision made. Thank you for that."

Sydney shouted from around the corner. "Hurry! I'm holding the door!"

The two sped up and stepped inside to join her.

Going out on a limb, he asked, "Maybe you ladies want to join me?"

Moving her sights to the floor, Julia didn't know what to say. "Umm, thank you for the invitation, but we still have some things to do tonight. We've already planned to get take-out and bring it upstairs with us. Sorry about that."

"Oh, that's okay. No problem. Just thought I'd ask."

Waiting in silence, Ty asked Sydney, "So, what are you having for dinner? Your Mom suggested I get the Carling Burger."

Thinking a second, Sydney answered, "Well, I'm getting the fish and chips. That's my favorite, but you can't go wrong with the burger. Make sure you get the..."

"Truffle fries?" he laughed.

"How did you know?" Syd was surprised.

"Your Mom suggested that too."

"Well, then you are all set," the girl confirmed.

Watching the doors open on the main floor, Ty waited for the ladies to exit first. Walking side by side, they reached the hostess area and saw Lisa finishing her shift.

Shooting Julia the eye, immediately interested in what was happening between the handsome stranger and her, Lisa greeted them joyfully, presumptuously suggesting, "Table for three?"

"No. Unfortunately not. Sydie and I are grabbing take-out and going back upstairs to the room tonight. We have a few things to finish so that we can spend some time outdoors tomorrow."

Reminded of the activity they had registered for, Ty stayed quiet.

"I think Mr. Reynolds will be eating here, though. He will need a table," Julia said kindly.

Nodding, he agreed with her. "It appears I will be dining alone tonight."

Before escorting the handsome baseball player into the dining room, Lisa handed her friend a piece of paper. "Before I forget, Ruth wanted me to give this to you."

Skimming the note, she said, "Thanks. That's perfect."

Lisa motioned for Ty to follow her by waving a menu in hand. "Right this way, Mr. Reynolds."

"Guess that's my cue, ladies. Have a good night."

Waving at Ty, Syd said, "Bye."

Julia also waved gently before looking at the menu. Although she was relieved, she felt terrible that he would have no choice but to eat alone. Having had to do that recently while Sydney was out with friends, she knew she would never bless that feeling on anyone.

Placing their orders with Lisa upon her return, Julia joined her daughter in the Lakes lounge to watch a little TV while they waited. With a sports news anchor spilling the latest on the hockey world, the topic of conversation soon changed to the Hot Stove and how things were heating up. Julia noticed a player's picture on the screen's top right-hand corner. Dressed in a Boston uniform, she focused and realized the guy looked a lot like Ty. Sitting up, trying to hear the announcer's faint words, she heard the name Reynolds. Wanting to turn up the volume, not seeing a remote anywhere, Julia missed most of the announcement before they moved on to the next player in question. Seeing Sydney immersed in a text conversation with friends, not having seen the screen, she decided to keep the information to herself. Later, once Syd was in bed, she hoped to check her phone and find out why Ty Reynolds was hiding out at the Carling for the holidays.

17

December 20th

Baking Tradition

Returning to their room with food in hand, Sydney and Julia sat at the dining table to discuss which cookies they would bake first. After receiving the note from Manager Ruth confirming the hotel had a skeleton staff of thirty scheduled to work over the next couple of days, Julia did a few calculations.

"So, maybe we should make around one hundred and fifty cookies. That would give the staff three each, and we will have enough left for Christmas Eve. How does that sound?"

"I think that's good," Syd agreed. Pausing, she then suggested, "But I was thinking.... How about you bake while I finish the ornaments? We can get more done that way. Like a divide and conquer kind of thing."

"Are you sure you can finish them all on your own?"

Convinced she would be fine, Syd replied, "Mom? Really? Yeah, of course, I can."

"All right, then. Let's get started."

Pulling her hair into a ponytail, Julia secured it with an elastic and stepped into the kitchen. The recipe book lay open on the counter, its pages well-worn and smudged with the evidence of past baking adventures. A soft hum escaped her lips as she arranged rows of sugar, flour, and chocolate chips, setting the stage for the triple batch of cookies she planned to conquer.

From the dining room, the gentle scrape of a chair and the rumble of small wheels signaled Sydney's movement. The craft trolley, brimming with supplies, came to a halt by the table. A felt-lined plastic table-cloth was unrolled and smoothed over the surface, a shield against the inevitable glitter and glue.

Connecting her phone to the Bluetooth speaker, Sydney scrolled through playlists until the room filled with the cheerful jingles of Christmas music. The upbeat rhythm drew a chuckle from the kitchen.

"Nice choice, DJ extraordinaire," Julia called without turning from her work.

A playful voice answered back. "I thought we needed something catchy."

Julia pulled an apron over her head. Vibrant red and adorned with holly berries, it was tied snugly around her waist before she turned her attention to the flour, carefully sifting it into a large mixing bowl. Nearby, another apron sat folded neatly on the counter, untouched.

A brief pause hung in the air as Sydney glanced at the craft supplies set out in front of her. But the sight of her Mother working alone stirred a pang of guilt. In that moment, she no longer believed the best course of action was to tackle the work separately. Stopping what she was doing, she walked into the kitchen and slipped the apron on with a smile.

Thrilled that her daughter joined in, Julia revealed, "Baking cookies with you every Christmas has been the most memorable part of my holidays. I love doing this together. You know, Grandma, my Mother, never really wanted to share her baking time with me. Not exactly sure why. She normally made the Christmas cookies and squares while I was at school, even though I always asked to help her when I returned at the end of the day. I'm glad we've created this tradition." Holding back the tears, she tried to stop them from welling up.

Sydney quickly reached out to hug her tightly. "Love you, Mom."

"I love you too, Sweetheart. I'm sorry. Around this time of year, I'm overly grateful for all the little things we share."

"Me too."

As the emotional moment passed, Julia located a tissue box inside their bathroom and blotted her face.

"Okay, I'm ready to bake. Are you?" she asked with a happier expression.

Sydney's eyes lit up. "Yes, for sure!"

18

December 20th

A Christmas Spark

Feeling like this Christmas break was probably the loneliest in years, Ty sat alone in the dining room and finished his dinner. Catching up on the sports highlights, seeing his situation plastered all over the internet sports pages and on TV, the baseball player checked his emails and texts almost every fifteen minutes. After signing the bill, he bid Lisa goodnight before slowly walking back through the desolate lobby. Thankful to see Nick at the Concierge desk, he strolled over.

"Nick, don't you ever go home?"

"Good evening, Mr. Reynolds. No, I work as much as I can. I don't sleep much anyway. Might as well fill in the time."

Not sure how to ask, Ty rested his forearms on the counter and said, "So, is there any way I can get a Christmas tree to make my room a little more festive?"

Surprised by his request, assuming he was against anything holiday-related, Nick's face erupted into a smile. "Why, yes. I think we can arrange that for you. We have a Christmas Tree Farm excursion scheduled for the day after tomorrow. It leaves at eleven o'clock, I believe. Would you like me to put you on the list?"

"List? Is that really necessary? There are only three guests in the hotel right now unless Julia has more family joining them later. Like a husband, perhaps?"

Staring at Ty, Nick knew what he was asking. "I'm sorry, Sir, but I am not at liberty to share personal information about guests." Looking left and right, he made sure they were alone before leaning forward to whisper, "I can assure you, no one else is expected."

Acknowledging him, Ty was secretly happy for the heads-up. "Thanks for that. Appreciate it."

"So, as for the list? Would you like to partake in the Christmas Tree Farm excursion then, Mr. Reynolds?"

"Fine, yes, put my name down," Ty confirmed, "Just to clarify, the other hotel guests are on that list, too, correct?" Using hand gestures to emphasize his point, he hoped the guy understood what he was implying.

"Yes, Sir," Nick whispered.

"Perfect. Thanks, man."

Before Ty departed, Nick felt the need to offer him some advice. "Oh, Mr. Reynolds, if I may - have patience. Certain things happen in their own time."

Confused by what he said, Ty turned around, hoping to get clarification. Strangely, he found the desk area empty. "Weird," he mumbled quietly to himself. "Why does this guy keep ducking out during conversations?"

Pressing the elevator button on the main floor, waiting for one to open, he wondered what Julia and Sydney would think of him invading on their Christmas tree trip. He hoped his presence wouldn't upset them. Nervous about the whole thing, second-guessing himself, he couldn't ignore the strange feeling he got around the pretty blonde woman despite barely knowing her. He often found her invading his thoughts throughout the day.

"What are the chances that we both converged on this remote hotel at the exact same time?" he whispered, stepping inside the elevator as the doors closed.

Not believing in coincidences or just plain luck, he was curious about what would transpire in the coming days. On top of that, he was pretty sure Julia did not know his identity. That was a nice change. It was rare for him to meet someone who had no idea he played first base for Boston.

With visions of his Mother again coming to mind, he recalled how she often asked if he had met anyone when they spoke on the phone over the years. Never having given her the gift of getting married and having a family of his own, Ty carried a certain level of guilt. He wished he could have shared that joy with her.

Feeling defeated while the doors opened on the fourth floor, a heavenly aroma suddenly wafted past. Slowly walking down the corridor, Ty tried to identify the familiar smell. Reaching his room, about to touch the card key to the reader, he realized it was emanating from across the hall.

"You gotta be kidding? Come on? Who bakes cookies in a hotel suite?"

About to knock and boldly see if they needed someone to taste-test the baking, knowing he would wholeheartedly volunteer, Ty raised his hand, then quickly stopped. Listening to the two laughing inside their room, singing along to the Christmas music, he knew he couldn't interrupt. Upon stepping across to his side, he unlocked the door. Standing there, Ty eavesdropped for a few minutes. The laughter and singing made him smile. Soon, feeling more alone than ever, he had no choice but to let the door fall shut behind him.

19

December 20th

A Little Kindness

Across the hall, Julia heard a door close and assumed their neighbor had returned from dinner. Not giving the guy a second thought, she called down to Nick at the front desk. He promptly answered the phone.

"Yes, Ms. Mariani. What can I do for you?" he said.

"Hello, is that you, Nick?"

"Yes, Ma'am."

"Can you do me a big favor?" Julia paused.

"Certainly."

"We have just finished baking the first few batches of the staff's Christmas cookies. Can you page them and announce that they are all welcome to visit our suite whenever they are ready."

"I'm sorry?" Nick was confused. "Cookies, Ma'am?"

"Yes. It is a tradition every year. We bake Christmas cookies before the holidays and share them with the staff."

"That is so very kind of you."

Julia smiled. "It's a long story, but years ago, the people who work here helped us in our time of need. So, we do what we can to show appreciation."

With a nod of his head, his face beaming, Nick said, "Very good. I will let them know."

"Thank you so much. We are on the fourth floor. Tell everyone to follow the yummy smells. Make sure you drop by to pick some up, too."

"Well, thank you. I certainly will."

"Okay, then. We will see you shortly."

"Yes, indeed."

After hanging up the phone, Julia put on her oven mitts to remove the baking from the oven. "Nick is telling the staff that we are ready. They should be converging on us shortly."

Syd went to prop their door open. Having heard Ty's door close moments before, she thought for a second. Taking a chance, she stated pretty concretely, "Should we give him a few to try?"

Julia asked, "Who?"

"Ty."

While placing multiple cookie dough mounds on the parchment, Julia stopped and said, "I don't know, Syd...."

"Come on, Mom. Shouldn't we show a little kindness? The guy is all alone and probably never gets homemade – well, anything."

Staring at her in desperation with puppy dog eyes, hoping she'd agree, her Mother finally caved. "Fine."

"Perfect," Syd replied. Not missing a beat, she placed some on a plastic party plate. "I can hardly wait to see the look on his face. Hope he likes them."

When the girl crossed the hall and knocked, Julia stood in the doorway to keep watch as her daughter waited.

Within seconds, he answered, surprised to see them. "Well, hello there," he said with a smile.

"We are baking cookies." The little girl lifted the napkin off the plated snack. "Would you like to give them a try?"

"Sure, I'd love to." Taking hold of one, he took a bite. "Wow, they're still warm. I don't think I've had freshly baked cookies since I was a kid. Thank you so much. Thought I could smell something good when I stepped off the elevator."

Taking another bite while Sydney and Julia watched, his eyebrows went up as his eyes fell closed, savoring the shortbread. "This cookie is amazing. How did you get it to taste like that? It's so...umm..."

"Fluffy?" Julia quickly answered.

"Yes."

"There is cream cheese in the recipe."

"That explains it."

Happy he loved them, Syd handed him the plate. "Here," she said. "We've got lots."

Taking the treats, Ty looked at both of them. "Thank you for thinking of me. I appreciate that."

"You're very welcome. Enjoy," Julia responded as Syd looked on happily.

"I certainly will. Thanks."

Watching the two return to their room, he noticed they'd propped their door open. With the plate in hand, his closed automatically behind him. Unable to resist, he ate the third cookie, trying to savor it.

In minutes, voices erupted from down the hall.

As the chatter grew louder, he couldn't help but sneak a peek as the staff arrived. Their easy laughter and lively conversations with his neighbors were hard to ignore. Settling on the bed, he fluffed the pillows behind him and attempted to relax and lose himself in a movie. It seemed like a simple enough distraction, but keeping his focus proved challenging. Deciding to turn up the volume on the television to block out the noise, the high pitched laughter and bursts of merriment kept slipping through. Before long, the story on the screen faded into the background as his thoughts wandered.

Unable to resist his curiosity, he eventually walked back to the door and squinted to look through the small fish eye. The hallway buzzed with activity while visitors lingered about inside the Marianis' suite. That's when the enticing aroma of gingerbread seeped under the door, wrapping him in a warm memory. The scent tugged at his heart, stirring thoughts of home and simpler times. Pacing, he wrestled with himself, debating whether to venture over, unsure if he was welcome.

Greatly lacking patience, he said, "Maybe I should just go over there? What's the worst that can happen?"

Peeking out again, he spotted Bryce and Nick leaving with gingerbread on their plates. That settled it. Ty checked his hair in the mirror and ran his hand through it a couple of times. "Okay, man, you can do this. Just knock and say hello. Don't forget to smile – but not a creepy smile." Testing out a few facial expressions in the mirror, trying to rehearse the one he thought would work the best, he added, "Tell them the smell of gingerbread reminds you of Mom. Yeah, yeah. That's good – it's not creepy. Hopefully, after all that, they'll invite you in."

Waiting for a few people to leave, seeing a lull in the activity, Ty left his room and walked over just as a lone staff member exited carrying some freshly baked cookies on a plate. Eyeing up the baking while saying hello to them, he knocked on the door frame. "Hello?" he said timidly.

Leaning forward, peering around to the left, he found Julia standing in the kitchen, just about to place another batch in the oven. Amidst it all, he heard her joyfully welcome him.

"Hello? Come in!" She did not know who was there.

Taken by her red apron as it brought back memories of his childhood, he stepped inside the rather large suite and tried to remember the lines he had rehearsed. "Hey, umm, the smell of gingerbread brought me here." Nervously spitting out that introductory line, it seemed her presence left him utterly mindless.

"Would you like to try some of these too?" Sydney questioned, surprised to see him, already knowing what he would say.

"Sure, if you don't mind sparing one."

Making eye contact with her Mom, the girl said, "Nope, not at all. That is what Christmas is all about—giving and sharing." She placed a couple of warm gingerbread cookies on a plate and passed them to him. "Here you go," she said.

"Have a seat if you like," Julia offered, still wearing her oven mitts.

"Are you sure? I don't want to intrude," the handsome man replied shyly.

"Don't be silly. The staff are coming and going while on their break. It's okay if you want to stay."

Having a seat in the living room, he finished the two cookies Sydney had given him.

"Do you want another?" The young girl asked, seeing his empty plate.

"No. I'd better not. If I eat any more, I'll have to go back to the gym tonight."

Sydney tilted her head. "It's Christmas." Scolding him, she added, "You need to live a little."

"Moderation is key at our age," her Mother snickered.

"Is that the secret to getting old? Always wondered," he chuckled, feeling a bit older this past season.

Trying to continue their conversation, Julia asked, "So, Ty? Where are you from?"

"Originally from Wyoming, then relocated to Texas, and now live in Boston."

Eyebrows raised, she replied, "Wow, that is a series of big moves."

Not wanting to let on it was part of his job, he said, "Yeah, umm. It's just me. So, I don't have much to pack. Makes it easier." Wanting to step away from the topic, he changed the course of the conversation. "I can't believe you are baking in a hotel suite. But have to say, this kitchen is pretty nice. You have everything you need."

"Yes, we always reserve this one over the holidays. We don't have extended family to visit with, so we spend the time here. The hotel staff has become our family. Of course, new faces always join us, but we don't mind. Our cookie baking became a tradition about five years ago..."

When Julia stopped, Sydney knew she would never elaborate on the tragedy their family endured. It was something that never came up in conversation anymore.

Ty's sights bounced between the Mother and daughter, knowing there was something they weren't saying. Noticing the awkward pause, he revealed, "Well, I want to thank you for your hospitality. These cookies have certainly made my day. I recognized the smell of gingerbread right away. You know, my Mom used to make them, too. One of my fondest memories as a kid was seeing her in the kitchen with a dab of flour on her nose, dressed in an apron, quite like yours, actually." Waiting for a second, unsure whether or not he should say what he was thinking, the famous baseball player continued, "She passed away a few years ago on December third."

Focused on him, not moving a muscle, Julia said sincerely, "Oh, I'm so sorry. My sympathies."

"Thank you. My father was already sick for a year before she died. Sadly, he passed three weeks after her on the twenty-fifth." Ty took a bite of the cookie and lowered his head.

Knowing he, too, had suffered tremendous loss, Julia felt conflicted. About to place another batch in the oven, she made eye contact with Sydney. "Well, we certainly know how you feel."

Bouncing his sights between them again, wondering what was happening, Julia divulged, "Five years ago, we were planning our visit to The Carling and had booked from December 18th through to New Year's Day as we normally do. My son, Ben, played high-level, triple-A hockey, and my husband was the team's assistant coach. Checking the schedule, they found out Ben had a game the day we were supposed to leave, so Sydney and I decided to come ahead and prepare everything."

Exchanging two cookie sheets and placing more in the oven to bake, Julia carefully transferred the baked cookies onto the cooling racks. While prepping another pan with fresh mounds of dough, she did not make eye contact with him. It was just easier that way.

"When we arrived here, we got settled in as planned. Sydney was just little. I finished some work while she colored a few wooden ornaments to hang on the tree we usually get a couple of days before Christmas. That night, when my husband and son returned home from the game, they called to share the exciting news that they had won. Ben told me that he had scored the first goal. Congratulating him, he was humble but yet so happy." She sighed. "Knowing we'd see them the following day, hoping the snowstorm wouldn't make their travel too difficult, we said goodnight and went to sleep. In the morning, they called and said they'd slept in and were running late. That was the last time I spoke to my husband."

With a shocked look, Ty watched Julia stop what she was doing.

Taking a deep breath, she calmly said, "My husband, David, and our son, Ben, passed away that day in a car accident on the highway about two hours after that phone call." Waiting for a second, with the room eerily silent, she explained, "So, we can certainly relate to your suffering and loss around the holidays... You are not alone."

"I'm so sorry... I know there is nothing I can say to lessen your grief."

"This was the first time I've shared that with anyone in a while... Everybody here pretty much knows. A few of the long-term staff were around when we got the news. They supported us through the aftermath. Now, Syd and I do everything we can to thank them for that. Sometimes, it never feels like we can do enough. Thus, the cookies and the ornaments, among other things." Stopping a minute, resting her hands on the counter, she looked over at Ty. "Suffering the loss of a loved one can only be understood by those who go through it too. Otherwise, people don't fully get it," With a tear running down her face, she concluded, "Despite it all, we are doing okay. We've had to downsize from our family home, which was hard. I could not afford to keep it any longer. We moved into a new townhouse a while ago. It is a house but doesn't yet feel like a home. Maybe over time, it will. Right, Syd?"

"Yeah," her daughter agreed.

Hearing the timer go off, Julia grabbed an oven mitt. She turned around to open the oven door and removed a fresh batch of gingerbread. "One day at a time. That's all we can do." Wiping another tear from her cheek, she asked, "Anyone for a freshly baked cookie?"

After their solemn conversation, Ty and Sydney silently raised their hands simultaneously, which gave way to a light chuckle because their timing was impeccable.

Each given a cookie, Ty scanned the room and noticed the dining table covered in crafting supplies while Sydney worked with her glue gun.

Walking over, he sat opposite her and asked, "Hey, what are you making?"

About to carefully add a dab of hot glue to the glass ball, she replied, "Trying to finish the ornaments. I'm a little more than halfway."

"Sydney usually makes something different every year for the staff. It's a good way to get through the holidays too. Keeping busy and doing nice things for others helps," Julia explained.

"Wow, that's pretty cool." Waiting for a second, he wondered, "Maybe you want some help? I think I need to keep busy through the holidays also."

Smiling, she looked at her Mom to get permission.

Julia winked at her to signal that it was okay.

"Yes, you can help me."

"That's if you don't mind," Julia interjected.

"I don't mind at all." He grabbed a glass ball, not knowing what to do next. "Give me step-by-step instructions. I don't want to screw it up."

"Well, have you ever made ornaments before?" the young girl questioned, a little concerned about his skill level.

"Technically, no, but I watched my Mom do this every December when I was a kid. She'd make a special ornament for every person's gift under the tree. So, when we opened our presents, we got two things, not one. The ornament was first, and the wrapped gift was second. I wish I would have paid more attention to that as I got older." Pausing to reflect, Ty shook off the sentiment that weighed him down and looked up at Sydney. "Okay? What do I do first?"

"Well, these are the pictures of the ornaments I am making. There are three types. Pick a style, gather what you need, and start assembling. If you need help with the glue gun, let me know. I don't want you to burn yourself."

"Got it," Ty said, gathering the materials in front of him while Sydney monitored his progress. "Let me see if I can do this."

She was happy that he had successfully created one button wreath ornament without much trouble. "Perfect. Now, can you do that thirty more times?"

Over the next hour, Syd and Ty created over ninety ornaments for the staff while Julia made one hundred and sixty cookies. By nine-thirty, only sixty remained. The staff had eaten the rest.

Ty helped Sydney place each ornament in a festive bag, ready for Christmas Eve distribution. Tying ribbons and making bows, Syd put them on the far side of the living room.

When Julia started cleaning the kitchen, the baseball player could tell she was tired. "Do you need help with the dishes? I don't mind washing or drying."

Not sure what to say, she happily accepted the help. "Sure, that would be nice. Thank you."

"No, thank you for the wonderful cookies and for giving me something to do to pass the time. Being on my own hasn't been as enjoyable as I thought. Spending time with you both has been fun."

"You are very welcome." Handing him a dish towel, Julia started washing the mixing bowls, cookie cutters, and measuring cups. Ty dried anything passed along to him. Both watched Syd gather all the crafting materials and organize them neatly in the trolley.

"She's an amazing kid."

"Yes, she is. She's been my saving grace these past few years. My rock, basically. Sadly, given what happened, she's had to grow up fast."

"I can't even imagine..." he whispered.

Noticing something on Julia's temple, Ty grabbed a napkin and said, "Umm, you've got some flour on the side of your face. One second. It's kinda right there."

Julia took it from him while he tried to help her pinpoint where it was.

Completely missing it, he stepped in and said, "Wait. Let me get it for you."

Gently taking the napkin, he swiped it past her temple a few times. "There. Got it." Looking her way awkwardly, he quickly grabbed something from the dish rack to dry.

"Umm, thank you," Julia nervously replied, separating herself from the situation and not saying another word, knowing they had almost finished.

Once the kitchen was tidy and clean with everything returned to its place, Julia remembered, "I'm so sorry. I didn't even offer you something to drink this whole time."

"Don't worry. I'm good. I should get going. I've already taken up so much of your time. Hope I didn't overstay my welcome. It's pretty late."

"Yes, I suppose it is." Julia looked over at Sydney. "Time for bed, kiddo. Busy day tomorrow."

"Ah, Mom?"

"Well, that's my cue. Goodnight, Sydney." He moved toward the door.

"Goodnight, Ty. Thank you for helping me."

Her comment made him smile. "You sleep well." Focusing on Julia, he said respectfully, "Thanks again. For everything."

Somewhat nervous, hoping she wasn't giving him the wrong impression, she answered, "You're welcome. You cut my clean-up time in half."

He stood in the doorway. "Again, it was the least I could do." A strange feeling erupted in the pit of his stomach, and it wasn't from the cookies. "Well, Goodnight then. Maybe we will see each other sometime tomorrow?"

"Yes, perhaps. Goodnight."

Ty walked across the hallway and into his suite, hearing Julia's door close behind him. A little overwhelmed, he smiled with a wash of unexplainable contentment. Quickly brushing it off, believing he was getting soft, for some reason, he couldn't shake the feeling.

Over the years, he'd learned to keep things straightforward—relationships weren't worth the hassle when people were more interested in his name and career than the man behind them. Sitting in the chair by the window, he rubbed a hand over his jaw, his thoughts circling. Julia wasn't like the others, and he knew it.

But why is she so different? He thought as her late husband and son came to mind.

"I guess we bonded over grief. That's all..."

As he got ready for bed, the answers didn't come easily. Many of Julia and Sydney's traditions mirrored those of his own Mom. That struck a chord.

"Maybe that's part of it, too..." he murmured, trying to reign in his feelings.

The two radiated the same warmth and generosity she once had—a polite, giving nature that was hard to find. Julia, in particular, struck him as a devoted mother, genuinely kind and effortlessly gracious despite their rocky start. She embodied everything he had quietly hoped to find one day but thought he never would. It felt almost magical, like fate had dropped a miracle right across the hall.

Taking one last look at the snow falling outside and the light of the moon fighting to break through the storm, he got into bed and pulled the covers snugly across his chest. As he stared at the ceiling, a quiet smile formed. "Life just got a little more interesting," he mumbled, rolling onto his side. Closing his eyes, he wondered what tomorrow would bring. Eager to finally spend some time outdoors, he hoped they wouldn't mind him tagging along on their excursion.

20

December 21st

Misjudged

A single beam of light filtered through the sheers and spread across Julia's fluffy pillow. Rolling over, feeling tired, she pulled back the covers and checked the time on her phone. Securely resting her feet on the floor, she waited a moment before standing to stretch her arms above her head. Wrapping herself in the cozy robe, she tied the belt around her waist before walking to the window. Gently opening the drapes, it was surprising to see blue skies with not a snowflake in sight. The rugged Muskoka landscape greeted her, the sunshine illuminating the heavily snow-laden trees, making them sparkle like diamonds. Excited to start the day and explore the winter wonderland, she got a burst of energy.

After taking a shower, she put on a little makeup to brighten her face. Thinking about the time spent with their visitor last night, she recalled the solemnity of their conversations. Like them, Ty was grieving through the holidays. Believing his intentions were harmless, she figured she'd give the guy the benefit of the doubt and not be too hard on him.

With her hair in a towel, about to go and get dressed, she went to see if Sydney was awake. Finding her rummaging around in bed, she knocked and said, "Rise and shine. How are we this morning? Did you have a good sleep?"

Syd was able to squeak out one word before yawning a second time. "Yes. Pretty good."

Sitting on the edge of the bed, her Mother asked, "Ready to go on our ski-shoeing trek today?"

"When do we leave?"

"We need to have breakfast first, then we'll meet our guide at one o'clock."

Not about to get out of bed, still half asleep, Sydney sat up and hugged her Mom. "What time is it?"

Julia giggled. "Nine-thirty, why?"

Her little girl fell back into the pile of pillows and pulled the covers over her head. "Just five more minutes?" she pleaded.

"Okay, Sweetie pie."

"Can you stop calling me that?" Syd whined. "I'm not a little kid anymore."

Her Mother squished her daughter's cheeks between her palms and said, "You will always be my sweet baby."

"Uurgghh..." Syd groaned. "Why?"

Done teasing her for now, Julia went to her room to get dressed. "Who will be ready first?" Julia shouted, knowing the challenge would light a fire under her.

"That'll be me!" Syd yelled back, determined to beat her Mom at her own game.

Minutes later, they emerged from their rooms at the same time.

Julia called it a tie but realized her hair was still damp.

"We can leave as soon as I dry my hair a bit more."

"Okay," Sydney said, tying her running shoes. "I feel like it is going to be an amazing day."

About to turn on the dryer, Julia agreed. "I think so, too."

21

December 21st

A Fresh Start

Forcing one eye to open upon hearing the muffled sound of a blow dryer resonating from across the hall, Ty rolled on his stomach. Partially awake, he slowly glanced at his phone and figured it was time to get moving if he wanted to keep up with Julia and Sydney today. Rolling over on his back and looking at the ceiling, he wondered how the day would go. Nervous about the ski-shoeing excursion, hoping everything would go smoothly, Ty sat up and stretched before making the bed.

Showered in a matter of minutes, he got out and wrapped a towel around his waist. Hearing the sound of his neighbors closing their door, the Mother and her daughter walked past quietly. He assumed they didn't want to wake him.

Casually getting dressed in his joggers, a t-shirt, and a hoodie, he quickly slipped on his running shoes, opting to go without the ball cap today. Running his hands through his hair, he noticed a hint of grey creeping in on the sides.

"Guess retirement and grey hair go hand in hand," he said, frustratingly.

Checking his emails, not seeing anything new, he stuffed his phone in his pocket and left his earbuds behind. Swiftly making his way downstairs, he drifted into the Cottages restaurant. Not seeing a soul around,

Ty searched for Julia and Sydney. Finding them sitting at their table by the windows, he waved to Syd, who had spotted him first.

"Good morning, Ladies. How is everybody doing this morning?" he said charismatically. "Mind if I join you?"

Julia looked up from her menu and smiled. "No, we don't mind. Please, have a seat."

"Thank you." Ty pulled out a chair. "Have you ordered yet?"

"No, just about to," Sydney said, barely glancing up from her iPad.

Nervous for them to know he was tagging along on their ski-shoeing trip today, Ty hesitated and said, "So what's on your agenda?"

Julia took a sip of her coffee. "We scheduled an activity early afternoon. How about you?"

"Yeah, I'm doing something too. I spoke to Nick yesterday at the desk. It was surprising to learn how much there is to do around here. He offered quite a few suggestions and said I'd probably like this ski-shoeing thing. He described it kinda-like a guided tour through the forest on these short, wide-planked skis. Apparently, the most exciting part is the hot chocolate and lunch on the mountaintop. I figured it would allow me to exercise and get some fresh air. So, I went with that."

"Wait? You are going ski-shoeing today?" Julia questioned in disbelief.

"Yes. He said to meet in the lobby at one o'clock. Why?"

Directing her attention to Sydney, Julia snickered and motioned for her to remove her earbuds. "It looks like we have company this afternoon."

With one earbud out, the girl's eyes bulged with excitement. "Does that mean you're joining us?"

Trying to act casual, he laughed. "So, that's what you're doing, too? Here, I figured I'd be going by myself with a Guide." With a curious expression on her face, Ty wondered if Julia believed the whole thing was indeed a coincidence. Knowing they were the only guests at the hotel, he figured she would think it was almost unavoidable.

Greeted by the new waiter, Jun, Julia, and Ty ordered their Eggs Benny while Sydney decided to change it up and requested Belgian waffles with fruit.

Scanning their faces at the table, Ty asked, "So, have you done this ski-shoeing thing before?"

"No. First time. I can't see it being too hard if you've been on skis already."

"Guess we will soon find out." Hitting a lull in the conversation, Ty thanked the waiter for warming his coffee after he poured Julia a second cup. "So, umm, Julia, what do you do for a living?"

About to take a sip from her cup, their eyes met, causing a slight flutter.

"If you don't mind me asking, that is?"

"I'm a landscape designer and parks and recreation urban planner."

"Impressive. How did you get into that?"

"One of my uncles was an architect, and the other a contractor. Both were excited to learn I had design talent. They kept me in the loop on their projects when I was young and allowed me to tag along from time to time to learn the ropes. I could visualize what the blueprints showed. It was easy for me. So, when it came time to decide what career to focus my energies on, I chose landscape design. I love taking a blank canvas and creating amazing spaces where people can immerse in nature and enjoy the outdoors."

"That sounds exciting."

"I like it. Currently, I'm working on a two-acre backyard for a client who plans to break ground in the spring. When we return to Toronto after the holidays, I'll meet with them, present my designs, and see which one they choose. There are usually some changes and additions, but for the most part, my creations stay intact."

"So, how about you? What do you do for a living?"

Startled, Julia heard a loud thump. "Oh, my," she said, witnessing what happened.

"Nooo!" Sydney said as her orange juice spilled across the center of the table. "Oh! I'm so sorry, Mom. I was going to put my phone down, and I hit the glass."

"It's okay, Syd. It was an accident." Julia tried mopping up the spill with her napkin.

Jun saw what happened and immediately ran over, suggesting they move to a clean table.

"I'm so sorry about that," Julia said, moving their drinks to the table on their right. Ty helped her.

"No problem at all. Don't worry." Their waiter hoped to diffuse the young girl's embarrassment. Placing a few cloth towels down to soak up the spill, Sydney walked up to him.

"Here, let me clean this up. It is my fault." Doing what she could to assist him with the cleanup, not having to be told to help, she apologized countless times, feeling so bad.

Noticing Syd's reaction, Ty commented while taking a seat at the other table, "Would you look at that?"

"What?" Julia sat opposite him.

"I have never seen a child offer to help like that."

"Yes, Syd is very thoughtful. I'm sure she feels bad, so that's her way of making it right."

"Amazing..."

"So, what were we talking about? I forgot?" Julia took a sip of her coffee.

Wanting to sway the conversation away from his life, he stayed on the subject of her work. "Did your creativeness take a hit after everything that's happened with your husband and son?"

"Sydney believed I used it as a crutch. It was a good distraction, though."

"All you did was work back then, Mom," Sydney interjected upon joining them again.

"Well, in all fairness, it was an escape from reality for me. The landscaping helped my brain conjure something beautiful instead of reminding me of our loss. It did get to a point where I found my-self always working, day and night. I did it to avoid feeling anything, really. Soon, I realized it was affecting Syd, so I took a step back and re-established a new normal for us. Gradually balancing our life, she became my main priority."

"You know, I did the same when my Mom died - dove into work and tried to avoid dealing with all of it. December has not been the best month for me. Guess that's why I'm here."

"Well, for us, it is like coming home for Christmas. Like I said last night, these people were there for us when we needed support through a rough time in our lives. Through this experience, we quickly learned how everyone in the Carling community bands together. Because we were stuck here for a few days with the storm, unable to drive on the roads after receiving the news, people brought us food, kept tabs on the weather, and even arranged for a driver to take us home once the storm subsided. Someone drove our vehicle behind us, knowing I was not in a state of mind to attempt that. They went far beyond what we could have ever asked of them. That is why they are truly family to us. You will see?"

"How's that?"

"I assume you will be around for Christmas Eve?"

"Yes, I plan to be."

"That night, I make a full turkey dinner to share with the staff. Those working that day, even those who aren't, all join us between family commitments. We have turkey, potatoes, stuffing, and a few casseroles. We cook all day, technically. Maybe you want to join us? You know, to help you stay busy."

Staring at her in amazement, Ty smiled shyly. "Thank you. I'd love to join you. I think that would be great."

"Good, then it's settled."

"Have to warn you, though, I don't cook much," he laughed.

"Can you cut vegetables or peel potatoes?"

Agreeing, knowing he was up for the challenge, he said, "I think I can manage that. I'm not afraid to try. I'll do whatever you need."

"Perfect."

Seeing Jun approaching with their breakfast, they watched him set each plate in front of them.

"Wow, this looks great," Ty complimented while sitting back in his chair.

"No matter how often I have Eggs Benny, it is still my absolute favorite thing on the menu," Julia declared. "Thank you, Jun."

"You are so welcome. Enjoy," he said.

Sydney eyed her waffles and reached for the warm syrup.

Throughout breakfast, Ty learned more about Julia and Sydney's adventures at The Carling Hotel, including their dog sledding excursion from last year. Intrigued by how much fun they had, he hoped that was something they could do together after Christmas. The thought then occurred to him - *What if they get tired of me continually invading their holiday fun?*

Eating the last bite on his plate, Ty watched Jun return and leave their billfolds between them on the table before removing their dishes. Fueled for the day, the baseball player slid both checks his way.

Surprised, Julia asked, "What are you doing? One is mine."

"Breakfast is on me." Smiling while flipping open the folders, Ty wrote his room number and splashed his signature across both slips of paper before casually stacking them and placing the pen on top neatly.

"Thank you so much, but you shouldn't have..."

"Yes, I should. You made me cookies and helped me get through the evening last night. So, thank you for that." Getting up, he pulled their chairs back when they were ready to leave.

Taken off guard by yet another gentlemanly gesture, Julia replied, "Thank you."

Offering a smile, he tucked the chairs in. "No problem," he said, requesting that the two ladies lead the way. "After you."

She appreciated the courtesy that had become so rare these days.

Strolling out of the restaurant, they saw a man standing at the Concierge Desk.

Moving past the lobby, Ty pointed in his direction. "Maybe he is our guide for this afternoon."

"Guess we will find out shortly," Julia said, moving along to the elevators.

Not saying much more while waiting for the doors to open, Sydney shouted, "Left or right?"

"What do you mean?" Ty did not understand what was happening.

Syd raised her arms and pointed to both sides. Which door will open first—left or right? It's a game we play."

Her Mother exclaimed, "I pick left."

"Alright, alright. I get it. I'll say – right," Ty spouted, pointing to the door he chose.

"Okay, guy against the girls! I'm saying *left* side with my Mom."

Waiting to see who won, the three silently listened to hear which elevator was on the move. With anticipation building, glancing at each other with curious expressions, the doors to the left suddenly opened.

Jumping up and down, Sydney was ecstatic. "Yeah! We win! Sorry, maybe next time, Ty."

Witnessing their excitement, he graciously conceded. "Yes, next time, for sure," knowing in his heart that all these meaningful moments were slowly becoming part of a much bigger picture.

First, to step into the elevator, Sydney pressed the fourth floor.

Ty offered for Julia to go ahead of him.

Seeing the handsome man standing straight and tall, with his hands positioned militarily behind his back, Julia could not deny that she was beginning to like him. "Do you want to meet outside our rooms in fifteen minutes?" she asked.

"Sure. That works for me."

"Remember, it is freezing outside, so dress warmly in layers. Wear everything you have," Sydney laughed.

"Good advice. I will take that under advisement," he said humorously.

Turning to her daughter, Julia chuckled, "Let's see how long he lasts before the cold starts to get to him."

Looking at her, raising his eyebrows, he cautioned, "Do I hear the makings of a challenge?"

"Maybe?" she snickered.

Taking a second, Ty tried to think up a penalty. "Okay, whoever complains about being cold first...."

"Gets snow, put down their neck!" Syd shouted.

"Oooh! That's perfect. Deal!" Julia put her hand between them as each followed suit, making a pact as the elevator doors opened.

Not wasting time, the three walked down the hall to get dressed for an extended stay outdoors.

"Okay. Fifteen minutes?" Julia reminded, tapping her card to the reader and opening the door.

Ty stood in his doorway. "Got it. See you shortly."

22

December 21st

Ski-Shoeing

The ladies gathered their winter gear from the closet and got dressed. All bundled up in warm clothes, Julia grabbed their card key from the kitchen counter and zipped it into her pocket for safekeeping. Carrying their hats and mitts, they walked out to find Ty waiting.

His head jerked up from his phone when they opened the door.

"All ready?" Julia asked, wondering why he had such a serious look.

"Yep, ready," he replied, securing the device in an inside pocket. "Let's go."

Sydney barreled down the corridor to the elevators and pressed the button while Ty and Julia tried to catch up. Once again, descending to the main floor, Sydney reminded the two of them. "Now remember, whoever complains about the cold first gets snow down their neck. Agreed?"

"Agreed," the two said at the same time.

Off the elevator, rounding the corner into the lobby, they saw the same man still standing near the front doors, waiting for someone. Figuring he had to be their guide for the day, Sydney walked over to him without fear and stopped.

Greeting her with a smile, he said, "Hello there. Are you part of my ski-shoeing group?"

Sydney swiftly nodded.

"What's your name, dear?"

"My name is Sydney."

"It's nice to meet you, Sydney," the man said happily, shaking her hand while Ty and Julia joined them.

"Hello. We signed up for the one o'clock excursion," Julia said.

"Wonderful, you are right on time. My name is Sam Mask, and I will be your guide today."

"I'm Julia, and this is Ty," she quickly introduced.

"Nice to meet you both." Sam shook their hands also. "Now that the introductions are out of the way, are we ready to get suited up?"

"Yes! Very excited," Sydney gushed.

"Great! Follow me."

Adjusting their mitts and hats, making sure to zip their jackets closed, the three followed Sam outside and veered to the right. Seeing him walk toward four sets of ski shoes and a few pole options, they gathered around for more instructions.

"Alright," he said, taking note of Sydney's height. "Let's get you fitted first." Setting the equipment beside the little girl, he knelt to place each of her feet in the bootstrap binding. Handing her a set of poles, he asked, "So, how's that?"

"Good," she replied, immediately taking off to try them out.

He watched the bindings to ensure they were acting accordingly and turned his attention to Julia. "Okay, you're next, Ma'am."

Still watching Sydney slide along, having picked up the motion of the sport quite well, Julia stepped up and placed her feet into the straps held open by Sam. Buckling her securely, he instructed Ty to grab a pair and do the same.

Having snowshoed before, the athlete managed to get ready without much assistance.

Standing up straight, Sam put his on. "Before we head out, please double-check your equipment. Make sure everything is good." Believing his guests were ready, he added, "The trail is just past the end of the building. We cross the roadway and begin our trek up the hill on the other side. The routes are marked clearly."

"You go on ahead so that you can keep an eye on Syd. I'll ski behind you," Ty urged.

About fifty feet away, Sydney shouted from the very end of the building. "Come on, everyone! Let's go!"

"We're coming, Syd!" Her Mom moved in her direction. "Wait there for us."

"This way," Sam said, taking the lead when the group reached the start of the trail.

When they crossed the private road, they noticed the trail map had many color-coordinated paths, each highlighted based on skill level.

Sam showed them where they were going by pointing to the selected route with his pole in hand. "Today, we are taking the trail marked in blue. You will often see a map like this along the route, should you need to refer to it. Since our group is small, it will be easy to stay together, so the chances of getting separated today are very slim." He started moving along the trail. "Let's enjoy the beautiful outdoors, shall we? The sun is shining, and it's not too cold yet. On the way back, we will be facing the setting sun. The temperature might drop slightly, especially if the wind picks up."

They concentrated on the poling motion, trying to coordinate it with the ski shoes. It was similar to cross-country skiing, but the short skis seemed to give them more control. Approaching the first hill, Sam turned around to provide safety instructions.

"Once we start climbing the hills, eventually, we need to come down the other side. Your ski shoes will stay on top of the snow. If you find you're gaining speed and want to stop, safely fall on your backside, and it will slow you down."

Outstretching her pole, getting Syd's attention, her Mom repeated, "You heard what Sam said. Sit on your bum if you think you are going too fast, okay?"

"Yes, Mom," Syd groaned, tired of her overprotective nature. "I'll be fine. You worry too much."

"Most of the path will be easygoing. A bit of up and down, not too bad," Sam concluded while everyone acknowledged and pressed forward.

Upon veering to the right, their group slowly traversed the steep hill to join the wooded path along the lake. Now, on level ground, they got in line behind their guide, who was leading the way. Sydney was first, followed by Julia then Ty. The snow crunched beneath their feet, and a series of little hills helped them practice controlling their stride.

With confidence building, Sam turned and said, "Just ahead, the terrain will get a bit steeper. The best way to attack the hills is to act like you're running up. Create a V with your ski shoes. Use your poles to stabilize yourself and to help push your body along." Demonstrating for them, they watched their guide ascend the incline effortlessly.

Ready to give it a try, each of them made it to the top, feeling like they'd conquered a mountain.

Getting everyone's attention again, Sam offered some more instruction. "When descending on this other side, keep your center of balance and your arms out front. Ride down the hill, and the ski shoes will slow you down at the bottom. Again, sit or safely fall to your side if you need to slow down. Be mindful of your proximity to any trees or shrubs."

Everyone nodded their head after hearing his advice. Thankfully, their group successfully descended the slope. It made them feel confident about attacking The Pointe coming into view.

Immersed in the majestic forest, Julia spotted a couple of deer walking amidst the trees.

"Syd?" she whispered to her daughter, a little further ahead of her. When she turned around, Julia pointed her poles at them. "Look. Do you see the deer?"

The young girl leaned left, then right. "Oh, I see them," she whispered. "They're so pretty."

Ty watched the animals peacefully walk along, unphased by their presence, and recalled the deer that used to reside near his parent's house.

Moving on, they soaked up every ounce of serenity they could. The whistling wind passing through the treetops was so calming, and the sun's rays peeked through the clouds periodically to warm their frozen faces.

Ahead of them, Julia heard Syd laughing at a pair of active rabbits chasing each other nearby while she moved along steadily.

At the base of the hill in front of them, Julia wasn't sure if she could reach the top. It was steep. Standing there, surveying the incline, seeing Sydney and Sam already partway to the peak, Julia started to move forward, pushing herself as they had. About mid-way, she struggled when her arms got tired, and her legs felt like Jell-O, making it challenging to keep her momentum. Digging in her poles, pushing herself to her limits, she felt her extremities burning and stopped to take a breather. Suddenly, she felt her skis slowly slide backward.

"Umm, Ty?" she said nervously, peering over her shoulder and seeing him a few feet behind her. "A little help, please?"

Noticing Julia heading toward him and picking up speed, Ty braced for impact and firmly stood his ground, open-arming himself to catch her.

She knew there was no way to avoid hitting him.

"It's okay," he said, "Don't worry. I got you."

Trapping her awkwardly, wrapping his arms securely around her, she giggled. "Oh! I'm so sorry." Unexpectedly knocking him off balance, they fell and landed in a heap, partially buried in freshly fallen snow.

She laughed while lying flat on her back to rest before attempting to get up.

Raising his head, he chuckled to find her looking so defeated. "Are you alright?" he asked humorously, her ski shoes mangled with his.

She opened her eyes, offering a bright smile. Overly embarrassed, she replied, "Yes, I think so."

"Are you hurt?" Pinned by her body pressing against his right arm, Ty couldn't move.

"No, just my pride," she giggled again.

"Okay, well, that's fine."

"Are you okay?" she questioned, hoping she didn't hurt him.

"Yeah, I can't get up."

"Oh? Why? What's wrong?" Julia turned to him, concerned.

"Well," Ty chuckled, "You are lying on my arm."

Closing her eyes, giving a subdued sigh, she said, "Okay, okay. Wait. One second."

Rolling over, taken by her light-heartedness, untangling their legs, Ty stood up with absolute ease. "Here. Take my hand. I'll help you."

Focusing on it, she slowly reached out and took hold.

In seconds, he effortlessly lifted Julia off the ground and onto her feet. Staying close, he looked into her eyes and rested his hands on either side of her shoulders to keep her stable. Carefully brushing the snow off her parka hood and hat, he bent down to pick up her poles. Helping to thread them onto her wrists, Julia looked up at him, taken by his attentiveness.

Securing the last pole strap, Ty quietly said, "There we go. All good?"

Butterflies took flight inside Julia's stomach. Having almost forgotten what it was like to have someone to watch over her, she mumbled, "Umm, yes. I'm okay."

With perfect timing, Sydney shouted from the next hill. "Hey! Are you guys coming?"

Caught off guard, they broke from the awkward moment.

"We are on our way!" Julia called out.

Glancing over at her, he whispered, "Ready?"

With a slow nod, she saw Ty in a different light. She felt protected, knowing he was there if she needed him. A part of her considered the thought of someone else—something she promised she would never do.

Slowly ascending the hill together, Julia and Ty side-stepped to the top, taking a break every fifteen feet.

"Come on! We got this!" he encouraged.

Even though she felt her strength dwindling, she moved along, trying to keep up with every step he took.

Glancing her way, Ty turned his ski shoes to prepare for their descent into the gorge.

Out of breath, Julia quietly confirmed, "Wow, we actually made it."

"Yes, we did." Feeling a connection develop between them, he knew he would have to be mindful, given her history.

Moving cautiously down the hill, Ty stayed close to Julia in case something happened. A skilled skier, he felt comfortable and missed the speed of downhill racing.

They spotted Sydney leaning up against a tree, seemingly a little bored. Her Mother knew they weren't moving fast enough for her.

"Finally!" Sydney voiced, with a look of frustration.

"Sorry, Syd. We had technical difficulties. It's all good now," Ty responded, smiling reassuringly at Julia.

"I want to get to the top, Mom. Sam says the view is awesome."

"It's not far now, right, Sam?"

"Almost there, Ma'am."

Continuing for another fifteen minutes, keeping up to Syd and Sam, they successfully maneuvered the novice trail to the base of The Pointe. Looking up at the two-stage incline, happy to have a spot to rest partway up before tackling the top section, their guide demonstrated his skills and effortlessly made it to the first ridge, urging Sydney to follow.

"He's so good at this," Julia said to her daughter.

"I know, right?" the young girl agreed before shouting to their leader, "Okay, I'm going next."

Keeping a close eye on her, Sam encouraged the enthusiastic girl the entire way: "Now, turn your ski shoes horizontally across the hill if you need a break. Traversing them will help you move up the rest of the way using the side-step method." Sam used hand gestures to demonstrate what he meant.

"Got it!" Giving a thumbs up, she was more than ready to mimic everything he just did.

Amazed by her daughter's abilities, Julia knew she would have to push beyond her limits if she was going to reach the top. She hoped she had enough energy left.

"Here I go!" Sydney took a run at it.

Sam kept cheering her on, expressing how well she was doing the entire time. Having attacked the incline using shorter strides, Julia watched her daughter turn sideways a few yards away from Sam. She was almost out of steam.

Reaching the first pinnacle, she raised her arms in triumph and celebrated, "I did it, Mom!"

"Yes, you did. Good job, Sweetie!" Julia clapped her hands. "So proud of you!"

"Great work, Syd!" Ty applauded.

Seeing Sam and Syd continue up the second section toward the top, Ty turned to Julia. "Okay? Who's next?" he asked with a mischievous twinkle, "Maybe you'd better go first in case I have to catch you again."

Smirking, Julia wholeheartedly agreed. "Fine, but if I start sliding, be prepared."

"Don't worry. I'll save you."

Hearing those words took Julia by surprise. Unable to ignore the schoolgirl flutter, she began the climb and pushed to the top of the first plateau without any problems. Proud of herself, she turned her ski shoes sideways and waited for Ty to catch up.

Ascending with ease, he joined her in seconds, making it look like a walk in the park. Stopping alongside Julia, positioning his skis horizontally with hers, they faced each other and decided to side-step the rest of the way together.

Breathless, Julia said, "I hope that the way back is all downhill."

"I'm sure it will be. I'm looking forward to that," he said, punching the ski shoes through the powder. "Kinda missing downhill skiing right now."

"Is that something you used to do as a kid?"

Looking at her, he replied, "Yes. I used to live in Wyoming, remember? We skied a lot. Haven't done it in years, though."

Step by step, they encouraged each other to keep going despite every muscle burning in their legs. The banter back and forth was light-hearted and fun.

"Come on! Almost there!" The baseball player rallied.

"I'm trying!" she giggled.

"Go! Go! Go!" He laughed, increasing his speed.

Reaching the top, the two almost collapsed.

"There's the tent! We survived," he stated humorously.

Tilting her head, offering a bashful expression, trying to contain herself, Julia said, "Yes, we did."

In an instant, he became aware of her effect on him. For the first time in a long while, he was having fun. He'd forgotten about the pressure of the Hot Stove and had not once checked his email. Somehow, the stress he'd been experiencing had slowly faded throughout the afternoon.

Able to take a break, Julia and Ty joined Sam and Sydney at the camp.

Immediately gravitating to the bonfire, Julia looked to one side of the tent and found hot chocolate waiting, along with their sealed lunches, piping hot in individually insulated bags. While walking beside the shelter, she found Sydney lounging on one of the fur-blanketed Muskoka chairs, positioned perfectly to enjoy the beautiful view away from the wind.

After removing the straps from their boots and stabbing their poles upright in the snow, Ty allowed Julia to lead the way and instinctively hovered his hand behind her back, believing she could fall into the almost knee-deep fluffy powder. Stepping onto the packed path, the two entered the tent and collapsed in a couple of chairs while Sam stoked the fire.

"Help yourself to the hot chocolate and the lunches," he suggested.

Sheltered from the elements, Ty saw Julia go over to their neatly organized food containers sitting on a red and green plaid tablecloth.

Preparing to distribute them, Ty went to help. "You go ahead and sit down. I've got this."

While Sam served their beverages in hammered tin mugs, Ty handed out the food.

After getting Sydney settled first, he handed it to her. "Here you go, Kiddo. Be careful; the outer container is a bit hot." Turning his attention to Julia, he did the same. "I believe this is yours."

"Thank you so much, kind Sir."

"You are very welcome, my Lady."

Having a seat between Sam and Julia, Ty stretched out his legs in front of him.

Enjoying the comforting homemade macaroni and cheese with chicken, everyone went quiet, having mustered quite an appetite. Amazed by the view of the frozen lake, with open water in the center, they watched the sun's rays sparkle on the snow while the clouds moved past swiftly.

To keep the conversation moving, Syd asked, "So, Sam? How did you get this job?"

Happy to share a little about himself, their guide finished his last bite of chicken and responded, "So, I grew up in a small town just north of here. I've always been an outdoorsy person. I can thank my grandfather for that. As a kid, he always spent time with me, fishing, snowmobiling, and talking about trees, birds, animals, and such. Eventually, I got an environmental engineering degree. After that, I could not find a job, so I returned to school and got into Parks and Recreation. That path got me back into nature, and finally, one day, after working for about three years, I noticed a job posting for an outdoorsman needed at the Carling. Asked to visit for an interview, I fell in love with the town. It's location, the people, the community, the traditions; everything I could ever want in a place to live and work."

Happy to hear that he loved being there, Sydney and Julia turned to each other.

"That is why we keep coming back, too," the Mom revealed, looking out at the view. "I never get sick of seeing this every day. It is just amazing to me."

"I quite agree," Sam replied. With the wind whistling through the trees, he noticed Sydney had finished her lunch. "So, Miss Sydney? Do you want to search for animal tracks? Maybe take a nature walk around the camp? There is so much to see here."

With excitement dancing in her eyes, she asked her Mom, "Can I go?"

"Sure. We will move the chairs out to the fire to see you better."

Standing up, Ty said, "Here. Let me help you with your chair." Doing that, she walked beside him as he lifted the heavy piece of wood furniture outside the tent and set it down four feet from the firepit.

Julia had a seat. Able to see Sydney clearly, she watched Ty bring his chair over and set it beside hers. Happy to have the heat of the fire keeping them warm, the two went silent.

"Are you having fun?" he asked her, afraid to break the peacefulness.

"Yes. You?"

"I am. Haven't enjoyed myself this much in a very, very long time." He glanced over at her with the sincerest look.

Lost in the eyes of a stranger, it unexpectedly made her shiver.

Then, amidst that perfect moment, they heard his phone faintly ringing and vibrating.

Standing up quickly and digging the device from his pocket, Ty apologized, "I'm so sorry. Please give me one minute. I need to take this."

Nodding her head, Julia was not bothered by the interruption. "Sure, no problem."

Swiftly moving away from the fire, he answered, "Yeah, hello?" while ducking in behind the tent.

"Hi, Michael. What's the word?"

Julia overheard his conversation. She felt like she shouldn't be eavesdropping, but his proximity didn't give her a choice. Everything he said she could decipher - plain as day.

"That is not what we agreed upon, Mike. The deal is seventeen mill plus 1.5 in incentives, no less. You have to bring 'em up. It's my last kick at this. I am still valuable, healthy, and willing to play, and I'm coming in at six million less than the rookies want per season. Come on, man." With a short pause, she heard him say, "Okay. Okay. Right. Yeah, call me back when you hear something." Ending the call, Ty returned to Julia and sat quietly. "So sorry about that."

"No problem."

"Guess you heard everything?"

"Sorry, a little, yes."

"No point in keeping this a secret any longer. I should tell you then. Umm, I play baseball for Boston. You asked me earlier what I do for a living, but if I recall correctly, that conversation got interrupted by an orange juice incident."

Laughing, she nodded her head. "Ahh, yes," and remembered that Sydney spilled her juice across the table when that topic came up that morning. After that, he had purposefully diverted them away from the conversation.

"So, I'm kinda in the middle of something the baseball world coins the December Hot Stove. Many teams shuffle things around at the end of the season, especially after the World Series. New contracts are up for grabs for certain players, while others need to renegotiate if they are on the move."

"It sounds complicated. I'm embarrassed to say I know absolutely nothing about baseball."

"That's okay. My Agent, Mike, was on the phone. We are trying to finalize my contract with upper management. I am looking to play one more year before retiring. In the coming days, I hope to get things squared away."

"So, one more year, and that's it?"

Staring out across the lake, he sighed. "Yeah, I think it's time to hang it up. My body has taken a beating over the last while, and the older I get, the longer the recovery time is. With the off-season being short, I often feel we finish the series, and suddenly, in a blink, we are headed back to Florida for spring training. Everybody gets a few months off, but still. There are things I want to do, places I want to visit, you know. I've given so much of myself to this sport. Sacrificed everything."

"If you feel that way, then it's probably time to move on," she replied, not knowing what more to say. "So, you live in Boston, then?"

"Yes, I do, and you?"

"We live in Toronto."

"So, you're not that far from home."

"No. For us, it is a hop, skip, and a jump. It's about a two-hour drive door to door."

Hearing that he was from Massachusetts, Julia experienced a sinking feeling as she looked out over the frozen lake. Realizing that a piece of her was unexpectedly disappointed to hear that he lived so far away and would return home when the holidays were over, she felt foolish for even contemplating the possibility of something developing between them. Believing Ty could have anyone he wanted, models, actresses, beautiful women, she knew she would never be able to compete. Reality set in. She assumed he was looking for someone to hang out with for the next ten days, nothing more. Knowing he was having difficulty being alone, she took a deep breath and reminded herself of the promise she had made David. Upset, Julia's mind drifted outside the wavelengths of her vows.

"Umm, I'm going to apologize in advance if my phone rings again in the next couple of hours. I'm sorry, but I'll need to stop and answer it. Hope that's okay?"

"Yes, that's fine."

Arriving at a lull in their conversation, Ty said, "Can I, umm..." hesitating a second, he continued, "Can I ask you a personal question?"

Glancing his way, Julia did not know how personal he would get.

"Have you dated anyone since..."

Understanding what he was implying, she responded bluntly. "No..." feeling quite uncomfortable with the subject.

Ty raised both of his hands between them sincerely. "I'm sorry... I didn't mean to....."

"It's okay. To be honest, I haven't dated anyone because I still feel connected to my husband. Like we are still married, you know? I realize that once your spouse is gone, the bonds of marriage no longer exist, but, to me, it's too soon." Finding it difficult to explain, Julia added, "It's complicated."

"Understood."

She felt their conversation get awkward. "Can we change the subject?"

Ty nodded, sensing her discomfort. "Fair enough." Giving a small nod, letting her words settle between them, he leaned back in his chair and turned his gaze toward the fire crackling softly.

Falling silent as her eyes drifted to Sydney and Sam returning to camp, deep in conversation, her daughter animatedly gestured as their guide chuckled, clearly amused by whatever story she was telling.

When plunging herself into the snow in front of them, she immediately shared their findings in great detail.

While listening to her intently, Julia couldn't help but reflect on how far they'd come in the past five years—through the heartbreak, the healing, and slowly finding joy again. But today felt different, as if a new chapter was beginning to unfold. Her gaze drifted to Ty, and a thought flickered in her mind—could he be the reason?

23

December 21st

Hero

On top of The Pointe, Ty discovered why Julia sometimes kept a barrier around her and seemed guarded and cold. Thinking of their collision earlier and the feeling he got when he caught her in his arms, a part of him hoped their conversation would address that moment. Finding out she was not open to pursuing a relationship with anyone, he sadly conceded but hoped they could at least be friends if he were lucky.

As Sydney climbed back to the white tent to warm up by the fire, Julia said, "Okay, Sweetie. Are you ready to go then? Should we head back now?"

"Okay, Mom," she replied, collapsing in a chair, needing to take a short break before moving on.

Confirming their request with Sam, he radioed to the hotel for a team to come and close down the Pointe while the group strapped on their ski shoes. Reminding everyone about the hills and stressing that they needed to control their speed, everyone secured their poles around their wrists to begin the descent.

While strapping his feet into the equipment, Ty thought about what Julia had said earlier and felt he'd overstepped his bounds. He felt bad for intruding on her private life. Picking up a strange vibe from her, he wondered where this left them.

Sam led the way and blazed a trail in the direction of the hotel on the opposite side of the mountain while Sydney followed behind him.

Julia moved along, punching her ski shoes through the deep snow.

"Do you want me to go first in case I need to break your fall?" Ty asked humorously.

She offered a relatively flat reply. "No. I think I'm okay."

Deciding to give Julia some space, he caught up to Sydney and Sam. Now, a few feet from them, Sam shared instructions on their descent and tested the snowpack.

Pointing down the incline, he said, "Just a reminder. Traverse the mountain on the way down and create a zigzagging pattern from left to right."

Sydney and Ty nodded while Julia wanted to confirm, "Did you hear that, Sweetie?"

"Yes, Mom!" The girl rolled her eyes. "I know. I know."

A loud rumble startled the group, and without warning, the snow-covered ledge under Sydney and Sam's feet gave way.

"Syd!" Ty shouted, launching his arm outward to grab her jacket. Unable to secure a grip, he watched the little girl and their guide get swept up in a wide, thin-slab avalanche.

Instinctively, he took off down the mountain after her and noticed she was sliding faster and faster but, thankfully, stayed above the snow.

Horrified, unable to see anyone, Julia's heart pounded in her chest as she rushed to the edge. "Oh, my god!!" she screamed fearfully.

Witnessing Ty courageously attempting to rescue her, she watched him fly down the hill, hoping not to lose sight of her. Maneuvering himself to the left, with a dense forest of trees below them getting closer and closer, he found it hard to see. The snow kicked up in a cloud, impeding his vision. The wind froze his face. Focused in, squinting his eyes, Ty knew it was now or never. Reaching his arm out to the girl, his fingers less than an inch from her shoulder, he grabbed hold of the jacket, but his glove slipped off the fabric.

"Ty!" The frightened girl screamed.

"Damn it!" he said. Quickly yanking it off and letting it fall, he quickly made a second attempt. Inches away, he successfully lunged his arm forward and got hold of her. Pulling her backward, digging his ski shoes in, he saw the wave of snow race by them. Seeing the trees to their left and a cliff to the right, Ty had no choice.

"Hang on!" he yelled, falling to the ground. Ty wrapped his arms around her and rode the snow wave until it stopped.

Finally, the forest returned to a peaceful state. Sydney opened her eyes to find the baseball player clinging to her tightly. Hearing him breathing heavily, he exhaled before lifting his head to see how close they were to the edge.

Noticing the drop-off about ten feet away, Ty panicked and clung to her so she wouldn't slide further down. "Holy shit," he muttered, trying to get his bearings. Turning to Sydney, he asked, "Are you hurt? Are you okay?"

Shaking her head, she said, "No," then "Yes." Unable to speak, she began to whimper. Removing his ski shoes with one hand and doing the same with hers, he tried to keep her calm while carrying her a safe distance away from the edge. Looking up the mountain, he saw the size of the section that had let go.

"Don't worry. I got you, Kiddo?" He refrained from hugging her too tightly in case she was injured. "You're okay. You're okay," he reassured. "I got you."

In the distance, hearing Julia screaming her daughter's name, Ty took a deep breath and called out, "She's here! She's fine!"

Running and stumbling, Julia finally reached them. Kneeling beside Sydney, she grabbed hold of her. "Oh, thank God! Are you hurt? Are you okay?" she cried hysterically.

"She's good. There's just a small cut on her cheek." Ty explained, looking back up the mountain. "Julia? Where's Sam? Did you see him?'"

"No. I didn't... No, I didn't see him." Julia stood up and scanned the mountainside.

"Stay here. Don't move. I'm going to find him."

Rushing up the incline, scouring for any sign of their guide, he shouted, "Sam! Sam? Where are you?"

Ty found his glove and slipped it on his frozen hand. Stopping and listening, hoping to hear the man's voice, he called out again, "Sam!" Listening, he heard a man groan. Swiftly heading in that direction, Ty shouted, "Come on. Say something!"

"I'm here." A weak voice shot through the trees.

Turning to his left, he saw Sam propped up against a large rock. As he walked through the mounds of snow, he noticed scratches on the man's face, and he was holding his arm.

"You okay?" Ty asked, kneeling beside him.

Sam nodded, "Yeah, I'm fine. Just got the wind knocked out of me. Nothing major."

"Is your arm broken?"

He moved his fingers and flexed his arm. "No, not broken. Shoulder feels a little messed up, though."

Taking hold of Sam's radio, Ty pressed the button and called the Carling for help before the two inched their way down to where the girls were sitting.

Happy that their guide was okay, Julia clung to her daughter tightly.

"Is she alright? Is she hurt?" Sam asked as they got closer.

"No, she's fine. Just shaken up."

"I'm sorry, Mom. I couldn't stop."

"There was nothing you could do, honey. It wasn't your fault. Thank God you're safe," her Mother replied.

"Ty saved me," she whispered gently, looking up at her hero getting closer.

With tearful eyes, unable to speak, Julia mouthed the words, "Thank you."

Slowly helping their guide sit on the ground, he nodded and had a seat himself, thankful that everyone was safe. In minutes, they could hear snow machines headed their way.

Sam pulled a warming blanket from his backpack and handed it to Julia. "Here. Wrap Sydney up. We don't want her going into shock."

She did what he instructed.

By this time, the sun was low on the horizon, and the cold seemed more bitter.

Their guide handed Ty a flare from his backpack and said, "Crack this over there, a few feet away, so that the crew can find us."

Taking it, Ty removed the cap and struck the pieces together to spark it.

Within minutes, multiple snowmobile lights were moving in their direction.

When help arrived, Ty picked Sydney up in his arms and set her in the sleigh behind the snow machine. Julia sat behind her daughter and held onto her. Going back to help the rescuers with Sam, he returned to Julia and Syd and sat on the back of the machine facing them when they were ready to leave. He made sure they remained safe the entire way back to the hotel.

24

December 21st

Indebted

Escaping the forest, they made it to the Carling. When the machines rounded the corner at the bottom of the roadway, they raced towards the front doors. Stopping under the covered portico, Ty jumped off the snowmobile.

Not wanting Sydney to walk, he looked at Julia and quietly asked, "Can I carry her?"

Nodding, she agreed.

He helped Julia up first, then focused on Syd. "I'm going to carry you to your room, okay?"

"Like a piggyback ride?" the girl questioned, having perked up.

"Sure, if you like," he replied, trying to keep the air light.

Sydney accepted in an exhausted tone. "My legs feel like Jell-O anyway."

Jumping onto Ty's back when he knelt beside her, he stood up effortlessly while she clung to his neck.

Outside the doors, needing a minute to process what happened, so many things went through Julia's mind. Hearing someone walk up behind her, she turned to see Sam standing there.

"I am so sorry, Ms. Mariani. It's my fault." The man apologized, feeling bad about everything, knowing how the whole day could have ended differently.

"No, it's not. You could never have predicted the snow would let go like that. I'm happy you are alright."

Walking away, he still felt terrible knowing this happened on his watch.

Hoping to reassure him, she said, "Hey, Sam?"

Turning around, he replied, "Yes, Ma'am?"

"She's fine. We all are. That's the main thing." Offering a thankful smile, she went over and tapped his arm.

Returning a flat grin, he appreciated her words.

Julia saw Nick and Bryce gathered around inside the lobby. With a group of them talking up a storm, she was thankful to see Sydney laughing.

Immediately spotting her, Bryce walked over. "You guys gave us quite the fright. I thought the worst when the call came in."

"Don't worry. We are fine." Julia hugged Bryce, who said he would check on them later.

Ready to head upstairs, she mentioned, "Well, we better let this girl get some rest."

On their way to the elevators, the two men waved.

Ty still had Sydney on piggyback.

Waiting for the doors to open, wishing it would hurry up, all three seemed emotionally exhausted while they stood in silence.

Out of the blue, Sydney said with limited enthusiasm, "I take, right." Positioned at the adult's level, she pointed to the side she figured would arrive first.

Knowing what she was implying, Julia played along. "Okay, I'll say left."

"I'll side with your Mom," Ty mentioned, hoping to bring a smile to her face.

They listened intently. When it opened, Sydney's arm went up in victory while the other remained tightly wrapped around Ty's neck. "Yes!" she said with a pump of her fist. "I win!"

"Oh no, not again," Ty joked, moving forward a few feet before stopping abruptly. "Hey, Kiddo, duck your head."

Mindful of the ceiling, Sydney hung on tightly and curled up.

The ride to the fourth floor was a quiet one. When the doors parted, they exited and strolled down the hallway before stopping a mere eight feet from their suites.

Ty knelt to lower Syd to floor level. "Here you go, Ms. Sydney. Safe and sound."

She dramatically collapsed. "Hurry, Mom. Open the door. I'm exhausted."

"Okay, okay," Julia said, believing her daughter was bouncing back, given the dramatic behavior.

Tapping his card to the reader, Ty asked, "So, umm, are you going downstairs for dinner?"

Seeing Syd shake her head, Julia replied, "No, I think we may order room service. Maybe some chili and buns. Last year, after the dog sledding, we ordered that. It hit the spot."

"Oh, okay." Swinging open his door, he was disappointed.

Waiting for a second, feeling somewhat indebted to him, Julia knew what she needed to do. "You are welcome to join us if you like?"

Smiling, he answered, "I'd love to."

"Great. We will probably shower and change into pajamas. Are you okay with a low-key evening?"

"That sounds perfect. I'm sure I have something that will fit the dress code."

"Knock on the door in about forty minutes? That should give us enough time," she suggested, making little eye contact with him.

"Alright. I'll see you shortly."

Walking into the room and closing the door behind him, Ty rested his flat hand against it. Lowering his head., he said aloud, "Thank you, God, for keeping that little girl safe today." Emotionally taxed, he started the shower and waited for it to warm up. Feeling this unexpected attraction for Julia intensifying, he outwardly insisted, "If you truly feel something for her, man, you will have to gather the courage to let her know. Complicated or not."

25

December 21st

The Bond

While hanging her jacket in the closet, Julia saw Sydney sprawl out on the floor and raise one boot toward her, implying that she needed help removing them. Obligingly tugging on each foot, she set the boots on the tray and hung up her little girl's jacket before taking their mitts and hats over to the fireplace to dry out.

Running a bubble bath for Sydney, she knew they needed to warm up and relax, given their stressful afternoon. Despite her fatigue, Julia urged her daughter to take a quick soak before getting into her pajamas.

After Sydney left the tub and drained the water, Julia started the shower and draped the towel over the glass door. The warm water cascaded over her shoulders when she stepped in, washing away all the tension. Thoughts of Ty surfaced. A debate of feelings ignited inside her. Running through the horrific events, she continuously returned to the same conclusion, time and time again.

"He risked himself to save her today."

Confident her husband David would have done the same, Julia realized Ty and Sydney would always have a special bond now. She thought about her daughter growing up without a father figure. Understanding all too well that she was no longer married, regardless of trying to ignore that fact, Julia was scared to love someone else. The guilt of even thinking the thought made her heart ache. It felt like she was cheating on her husband, even though she wasn't. Recalling what Sydney said about leaving for university, not wanting her to be left alone, a part of her didn't want to be either.

"You're turning thirty-seven this year," Julia mumbled. "How can you spend the rest of your life by yourself? The past few years have been difficult enough." Inhaling deeply, she added, "Promise you will open your heart and see where this goes. Promise you will not back away if he says he has feelings for you. You know there is something about him, too. It is not wrong to feel this way. It's just not."

Turning off the shower, Julia wrapped herself in the fluffy white towel. Hearing Sydney in the kitchen not long after, she heard the TV turn on. Hurrying, putting on a light dusting of makeup and a little lip gloss, she brushed her wet hair and used the blow dryer to remove most of the dampness. Walking into the bedroom to get dressed, finding a pair of black tights, a white cotton t-shirt, and warm fleece, she finished the ensemble with a pair of cozy socks. Glancing in the mirror to see if it coordinated, Julia heard a knock at the door.

"Syd, can you see if that's him? Check before you open it!"

"Okay!" her daughter shouted from the other room.

Listening to make sure everything was okay, a manly voice drifted under her bedroom door. Ready to step out, she took one last look in the mirror before turning off the lights.

Casually appearing with her damp blonde locks flowing freely over her shoulders, Ty couldn't help but smile nervously.

Lost for words, he said, "Hey? Feeling better after the shower?"

"Yes, I finally warmed up."

"Yeah, me too. My feet were pretty cold," Ty laughed, remembering their pact.

Sydney immediately turned and reminded him, "Hey. It's a good thing you didn't say that earlier. You would have gotten snow down your neck."

"Yes, I know. I think I'm safe now, though."

"I guess so. I'm too tired to get the snow from the balcony." Sighing, the little girl plopped down on the sofa in a heap with three blankets rolled in a ball.

Chuckling at Sydney's humor, Julia realized she hadn't fully invited him in since he remained close to the door. "So sorry. How rude of me. Please come on in and have a seat. I am going to call down and order the chili and buns. Anybody like anything else?"

"No, that sounds great. I'm okay with that."

"Alright, give me two minutes. I will be back."

Dipping into her bedroom, Julia called downstairs to place their order. Emerging afterward, she found Ty and Sydney sitting on either end of the sofa, with their feet on the coffee table. Just chilling, watching the movie Home Alone, Julia walked in when the robbers got hit in the face with paint cans.

"Syd and I must have seen this movie forty times already. It is one of the holiday classics that never gets old."

"Think I may have seen this once."

"That's all?" The young girl questioned.

"Yes. As a rule, I never watch Christmas movies."

"Well, that's sad," Syd said. "Why?"

Ty thought for a second. "I'm not entirely sure." He could feel his hatred for the holidays slowly dissipating. For once, it was bearable.

Ready to play hostess, Julia clapped her hands. "The food should be here shortly. What would everyone like to drink?"

"Syd? How about you?" Ty asked, allowing her to go first.

Opening the fridge, Julia rhymed off a few options. "I have a selection of mini cans. Sprite, Gingerale, Iced Tea, Lemonade? Which one would you like?"

"Maybe iced tea, please."

Ty got up from the sofa and moved toward the island in the kitchen.

Grabbing the drink from the fridge, Julia got a glass from the cupboard and poured it.

"Here. I will give it to her if you like," he offered.

"Perfect. Thank you," Julia replied.

Passing the drink to him, Ty walked over and set it on the coffee table in front of the little girl.

"Thank you," Syd politely said while watching the movie intently.

"You're welcome, Kiddo."

Eyeing up a few options for them, Julia asked, "What would you like?"

"What are you having?"

"I am opening a bottle of red. Would you like a glass?" Julia said while taking the stemware from the cupboard, assuming he would agree.

"Sounds good," he replied. "Here, let me help you." Skillfully opening the bottle for her, Ty poured two glasses. Looking out the window, he said, "It's five o'clock, and it's already pitch dark."

"Yes, I'm missing the sunlight these days."

"Me too," he said, handing Julia the glass. "Cheers."

She offered the same. "Cheers." Taking a sip, it felt a little awkward, like she was doing something wrong.

Moving to the living room, they all sat on the couch to watch the movie. Laughing so hard they needed to wipe away the tears, Ty was amazed by Julia and Sydney's sense of humor. Constantly giggling, their actions were infectious.

Welcomed wholeheartedly, he was thankful to be included in their evening. Surprised they didn't mind spending time with him, he glanced across the sofa at Julia sitting on the opposite end and unexpectedly felt so fortunate to have met her.

Amidst his thoughts, a knock came on the door. The sound startled Sydney so much that she jumped in her seat. In true dramatic fashion, she giggled at the degree of fright it gave her.

Getting up, Ty followed Julia to the door and opened it but stayed out of the way.

"Hi, Lisa," Julia greeted her friend, who guided the trolley cart into the room.

"Hey, Marianis. How is our little Syd doin'? I heard about what...." Stopping dead in her tracks upon seeing Ty standing behind the door casually dressed, Lisa immediately clammed up, unable to finish her sentence.

"Hi, Lisa!" Syd exclaimed with a bright smile.

Switching her attention to the youngest in the room, their friend said, "I guess our patient is doing much better?" She was relieved to see the little one nod in agreement. Dying inside, shooting Julia a curious eye, Lisa wanted to know what was happening with the baseball player but knew she couldn't ask.

"I have three orders of chili and a selection of buns for you. Enjoy your dinner." Lisa winked at her friend when Ty turned his back for a second.

Julia quickly waved her off. "Thank you, Lisa. We should catch up later. We still haven't had time to do that."

"Yes, maybe during my break tomorrow around two," the woman hinted strategically.

Thinking, Julia quickly replied, "Oh, we won't be here. Sydney and I are getting our Christmas tree tomorrow and won't be back until late afternoon."

With his interest piqued, Ty asked, "Wait? What Christmas tree?"

Taking an order of chili off the cart, Sydney went over and sat at the table before describing yet another Carling tradition while dipping her fresh bun in the chili and taking a bite.

"Oh, Ty. You should join us. We visit this magical tree farm, pick a tree, and then go to Clarence and LeeAnn's store to get its decorations and lights. It's the best part of our Christmas in Carling."

Not saying a word, Ty whispered, "Well, we'll have to see. That's up to your Mom."

Lisa felt an awkwardness fill the room. "Right! Well, I'm off. Goodnight, everyone. Bon Appetit." She waved while going out the door, still giving Julia the eye.

After it closed behind her, Ty wheeled the cart beside the dining table while Julia set the food out and placed the basket of buns in the center. The two had a seat across from each other.

Opening the container, Julia explained, "So, umm, every year, Sydney and I get a small Christmas tree for the room. Usually, they don't allow it, but they've made an exception for us."

"Wow, that's nice of them."

Thinking things through, remembering what she told herself an hour before, she confirmed, "If you would like to join us, you are more than welcome. We don't mind."

"Ty, please come with us. It'll be fun," Syd begged, eating a spoonful of chili.

"Okay, thank you. What time does this exciting adventure start?" He didn't let on that he already knew.

"We leave early because the tree farm is a little further away. In the past, we departed around ten-thirty or eleven and returned to the store in Carling early afternoon."

"All right. I'm in."

Noticing Sydney had finished her dinner, Julia watched her walk into the kitchen with her dishes, looking tired. Landing on the sofa, seeing her curl up on one end, she placed her head on the pillow and quickly fell asleep. The room went quiet without the tween's giggles and laughter.

"This is probably the best chili I've ever tasted," Ty divulged, hoping to keep the conversation alive, feeling a heaviness blanketing the space around them.

"On cold days, there is nothing like having a hearty meal to warm you up."

"Yes. It certainly did. Thank you for inviting me to stay."

"No. Thank you." Getting up from the chair, Julia lovingly went to check on Sydney and covered her with the blanket before returning to the table to finish her last few bites. Dipping the bread into the yummy sauce to clean the bowl, she relived the day's events in great detail when they hit a lull in the conversation. The reality of what happened struck a chord. If they had gone with just the guide, she could have lost Sydney, too. A lump developed in her throat. Anxious, she got up from the table to clear the dishes.

Ty helped bring everything over to the kitchen.

Stopping what she was doing, unable to look him straight in the eye, she concentrated on what needed to be said. "If you weren't there today, I hate to think what would have happened...." Tearing up, raising her hand to her mouth, Julia glanced at her daughter, now sleeping soundly.

Standing to her left, he could see she was getting emotional. "I'm just happy that I was there to help. Right place, at the right time, I guess."

Forcing herself to look up at him, she found eyes affixed to hers. "It wasn't just the right place at the right time. You saved her and risked getting hurt yourself."

Ty wrapped his arm around her shoulders, hoping to console her without making her uncomfortable.

Indebted and overwhelmed, she suddenly turned and slipped her arms around his waist. Whispering, she said, "Thank you... Thank you for what you did today."

Surprised, gingerly holding her at first, Ty slowly tightened their embrace. He knew the trauma experienced today had inevitably brought them closer. Thinking back to being on the hill, not giving it a second thought, he knew he would do it all over again.

While she slowly pulled away, Ty felt his phone vibrating in his pocket. The sound made Julia take a step back. Sighing, he knew the interruption had ruined the moment.

"I'm sure you need to get that," Julia stated quietly, looking into his eyes. It made his heart skip a beat.

Great timing, Matt. Impeccable, he thought while pulling the device from his pocket. Assuming the team had an offer to present, he replied, "I'm sorry. Give me a second."

"It's okay. Take all the time you need." Leaving him, she continued to tidy the kitchen and began quietly placing the dishes in the dishwasher.

Going to stand in the far corner of the room, he checked who it was. Having missed the call, he waited for Matt to leave a message. Unfortunately, while listening to it, he only found disappointment on the other end.

"Any news?" she questioned when he walked over to set the phone on the counter.

Ty shook his head. "No. It was just Matt. There is nothing new to report. He said maybe tomorrow."

With arms crossed in front of her, Julia encouraged, "Don't worry. I have a feeling this will turn out fine. Everything happens for a reason."

"Hope you're right. I want to get this done so I can enjoy my time here without all this stress. I'm looking forward to the Christmas tree farm tomorrow."

"It will be fun. You'll see."

"Yesterday, while spending most of the day alone, I thought I made a mistake by coming here."

"Oh? And now?" Pausing, she added, "Well, despite the makings of this afternoon."

"I am having a good time."

Julia blushed. "I'm glad."

"I'm certainly happy the two of you are here. Otherwise, my holiday would be a lonely one."

"We've enjoyed spending time with you too."

Noticing the romantic movie The Holiday coming up next, Julia offered to extend their evening. "I love this one. Do you want to watch it with me?"

Happy to stay a bit longer, Ty agreed. "Yeah, I'd like that."

"Me too."

About to walk over and sit on the sofa, Julia forgot Sydney was still sleeping there. Needing to put her to bed, she mentioned, "I'll move Syd to her room."

Ty waited before offering some assistance. "Umm, do you want me to carry her? I can help."

At that moment, Julia thought of how often her husband had done that for her. "Umm, sure. If you don't mind."

"No, not at all. Happy to."

Lifting Sydney and cradling her in his arms, Julia led him to the room and pulled back the covers. He set her down gently and noticed Syd didn't move an inch.

Tucking her in, Julia quietly crept out and closed the door, leaving it open a little in case Sydney needed her. Following Ty, seeing the movie was about to start, they grabbed their wine from the table and brought the glasses over to the sofa.

Getting comfortable on one end, he tried to keep his composure despite a nervous feeling filling his chest.

Julia turned off the bright lights one by one, leaving only the table lamps on. The softer atmosphere allowed them to enjoy the flames flickering from the fireplace. Seeing the baseball player sitting there, Julia felt her heartbeat increase. She was anxious at the thought of being alone with him.

Where do I sit? She thought frantically. *What do I say?*

A million questions flooded her mind. Deciding to take a seat on the other end, she timidly lifted her legs and curled up with a cushion.

With barely anything said between them for the first five minutes of the opening scene, thankfully, Ty broke the silence.

"If you don't mind me asking, what was your son Ben like?"

Not expecting that topic of conversation, Julia fidgeted with the tassels on the pillow, unsure how to respond. "Ben? He was, umm, the most caring boy. He always helped me around the house when David was working late or if he was away on business. He was very athletic - not as studious as I would have liked, but he did well in school. He accepted others despite their faults and was in tune with his friends, who seemed troubled. He was known for cheering up those who were having a bad day. I think that was why he had so many friends." Julia thought a minute about what more to add. "He and Sydney never fought or argued much. Ben never teased her, as most brothers do. If anything, he was more protective of her - always watching out for her at school in the early grades." Tearing up, she said, "Ben was so proud that night he scored the first goal. He thought it set the tone for the rest of the game." She paused. "So, umm, that was my Benny-Bear."

"Well, he sounds like he was an amazing young man."

"Yes, he was. Very much so. You know, sometimes mothers complain about their children talking back and saying mean things to them in anger. I can honestly say Ben never showed any level of disrespect to either David or me. He had a kind soul and could never hurt anyone. Unless, of course, he was in the midst of a hockey game and followed a puck into the corner. That was different," she laughed. "Players went in at their own risk. He was quite competitive." Staring straight ahead, deep in thought, she added, "I don't know; maybe it's because I was his biggest fan. Perhaps that's why I find it easy to say these things. I loved being his Mother," she revealed as tears rolled down her cheeks. "Every morning, he came downstairs and greeted me with a hug. It was something I looked forward to. Often, I make sure to hug Sydney throughout the day." Using her fingertips to wipe away the tears, she said, "Because you never know when it could be your last one..."

Unsure what to say, Ty's instinct was to comfort her. Cautiously sliding over, he slipped his arm around her shoulders and offered a side hug, hoping to reduce the pain he had unintentionally rekindled.

Finding herself in unfamiliar territory, Julia wasn't sure what to do. He was still a stranger, yet it felt like she'd known him forever. But today, above all else, he was the man who saved her daughter - the man who had been nothing but respectful and kind to them. Granting solace, she leaned in and casually rested her head on his shoulder.

"I'm sorry. I probably shouldn't have asked you about him," he whispered.

"No, it's okay. It's nice to talk about Ben. I guess I don't do that as often as I should."

Refocused on the movie's storyline, Julia was surprised that Ty remained close and didn't return to the other end of the sofa. Their conversation seemed to flow more freely afterward.

"So, which place would you prefer?" he asked, pointing at the screen.

"Like from the movie?"

"Yeah. Which house would you gravitate to?" Taking a sip of wine, Ty set his glass down.

"I'm not sure. Both have advantages and disadvantages. The English cottage reminds me of the town of Carling, and I'm sure that Amanda's LA house must be like something you'd live in."

"Actually, no. I live in the Ritz residences in downtown Boston. A far cry from suburbia."

"Oh, really?"

"Well, because I travel a lot, it's easier that way. No maintenance or worries. Plus, there's built-in security."

"Yes, that makes sense," she nodded.

Watching the character Amanda kiss Iris' brother, Graham, Ty, and Julia stayed silent during the romantic scene. Not turning to look at the man sitting beside her, fearing it may spark something escalating between them, she thought of her husband David as a pang of guilt washed over her. It was like he was watching from heaven and was disappointed. The cheating feeling was hard to shake. In an attempt to redirect her thoughts, she noticed her glass was almost empty.

"Would you like to split the last of the wine with me?" she asked, about to get up from her spot.

"You stay," he replied. "I'll get it."

Bringing the bottle from the dining table, he returned to the sofa.

"Just a splash for me, please." She watched him pour some into her glass first. "That's good, thank you."

Stopping there, he emptied the little that remained in his.

Julia leaned forward to take hold of the glass. Doing this brought them face-to-face. Drawn to him, she was unable to ignore their connection. Peering into his eyes and seeing him glimpse intermittently at her lips, Julia picked up on the signals and met him partway. Her heart raced at the thought of what he was about to do. A flood of heat flowed through her from head to toe. Her body trembled in anticipation. Merely an inch apart, both barely breathing, Julia waited for his lips to touch hers while her eyes drifted shut.

"Mom?" A voice cut through the silence.

Julia stopped abruptly and diverted her head to one side, as did Ty. An awkwardness followed.

"Mom?" her daughter said a second time.

"I'm so sorry. Give me a minute." Needing to tend to her daughter, Julia left him and walked into Sydney's room. Returning to the kitchen to get a bottle of water from the fridge to satisfy her request, she closed the door slightly behind her, knowing their moment had passed.

On her way over to the sofa, she noticed he had moved a couple of feet from where he was.

A little embarrassed by the interruption, knowing she was no longer a free-spirited young woman, she said, "I'm so sorry about that. When duty calls, Moms drop everything."

"Never apologize. That little girl should always take priority."

She very much appreciated what he said. It helped calm her nerves.

"Can I ask you something?" Ty sounded sincere in his tone.

Afraid of what he was about to say, she replied, "Sure," while turning sideways on the sofa, cuddling a pillow.

"This is not something I'm good at – like at all. Umm..." Ty rubbed his palms together nervously.

Hanging on his every word, Julia watched him lean forward and rest his elbows on his knees. Tightly gripping his hands in front of him, he could not look at her. "I just wanted to say...." Taking a deep breath, with a concerned look on his face, clearing his throat a few times, undecided on how to formulate his sentence, he finally gathered his thoughts. "I find myself developing...umm...certain feelings - for you." Quickly raising his hands between them to stop her from commenting, he continued, "Now, before you say anything, I realize your life is complicated, and mine is far from ordinary; I respect that, I do, but I am hoping in some small way you feel the same? I know this sounds crazy since we only met a few days ago. But, I thought I'd throw it out there."

"Yes," Julia answered spontaneously, interrupting him, waiting for that feeling of extreme guilt to follow.

Lifting his head, Ty caught the smitten smile playing on her lips. The way her eyes sparkled, unguarded and alive, told him everything he needed to know. His voice softened. "Really?"

"Yes." Her voice was barely above a whisper, her nod timid.

Hearing her answer, Ty exhaled a breath he hadn't realized he was holding. Relief, joy, and something far more profound swept through him all at once. His hand, deliberate yet gentle, moved to her waist, his fingers tracing the curve as if committing the moment to memory. Drawing her closer, he felt her warmth against him, her presence grounding him like nothing else ever had.

Julia tilted her face up to him, her lashes lowering nervously. Relying purely on instinct, they met in the space between, lips brushing softly at first, then lingering. Each - a discovery. A connection deepening. The world around them blurred amidst the intimate rhythm they created.

His heart raced, yet his mind remained startlingly clear. How had he survived all this time without knowing the feel of her lips, the intoxicating closeness of her? For the first time in his life, the first baseman believed fate must exist. It had to. There was no other explanation for the way she had walked into his life, wearing a cozy sweater and slippers, somehow stealing his breath away. The most perfect love-at-first-sight meeting.

As they pulled back slightly, their foreheads rested together in the faint chill of the room.

Ty's lips brushed over hers once more in a series of featherlight pecks, each one a promise. His cheek drifted against hers, the stubble on his jaw teasing her smooth skin. "I believe I'm falling for you, Julia Mariani," he whispered, his voice carrying the weight of a confession and the lightness of hope.

Her fingers curled into his shirt as her lips curved into a smile against his cheek.

"Is that right?" she replied subtly.

"Wholeheartedly."

"You seem to be growing on me, too." She felt like she was living someone else's life.

"I'm glad to hear that."

Without warning, that expected feeling of guilt appeared. Her heart sank. Pressing her hand against his chest, she said, "Please be patient with me. We need to move slowly."

He reassured her, "You can have all the time you need."

As a heavyweight lifted off them, they both felt light as a feather. Kissing her forehead, then her cheek, he couldn't help but gravitate to her lips again. Shyly unable to look her in the eyes, he hugged her intermittently and lowered his sights to the floor. His heart rate increased - maybe too much. "Being the gentleman I am, I must bid you Goodnight. I hope to see you both at breakfast."

"Yes. We will be ready to go downstairs by nine o'clock."

Leaving the sofa, holding her hand, Ty reached for his phone on the countertop and walked toward the door. Julia stayed by his side. Opening it, he waited a second.

Kissing her, offering one last tight embrace, he whispered, "I am thankful Sydney's okay."

"How can I ever repay you for..." she stated, still feeling indebted.

Putting up his hand to stop her, Ty confirmed, "No thanks necessary. I would do it again in a heartbeat." Hugging her, hoping to offer even more reassurance, he said, "Goodnight, Julia. I'll see you in the morning."

"Yes, Goodnight."

While crossing the hallway, Ty let go of her hand. Watching her lean on the door frame, resting her head against it, he waved before closing them simultaneously.

Hearing his slide shut with a click, Ty locked it and moved toward his bedroom. Sitting on the edge, he checked his emails and found nothing new. When he placed the phone on the side table, he hoped everything would work out the way he always believed it would.

Raising his head to stare at the ceiling, he whispered, "Hey, Mom. I met someone. Did you have something to do with that?"

26

December 22nd

Decisions

Up early that morning, unable to sleep most of the night, Ty headed downstairs to the gym for a workout around seven. Almost putting in a full ninety minutes of weights and cardio, he used the quiet time to take inventory of his life and wondered what direction the New Year would bring, given the career decision still weighing heavily upon his shoulders. Quickly checking his messages, there was still nothing.

"What if the one-year contract falls through?" he muttered, wondering what the chances were of finishing his final year in Boston. "Do I call it quits?" He didn't want to retire on such a low note, especially after losing out on the Series this season. "For the first time in sixteen years, your life is in complete turmoil, and you have no control over it. What's your plan? You need a plan."

Julia crossed his mind more than once. Thoughts of her helped douse any negative thinking. Having shared her feelings, he was happy she, too, felt the same way. Without a doubt, Ty had never found a woman with the qualities that Julia possessed. She was kind, considerate, and giving, not to mention a wonderful mother to Sydney. She treated everyone around her with the utmost respect. Her smile was embedded in his mind now. He bashfully lowered his head and grinned ear to ear, recalling their kiss the night before and the warmth it gave him. He could hardly wait to see her today.

Toweling off after his run on the treadmill, Ty sat on the bench to catch his breath. Checking the time, he said, "Damn. I'm running late."

With urgency, he left the gym and stopped at the elevator. Pressing the button repeatedly, he got impatient. Not wanting to waste another minute, he opened the door to the stairs and energetically ran up the five flights. Reaching the top and swinging open the door, he hoped he hadn't missed them since Julia said they were meeting in the hallway at nine o'clock. With a little less than twenty minutes to spare, he quietly leaned a listening ear toward Julia's door. Happy not hearing a peep from them, he got moving.

With a jump in his step, he whispered, "Good. I still have time," before opening his door to get ready for the day.

December 22nd

Aftermath

With another five inches of snow blanketing the ground that morning, everything looked naturally unspoiled. Still seeing residual lazy flakes falling, the Hotel lived up to its reputation. Lovingly creating a picture-perfect winter wonderland backdrop, Julia was excited about the day's festivities.

Brewing her coffee, she let Sydney sleep a little longer. Yawning, since she had only slept about three hours, she recalled the feeling she got when Ty left last night. Replaying their goodbye in her head, Julia had closed the door quietly behind her, making sure not to wake Sydney. Securing the deadbolt and the swing lock, she remembered turning around and resting her back against it. With hands clenched together tightly, unable to fathom what just happened, she felt a surge of energy and excitement not felt in a very long time. That feeling slowly faded at the thought of David and their memories still haunting her.

Hearing Sydney groaning in bed, Julia walked over to her door.

"Good morning, sleepyhead. How are you?"

Yawning considerably, Syd squeaked out one word. "Good."

As if contagious, Julia yawned, too. "Are you feeling okay? Does anything hurt?" She wasn't sure if she had suffered any post-traumatic effects from yesterday.

Barely able to open her eyes, she mumbled, "No, I'm fine. Nothing hurts."

The cut on her face looked a little redder this morning when Julia looked at it. "Here, let me put some more Polysporin on that."

"Okay," she said, sitting completely still.

"There. How's that?" she asked her.

Without an ounce of complaining, the girl offered a thumbs up.

"Ready to get our Christmas tree today?"

"Oh, yes. I almost forgot. How do you think Ty will do?" She rolled over for Julia to offer a morning hug.

"What do you mean?"

"Isn't he from the city?"

"I suppose so," her Mother confirmed.

"Does he know anything about getting a Christmas tree from a tree farm?" she laughed.

"That I don't know." Not sure what the day would bring, Julia clapped her hands to light a fire under her daughter. "Well, I guess we will soon find out. Let's get moving. We need to get dressed. It's already 8:35."

"Why?"

"We are meeting Ty for breakfast at nine."

"Oh. Okay," Syd said, jumping out of bed. "I can hardly wait to see Clarence and LeeAnn."

"Yes, me too. It's been a while since we've seen them."

"I bet they'll think I've grown again."

Julia kissed her daughter's forehead and laughed. "Oh, I'm sure they will."

28 ▌

December 22nd

History

Knowing he had to hurry, Ty quickly jumped in and out of the shower and dried off before getting dressed at a rapid pace. Still not hearing anything from across the hall, the baseball player looked in the mirror and ran his hands through his hair to make sure it looked presentable. More than ready to start the day, breakfast with the ladies was the first order of business. Questioning whether he should bring along the winter gear, Ty placed everything on the chair just in case.

Moving across the hall, he listened to hear if the Marianis were mobile. Hearing voices, anxious about seeing Julia, he took a deep breath. Nervous energy flowing over him, he rapped his knuckles on the door. Watching the barrier between them swing open, Ty found Julia and Sydney prepared for winter. They had everything they needed already packed in a backpack with coats in hand.

Greeted with the biggest smiles, warming his heart, he said, "Good morning, you two. Sleep well?"

"Good morning," the ladies said simultaneously.

"I know I did. I don't know about Mom." Sydney sounded tired.

Waiting for Julia while she gathered their things and closed their door, Ty grabbed his winter gear from his room and returned to them.

Letting Sydney lead the way, Julia and Ty walked side by side. It felt strange. Not knowing how to act given the makings of the night before, having Sydney present now changed the dynamic between them.

At the elevators, the young girl pressed the button to go downstairs.

"How are you doing this morning, Syd? Recovered from yesterday?"

With a smile, she replied, "Yes. I'm good."

Without missing a beat, Ty thought he'd ask a question to initiate a conversation. "So, can you tell me more about how this tree farm thing works?"

Sydney flashed an - *I told you so*, look. "See, Mom. Remember what I said? I was right."

Both Julia and Sydney giggled.

Ty's sights bounced between the two of them. "You were right about what?"

"This one mentioned this morning that this Christmas Tree Farm excursion might be out of your scope for a city boy like yourself. She thought you might be in over your head."

"Is that so?" Laughing, he revealed, "What I failed to share about myself the other night is that I was not born and raised in the city." Seeing their surprised reaction, he added, "Ha! Yes, that's right. I grew up in a small town outside of Jackson, Wyoming. It had a population of about 1200 people at the time. I think it may be more now."

The elevator doors parted.

While holding them open for the girls, Ty let the two go first. "I used to chop wood for the fireplace and shovel snow in the winter. I tilled the garden in the spring and raked leaves in the fall. So, does that still make me a city boy?"

Stunned by that, Sydney looked sheepishly at her Mom. "I think we may have underestimated him."

"We'll have to see, now, won't we," Julia challenged, locking eyes with his, offering him a smitten smile.

Upon reaching the main floor, the group passed by the lobby. Ty was the first to notice, "I wonder where Nick is this morning."

Laughing, Julia thought the same. "Oh, he probably has taken the day off finally."

On their way to the hostess podium, not waiting for anyone to greet them, they found a seat at their regular table by the window in the Cottages Restaurant. Thankfully, the storm had passed, and the snow had stopped. Having left a thick white blanket over the entire view, all that remained was a perfect backdrop for a Christmas tree excursion.

They were greeted by Lisa when she emerged from the kitchen. "Well, good morning, everyone. How are we doing today?" She gave Julia the eye.

"Good morning, Lisa. We are all doing well." Julia hoped she wouldn't ask for the inside scoop this morning.

Lisa poured their orange juice and two cups of freshly brewed coffee. "What can I get everyone?"

Sydney ordered her waffles with whipped cream and fruit while Julia and Ty went for the usual. It wasn't long before the young girl inserted her earbuds to connect with friends.

Reaching for the cream and pouring some into her coffee, curious about Ty's childhood in Wyoming, Julia passed the creamer over to him. "So, how does a guy from Wyoming end up playing pro baseball for Boston?"

Concerned about sharing anything regarding his past, Ty nervously cleared his throat. "That is a long story." Seeing her waiting for a response, he opted to give her the Coles Notes version. "So, we lived in Jackson until I was seventeen. Our house was close to the ski hill, so I worked odd jobs there to ski free of charge when I was off. Couldn't afford it otherwise. Over the years, I looked forward to taking even an hour to ski the hills. It was so peaceful." Pausing a second, unsure if he should share his thoughts, he took a deep breath. "Umm, my life wasn't as peaceful during the spring and summer months. My Dad got me into baseball when I was very young. He coached my little league teams for many years, making my life overly complicated. For him, it was all about winning. The kids on the team resented me for it. Knowing how stressed

I was, my Mom tried to be quietly supportive. Not wanting to anger my father, she said to keep my head down and play as hard as possible. She told me to think of only her cheering me on, nobody else. Every time I stepped up to bat, I wanted to make her proud. Doing this helped me not give the guy a second thought 'cause nothing I did pleased him anyway. Every catch made, every hit, and every out I made was for her. That led to a long year of scouts watching my games from age fifteen to sixteen. Dad invited them, adding to the pressure. In the spring of my grade eleven year, I got asked to join a junior team in Texas. We moved from Jackson to Houston in a blink. My sister hated me for it because it forced her to leave her friends behind." Recalling the makings of that time in his life, he continued, "When I got there, I always did what the coaches said, but my father argued with them from time to time, and that caused friction. Despite it all, I played exceptionally that year and earned a full-ride to Rice University, allowing me to play NCAA. When finishing my fourth year of school, our team ended up in the playoffs, where I attracted a lot of attention from the MLB scouts, giving me a shot at the major leagues. Getting drafted to Houston's farm team, I soon got called up and was eventually traded to Atlanta a couple of years later. After having the best season of my career, I got traded to Boston and have stayed there ever since." Pausing a second, moving his food around with his fork, he finished the story. "Yeah... That's it. Many people think your life is easy when you make it and become successful in pro sports, but most don't realize the backstory that made the person who they are. When my Mom died, I knew she would always be with me on the field. To this day, I still believe she is my biggest fan. I wasn't there for my sister when my Dad died. For whatever reason, I couldn't bring myself to attend the funeral. Many would say that I made it this far because of him. I suppose that is true to an extent because of how he treated me and pushed me, but in the end, I know I played for my Mother. She was the one who got me through. She is the one who made me who I am — not my Dad. I promised myself that if I ever became a father, I would never put my children through that. Ever. So, as luck would have it, it looks like that isn't in the cards for me anyway."

Julia didn't know what to say.

Picking up on it, Ty assured, "I know... You don't have to say anything. Hard to believe, huh?"

"I'm sorry your Dad treated you like that. I would have loved to meet your Mom."

Reaching his hand out to her under the table, he grasped hold and said, "I know she would've loved to meet you, too."

When their food arrived, Sydney removed her earbuds, ready to eat. That set the tone for an abundance of conversation, something Ty could never get enough of.

December 22nd

Getting to Know You

"So, Sydney? What is a typical day like for you with school and all?" He cut through his eggs benny and took a bite.

"Well, Mom drops me off at eight-thirty each morning. I usually meet up with friends outside. Two days a week, we pick up my friend V. It's short for Veronika. She needs a drive because her mom works in the city those days." Sydney took the syrup bottle and poured extra on her waffles. "My classes are okay. The teachers are a bit mean at times. I hate when they yell at the boys who are misbehaving. Wish they'd act more mature. But no. They continue to do stupid things. Not sure why?" Cutting the waffle, she took another bite. "Oh, this is good."

"So, are you in any clubs? Sports? Things like that?" he wondered while Julia looked on.

"Yes. I'm on the yearbook committee. I mostly take pictures for them. Sometimes I write articles for the newspaper. That's if I feel strongly about something. I always write anonymously. Never use my real name. It's easier that way."

She was surprised to hear this. "I didn't know that, Syd."

The girl laughed. "You never asked."

The comment caught Julia off guard. Ty could see it. It was like a knife to the heart. It made her realize she would have to do better at getting involved in her daughter's daily activities. With work, the new house, and adjusting to life after losing David and Ben, saying things were stressful was an understatement.

"As for sports, I don't like being the center of attention, so the cheerleading team is not for me. But I run track and cross-country. I play basketball, badminton, and tennis."

"Have you ever played baseball?" Ty was curious.

"Just in gym class once or twice." Syd looked down at her food before she whispered, "I recall Dad playing catch with Ben in the backyard, though. I think I was too little to join them."

Ty wished he hadn't brought it up.

"Yes. We used to watch the boys. I remember you'd run after the ball when it got away from them." Her Mother said almost solemnly. "You would try throwing it back, but it would roll off your fingers and fall a few feet in front of you."

"Mom...." she groaned, her voice stretching the word into an exasperated sigh, colored by the unmistakable blush of embarrassment.

"What did I say? You were little, and it was adorable." Julia tilted her head, recalling those memorable moments.

"Maybe we could throw the ball around and play catch. I would love to teach you. No pressure. I'm sure we can pick up gloves and a ball at a sports store around here somewhere."

Sydney's face lit up. "Yeah. I'd like that."

"Great." With that settled, Ty moved along to Julia, wanting to know more. "So, what does your day look like when Syd is at school?"

"My day is boring compared to hers, I'm sure."

"No, it's not. There are times she takes me to her building sites. You should see how pretty some of her landscape projects are. They don't start that way, though. It's usually messy until the very end. I love the great reveal. It's my favorite part. I especially like the backyard builds with pools. They are so nice."

"Oh, really?" Ty was happy to hear that perspective.

Turning to her Mother, she said, "Show him some pictures." Before returning her sights to Ty. "She's got so many."

He glanced over at Julia, who was blushing.

"Show him, Mom."

"How about we finish our breakfast first? We can do that later."

"Okay..." her daughter said, taking another bite of waffle with fruit and whipped cream, drenched in syrup.

"So, how about you, Ty? What's your day like?" Julia questioned.

"Mine? Well, I usually get up early and head to the gym. Practice begins at eleven and ends at four most days. When we travel, it's different. While we are on road trips, it varies also. It's mostly workouts, practice, eating, and sleep. That's it."

Sydney stared at him. "Wait, wait, wait. Did I miss something? What do you mean you practice, eat, and sleep? What's your job?" Not wanting to get Nick in trouble, she didn't let on that she'd investigated him already.

Her Mother got her up to speed. "Ty plays professional baseball."

"So, like, you're famous." The little girl stated point blank.

"I don't think of it like that."

Taken by how humble he was, Julia's opinion of him softened even more.

"Do you have any friends?" Syd questioned.

"My teammates are all friends. Sadly, I don't have many outside that circle. In my line of work, it's hard to trust people."

"Do you trust us?" she said innocently.

Smiling, he lowered his head. "I believe I do."

"That's good."

"Can you tell us more about your sister? What's her name?" Julia hoped she wasn't prying too much.

"Yeah, what is she like?" Sydney sat up in her chair, ready to listen.

Turning his plate clockwise, seeing two sets of eyes on him, he contemplated his answer. "My sister? That could take a while."

Julia checked the time. "We have a few minutes still."

Ty leaned forward and rested his elbows on either side of his plate. "Her name is Jenna. She married a Texan named Dan Ducane, and they have two boys, Alex and Brayden. Since I got traded to Boston, we haven't kept in touch for a few years."

Saddened to hear that, Julia said, "You haven't spoken to her at all?"

"No. Not since Dad died."

"Don't you think she would like to hear from you?" Julia hoped she wasn't overstepping her bounds.

Pretty sure that was not the case, he said, "I don't think she will ever speak to me again. I've been the cause of so much disappointment and anger in her life. I can almost bet that she hates me. So that's the end of that."

A heaviness fell upon them. Believing Ty wanted to leave that conversation alone, Julia and Sydney didn't press him further.

Seeing Lisa making her way over with the bill, Ty swiftly took hold of both folders again. Before Julia could argue, he splashed his signature across the two slips of paper.

"Wait. What are you doing?" Julia replied as he stacked the booklets and set the pen on top.

Prepared to argue, he said with great sincerity, "You paid for the chili and buns last night, so I am buying you breakfast."

"But you can't do that."

"Just did," Ty said quietly.

Julia had no choice but to concede. "Then, we will pay for your breakfast tomorrow."

"So, you want to have breakfast together again?" He replied with eyebrows raised, offering a sexy smirk.

"Guess so. I've got to even the score."

Ty laughed, appreciating the sports analogy.

Julia could feel a tiny spark ignite between them as she tried to fathom how, out of all the women in the world, Ty Reynolds would even look her way and be remotely interested.

Excited to start the day, he suggested, "Shall we go?"

"Sure," she said, seeing Lisa giving her a thumbs up from the other side of the room.

Leaving the restaurant with their winter gear in hand, they walked toward the lobby. Upon rounding the corner, they found Nick standing by the front doors.

"Nick!!" They all shouted in unison.

Startling the man, he happily said, "Hello, everyone. Are you ready for your Christmas tree excursion?"

"Oh, yes!" Syd replied with an abundance of energy. "I'm so ready."

While getting dressed for the cold weather, Ty watched Julia help her daughter with her jacket. Zipping it up to her chin, the two were quite giddy. He thought she was so attentive, much like his Mother. An unparalleled joy revolved around the two of them. It was infectious.

Opening the entrance doors, Nick announced, "Follow me, everyone. This way. I have the truck waiting for you."

"Is Grandpa Bryce not driving us?"

The man answered her, "Sorry. I believe he has the morning off but might be working later today. Is it okay if I drive you?" His face went rosy, and his eyes twinkled.

Mesmerized, Sydney said, "Yes, that's okay."

"Alright. Let's go - daylight is burning."

December 22nd

Christmas Tree Excursion

All bundled up, the group walked out to a black extended Cadillac Escalade with The Carling logo on the side. Nick opened the back door for Sydney and Julia to hop in.

Not sure what to do, Ty got in the front seat. He didn't want to invade their mother-daughter space.

Seeing this, Julia was disappointed.

Settling in behind the wheel, Nick announced, "Everyone buckled up, ready to go?"

"Yes, ready!" Sydney exclaimed while peering out the window.

"Perfect," Nick said, shifting the vehicle in gear. "We are off."

Leaving the hotel, they marveled at the majestic scenery on all sides - tall trees hanging with a thick layer of snow and the sun's rays peeking through the clouds, glistening over the fields of white, untainted, and smooth. A picture-perfect winter wonderland.

Not having seen anything while arriving in the middle of the night in a snowstorm, Ty scanned his surroundings, surprised by the rugged landscape and the large cottages lining the lake.

"Wow, this place is beautiful. I bet it's amazing in the summer months."

"We wouldn't know," Julia laughed, leaning between the seats. "Sydney and I never visit during the summer. Not sure why. I guess we could if we wanted. It is just such a popular place. The summer is jam-packed usually."

"I bet."

"If we owned a cottage here, it would be different. But to stay at the Carling would be hard with the crowds. We are used to having the hotel to ourselves. Guess we've gotten spoiled over the years."

"I'd like to see if there was a vacation rental on this lake. I'm sure there's gotta be something. That way, you don't have to commit to the expense of buying and maintaining a place all year round. You enjoy your time off and leave."

"Never thought of that." It got Julia thinking. "Given the price of real estate in this area, I'm sure if there were a rental, it would be thousands of dollars for a week, which is out of our price range. But we should still look into it. What do you think, Syd?"

"Yeah, that would be fun."

Ty suggested, "Maybe I'll visit in the summer, and we can meet up?"

Surprised, Nick glimpsed at the baseball player, then in the mirror at the young woman behind him.

Sitting back in her seat, Nick could tell Julia's mind was racing as she looked at Ty's reflection in the side mirror.

"Thankfully, the roads are somewhat clear today. I was doubtful," Nick said to help change the subject.

"Yes, the way you talked yesterday, I expected we'd be snowed in for days," the athlete replied.

"Around here, the plows don't venture out until the storm subsides. Luckily, it tapered off late last night. It seems the trucks got an early start."

Expertly maneuvering the vehicle along the back roads to another nearby town, Nick offered his knowledge of the historical landmarks that peppered their route.

Sydney's anticipation began to build when she recognized how close they were to their intended destination.

Signaling left, Nick veered down a laneway lined by traditional wood and stone fencing leading to the most beautiful garden center. Festively decorated for the holidays, the first thing Ty noticed was the two six-foot Nutcrackers guarding the main entrance. Countless wreaths and trees filled with ornaments surrounded the long building draped in Christmas lights. While parking close to a traditional red sleigh staged for photo ops out front, Ty thought it resembled the one showcased in his hometown square. The vibe felt like he'd stepped into a Wyoming holiday Christmas card.

"Well, here we are. Enjoy your visit to the tree farm," Nick said before helping Sydney jump out.

Curiously looking around, Ty left the front seat and held open Julia's door for her.

"Thank you," she said before catching up to Sydney.

He closed it behind her. From a distance, he watched the two lead the way through the welcome gates. It seemed they knew where they were going.

Seeing him falling behind, Julia stopped and allowed him to catch up. "So, what do you think?"

Surrounded by festive décor, infusing him with the spirit of Christmas, he couldn't help but smile. "It's nice. Reminds me of home."

While keeping a close eye on Sydney skipping ahead a little further, Julia walked alongside Ty and placed her hands in her jacket pockets. In minutes, she knew she would soon start to see familiar faces around the greenhouse, and the thought made her anxious.

What will they think of me? Julia thought. *Will they get the wrong idea?*

Given the number of eyes staring at them when they entered the building, Ty assumed each person knew of the Marianis and their tragic past. Staying mindful of his proximity to the girls, he tried not to infringe too much on their outing.

The plantation shuttle line was short, indicating that the season was noticeably winding down. Most people had already picked up their trees weeks beforehand.

Sydney spied the horse-drawn sleigh emerging from below the hill.

"Here it comes, Mom. Hurry!" she shouted.

When it stopped in front of the platform, sectioned off with thick red Christmas ribbons and bows, the three climbed aboard and had a seat. On their way up the hill, the wind picked up, prompting Ty to help them spread the wool blanket across their legs.

Hearing the sound of jingle bells, the horses galloped steadily. Making it to the top, they traversed the pinnacle and looked down on the rows and rows of Christmas trees.

The girl threw her hands in the air. "This is the best part! I love the view from here!"

Overjoyed to see her so happy, loving every treasured moment with her, David and Ben crossed Julia's mind. It was hard not to recall their first sleigh ride here years ago. In a series of flashes, she could not stop the memories from flowing. It was an exciting adventure for such a young family. The children were so small. Able to hear their laughter and see the smiles on David and Ben's faces clear as day, a gust of wind made her return to the present.

How strange to be sitting here years later without them. It all ended in a blink. David and Ben seemed to disappear.

Her heart ached as remnants of that fateful day returned, making Julia feel a great deal of sadness. Hoping not to dampen the mood, she forced herself to block out the grief creeping in – something that often happened when they visited the farm.

Glancing over at Ty, she felt guilty about spending the day with him. Christmas tree shopping was a Mariani tradition, and she was allowing a stranger to invade it.

An internal battle erupted. *Stop, Julia. You're not doing anything wrong. It's fine.* She tried to reassure herself.

Ty could feel she was uncomfortable. It made him question if he'd said or done something wrong. Afraid to ask, he just let it go.

As the horse-drawn sleigh slowly stopped beside lines and lines of perfectly shaped Christmas trees, Ty was amazed by the organized rows.

"Wow," he said. "This is incredible. Look at these trees. It won't be hard to pick a perfect one."

Jumping off into the snow, the three of them met with a Greeter.

"Hello! How is everyone this fine day?" The man was dressed warmly from head to toe.

"Hi, there. We are doing well, and you?" Julia politely replied. Not recognizing him from previous years, she knew the man was new.

"Have you been to our plantation before?" he asked cheerfully, dressed with a green and red plaid scarf around his neck.

She answered, "Yes. We have been visiting for ten years now."

"Then, I don't need to explain the process to you. You are veterans."

Sydney giggled. "Yes, we know what to do."

"What name do I put on the tag?" he asked, holding a Sharpie, ready to write on the red ribbon.

"Mariani. M-A-R-I-A-N-I," Sydney spelled out letter by letter.

Thinking a second, knowing he didn't want to pass up this opportunity, Ty said, "Umm, can you make that two? One for Mariani and the other for Reynolds?"

"Two?" Sydney asked, confused.

"Would the hotel mind if I got a tree also? Nothing big. What do you think? Is that alright?"

"Syd? Think you can help him out?" Julia wanted her daughter to share her thoughts.

She confidently nodded. "Leave that to me. I have connections and will make sure it's fine."

Laughing, he pointed to Sydney and said, "Perfect! It looks like I have someone on the inside willing to put in a good word. Thanks."

"What was the name again, Sir?" The man asked.

"Reynolds. R-E-Y-N-O-L-D-S."

The guy printed his name on the ribbon.

Sydney approached with a serious look on her face. "So, if you do this, it means you must decorate the tree, too - the works. No skimping," Syd insisted with hands on her hips. "No shortcuts. All or nothing."

"Deal. I can do that." Ready for the challenge, Ty took hold of his red ribbon. "Let's go and find our trees."

Strolling along the ends of the rows, Julia asked, "So, where should we start?"

"This way!" The girl waved them on, pointing down an aisle nearby.

Watching the little girl stroll up and down the rows, seemingly skimming each line, passing over some very nicely shaped trees, Ty came across a smaller-sized one and asked, "How about this? It looks great. It's nice and full, very green, and perfectly shaped. What do you think?"

Laughing, Sydney immediately stopped and offered a disappointed smirk. Shaking her head, she decided to teach him how they tree shop.

"No, no, no..." she said with a humorous expression, "Let me explain something to you." Walking over to the tree that Ty had chosen, she divulged, "This tree is beautiful in many ways, yes, but we are not interested in the trees that will get picked. We look for a tree that is not doing so well - one that runs the risk of being cut down and replaced by a seedling in the spring. After all, the greenhouse is running a business."

Somewhat confused, Ty replied, "Okay?"

Walking over to one about four feet tall, with a lack of needles and sparse branches, Sydney surveyed it. "Take this one, for example. This little tree will never get selected like the perfect trees you see here. It will never stand proudly in a family's living room and shine brightly with pretty lights and ornaments. It will never get the chance to celebrate Christmas and bring joy to a family – unless...."

"We buy it, and it comes home with us," Julia said, proudly finishing her daughter's sentence.

"Precisely!" Syd's face brightened.

Speechless, he didn't know what to say. Taken by their family tradition, he asked, "Well, if that is the tree you are getting, what should I choose?"

Tagging theirs with the ribbon secured to a branch, Sydney searched for a similar one. Finding a tree a few rows over, she shouted, "Here, Ty! I found one for you!"

Joining her, Julia smiled while he surveyed what Syd had selected. It was almost identical to theirs.

"What do you think? It's perfect, isn't it?"

Nodding her head, Syd agreed. "You are going to make this cute little tree very happy."

"This is kind of exciting. So, what happens next?" he questioned.

Julia turned to him. "Well, they come by and cut it for us and wrap it up. Once we get it loaded in the truck, we head to the local hardware store to pick up lights and a few ornaments."

While waiting for the cutter to visit their rows, the three watched a few perfect trees pass by, with excited young families not far behind.

Analyzing what the girls just said, Ty wondered, "Wait? Do you buy new ornaments every year?"

"Yes," Julia answered.

"Why don't you reuse them?"

Smiling at her Mother, she nodded, motioning for her to share their secret.

Syd walked over and quietly confided, "Only two other people know that we do this, so you can't tell anyone."

Intrigued by what she was about to say, Ty knelt on one knee when Sydney prompted him to whisper in his ear.

"This community has a special place for families who are escaping scary situations," she mumbled. "Here, mothers with young children hide to escape abusive homes. If they assign them to this area, it is because their file is considered high-risk. Many leave in the middle of the night with only the clothes on their backs. Once they get to the facility, they walk into a sparsely furnished room. We wanted to change that. So, we choose a different theme for our tree every year, and after the holidays, we donate the lights and ornaments to the shelter. We buy a pretty box to store it all in and deliver it to a wonderful woman named Betty, who runs the place. They reuse the ornaments and decorations. The ones we buy today will bring joy to yet another family next year. So far, we have donated enough decorations for ten trees. It helps the shelter provide a Christmas to those families who wouldn't otherwise be able to have that. We've also brought wrapped toys and other gifts for all ages and provided gift cards to the shelter so the mothers can have a Merry Christmas, too."

With a lump lodged in his throat, Ty suddenly felt very insignificant. Letting the gravity of their tradition sink in, he thought, *You've done all these charity events countless times. Each was a successful team initiative, but nothing as genuine and heartwarming as this.* Staring at the two of them standing side by side, thankful to be trusted with their secret, Ty said, "That is the most honorable thing I've ever heard..." He saw tears developing in Julia's eyes.

"Well, it's not much, but to them, it is everything. When buying some ornaments today, you can do the same if you like." Julia went out on a limb and planted the seed.

"I would love to do that," Ty sincerely agreed.

Once the man had cut their trees with a chainsaw, he brought them to his trailer and carefully loaded each for processing back at the greenhouse.

Sydney oversaw the whole operation. She was very particular about how the tree should be handled and respected.

The baseball player was amazed by this. The young girl was so very different than most her age.

Ready to board the horse-drawn sleigh back to the main building, the driver decided to take them for a ride around the plantation. Enjoying the sights and sounds, they marveled at the scenery - the vast open fields to one side and the perfect rows of evergreens to the other. Dashing down the hill, the driver slowed their speed once they reached the tree line. In contrast to the dark tree trunks and branches, the snow stood out, creating a magical backdrop for their Christmas sleigh ride. Snow-laden boughs arched overhead, creating a wintery tunnel. To Sydney, it was the perfect end to their tree excursion.

Returning to the Garden Center, stopping alongside the platform, Julia watched her daughter and their new friend get out and walk ahead, talking and strategizing about the tree decorations. Hearing them discussing themes, Julia discovered another side of the handsome man. He wasn't just a famous baseball player who had the world in the palm of his hand. He was a man willing to take the time to listen intently to a girl's wisdom. It was easy to see he valued the little things in life. Something both she and Sydney learned to appreciate years ago. It got her thinking if they'd met him to influence change in his life or whether he would bring about a change in theirs.

31

December 22nd

Clarence and LeeAnn's

While Julia lingered, she listened closely to Ty and Sydney's conversation. It was effortless. Her daughter laughed and joked with him as though she'd known him her whole life.

Glancing back, noticing her lagging behind, Ty stopped. "Everything okay?"

"I'm fine," Julia replied, catching up to them.

With his eyes locked on hers, he couldn't help but feel good about the friendship they were building. Thankful to be included in this overly personal and thoughtful experience, secretly shared between a mother and a daughter, Ty believed it to be an unforgettable day.

Walking alongside the tall, handsome man, Julia asked, "Are you ready for our next stop on the Christmas tree excursion?"

He nodded. "So ready."

"Great. Let's get our trees packed up, and we can head to Clarence's."

"Clarence's?" he replied. "Is there anything, in particular, I should know about him? You know. Inside information to break the ice." A youthful level of curiosity took him over.

She revealed, "No. Clarence and LeeAnn are good people we consider family." Julia neglected to tell him that Clarence might be slightly protective of her and Sydney.

Exiting through the red barn on the way to the truck, Ty found the tree cutters packing up their trees. He sneakily paid the bill while Julia spoke to a few ladies who worked there.

After seeing what he had done, she offered a stern look on the way over. "Why do you keep doing this?"

Genuinely happy, he said, "Why not? I want to. Isn't that reason enough? It is better to give than to receive at Christmas, isn't it?"

"I suppose, but it makes me feel like I'm not contributing."

"Let's recap, shall we?" Ty crossed his arms in front of him. "You've made me three different types of freshly baked cookies, allowed me to help make ornaments for the Carling staff, paid for chili and buns, offered me wine, and did not say anything when I invaded your ski shoeing activity."

"Yes, but you...." Julia interjected.

He put up his hand between them. "Wait. Yes, I know what I did for Syd." Wanting to explain, he took her aside. "All these years, I've hated Christmas. Like, I mean hated it ever since my Mom passed. Every year, I'd do anything I could to escape it. But now, I feel a renewed excitement for the holidays because of you," Ty stated most sincerely. "So, please. Let me repay you for that."

Unable to respond, touched by the sentiment, her heart went out to him. "Well, you can't make a habit of it," she chuckled nervously, trying to lighten the mood.

"We'll see," he replied with a smile.

She could tell he was not about to refrain from that behavior.

Loading their trees into the SUV, Nick helped the attendant with everything. Ready to leave, Ty held the door open for Syd and Julia. Offering his hand in a gentlemanly way for them to step up into the vehicle, the two removed their hats and mittens while Ty closed the door. Julia watched the rugged baseball player swing around the front of the vehicle to the passenger side to find a seat. For a second, her heart fluttered, catching her off guard. Nervously fidgeting, she didn't know what to do. Unexpectedly leaning forward between the seats, she whispered, "Don't you want to sit back here with us?"

Surprised, Ty glanced over his shoulder. With a sexy smirk, he asked, "Is there room for me?"

"Of course, there is."

Nick overheard their conversation. His rosy cheeks brought about a joyful expression. Starting the engine, he waited for everyone to get settled before departing.

Ty got out and opened the passenger side door. Stepping up into the vehicle, he took a seat beside Julia. Looking over at her, he felt a nervousness in his chest. Something very unusual but welcomed. Rubbing his hands together, trying to warm them up, ready to be on their way, Ty rested his hand on his left leg. To his surprise, Julia's hand found his and brushed against it seconds later. With their hands touching, Julia placed her scarf overtop to keep Sydney from seeing. Anxiously clearing his throat, he took hold of her hand and gave it a few gentle squeezes while she did the same.

Nick pulled away from the greenhouse and passed through the main gates onto the highway. Christmas music joyfully played on the radio. To her surprise, Ty didn't mind.

While maneuvering the many twists and turns on the county road, they headed back towards Carling's downtown core. Sydney was quiet the whole way there.

"Is she falling asleep?" he whispered, seeing the girl's head dip uncontrollably from time to time.

"Quite possibly. She usually does this on long trips. When we drove to the Hotel, she must have slept about three-quarters of the way. It was lonely for me – but fine for her." Julia chuckled. "It must be a teenager thing. You'll see. She will perk up when we get to Clarence and LeeAnn's."

"So, are you sure there is nothing I should know before we get there?"

"No. They are wonderful people, that's it. Very involved in their community. We always brought the kids to their store to pick out decorations for the tree. They were the first to rush to our side and offer support when David and Ben passed. LeeAnn

brought us food every day and sat with me in silence as I cried. She is like a second mother, and Clarence is like a father. The same goes for Bryce. They have all been like grandparents to Sydney, and I would not have it any other way."

Ty nodded, processing what she said.

Secretly listening to their conversation, Nick drove along with a twinkle in his eye.

Tapping Ty's knee, she said, "Don't worry. They will like you. I promise."

He hoped she was right.

32

December 22nd

It's Complicated

It was mid-afternoon when they returned to the town of Carling. While approaching the hardware store, Julia pointed it out. Ty could see how modern it was. Initially expecting a mom-and-pop shop, given the size of the community, to his surprise, the place was massive and looked brand new.

"Wow, this is a nice store."

"Yes. It's the only one in about a two-hour radius. Clarence has a steady flow of customers here." With many thoughts rolling through her mind while pulling into the parking lot, Julia was concerned about going inside with Ty.

What would they think? Would they get the wrong idea? It could make their visit awkward. Julia suddenly felt sick. "It's so complicated," she whispered, shaking her head, wondering how to blend these moments in time.

"What's complicated?" he asked, having heard her.

Realizing she'd said the words out loud, Julia muttered, "Oh, nothing."

Nick found an open space close to the main entrance. "Here we are. Stop number two on your list." Slipping out of the driver's seat, Nick saw Sydney wake up. Opening and closing her door when she'd gotten out and stretched, he stayed with the vehicle and kept it warm for them.

Ty exited on their side and offered his hand to Julia again so she could step out carefully. Pausing for a minute, she took hold of it briefly, looked his way, and took a deep breath. "Get ready to meet Clarence and LeeAnn," she said.

He couldn't help but feel nervous. These people were important to her, and he wanted to make a good impression. For some reason, it felt like he was meeting her parents.

Hearing Syd calling out, Ty said, "I think she is summoning us."

"Yes. I believe so."

Ty let Julia lead the way. Strolling in front of the SUV, she prayed their visit would go well.

"Hurry up! Come on!" Syd belted, holding the door half open for them.

"We're coming," Ty said on their way over, allowing Julia to enter before following in behind her. Tense, unsure what to expect, he watched Sydney scan the aisles.

"Hello!" she shouted loudly, looking from left to right, keeping her eyes peeled. Knowing they always visited on December 21st, Sydney assumed Clarence and LeeAnn had probably been patiently waiting for them all day.

"Hello? Who's there?" A voice said from afar. Spotting the little girl in the center of the store, Clarence approached. "Sydney Mariani? Is that you? Finally!"

She swiveled around, trying to find the direction the voice was coming from.

Soon, Clarence emerged from the elevated office area on the right-hand side.

Waving at him, grinning from ear to ear, she shouted, "I know! Sorry, we're late."

Julia turned to Ty. "Clarence loves her to bits. He and LeeAnn couldn't have children of their own. So, we've kinda filled that gap for them."

In awe of the woman he was spending the day with, he realized his feelings for Julia were growing exponentially. It wasn't hard to see.

Onward to their happy reunion, the man stood six-foot-four and towered over Sydney. With almost snow-white hair, he also put out his arms for Julia.

"Hi, Clarence. How are you?" she asked, hugging him tightly.

"I'm great. We've been waiting patiently."

"I figured as much."

Spotting Ty waiting in the wings, Clarence curiously asked. "So, who's your friend?"

Before Julia could say anything, Sydney immediately answered, "This is Ty Reynolds. He's staying at the hotel this Christmas. We're showing him the ropes around here."

With a chuckle, responding to Syd's introduction, Ty stepped forward and kindly reached out his hand. "Very pleased to meet you, Sir."

"Ty Reynolds? Wait, not the Ty Reynolds of the Boston Red Sox?"

"You're a baseball fan, I take it?" He was surprised he recognized him.

"I watch you every time you play the Jays. First base, right?"

"Yes, Sir."

"Very good. Rough Series this year."

"Not exactly the outcome we'd hoped for."

"You win some, and you lose some."

Concerned about Julia and Sydney's association with the ball player, familiar with professional athlete reputations, Clarence took a few steps back and pointed toward the Christmas aisles. "You go ahead and look at the decorations. I promised LeeAnn I'd call the moment you arrived. She will drive over and join us shortly."

"Okay," Julia said, getting a strange vibe.

The elderly man walked to his office and disappeared.

The three went off and immersed themselves in the well-merchandized Christmas décor section.

Not sure what Clarence had picked up on, Julia's mind reeled. She hoped he wasn't disappointed in her. Desperately trying to refocus on their task, she watched Sydney drift into the aisle filled with colorful lights.

"First thing's first, Ty. What color would you like?" Syd asked point-blank, opening her arms to the expansive selection available.

"I'm not sure. What are you doing?"

"Me? I'm going festive. Multi-colored. They are joyful and bright. Kids love them."

"Good point." Crossing his arms over his chest, he went deep in thought. "How about I go with icy white? I like their crispness."

"If you go icy white, they are more contemporary, not traditional at all, so your ornaments will have to reflect the same," she said, grabbing what he wanted and putting them in the cart.

"Oh, then wait one second. What do you think about warm white?"

"That is more traditional. If you are going for a pretty red, green, and white, or gold and silver, those are perfect for that," Syd explained with an abundance of knowledge.

He took hold of both boxes in hand, trying to decide what to do. Intending to create a tree like the one he had when he was young, he put the icy white box back on the shelf. "Definitely these then."

Placing the box in the cart, they turned the corner and headed into the ornament aisle. Scanning the shelves, Syd wanted to know, "So, what's your theme?"

"Theme?" He thought for a second. "Good question…"

"Remember, we talked about this back at the tree farm. What style of ornaments would you like to use? Color combinations, like red, white, silver, gold, or bright Dr. Seuss colors? Maybe snowmen or icy-looking? You know? Theme?"

Searching through the decorations, unsure what to select, Ty spotted a boxed set of handblown glass ornaments on an upper shelf. He couldn't believe his eyes. Reaching for them, feeling dusty, he stared through the clear window in the box, remembering his Mother's ornaments. He immediately experienced a flashback. His heart ached upon recalling her voice.

Now, Ty, remember to hang on to it tightly. These are glass. They will break if you drop them.

He could clearly see himself sitting on the floor beside their tree. One by one, his Mother asked for each ornament, which he carefully handed her. Every year, she would remind him they'd been passed down for generations from her great, great grandma years before.

Julia saw him lost in thought, staring at the box. "These are beautiful."

"Yes, I think so, too," he quietly muttered, proudly showing them what he chose. "This..." he pointed at the box. "This is my theme, Syd."

"Okay, I can work with that."

Standing back, Julia let her daughter do her thing. "Watch this," she said.

"Watch what?" Ty was not sure what she meant.

"My little elf is about to create a tree to remember."

The two marveled at Sydney walking back and forth, coordinating several elements. She matched colorful balls, fillers, and ribbons to compliment the ornaments Ty wanted as his focal point.

Placing two tree reservoirs underneath the cart, amazed by her daughter's artistic ability, Julia said, "Oh, by the way, we need to get you a box to put your ornaments in at the end of your stay. Come with me. This way." Getting Sydney's attention, she said, "We are just going to go and find Ty a decoration box."

"Okay!" The busy bee shouted back as Clarence returned to offer suggestions.

Going to the far side of the store, Julia peered down each aisle before locating the boxes. "Ah, here they are. This is it. There's quite a selection to choose from this time of year. Maybe we can also grab you some ribbon to wrap it with."

Stopping between two stacks of shelves with boxes piled high, Ty stood beside her while she picked out a few and analyzed the patterns and pictures. Seeing how much thought and effort she put into making the holidays special for others, he knew that Julia was the most remarkable woman he'd ever met in his entire life. With that crossing his mind, his heart began beating rapidly. Attracted to her beyond words, he didn't know how to act given her story.

Short-listing a couple of boxes, Julia picked one for their decorations and casually showed him the two options she thought would work best for him. "Either of these would be perfect. They are traditional, just like the glass ornaments you chose for your tree. What do you think?"

Ty stared at her longingly before coming to his senses. "I think this one," he pointed to the left.

She put the other back on the shelf and held what they chose in front of her.

"Here, I'll take it." Reaching out, his hands landed directly on top of hers.

Startled, the pretty blonde-haired woman looked down, feeling his warmth. Soon, she got lost in his eyes, and he in hers.

Stepping closer, he leaned forward with the boxes between them and gently kissed her lips.

It caused Julia's legs to weaken, and she could hardly breathe.

Backing away, anxious to make eye contact, Ty said quietly, "Let me carry those for you."

"Thank you," Julia said whimsically.

Sliding his hands off hers, he took both boxes, wanting to keep holding her hand. But given where they were, he thought he'd be patient and wait for the right time.

"We should probably find Syd," he said, hearing the little girl talking with Clarence a few rows away.

"Yeah, we should." Staying quiet, Julia walked alongside Ty down the center aisle.

Needing to break their silence, he said, "I think I'm going to buy another package of those ornaments to take home to Boston. You know, to have 'em. I swear they are the same as my Mother's."

33

December 22nd

Torn

Drifting amongst her thoughts, Julia tried to control the butterflies that had taken flight and forced herself to get her head out of the clouds. Like a fish out of water, she didn't know how to act. Not having dated anyone but her husband, this was foreign territory. Julia knew that as a Mother, the expectation was to set an example, and kissing Ty Reynolds in the hardware store aisle with her daughter a few rows over was not exactly a responsible thing.

Silently, deflated, Julia spotted LeeAnn and swiftly walked up to her with open arms.

"Oh, my dear! How are you?" the stylish white-haired lady asked, wondering who the handsome man was behind her.

Clarence immediately introduced him with an abundance of excitement. "LeeAnn? This is the famous Ty Reynolds from the Boston Red Sox." Turning to Ty, he revealed, "My wife is not a baseball fan."

Putting out her hand and staring him down, LeeAnn offered a firm handshake. "It's nice to meet you, Mr. Reynolds." It was like she was reading him like a book.

"Nice to meet you too, Ma'am," Ty greeted pleasantly.

"They met at The Carling. He's spending the holidays there," Clarence verified while helping Sydney grab a box from an upper shelf.

Amidst their conversation, Ty's phone rang. Slipping it out of his pocket, he apologized. "Excuse me a minute," he said, walking away to take the call.

"What's with the baseball player?" LeeAnn inquired sneakily. "He's cute."

Watching Ty talk on the phone, sternly pacing back and forth, she said, "We met a couple of days ago. He is here from Boston and is on the verge of retirement from the MLB. He needed a break from all the press mayhem. We bonded over our loss. His parents died around Christmastime. If anyone can understand what he's feeling, it's me."

"Hmm," LeeAnn said with a smile.

Ty finished his conversation and returned to them.

"Apologize about that," he said. "Work calling."

Clarence and LeeAnn's sights bounced between the two of them.

Thankfully, Sydney said, "Okay. I think I've got everything."

Swiftly coming to the young girl's aid, Ty placed a second set of glass ornaments in the cart and helped her swivel it in the direction of the cash.

Everyone followed.

Arm and arm, Julia and LeeAnn walked along together, allowing the rest to go ahead.

The pretty middle-aged woman wanted to fish for information. "So, what's really going on between you two?"

Not sure how to respond, Julia paused. "LeeAnn, it's not what you think."

"Sure, dear. You keep telling yourself that." She beamed.

Confused, she hoped to get some clarification. "What do you mean?"

"I think I'm a pretty good judge of character, among other things." LeeAnn smiled. "And I will bet any money that that man is smitten."

"You can't be serious?"

"Oh yes. In the worst kind of way, too." The woman grabbed her arm and pulled her aside. Standing in the aisle out of sight, she said, "Trust me. He has fallen for you, hook, line, and sinker."

"You've talked to him for what - five minutes? You sure you're feeling alright?"

"Think what you will. I am never wrong when it comes to the subject of love." She was so confident in her observations.

"Love? That's impossible. We barely know each other."

"Sometimes that's all it takes," LeeAnn giggled.

Contemplating the butterflies she had earlier, Julia paused. "Can I ask you something?" She looked straight ahead, deep in thought.

"Sure. Shoot, buttercup."

"Is it wrong? If I was interested in him, I mean."

"Julia, your life with David was wonderful - a blessed union that lasted for a season. Sadly, your time together was short." She tapped Julia's arms gently. "It is not wrong to want to explore a relationship with someone else, especially after five years. I assume this whole thing came out of the blue?"

"Yes. We seem to have this connection. As I said, sharing our grief is what started it all."

"If God brought the two of you together when you least expect, against all odds, I might add, then you should see where this path takes you, or you may live to regret it otherwise."

"But I feel this guilt for even considering it. It's like I'm cheating on David, even though, logically, I know I'm not. There's this internal battle. It's pulling me in all directions. Is it right? Is it wrong? I don't know for sure."

"Finding love with someone should never be considered negatively."

That word caught Julia off guard again.

"Have you not felt a spark between the two of you, dear?"

"Yes, I suppose."

"Well, those are feelings of love creeping in - the beginning stages of something bigger. Remember how it was with you and David? The rush of excitement and the newness of a budding relationship."

A bit frightened by the obvious, Julia took a deep breath. "I suppose."

She grasped the young woman's hands tightly. "It is rare to love twice in a lifetime. Remember that. Do not let go if you are lucky enough to find it again."

"But he's returning to Boston, and we are heading home. There is no future if we aren't in the same country."

"How do you know? Maybe the timing is right? Miracles do happen. What is meant to be will be."

Not fully ready to move on, Julia whispered, "I hear you. I feel I need more time."

"I understand that. Ultimately, it's your decision."

That got Julia thinking.

"You will have to tell me what happens," LeeAnn gushed before emerging from the aisle. "Thank you so much for visiting."

Ty glanced over at them.

"Are you coming for Christmas Eve dinner?" Julia double-checked to make sure they could join them.

The two approached Ty, Syd, and Clarence at the front of the store.

"We wouldn't miss that dinner for the world," she said, letting go of Julia and slipping her arm around her husband's waist, prompting him to cuddle his loving wife.

"We will be there with bells on," Clarence stated.

"So happy to hear that. We look forward to seeing you in a couple of days."

Cashing out, Ty ended up paying for everything, to Julia's dismay. "It was very nice to meet you," he said to the loving couple.

"Very nice to meet you as well. We hope to see you more often," LeeAnn said mischievously, planting the seed.

Julia blushed while she and Sydney took turns hugging them both.

"Bye!" Sydney waved on the way out the door.

"Goodbye, Sydie," Clarence shouted from the center aisle.

With countless bags in hand, Julia told Ty, "You did it again."

"Yes, I did," he said with a smile.

She shot him a disapproving look.

Ty shrugged his shoulders. "What's the harm? It's fine."

Waiting for Nick to open the tailgate remotely, Ty placed most of the bags in the back of the SUV beside the wrapped evergreen trees. After opening and closing the door for Syd, Nick returned to the driver's seat. He watched Ty and Julia walk to the opposite side of the vehicle. He could tell something was brewing.

Opening the door for her and offering his hand again, the handsome guy courteously said, "Ladies first."

"Thank you," Julia replied.

Once she got settled, he got in and sat beside her, leaving some space between them, hoping to keep her at ease.

When Nick pulled away, Julia spotted LeeAnn resting her praying hands against her lips. She then gave a cheery wave as they drove away.

Leaving the town of Carling, turning onto the hotel's side road not long after, Syd started to ramble off a series of tasks they needed to accomplish upon their return. Seeing the sun beginning to lower on the horizon, Julia marveled at the snow glistening on the trees. She didn't want the day to end. That is when it hit her. Without a doubt, she could honestly say she had fun. It had been so long since feelings like these had surfaced. The thought of moving on was scary, especially knowing she had to bring the pieces of her past into the future. Taking a deep breath, she thought about what LeeAnn said and wondered if Ty Reynolds was truly heaven-sent.

Guess time will tell, she thought.

34 |

December 22nd

Conflicted

Climbing the hill to the Carling, Nick stopped at the main doors and quickly got the bellhop on duty to grab a cart for them. He promptly handed the bags to the young man, who threaded each of them on the cart posts. Ty jumped out and held the truck door open for the ladies, offering his hand.

Syd walked around the SUV and over to the bonfire, crackling and smoldering in the circle. Standing there warming herself, feeling the heat on her cheeks, she looked up at the lazy flakes starting to fall from above.

Seeing her standing there alone, Ty joined her, having never seen a bonfire in a hanging iron cauldron before.

While he stood beside the little girl, she confided, "This has been the best day I've had in a long time."

Not knowing what to do or say, he got down on one knee while Julia watched from afar.

"Syd, I have to tell you, I have never met anyone like you and your mom. You are the sweetest, most caring little girl I've ever met, and your mom is so giving and kind. Thank you for showing me what is most important at Christmas. Thank you for sharing all of your traditions with me."

Granting him a smile that warmed his heart, she patted his shoulder and hugged him. "You're welcome."

That moment caused tears to stream down Julia's face.

Ty glanced her way just as she wiped her cheeks.

"Come on," Sydney said to Ty, "I'm sure they're giving out hot chocolate and apple cider in the lobby right now."

"Okay. Lead the way."

Meeting up with Julia, she looked at him. "We need to talk later. Once Syd is asleep."

Knowing something was wrong, he answered, "Umm, yeah. Okay."

They each poured a cup of hot chocolate to take upstairs. The new bellhop brought their decorations and trees to their rooms. Propping open their doors for him, Sydney began separating the décor based on themes while the guy brought in their tree. Taking a reservoir, Ty went into his room and removed his coat and boots. He filled the stand with water from the kitchen sink and selected a spot to put it. Spreading a towel on the hardwood floor and setting the reservoir down, Ty tightly secured the tree trunk with the screws. Walking across the hall in sock feet, he knocked before entering.

Not missing a beat, Syd said, "Come in!"

Ty noticed her at the dining table, grouping the ornaments accordingly.

Seeing Julia emerge from her bedroom with slippers and that same cozy sweater from the first night he saw her, she went to the fireplace and turned it on before grabbing the reservoir and filling it in the kitchen.

"Here, let me help you with that," he said. "It's heavy."

Julia moved aside and accepted his help. "Thank you."

He filled it with water and carried it over to the living room. "So, where are we putting the tree? Do you have a special spot in mind?" He asked.

Syd instructed, "We always put it here." Standing straight as a pin, the little girl stood in the exact spot their tree had been year after year. "We center it between the two windows and keep it far away from the fireplace."

"Okay," he confirmed, setting it on the plastic sheet they'd put down. Grabbing the tree, he inserted the trunk in the stand and secured it at the bottom.

Bringing over a pair of scissors, Julia said with anticipation, "Ready, Syd?"

"This is my favorite part." She clapped her hands together. "Finally, the big reveal."

Julia carefully discarded the plastic netting, cutting it away to reduce the needles shedding on the floor. Suddenly, the branches fell to their natural position.

Standing back, Sydney looked at it. "Yeah, I can work with that. It's good."

While her daughter unboxed the lights, Julia stood nearby. "What can we do?" she asked.

Syd handed her the strands. "Maybe make a line across the floor with these. I don't want them to get tangled."

Ty opened the second box and said, "I can help too."

"Here, you take this end and go that way," Julia pointed towards the front door. "I'll go this way." The two stretched the line across the room before plugging them in. In an instant, the colors lit up the suite beautifully.

"Okay, mission accomplished. Now what?" Her Mother asked.

"Now, I need space to work. You guys go sit down over there."

Julia was surprised to hear that. "We can't help you?"

"No, not this time. Perhaps when we decorate Ty's tree, deal?"

"Okay, just say if you change your mind."

"Alright, Mom." She gave her a thumbs up.

On her way to the kitchen, Julia got Sydney an iced tea. Setting it on the island, she asked Ty, "Wine?"

"Sure. That would be great. Thanks," Ty responded, moving over to a barstool.

"So, now that the Christmas tree shopping is complete and we are decorating this evening, what are you doing tomorrow?"

Pouring two half-glasses of white, Julia said, "Tomorrow is kind of a mishmash day."

"Oh? What does mishmash mean?" He'd never heard the term.

"It means we do a few relaxing things throughout the day but don't plan anything. We go with the flow. Do whatever we feel like doing. I think the only activity Sydney and I put on the free-flowing agenda at some point was ice skating, so in between, we might play a bit of foosball or a game or two of pool. We need to finish placing all the ornaments in gift bags and add the ribbon. I think the paint is dry enough now to pack them. We might even take in a campfire tomorrow night for smores or perhaps go for a night swim - whatever we feel like doing. Edward Nelson usually does an astronomy session three evenings a week around nine o'clock for whoever signs up by eleven that morning. So, yeah..."

"Wow, that sounds like an action-packed day. Alright, a mishmash it is."

Conflicted, she needed to talk to him about what she noticed at the bonfire that afternoon. Believing she should implement some boundaries between them, Julia wondered if they were setting themselves up for disappointment. She knew Syd would be heartbroken at this point if Ty decided not to stick around. Being a mother, it was her job, regardless of her feelings, to protect her little girl. Julia sighed, realizing she'd failed by letting down her guard too much. For now, though, she watched Ty help Syd decorate the tree.

Before Julia moved to the couch, she played instrumental Christmas music. Watching the two of them work, she tried to figure out what she would say to him when the opportunity presented itself. She didn't want to hurt his feelings, so she planned her words carefully.

Ty looked around the room and felt a part of something. He wished they could do this every year. That got him thinking about extending his stay to the day after New Year's Day. Entrusted to place the Christmas bells on the tree, he stepped forward and strategically hooked each on a branch, trying to keep it balanced.

Laughing and talking with the famous baseball player, the young girl moved on to the colored ball ornaments and filled the open spaces between the festive bows.

Once every branch on the tree was sparkling with the beautifully displayed ornaments they'd hand-picked, Syd took the decorative box from the large plastic bag and slid it under the tree. When he saw this, Ty recalled the secret behind it.

"Voila!" Syd declared, collapsing in the chair. "Wow, that was a lot of work!" Grabbing her tummy, she said, "I'm so hungry. Can we get food?"

"How about we go downstairs for dinner and then come back to finish Ty's tree afterward?" Julia suggested. "Is that okay with you?" She wondered what he thought.

"Hey, I can always go for something to eat," he agreed.

Getting on their shoes, Syd gushed, "Wait, one second." Before leaving, she turned off all the lights. Staring at their tree majestically glowing in the dark, she placed her hands on either side of her cheeks and whispered, "Isn't it beautiful?"

With the room illuminated with a festive glow, she offered a side hug and complimented, "You did an amazing job, Sweetie."

"You have a talent for this," Ty insisted. "Maybe they would hire you at the North Pole."

Sydney cast a look of disbelief. "Yeah, sure. The North Pole," she laughed.

Casually making their way downstairs to the restaurant, the lit Christmas displays gave Sydney goosebumps.

"It's almost Christmas. Oh, I can hardly wait." Grasping her hands in front of her with enthusiasm, she turned to Ty and said, "I'm excited to see how your tree turns out. I bet the ornaments will look pretty."

"Yes, I think so too," he said.

Greeting Lisa at the hostess station, she quickly gave Julia a wink when Ty wasn't looking. Allowing Syd to lead the way into the dining area, he followed, leaving Lisa and Julia to toddle behind. "So, things are moving along, I see."

Julia wasn't sure what to think. "No, Lisa. It's not like that. He's returning to Boston after the holidays, then to Florida for spring training. We are just two people trying to make the best of the holidays."

Casting a sad look, Lisa grabbed hold of Julia's arm. While they walked along, Ty glanced back. Julia hoped he hadn't heard what she'd said.

Before dinner, Sydney shared a list of her favorite items on the menu as Ty listened to her suggestions. When they placed their orders, the air around the table felt different. Julia allowed Sydney to talk the entire time.

Rarely speaking to each other for some reason, Ty kept glancing over, knowing something had upset her. His mind reeled, trying to recap the day's events. Was it the people looking at them at the Christmas tree farm, the kiss in the hardware store, or his talk with Sydney at the fire? Kept in suspense, he needed to know what was wrong and how to fix it. That night was the longest dinner ever.

35

December 22nd

Clearing the Air

Upon finishing up in the restaurant, Julia insisted on handling their own bills when Ty was about to sign theirs again. It hurt his feelings, but he could see why she wanted to pay her way.

Bidding Lisa goodnight, they slowly strolled toward the elevators. Tired from their busy day, he hoped they would have time to clear the air and planned to solidify his feelings when they spoke later. Hopefully, whatever she had to say would be similar.

Hoping to lighten the mood, while standing in front of the doors, Ty whispered, "I say – right."

That made Sydney spring into action. "Okay, Mom and I choose left!"

Waiting and waiting, listening for any indication of which door would open first, the three went silent until a winner was declared.

Arms raised victorious above his head, Ty said excitedly, "Yes, finally!"

"Wow. Good choice, Ty," Syd conceded, happy that he finally guessed correctly. When she stepped into the elevator, she pressed number four before the doors slid closed.

Still feeling something looming on their way to his room, he pulled his card from his pocket and touched it to the reader. Holding the door open, allowing the girls to enter, he propped it with the stopper.

Seeing the tree in the stand, Sydney went to their room to get the scissors.

With Syd gone, Ty quietly asked, "Are you okay? Did I do something wrong?"

About to answer, Julia saw Sydney return.

"I got the scissors to cut the netting."

He helped her cut the tree free of the binding before the branches fell into place.

Not wasting time, the girl began sorting the ornaments on the smaller round table and the sofa. Finding the second box, she said, "Here. You should put these somewhere safe."

Taking them, he said, "Thanks. I'll put them in my room."

Needing to talk, Julia made direct eye contact with Ty when he returned. "Would you like something to drink while you work, Sweetie? I can get you juice or iced tea?"

"I could go for an apple juice," she said, still grouping the ornaments.

"Want to help me, Ty?" She signaled for him to follow.

Understanding what she was doing, he said, "Yeah, sure."

"We will be right back. I'll prop our door open, too."

"Alright," her daughter replied, not paying too much attention to them.

When she went across the hall, he followed.

In the kitchen, Julia turned to him with her arms positioned defensively.

Clearing his throat, he said, "Before you say anything, can I please speak? There is much I need to say."

She nodded and gave him the floor.

"The past few days have been nothing short of amazing. I don't even know where to begin."

"Ty…" Julia interrupted.

He put up his hand to stop her. "No, please hear me out," he interjected, needing to say his piece. Pausing, gathering his thoughts, he lowered his voice and said, "You are the most incredible woman

I've ever met. You are kind, thoughtful, and caring, not to mention an amazing mother. I am drawn to you. I knew it the very first night we saw each other. Since then, I've developed these feelings - the kind that won't fade." Nervous about how she would respond, he quietly awaited her answer.

Scared to look him in the eye, she said, "No matter what is happening between us, my job is to protect my daughter. When you leave, I will have to pick up the pieces again and try to repair the damage. Sydney is getting attached to you."

"Are you getting attached?" he asked, desperately wanting to hear her say yes.

"Look, how I feel is beside the point. The bottom line is you are going home to Boston, and we are returning to Toronto. There is no future here if we are hundreds of miles apart?"

"So that's it?" he said quietly. "You don't want to explore this and see where it goes?" Ty stepped forward with open arms. She backed away. "Julia?" he said softly.

"I need to do what's best for us."

"Look, I could never understand the horror you've gone through in the aftermath of David and Ben's passing. I would never be able to fathom that kind of pain. You were left to survive alone, raise your daughter, and grieve. I get that you're scared. But what if by being with me, you could find happiness."

Julia tried to remain composed while her heart pulled in two different directions. On the verge of tears, she whispered, "I'm terrified."

"Of what?" he said in a gentle tone.

"Of having these feelings for you. Of moving on. Of you leaving and not coming back."

"I'm not going anywhere. You've captured my heart, Julia Mariani," he said with a sexy smirk, placing a hand on his chest.

"Really?" Julia whimpered and began to sob.

Reaching out to her, she slowly inched forward into his arms.

"There's this internal battle," she whispered. "Part of me thinks this is wrong. The other half knows I'm allowed to move on. But whenever we spend time with you, I think less of them. It's a constant reminder that they're gone."

"What do you need me to do? Name it. Just say, and I will give it to you - no questions asked."

"Please, be patient. I need more time."

Hearing Nick's advice, he replied, "You can have all the time you need."

"Are you sure?"

"I'll wait forever if I have to."

"You travel a lot. How do I know you won't find someone else and leave us?"

"I would never..." Ty tilted his head sympathetically.

"Did you see how Sydney reacted at the bonfire? Her heart is already vested, too. Are you sure you're ready to think of someone other than yourself?"

"Look, I am on the verge of retiring, and I don't want to live out the rest of my days alone. Meeting you has been the greatest gift. If things are moving too fast, I get it. We will slow down and take our time. Whatever you feel comfortable with."

That pulled on her heartstrings.

"Mom? Did you get my juice?" Syd shouted from across the hall.

"Can we talk more about this later? We should get back to her."

"Sure," he said, believing that to be best.

They found Sydney hanging Ty's glass ornaments.

Greeting the little girl with a smile, he complimented, "The tree looks great, Kiddo. I love it. Here, let me help you with those."

"Okay," she agreed, carefully handing him the box.

Not sure if Sydney had questions about what was happening between her and Ty, Julia wondered if she should talk with her before bed. They never had secrets, none that she knew of anyway.

Sitting on the sofa, Julia watched the two survey the placement of each decoration.

When they had finished, Syd ran over and turned off the lights to see how it looked in the dark. "What do you think?" she said, looking for opinions.

Julia smiled from ear to ear, "It's perfect."

While staring at the tree, Ty noticed how much it resembled his Mother's. It was then he felt she had a hand in him meeting Julia. The cookies, the red apron, the gifted homemade ornaments, and his tree were all signs sent from her.

"Ty?" Syd repeated, having not gotten a response.

He broke from his daze. "It's amazing."

Innocently looking his way, the little girl said, "Thank you for helping me."

"I should be thanking you," Ty smiled. Glancing over at Julia, he knew they still had unfinished business.

"Well, it's late. We have a busy day tomorrow. Better get you to bed."

Walking across the hall, Ty followed. Standing in front of their door, Julia told her daughter, "Go ahead and change into your pajamas and brush your teeth. I will be there shortly."

"Okay, Mom," she called out.

Allowing their door to fall closed behind her, she stood in the hallway with him. Not knowing what to say, she hoped the words would come to her.

Ty held out his hands. Seeing them waiting, she obliged and grasped hold. Peering into his gentle eyes, she saw such sincerity and knew he would never intentionally hurt either of them.

"Can I make a suggestion?" he asked.

Not sure what he was about to say, Julia nodded. "Sure."

"Can we move past the heavy stuff and enjoy our time together? Let things evolve like they were supposed to naturally. Not make it too complicated."

She sighed.

"I understand your concerns. But look at it this way. What are the chances that we both arrived at this hotel this Christmas and we are the only guests here? Doesn't that strike you as odd?"

"I suppose."

He wondered if she needed a break from him to gain clarity. "If you need time apart, please say. If you want to spend tomorrow alone with Sydney, I will bow out, no questions asked. Maybe I've been invading your holiday too much. Smothering you, perhaps? It wasn't my intention. I just wanted to get to know you better."

The comment grabbed her. "I like us spending time together. It's okay if you join us tomorrow. I don't mind."

"Are you sure?"

"Yes. Thank you for asking me."

"Well, okay. On that note, I should bid you Goodnight. I am excited to discover how a mishmash day goes. It sounds fun." Ty pulled her in close and wrapped his arms around her. He felt hers willingly curl around his waist. Kissing her forehead, he whispered, "Goodnight. I'll see you in the morning for breakfast?"

"We will see you then."

Letting her go, she walked back inside and waved before disappearing.

Ty stood there, hearing her lock the deadbolt and security bar. Returning to his room, with his hands in his pockets, he closed his door and locked up. Seeing the beautiful tree, he sat on the sofa and clasped his hands together.

"I need your help with this one, Mom. Anything you can do, I'd appreciate it." Desperately hoping she had heard his plea, he checked his phone. With no updates on his contract negotiations, Ty knew it would be a long night.

36

December 22nd

Straightforward

Julia stood alone in her bathroom, her eyes welling. Before closing the door, she peered across to Sydney's room. The conversation with Ty weighed on her heavily. Seeing the reflection of a confused woman in the mirror, she looked down at her wedding rings and could not deny that she felt something for him. But her motherly instincts kept warding her off. Life seemed complicated enough. Fixing her face and taking a deep breath, she went to say goodnight to Sydney.

Already settled into bed, she'd nestled into her blankets and arranged her pillows just right. Hugging her well-loved teddy bear close, she looked small and vulnerable in the warm glow of her bedside lamp.

Julia sat beside her, tucking the edges of the duvet around her.

"All snug and cozy now?" Julia asked with a soft smile, brushing a strand of hair from Sydney's face.

The pretty girl nodded but avoided eye contact.

Julia noticed immediately. "You're quiet tonight, Sweetie. What's on your mind?" she asked, pressing a kiss to her daughter's forehead. "Did you not have fun today at the tree farm?"

Without hesitation, she answered, "Yes, I did." But her fingers kept absently stroking the bear's ear. Finally, she whispered, "Don't be mad, but... I heard you and Ty talking earlier. Was it about me? I heard my name a lot." Her voice wavered as she glanced at her Mother, her wide eyes searching for reassurance.

Julia's heart sank. She placed a gentle hand on her cheek, tilting her face toward her. "You did nothing wrong. Nothing at all."

She searched her Mother's expression, her voice uncertain. "Then why does it feel like that?"

Grappling for the right words, she sighed. "It's just... Ty has grown to like us. A lot."

"I like him too," Sydney said quickly. "He's nice. It's been fun having him around."

"I'm glad to hear that." Julia's smile was faint, her thoughts heavy. "But I worry about what will happen when he has to leave and return to his life in Boston. As your Mom, it's my job to protect you. I don't want either of us to get hurt."

Sydney sat up straight. "So you're scared we'll miss him too much?"

Julia nodded, surprised by her daughter's clarity. "Yes."

"And you don't want to be friends anymore because he might leave?"

The comment caught her off guard. "I... I don't know."

"Well, I think we should stay friends with him no matter what." Her daughter's voice was firm, her innocence giving way to a surprising wisdom. "If he cares about us, and we care about him, why stop being friends?"

Chest tightening, Julia wished life were as simple as her daughter believed it to be. "Maybe you're right," she said softly. "But for now, let's focus on getting a good night's sleep. We'll see how things feel in the morning. Deal?"

"Fine." Her little girl's face brightened instantly. "Is he still joining us for mishmash day?"

Chuckling, she smoothed the blanket over her. "Yes, I believe he is."

"Good," Sydney said firmly, hugging her bear tighter.

"Goodnight, my sweet girl," Julia whispered, kissing her temple.

"Night, Mom."

Blowing her a kiss, she left the room. Hearing her daughter's straightforward approach to the situation, she wondered if she was over-thinking it. Still unsure if she was willing to allow someone into their life fully, no matter how lovely the past couple of days had been, she got into bed and slipped under the covers. That night, it wasn't surprising to see him appear in her dreams.

37

December 23rd

Ty's Plan

With the stormy weather clearing, the sun burned off the clouds above the Carling Hotel. The sleepy resort slowly came to life with staff clearing snow-covered pathways around the buildings. Hearing the machine moving past his window, rumbling as it went by, Ty opened his eyes and realized it was morning.

Reaching for his phone, seeing that it was only a quarter to seven, he returned it to the side table and decided to skip his workout. Lying flat on his back in bed, he racked his brain about how things went wrong yesterday. Understanding Julia's concerns regarding Sydney, he felt he had to take things a bit slower so her feelings could catch up to his.

Wondering what today would bring, hoping they could get back to a more lighthearted pace, Ty tried to think of something special to do for the girls, believing it might fix things, maybe even give Julia the confidence she needed to move forward. Remembering that today was going to be a mishmash of activities, going wherever the wind blew, Ty jumped out of bed. He started looking on the internet for things they could do in the town of Carling and beyond. Being winter, he was sure there wasn't a wide selection of options, but he thought he would at least research what he could. Knowing they allowed him to tag along on their excursions, he thought it would be a good idea to return the favor and invite them on one of his.

Finding a museum featuring local artists, a famous butter tart bakeshop, and a cottagey home décor emporium, he soon constructed a plan for the day. While scrolling through a list of popular regional attractions, he found one he certainly needed to see to believe - something the girls would love. Wondering then if this would help him show Julia how much he cares, he started jotting down notes on everything.

Quickly getting dressed, Ty headed downstairs to the concierge to get help making the arrangements.

Arriving in the lobby, he noticed Bryce at the concierge desk and approached him with a casual smile. "Morning, Bryce. Got a moment?"

The tall, broad-shouldered man in his early sixties looked up from his newspaper and folded it neatly. "Morning, Sir. What can I do for you?"

"I'm looking to make some plans for today," Ty began, keeping his tone light. "I've got two guests with me, and I was hoping to find some activities we could all enjoy. Thought you might have some good recommendations. Maybe something child-friendly."

Bryce arched a brow, immediately connecting the dots. "Two guests, huh? The Marianis?"

"Perhaps." Squinting his eyes with a timid grin, Ty did not confirm or deny it either way.

The gentleman leaned back in his chair, his expression unreadable. "What did you have in mind?"

"Something casual. I was thinking a mix of things—maybe the local art museum, that famous butter tart place, and some shopping around town perhaps," Ty explained. "Just want to make it a fun, memorable day."

He studied him. His sharp gaze was like a hawk sizing up its prey. "We can arrange a tour of those places for you. No problem."

Noticeably happy to hear that, the baseball player said, "Appreciate it. Thanks."

Protective instincts kicking in, Bryce added, "Tell you what, Sir. How about I drive you around? Makes it easier for you to focus on your plans, and you won't have to worry about navigating or parking. What do you say?" Having an ulterior motive, he wanted to see firsthand what the baseball player was up to. Keeping an eye on the girls would give him a chance to ensure Ty's intentions were pure.

"That'd be a big help."

Though his tone carried a hint of firmness, Bryce smiled faintly. "May I suggest this agenda, perhaps?" Jotting down a list of things in order, he pulled out a brochure and slid it along the desk before adding a restaurant suggestion.

Ty looked it all over. His face brightened. "Wow, that's awesome. Let's go with that."

"What time were you thinking of leaving?"

"I thought we'd head out around one o'clock. Does that work for you?" Ty replied.

Bryce nodded. "No problem, Sir. I'll have the truck waiting."

"Great." The guest slapped his hand flat on the desk. "We will see you later on then."

"Yes, see you in a few hours."

Returning to his room, Ty was determined to make the day meaningful. Happy with the loose plan in place, he hoped Julia would trust him enough to go with the flow without knowing what surprises he had in store. He sat at the small desk, thinking about how to set the tone for the day. Julia deserved a gesture, something thoughtful and heartfelt.

Pulling out a pad of paper and pen, Ty began drafting a poem to invite the girls on the adventure. Line by line, he poured his thoughts onto the page, ensuring each word reflected the lighthearted fun he envisioned. After several drafts and a few edits, he finally had something he was proud of.

After a few phone calls to add some personal touches, Ty finally hung up, a satisfied smile spreading across his face. With everything set —now all he needed were his guests.

By nine o'clock, he couldn't wait any longer. Quietly opening his door, he crossed the hallway with the folded poem in hand. Listening, he didn't hear a peep from Julia and Sydney, so he crouched down and carefully threaded the invitation under the door. Hesitating, he raised his hand to knock, hoping it wasn't too early to bother them. He smiled, wishing he would see their faces when they found the note. Rhythmically rapping his knuckles on the door, he let the mystery linger and slipped back to his room. Out of sight, his heart raced with anticipation for what the day would bring—hoping that by sunset, he could prove to Julia that some risks were worth taking.

38

December 23rd

Mishmash Day

Across the hall, Julia stared at the ceiling, unable to sleep any longer. Hearing a gentle knock at the door, she reached for her phone and checked the time. It was three minutes after nine. Concerned that something was wrong, she flung back the duvet and slipped on her robe. Tying the belt around her waist, she rushed to peek through the hole in the door. Not seeing anyone, she happened to look down at her feet. There, lying on the floor, was a note that read,

GOOD MORNING JULIA AND SYDNEY,

A BUNCH OF SURPRISES I'VE ARRANGED FOR US TODAY.

WHAT THEY ARE, I CAN NOT SAY.

I AM ANXIOUSLY OFFERING A SLIGHT CHANGE OF PLANS,

AFTER TODAY, I SINCERELY HOPE YOU'LL BE MY BIGGEST FANS.

MEET ME DOWNSTAIRS FOR BREAKFAST BY TEN-THIRTY IF YOU DARE,

'CAUSE IF YOU DO, YOU'LL SEE HOW MUCH I CARE.

DRESS CASUALLY, BRING EVERYTHING YOU HAVE TO STAY WARM,

IT SEEMS COLD TEMPERATURES AROUND HERE ARE CERTAINLY THE NORM.

PLEASE SAY YES TO THIS EXCITING ADVENTURE WITH ME,

BY THE END OF THE DAY, I'M PRETTY SURE YOU'LL AGREE,

THAT DOING THINGS TOGETHER FILLS YOUR WORLD WITH LAUGHTER AND FUN,

Julia noticed the instructions at the bottom. "*P.S.,*" she read. *To RSVP, please text "Yes" or "No" to 617-201-6996.*" Grabbing her phone, she sent him her answer of "Yes." When she sent it, she received a heart emoji in return, prompting her to send one back.

Smiling, she couldn't believe he had written her a poem and somehow planned a day out for them. Double-checking the time, she said, "Okay, it's just after nine o'clock. I'll let her sleep a bit longer."

Julia decided to go ahead and get ready. Her mind raced. While getting dressed, she wondered if they would be visiting another town or driving into the city of Toronto, perhaps. She didn't know.

When it came time to wake Sydney, Julia strolled across to her little girl's room and sat on the corner of the bed. Seeing her daughter move about, she patted her legs on top of the covers to get her attention. "Morning," she said as Sydney sat up.

Giving her a hug, she said to the sleepy little girl, "So, it seems we got invited on an adventure today."

"What kind of adventure?" Syd wiped her eyes.

"From what I can tell, it is a surprise."

"Huh? What do you mean?"

Reading Ty's poem, Sydney listened intently, intrigued by its mysteriousness.

"So? He didn't give us any other clues?"

"No, not a one. The note says to pack all of our warm clothing. That's it."

"Does that mean we will be outdoors all day? Hmmm." With her pointer finger pressed against her lips, she analyzed the words on the page.

Looking at the time on Julia's phone, Sydney exclaimed, "We'd better get going if we are supposed to be at breakfast for ten-thirty.

Hurry, Mom!" Sydney said, throwing back the bedding and jumping out of bed before running into her bathroom to brush her teeth.

The Marianis got dressed and gathered their winter gear. Julia took out a duffle bag from her closet and packed their snow pants and every stitch of warm clothing they had, including extra-base layers, scarves, mitts, and hats. Seeing a few Hot Shots, she enclosed enough for two packs per person and zipped them in the side pocket until they needed them. With hair brushed, all pulled back in low-positioned ponytails, making it easier to wear a hat that day, the girls prepared to head downstairs to meet Ty for breakfast.

Meanwhile, having gone ahead to Cottages, deciding not to meet the girls in the hallway, Ty stepped into the cozy breakfast room and glanced around, noting the warm morning light streaming through the windows and the faint scent of freshly brewed coffee in the air. His gaze landed on Lisa, the hostess stationed near the front. He approached her with a friendly smile.

"Morning, Lisa. Do you have a second?" Ty asked, leaning slightly on the podium.

Looking up from her tablet, taken by the handsome baseball player, she smiled bashfully. "Of course! What can I do for you?"

With a hint of nervous excitement in his voice, he said, "So, I've planned a surprise day for Sydney and Julia. A whole list of activities, just to make it special for them. But I was thinking—why not start the morning off on the right foot? I want to make the breakfast table stand out. Could you help me spruce it up? Make it look festive, perhaps?"

Lisa's eyes brightened, her enthusiasm evident. "That's so sweet! Yes, absolutely, I'd love to help."

"Thanks. Any suggestions?" Ty suggested, his voice laced with hope.

"Say no more. I've got this," Lisa replied with a wink. She quickly pulled a small team of servers into action, and they set to work. Sending one on a mission to collect a few flowers from the festive arrangements around the hotel, within minutes, Lisa had transformed the table. Arranging a delicate centerpiece of pinecones, sprigs of holly, ornaments, and small white flowers and pine branches from the resort's garden, tying it together with a red ribbon that gave the setup a festive flair. As an added touch, she sprinkled some silver confetti around it, placed folded napkins into intricate shapes and added a handwritten note at each place setting that read, *"Here's to new adventures and cherished memories."*

Ty stood back, marveling at the result. "Wow, this looks amazing. They're going to love it. Thank you."

"You're so welcome. It's all about the details," she grinned, admiring her creativity.

Checking his phone, he said, "They should be here any minute now. Thanks again for making this so special."

"Anytime. Good luck—and for what it's worth, I think you're doing something pretty incredible."

Ty nodded appreciatively and took a seat at the table, the excitement and nerves swirling within him.

On their way downstairs, Julia and Sydney were curious about what Ty was up to. Arriving at the elevators, laughing and talking with anticipation, the young girl referred to his note again. "It says to meet him downstairs for breakfast at ten-thirty."

"That's right." Her Mother checked the time on her phone. "We need to hurry."

"So, what do you think we are doing today?"

"I have no idea. We will have to wait and see," Julia replied, never having been surprised like this before. Feeling a little scared, a line from the poem popped into her head - *you'll see how much I care.* While descending to the Lobby, she believed his intentions were genuine. Telling herself to keep an open mind, she knew she couldn't let her guard down too much but was willing to let go and have some fun.

Reaching the restaurant, Ty saw them and happily got up from his chair. He stood with two roses in hand—one coral and one yellow. Never knowing the meaning of the colors when given together, he reminded himself to give Lisa all the credit.

As they walked over to him, Lisa looked on with raised praying hands, so happy for her two friends. Standing back, she watched and listened as they greeted Ty.

"Good morning, Ladies," he said with a smile.

"Morning," Sydney gushed, approaching first while Julia followed behind. "We got your invitation. I am so excited! What are we doing?"

"Well, if I tell you, then it won't be a surprise," he revealed.

Julia stepped closer. Staring into the eyes that captivated him, he passed each a rose. "These are for you."

Taking the flowers in hand, the girls smelled their sweet scents.

"I enlisted Lisa to help me this morning. Thankfully, she obliged."

Their friend waved at the girls from the far side of the restaurant.

Raising her hand, covering her mouth in shock, she turned to her friend and said, "Thank you," while Sydney looked on.

The woman blew them a kiss.

Ty added, "From what I understand, she says these flowers symbolize Happiness and Excitement when given together, so I thought that was fitting." He gave the woman a thumbs-up sign. "Thank you for agreeing to join me today. I wanted to start it off right. What better way than a festive setting and a hardy breakfast."

Smiling from ear to ear, peeking around Ty to find a table dressed in cedar bows, silver votive candles, pine cones, and Christmas ornaments intermixed throughout the greenery. "How beautiful is this," Julia said, resting her hands along her cheeks, overjoyed by the effort Lisa and Ty put into making it so unique. Reading the note, she clutched her chest while her heart melted.

Pulling a chair out for Sydney, Ty offered, "Here, Syd. Have a seat," before doing the same for Julia. He sat down with them while Lisa brought out the food he'd preordered.

Seeing Eggs Benny with a twist, finding lobster under the Hollandaise sauce, Julia remembered having it a few years back. "Oh, this looks so delicious."

Sydney spotted her Belgian waffles piled high with blackberries, bananas, and whipped cream. "Wow, Mom! Look!" she exclaimed with bright eyes.

Surveying their reaction, Ty rested his napkin on his lap. The ladies did the same.

With a bite of the eggs benedict, Julia rolled her eyes. "Oh, this is so good."

Not saying much, allowing the girls to settle in, Lisa walked over with freshly brewed coffee and juice. She tapped Julia's arm and smiled brightly, causing her friend to giggle.

Dying of suspense, Julia mustered some courage. "So, are you going to give us a hint as to what you have planned?"

"Umm, no," he snickered mischievously. "All I will say is, you mentioned today was a mishmash of things. I've stayed within the confines of your theme. I will say that we are leaving the resort for this excursion. I hope that is okay with you?"

Thinking about what was available outside the hotel, Julia's mind went into overdrive. There were only a few winter attractions nearby.

"Are you still game - knowing that piece of information?" he asked.

Sydney nodded and gave her Mom the eye, trying to sway her to say *Yes*.

Seeing her daughter's reaction, Julia agreed, "Okay. We're game. Think our life needs a little mystery and spontaneity."

"Perfect!" he said. "You will not be disappointed. I promise."

39

December 23rd

The Big Surprise

Within the hour, Julia, Sydney, and Ty thanked Lisa for everything she'd done to make their start to the morning extraordinary. While they walked past the lobby, Ty saw the Carling-logoed SUV waiting outside the front doors under the grand entrance.

Reaching the elevators, Syd blurted out, "I pick right!"

"Well, I guess I'll say, left. How about you, Julia?" Ty wondered what her response would be.

"Umm, sorry, Syd, but I'm going to say left this time."

"That's okay," Sydney replied, moving her ear closer to each elevator, trying to assess which one would open first. Excited to hear the right side on the move, suddenly, the left side arrived from the mezzanine level below. Oh, no! You guys win!"

Smiling at each other, believing the day had begun positively, the three stepped into the elevator before making the long walk down the hall to their rooms.

When they made it, Ty stood outside his door. "Okay, ten minutes, and we go? Does that work?"

"Okay," Julia replied with a deep breath, seeming quite nervous about the whole thing. "We will be ready."

The ladies went inside their suite to brush their teeth and get dressed. They put on coats and boots before double-checking their duffle bag with everything they needed for the trip. Julia tossed her phone charger in at the last minute and grabbed her crossover bag with her wallet and card keys inside.

"I suppose that's it. Are you doing okay?" Julia wanted to confirm.

"Yes, are you kidding? I am so excited to see where he is taking us."

Stepping out into the hallway, Julia found the great baseball player leaning against the wall. Waiting with a backpack hanging off one shoulder, anticipating the memorable day ahead, he said, "Well, Hello, ladies. Ready? Have you got everything?" He grinned from ear to ear.

"Yes, we are good. You?" Julia asked in return.

"Yep. All good."

While they moved down the hallway, Sydney pleaded, "I'm so excited. Can you give us one hint? Please? Please? Please?"

"Sorry, Syd," he smiled happily.

The young girl had no choice but to concede. Pressing the lobby button, almost vibrating with enthusiasm, Syd found the need to jump and fidget while waiting for the elevator to open.

On the main floor, strolling along to the entrance, Sydney ran ahead of them.

Julia turned to Ty. "So, I can't remember the last time someone surprised me with something special like this? It's been a while. I wanted to say thank you."

"Because you've included me in your traditions, I figured it was time to return the favor. So, when I got up this morning, I started researching and planning everything. Hope you have fun with it."

Bashfully smiling, not used to being spoiled, Julia walked with Ty and met up with Sydney, who had already started interrogating Grandpa Bryce. All decked out in Carling apparel, Bryce waved at Julia.

Ty nudged her shoulder. "Oh, by the way, Bryce is coming with us. He will drive just because he knows these places like the back of his hand. Hope that is okay?"

"Absolutely. I love that." Moving closer, Julia greeted Bryce. "Good morning! I hear you are joining us on this little surprise adventure."

He offered Julia a hug and confirmed, "Yes! I'll be honest. When he approached me this morning, I wasn't sure we could pull this off, but everything came together nicely, I must say."

"What came together exactly?" Julia snickered with a hint of curiosity. Bouncing her sights between Ty and Bryce, seeing an abundance of mysteriousness there, she squinted her eyes, wondering what they had up their sleeve. "Just a hint," she asked.

Not about to spoil it, Bryce closed his mouth and pretended to lock it up with a key. "I'm sorry. I have sworn to secrecy. You'll have to wait and see, my dear."

Ty gave him a thumbs-up, happy he went along with it.

He zipped up his jacket. "Everybody ready to go?" Finding definite nods from those around him, he said. "Great. Onward, ho!"

Nick waved and bid them goodbye. "You guys have fun!" He smiled with a wink and a twinkle.

One by one, they piled into the extended SUV. Julia, Sydney, and Ty found a seat in the middle row while Bryce got in on the driver's side after he helped Ty load all the bags into the back. "Buckle up, please. Safety first."

Hearing the clicks of three seat belts, Syd confirmed, "I'm ready."

"Well, here we go. Onto our first stop on this adventure."

While driving down the laneway, Ty searched his pockets for his phone, hoping to sync it with the Bluetooth on board so he could play Christmas music along the way. "Oh, great..." he said frustratingly.

"What is it? What's wrong?" Julia had never seen him react that way.

"I forgot my phone in the room."

"Do you want to go back for it," she asked. "We can. It's okay."

"You know what, no. I don't need it." He shook off the shock of leaving it behind. "Sometimes it's good to disconnect."

"Alright, if you're sure."

"Yes, it's fine. Let's keep going."

Bryce continued maneuvering the snow-covered roads to the main highway. Everyone enjoyed the view from all sides. Covered with a thick blanket of snow, the fields of white sparkled as they passed. Having turned left to go into the town of Carling, Julia couldn't help but wonder what they would be doing first.

Rounding the corner and descending into the hamlet, they slowed down along the main street. Veering right, he pulled into a parking lot behind a store. Julia didn't catch the name on the sign.

"We have arrived at destination number one," Bryce announced, stopping the vehicle.

"Perfect," Ty said, opening his door and holding it for Julia.

Sydney got out from behind the driver's side.

"Right this way, ladies."

The little girl and her grandfather figure led the way up the street.

"Are we close?" Sydney asked, turning around to Ty and her Mother trailing behind.

"Getting warmer," he replied.

While they approached the store on the right, Ty said, "Much warmer now."

"The Copper Canoe Gallery." Sydney read the sign and noticed a handwritten note at the entrance.

"Hey, I don't think they're open. It says right here. Closed for a Special Event from noon until two o'clock."

Ignoring the notice, Ty swung open the door and asked the ladies and Bryce to walk in.

Once inside, they found a woman with a silver-grey, perfectly sculpted bob. She was dressed in a tailored suit and stood in the middle of the gallery, seemingly awaiting someone.

Suddenly extending a hand, she said, "Mr. Reynolds, I presume?"

Responding positively, he obliged. "Yes, you must be Mable."

"I am. Welcome to the Copper Canoe Gallery. So happy to meet you."

Ty turned around to introduce everyone. "This is Julia, her daughter Sydney, and their family friend, Bryce."

"Oh, I know you," Mable said joyfully, pointing straight at the older gentleman.

He chuckled a bit, having known the woman for over forty years.

"Welcome! Are we ready for your tour of the gallery?"

"This is awesome," Sydney quietly mumbled. "I'm so excited." Clasping her hands tightly in front of her, she hung on Mable's every word.

"Follow me. Let's begin our journey through these walls of inspiration," Mable said warmly, gesturing toward the first display with an inviting smile.

40

December 23rd

Art & Tarts

The stark white walls beautifully showcased the colorful works of art. Beams of light cast a bright hue across each one-of-a-kind piece. Stopping to listen to Mable share insight into the lives of local artists and their talents, Sydney was in awe. Julia stood back and allowed her little girl to soak in all its splendor, so happy to see her keen interest in the stories shared. It warmed her heart to watch her gravitate to the many carvings and sculptures displayed throughout the main floor.

While walking around, a few hand-crafted wooden bowls caught Julia's eye. Set atop white pedestals, she marveled at how seamless they were. Pointing it out to Ty, she said, "I always wanted a wooden salad bowl like this. Aren't they beautiful?"

Taking note, Ty made eye contact with the gallery owner and asked her about the people who crafted them. Hearing that the local artist created them from a single piece of wood, each one taking thirty days to complete, Mable raised her eyebrows and smiled. She knew what he was signaling to her. "It would make a wonderful addition to any home, don't you think?"

He immediately responded, "Yes, I think so too."

Drawn in by a dye-cut metal tree anchored into a granite stone, Sydney quickly knelt in front of the sculpture, careful not to touch anything.

"What do you think of that, Sydney?" Ty asked.

"This reminds me of our drive up to Carling. The trees along the highway are embedded in the rocks just like this. I often wondered how they grew between the cracks and crevasses. I love this piece. What do you think?"

"I think it is pretty cool." Ty turned to Mable and shot her another eye while Julia strolled alongside a cabinet near the back, showcasing handmade jewelry.

Joining her as she gazed into the brightly lit display case, she took time to appreciate the uniqueness of each piece.

"Are these all handmade?" Julia questioned.

Mable walked up behind them. "Yes, each was created by a group of metal workers on the outskirts of town. The precious stones are native to this area."

Aware of what Ty was doing, Bryce's heart filled with happiness for his two girls, believing this man was more than just a guest passing through for the holidays.

Julia's face lit up upon finding a stunning sterling silver necklace with a pendant wrapped in wire. The blue stone in the center was very unique. Loving the necklace, seeing the expression on her face, Ty turned to Mable again and winked at her without Julia noticing a thing. The woman jotted down a note on a piece of paper.

"So, if there is anything you wish to purchase," Mable interjected. "Please refer to the attached tags. I am here to answer any questions you have."

"Thank you so much," Julia replied while moving away from the jewelry case. As she walked along, appreciating the many paintings and sculptures surrounding her, Ty left them momentarily and went to speak to Mable.

When they had seen everything, Julia asked, "Well, are we ready to go, Syd?" She had enjoyed their visit very much. After all these years, she finally got to stop in, never taking the time before this.

The young girl joined Bryce, who was standing near the main entrance.

"Umm, yeah, I suppose so," she said, still looking back at the tree sculpture.

Seeing her reaction to it, Julia walked around to look at the price. It was expensive. Sighing, she whispered, "Sorry, Sweetie. I can't buy that for you. Why don't you take a picture of it, and we can blow that up and place it in a frame to put in your room?"

Her face lit up. "That's a great idea, Mom." Taking her phone from her pocket, she snapped a few different angles and showed her to see if they would suffice. Julia loved the third one and thought it would be perfect. As the little girl put her phone away, she longingly looked at the sculpture, imagining it sitting on her side table beside her bed. It also got her thinking about how she could recreate something similar on her own.

Approaching Mable, Julia said, "Thank you so much. It was nice to meet you."

"It was nice meeting you as well."

Joining Ty and Bryce at the door, Julia asked, "So, where to next?"

Keenly listening in to see where they were off to, Sydney waited for Ty to reveal the next clue.

"Well, it seems we can walk there," he mentioned while Bryce smiled.

Saying one last goodbye to Mable, thanking her for taking the time to show them around her beautiful gallery, Sydney waved to the older woman who had escorted them to the door.

"Enjoy your day, everyone! Thank you for visiting the Copper Canoe," she said with a smile before removing the note from the window.

"Which way do we go?" Sydney questioned.

"Umm, turn right," he instructed. "Oh wait, I forgot my gloves on the table in the gallery."

Returning inside, he took a little longer than expected. The girls and Bryce talked while they waited. Emerging, with gloves in hand, he said, "Sorry about that. I forgot where I'd put them down. We are heading that way and will go into that store."

Happy the next stop wasn't far, Sydney again read the sign. "Wait? Abigale's Bakery?" She turned to Bryce, a little confused.

"Yes, that's the one," Ty confirmed.

The broad-shouldered gentleman swung the door open for Sydney and went inside, allowing Ty to hold it for Julia.

Gathering around, the baseball player explained, "From what the locals say," he pointed to Bryce, "This place has the best butter tarts in all of Cottage Country."

"I can greatly attest to that."

Laughing at the white-haired man, closing his eyes while smelling the pleasant aroma wafting through the store, they all made their way over to the counter.

"So, Syd, what will it be? Butter tart and hot chocolate?" Ty wasn't sure what she'd select.

"Yes, please. It looks so good."

"How about you, Julia?"

"Yes, I could try one of those, and coffee would be perfect, thank you."

"Bryce?" Ty asked, confirming everyone's orders.

He nodded, unable to pass up a sweet treat.

Greeting the woman behind the counter with a smile, the girls watched as he ordered four butter tarts, a hot chocolate, and three coffees.

The woman quickly plated their choices and poured their piping hot drinks into cute paper birch bark-printed cups with black lids.

With cash in hand, Ty made sure she did not take Julia's money as she reached into her crossover bag to get her wallet.

The second she did, he stopped her. "Hey, no. Today is my adventure and my treat. Put your wallet away. Don't even think about it," he said humorously.

Returning her wallet to her bag, she quietly replied, "Thank you so much. I appreciate that, but you can't always pay for everything?"

Chuckling, he smiled and said, "Who says?" Understanding what she meant, he added, "Please. Let me do this for you."

She nodded timidly.

Taking their treats and drinks over to a table by the window, the three listened to Bryce offer some inside information on the place.

"Usually, in the summer, Abigale's sells out all of the baking by eleven every morning, especially on the Fridays before a holiday weekend. They are the best desserts in town. So much so that they plan to move to a larger location in the off-season."

"Wow, that is impressive. Where is the store relocating?" Ty wanted to keep tabs on the place.

"Rumor has it they have bought a nineteenth-century church and plan to repurpose it. The church has come all the way from Nova Scotia."

"They actually moved it here?" Julia was surprised. "That is a huge undertaking."

Bryce was proud of their little town. "Yes, it is. But it will certainly add to our beautiful community."

"Well, we will have to visit their new location next year," Julia suggested.

"Yes, I'd like that," Syd added.

Almost finished their mid-morning snack, having people-watched out the front window, Sydney could hardly wait to continue their special day. "Okay, where are we going next?"

Happy to see such excitement directed his way, Ty hesitated a second before looking at Bryce. Raising his eyebrows, he said, "Should we tell them?"

"Come on!" Sydney pleaded, hoping he'd give in.

"Well, we can walk to the next place too."

"Which way? Left or Right," Syd inquired, wanting to get her bearings.

"Umm," Ty mumbled. Not sure himself, he hoped Bryce would help direct him.

The older man swayed his head to one side.

"Okay, he says it's that way." Ty pointed east.

Returning their dishes to the counter, bundling up to greet the cold again, and thanking the lady for the delicious snack break, they all bid her goodbye while she waved. Veering right, Bryce whispered to Ty and walked away.

"Hey, where is he going?" Syd was concerned.

"Oh, he will be back in a little while. I promise."

Strolling along the sidewalk, checking every storefront, knowing they were not going into the bank or real estate brokerages, Sydney stopped at this one place with red light fixtures and large picture windows. Pointing at it, not saying a word, Ty nodded and said, "Yes, that's the one."

Julia moved back from the curb to read the sign. "Morrison's Emporium. Interesting?"

When Syd stepped through the door, the scent of pine and cinnamon greeted her. The interior was a festive wonderland, with twinkling lights, garlands draped over shelves, and ornaments sparkling in every corner. She turned back to Ty and Julia, her grin widening. "I think we just stepped into a Christmas dream," she said.

41

December 23rd

The Emporium

Swinging open the heavy door for Julia and Sydney, Ty walked in behind them, ready to greet the man standing inside.

"Hello! Welcome to Morrison's Emporium. Are you Mr. Reynolds?" The man assumed as much.

"Yes, and you're Greg? We spoke on the phone?"

"Sure did. So nice to meet you. Good afternoon, Ladies."

Saying Hello, the girls stayed close to Ty while scanning the many shops under one roof. Some displayed home décor, filled with casual, comfy items to accessorize any room of the house. Others showcased bath products, candles, and sportswear. There was even an HBC-brand store with everything needed to stay cozy and warm in the winter.

Ty turned to Julia. "So, I brought you here in hopes of browsing, thinking you might like something for the new house. I recall you saying, during the cookie baking, that your house had yet to feel like a home. I'm not sure if this will help, but I thought something might catch your eye?"

Inhaling and taking a deep breath, Julia knew the answer to that. Their place didn't feel like home because it was missing two very important people. She stayed quiet, not wanting to spoil their visit by sharing that explanation.

"This was so thoughtful. Thank you." Julia held back her tears while strolling through the wonderfully spa-scented space. All natural, locally made soaps of every kind helped her relax and control her emotions. It was supposed to be a happy day. Despite trying to move forward, the past kept pulling her back from time to time, flashing little memories without warning, making it hard. She felt overwhelmed by it.

Drawn to a small cottage built near the back of the building, Sydney entered through the quaint doorway to find the inside decorated with signature HBC blankets and merchandise. Syd loved the knitted mittens with the traditional four stripes of color.

Taking note of what caught the ladies' interest, Ty walked along with the store owner – who happened to be a huge baseball fan. He answered his questions about the World Series and his career to date and even agreed to take a few photos and scribble an autograph for their wall.

While gravitating toward the handmade scented candles, Julia picked up a couple she liked before finding a clothing section with golf and tennis wear. There was even an elegant jewelry counter and a florist inside the emporium. The smell of fresh flowers was invigorating.

Syd walked toward the back with a pair of mittens in hand. "Hey, guys! Look a this!" she shouted, having found a giant plush moose. Taking out her phone, she handed it to Ty when he joined her. "Here. Can you take a picture of me, please?"

"Sure thing," he obliged.

Surrounded by the contents of all the little shops, Julia felt anxious and started analyzing what was happening. She knew Ty was only trying to help, but she couldn't bring herself to say the problem was not an easy fix. To her, the family was the heart of any home. It had nothing to do with the many things used to accessorize it. Sadly, nothing in this beautiful store could ever bring back the two people she'd lost.

The other two caught up to Julia.

He asked, "So, do you see anything you like?"

"Yes, of course. There is so much to choose. It is amazing," Julia shared with a forced sense of enthusiasm.

"...but?" he questioned, reading the emotion on her face.

"I've always loved the HBC blankets. We are always looking for something cozy to curl up under, right, Syd? They are the most practical."

"Yep, that's true." Her daughter agreed.

"There is a candle I'd like to get because it reminds me of the smell of the forest. I assume it's a pine or cedar smell. It's quite distinct. Anything you'd like, Syd?"

Holding up the signature mittens, she smiled. "Just these."

"Oh, good choice, Sweetie." Taking out her wallet, Julia walked over to Greg at the cash.

"I'll be right back," he said, disappearing around the corner.

Suddenly surfacing, he stood in line behind her while Greg cashed her out.

A mischievous grin appeared on the man's face as he handed Julia her receipt and corded-handle bag. "Thank you for shopping with us."

"Oh, thank you. You have a wonderful store. I'm sure we will be back."

"Happy to hear it," he replied, moving his eyes onto the baseball player.

Swiveling around, Julia was surprised to find him with three HBC-striped blankets in hand. "What are you doing?"

"I'm buying these," he replied casually.

"You can't buy three?"

"Why not?"

"Because you, umm, just can't...."

"So that I understand. Do you like the candles you bought?" He couldn't keep a straight face.

"Yes, I suppose so." She didn't know what he was getting at.

"Does Syd like her new mittens?"

"I'm sure she does."

"Well, if both of you bought those things, then I am buying these. We need three blankets, one for each of us, when we watch movies on Boxing Day."

"Boxing day?"

"I thought you would need a day of rest after having Christmas dinner for the staff, delivering ornaments, and baking a million cookies. How better than watching holiday movies covered in a signature blanket."

She stayed silent as he handed them to Greg.

"Good choice, Mr. Reynolds," he said happily.

Able to see Julia was a little upset at him, he excused himself. "Greg, give me a second. I'll be right back."

"Sure. No problem, Sir."

"Julia, can we talk?"

She followed him over to a spot away from everyone. Shoving his hands in his pockets, giving her ample space, he said sincerely, "Don't worry about the blankets. It's okay."

Finding it hard to look him in the eye, she turned away.

"What's wrong?" he whispered. Reaching out to her, he took hold of her hands. "Listen, I don't want you to be unhappy. I want you to enjoy this experience."

"But..." she teared up.

He stepped forward and gently brought her in close. "Whatever it is, please tell me."

"That's just it. I don't know what it is," Julia whispered. She found comfort in his arms. "Maybe you are spoiling us too much."

"Don't think of it that way. I wanted to make today special. That's all. I realize this time of year is hard. There is probably a lot going through your mind. I get it. But neither my parents, your son, and your husband would want us to be unhappy over the holidays."

"I know..."

"Just think, whenever you use the blankets, you'll think of me," he said, offering a smitten smile.

That comment hit Julia hard. It meant he'd be leaving. She was beginning to hate the mere thought of that. Emotionally pulled in a few different directions again, she sighed.

"Are we good?" he asked, peering down at her with a hopeful expression.

Nodding, she replied, "I suppose so."

Syd rounded the corner. "There you are. I've been looking for you guys."

"Sorry, Syd. I just needed to talk to your Mom for a second. Ready to get going?"

"Yes. Where to next?" she asked.

"Can't say," he teased.

"Come on! One hint? Just one," the young girl pleaded, "Please? Please? Please?"

"Nope."

Ty walked back over to pay for the blankets. Greg had already packaged each into special monogrammed storage boxes and placed them in sleek black Morrison's Emporium bags.

"Thank you for shopping with us, Mr. Reynolds," Greg said from behind the cash, handing him his receipt. "I'm a big fan. Is it okay to grab a picture?"

"Yeah, certainly," Ty agreed.

"Do you mind?" Greg asked Julia, passing her his device.

Carefully taking hold of it, Julia said, "No, not at all." Centering the two men in the picture, she took a few snaps. "There you go."

"Thank you so much." Greg got his device back.

"Is it alright if we place your photo and autograph on our VIP wall of fame?"

"Sure, no problem. I'm okay with it." He was used to this type of thing.

"Great. Thanks again. So nice meeting all of you. Have a good rest of the day."

"Speaking of that," Julia hinted. "Where are we headed next?"

Pointing to Bryce, who was sitting in the SUV now parked outside the store, Ty revealed while Sydney listened intently, "We have to drive for about forty minutes to reach our next destination."

"Forty minutes? That's so far," the girl replied, about to faint dramatically on their way out the doors.

Knowing the area reasonably well, Julia inquired, "North or South?"

"Hmmm, can't say?" Ty didn't really know for sure himself.

"Oh, come on," she urged, "Which way?"

"Well, I can't say because technically, I don't know," he laughed, shrugging his shoulders.

Reaching the truck, Ty opened the back door for the girls to jump in. Bryce automatically raised the rear hatch for Ty to pack the blanket boxes. Returning to his spot beside Julia, he closed the door behind him. "Okay, Bryce. We are off to stop number four."

"Roger that," Bryce acknowledged, backing out of the space.

As the truck merged onto the highway, the hum of the engine blended with the soft laughter from the backseat - the journey promising more adventures to come.

42

December 23rd

Two Men and a Stove

Intrigued, Julia tried to figure out which direction they were going. Watching Bryce continue East, Julia thought of a few places, but none as far away as a forty-minute drive. Not long after, her trusted friend signaled left. The turn made her pay attention to the compass on the dash. When it calibrated, Julia confirmed they were now headed north.

"So, is everybody having fun?" Bryce asked, looking in his rearview mirror a few times to read his girls' expressions.

"Yes, this is so exciting," Sydney gushed, "I love not knowing what's next. It's a real adventure for sure."

Smiling, so happy that Sydney was enjoying herself, Ty whispered to Julia, "So, are you having that much fun too?"

Amazed by what he'd planned, trying to enjoy herself and not over-think it, she replied, "Yes. Have to say, I'm intrigued. By the way, how did you know?"

"Know what?"

"That Syd and I have never been to any of these stores in town?"

"Never?" Ty wasn't aware.

Julia shook her head.

"Just thought it would be something fun for you guys. Ladies like to shop. Don't they?"

She quietly chuckled. "Yes, I am guilty of that from time to time."

It wasn't easy to be close to Julia and not offer affection, but he kept his distance, mindful of giving her space. The last thing he wanted was to stress her out.

Looking at him, she saw great sincerity in his eyes and knew she had to stop riding this emotional rollercoaster. It wasn't fair to him. Thinking about everything that had to happen to spend the holidays together, she recalled what LeeAnn had said yesterday.

What if they'd met for a reason? What if it was meant to be? She thought. *Why was she fighting so hard to hold onto the past when a bright future was sitting right beside her? Was there a way to strike a balance between her life with David and Ben and her life after? A world that included someone else?*

At that moment, Julia remembered the day Ty saved Sydney. That night, she'd permitted herself to fall if that were to happen. Somehow, she'd gotten overwhelmed and lost sight of that promise.

"Thank you for planning this day—all of it - no matter what comes next. I needed a day to relax. And despite my troubled heart, I am enjoying it."

He offered his hand to her. Reaching over, she took hold and gave it a few gentle squeezes. He did the same. Happy to rekindle their connection, he didn't know what brought on her change of heart, but it was nice to see a sparkle in her eye.

Bryce made another left in the middle of nowhere - only a lonely gas station for miles.

Her mind reeling, Julia wondered where they were going.

With about ten minutes left on the trip, Sydney curiously peered over Bryce's shoulder to look at their GPS location. "Hey, it says we are going to Forest Glen."

"Hmm," Julia mumbled, "Forest Glen, huh?"

"Yeah, you may think you know, but you will never guess what we are doing in a million years," Ty said confidently. "Trust me." Not giving up a single clue, he offered a sexy smirk, igniting a few butterflies in her heart that quickly doused any doubt and sadness lingering.

Bryce pulled off the highway into a parking lot on the far side of Forest Glen. Backing into a spot in front of the modern log house with a fire pit glowing with controlled flames, Sydney sat up and looked around before removing her seatbelt.

"I think it's a restaurant, Mom. It says Two Men and a Stove."

Turning off the vehicle, Bryce got out and opened Sydney's door. Given his hand, the little girl took hold and slid out, placing her feet firmly on the ground. "This way, my dear Sydney," he said with a smile, offering his arm in such a gentlemanly way. Syd grabbed hold and walked alongside him toward the entrance.

Mimicking Bryce, Ty followed suit. "This way, my lady."

"Thank you kindly."

Arm in arm, the two stopped at the doors and noticed another sign.

"Wait, it says closed for a private party," Sydney said. Quickly recalling what happened at the gallery, she swung around and asked, "Is this for us too?"

"I think so," Bryce replied.

Inside the foyer, two chefs dressed in white coats were waiting to greet their guests.

"Hello, there. Are you our Reynold's party of four?"

Immediately, Ty stepped forward. "Yes, we are."

"Thank you for joining us. I'm Lawrence, and this is William," he introduced.

"Very nice to meet you both. These lovely ladies are Julia and Sydney, and this is...."

"Oh, this guy needs no introductions," William confirmed jovially. "How are you, Bryce?"

"Doing well," he chuckled. "I'm enjoying the day tagging along with Ty and my girls."

"Well, follow me. Your table is ready. Right, this way, everyone."

The gentlemen led their group up the stairs to a table beside the fireplace, dressed in crisp white linen. Three pendant lights hovered overhead.

"Here we are. Please settle in, and we will be back shortly to take your orders," he said.

Courteously pulling out Sydney and Julia's chairs for them, Bryce and Ty took a seat after they got comfortable. There was a noticeable warmth to the room.

"This place is so cozy." Julia was excited to see the menu. Flipping the folder open, she found a piece of paper entitled *Reynold's Party of Four*. Finding a fixed five courses inside, Julia showed Sydney.

All smiles, she exclaimed, "Wow, everything they have on this list looks so good, Mom."

"How did you find this place?" Julia glanced over at Ty.

Lifting his hand, pointing to the man across from him, he said, "You can thank Bryce for the suggestion. He thought this would be a good spot to have dinner."

"Yes, this was where Bev and I would go when we needed a little change in scenery- especially since she didn't like venturing too far. The town of Forest Glen is the cutest spot, especially in the summer. They have a very active waterfront here, maybe something you would like to visit in the future."

"That sounds awesome. What do you think, you two?" Ty was game.

Seeing a positive reaction, they saw their first course en route along with their drinks. Setting the plates in front of them, Lawrence stated before departing, "This is our coconut shrimp, grilled calamari, and pita bread with goat cheese, black olives, and roasted garlic. Enjoy."

Unwrapping their cutlery from the tightly bound napkins on the table and placing the cloth across their laps, Ty proposed a toast. "To a wonderful day filled with laughter, fun, and the big surprise yet to come. Thank you to Bryce for helping me orchestrate it all."

"Of course, anything for my girls." The older man raised his glass. "Cheers."

Sydney's eyes almost bulged out of her head. "Wait? Did you say there's more after this?"

"Yes, that's right," the ball player responded confidently. "We saved the best for last," he added, "Didn't we, Bryce?"

"Yes. You will love every minute of it, ladies."

Happy to see their faces filled with wonderment, the athlete was pleased that things had gone well thus far. He hoped the next phase of his plan would allow him to spend one-on-one time with Julia. There was so much more he wanted to say.

43

December 23rd

Ty's Childhood Tradition

One delicious course after another, feeling comfortably full, they opted to take their desserts to go. Ty excused himself a minute and walked downstairs. There, he found William steaming the stemware.

"Hello, Mr. Reynolds. What can I do for you?" he asked. "Has everything been to your liking?"

"Beyond expectations. Wanted to thank you for closing for us tonight. I appreciate it."

"Absolutely. Things have been a little slower over the holidays, so it worked well for us too."

"Can I settle the bill with you?"

"Yes, sure. Right this way."

William led Ty over to the POS and handed him the machine.

Ty made sure to leave a substantial tip for their troubles.

Seeing the payment, the owner said, "Thank you so much, Sir. That is much appreciated."

"No, thank you. Dinner was amazing."

"We aim to please."

"And that you did."

"Hope to see all of you again."

"I'm sure you will."

Returning to the group upstairs, he said, "Okay, everyone. Ready to move on to our next adventure?"

Sydney grabbed her coat as quickly as she could.

With her all bundled up, Ty hinted on the way down the stairs, "So, Bryce, what do we have? A six-minute drive now?"

"Yes, that's about right." Bryce winked at Sydney. "Are you excited?"

She looked up at him. Her eyes sparkled. "Yes!"

Bidding the chefs Merry Christmas, the group piled into the SUV. A few snowflakes fell past the streetlights as they departed and rejoined the main highway.

Julia contemplated what activity they could do at nighttime while Sydney kept her eyes peeled and counted the minutes from when they left.

"Once we arrive, you will have to change into warm clothes. I'm sure you will discover what we are doing fairly fast."

"Are we going night sledding or tubing? Maybe taking a sleigh ride?" Syd asked.

"Nope," the baseball player smiled.

With great anticipation, the girls saw Bryce merge right at the next intersection. Driving up a long hill, he skillfully navigated through the country setting before turning onto another snow-covered road. Bearing right, with thick forest on either side, they saw a few cars here and there driving in the opposite direction.

Julia noticed a sign: *No Excessive Noise At Any Time. What does that mean? She thought. How strange.*

Still unsure where they were going and what they were doing, in minutes, they arrived at a parking lot with a small log building illuminated by Christmas lights. Seeing an orangey glow in the distance, Bryce parked the vehicle while the girls quickly surveyed their surroundings.

"So," Ty paused, "We are here."

"Where?" Syd asked, a little bit concerned about being in the middle of a dark forest.

"We are at Arrow Park. Behind this building is a path that leads through the forest, but it is not just any path. It is called the Fire and Ice Trail." Seeing the lady's eyes light up, he added, "Over the past few days, you have introduced me to your Carling Christmas traditions, something I was so grateful to be a part of. This morning, I figured I'd share a Christmas tradition of mine with you. We could have gone skating at the Carling, but this was too incredible to pass up."

The girls looked at each other – their eyes danced with delight.

"While living in Wyoming, over the holidays, my parents would take us to this rickety outdoor rink with strings of lights hanging from these wooden poles nailed to the outside of the boards. Some would shine brightly, and some were in need of replacement because they'd blown out."

Sydney hung on his every word.

"The ice wasn't perfect. Sometimes choppy. It depended on who did the flood that day since the community members took turns helping to keep it running. Around Christmastime, I recall it always being pretty cold, and it seemed to snow all the time. Adjacent to the ice surface was this old shack with a black wood stove. Throughout the night, people would fire up and keep the place warm so we could go and thaw out our toes from time to time. I hadn't thought of that childhood memory in years. It prompted me to search for a unique place to skate. I wanted to incorporate that tradition into the list of amazing things you do while celebrating Christmas in Carling. I hope that's okay?"

"This is wonderful," Julia fondly replied, with a tilt of her head.

They found the little girl with her nose pressed against the window, trying to see more. "Can we go now?"

"Yes. Our skating reservation is in fifteen minutes. Bryce brought skates from the hotel. He knew your sizes better than I, so...."

"I brought a few extra just in case Sydney grew a ton from last year," the man interrupted with a chuckle.

"Everyone head inside the building to change into winter gear. Afterward, we take our skates to where the path begins and change into them there. Soon, we will be skating on the Fire and Ice trail through the forest."

Excited, Syd quickly got out of the truck. Meeting Bryce, she helped him with their skates.

Opening his door, Ty offered his hand for Julia to step down carefully. "Bryce, I'll grab the bags if you want to go ahead inside with Sydney," he bellowed to them on the opposite side of the truck.

"Sounds good," Bryce said.

While walking with him, Syd shouted, "I've got our skates, Mom."

"Okay," Julia replied, seeing the baseball player move toward the tailgate. "Ty, wait." Julia gently grabbed hold of his arm to stop him. Nervous and lost for words, she slowly slipped her arms around his waist and pulled him in close. Surprised, he could not resist doing the same.

"I must say you are full of surprises, Mr. Reynolds. Thank you."

"I'm happy you're having fun. It's been pretty great for me too. Hope it hasn't been too stressful, especially not knowing where we were going."

"Yes and no." She paused. "I'm sorry I've gotten stuck in my head."

"Julia, I've learned over the years that grief sticks with you. It never leaves. But the thing is, we are still here, and they expect us to live and not wallow in our sadness. Promise you will enjoy the journey."

Taken by his words of wisdom, she nodded. "You're right."

His eyes affixed to hers, Ty pressed his lips upon her forehead, letting them linger until Julia looked up. There was no denying the feelings he'd developed - it was a connection that deepened by the day. His heart pounded. It was a rare feeling and seemed more intense than stepping out onto the field in front of millions of people watching him play. Seeing Julia raise herself on her tiptoes, Ty slowly leaned in to meet her halfway, knowing she wanted to kiss him as much as he needed to kiss her. A warmth spread from head to toe - so much so that it made Julia shiver.

Lowering his head, resting his chin on her shoulder, she held on tightly, as did he. Rocking back and forth, the two didn't want to part ways.

"Would you do me the honor of skating through the forest with me?"

Julia smiled from ear to ear. "Yes, I would love to."

Taking their bags from the truck, they joined Bryce and Sydney inside. After paying the fees, the ticket guy passed along their wristbands.

Fully dressed, waiting patiently, Sydney sat on the bench, bouncing her legs up and down.

Realizing she seemed off, her Mother asked, "What's wrong, Syd?"

"Yeah. I'm just nervous." Hesitating, she said, "Aren't bears and wild animals in the forest at night? What about wolves?" Syd fearfully described while Bryce sat beside her to calm her down.

"Oh, I think the bears are hibernating, and the wolves may be too scared to see and hear so many people around the park. Fire tiki torches are lining the skating trail, so I don't think they would like that either. Don't worry, Sydney. I'll keep you safe."

Nodding her head in agreement, taking hold of Bryce's hand, knowing he would skate with her, she smiled. "Okay. I trust you," she declared.

His face lit up.

With everyone dressed, the guys walked hand in hand with their girls to the starting area. Arriving at the well-lit clearing with picnic tables and box shelves, each took a seat and put on their skates. Soon, they were all laced up and ready to go. Ty placed their boots and bags inside the top storage box before starting their nighttime skate on the icy path. With flaming torches set every ten feet, scouting the majestic winding trail ahead, Bryce held onto Sydney's hand, and they were off. Noticing her scanning the dark forest from left to right, he asked how school was going. That sparked a string of conversations from teachers to friends, fights, and everything in between. Syd was then too busy talking to take notice of where they were.

Skating a few yards ahead of Julia and Ty, Bryce hoped to give them time together.

Asked to share his knowledge of the forest and wildlife, the little girl looked inquisitively at him. Spouting an abundance of facts, he was surprised by what she knew about animals, too.

Shyly glancing Julia's way, Ty offered his hand to her. She took hold while they skated along behind Bryce and Sydney. Somewhat relaxed, she knew her daughter seemed more comfortable with the experience now. In awe of how beautifully peaceful the forest was at night, Julia stared at the flame's reflections gleaming and shimmering off the ice surface. The skating trail seemed magical like they were in an entirely different world.

"Today has been so lovely. I don't even know what to say. This has got to be a bucket list item." Pausing a moment, she said, "Other than wanting to share one of your Christmas traditions, why did you do all this for us?"

"Well, as my poem said...."

"Yes, the poem. You wrote that all by yourself?"

Proud of what he had accomplished, he lowered his head, a bit embarrassed. "Yes, I did. Thought you would appreciate that. It took me a half-hour, but I think it was good. Right?"

"It was perfect."

"So, like the poem read, after today, you will see how much I care."

"I know you care. I truly do. It's just....."

"I know it's complicated," Ty said casually. Stopping to pull her towards him gently caused her to glide straight into his arms. "Can't we just see where this goes? Please?"

With a bit of vibration in her voice, she whispered, "Yes."

"I know there are some logistics we need to work out, but I am willing to do whatever it takes to make you happy - if you'll have me. I want to build a life with you and Sydney."

"What are you saying?"

"Julia, I've told you. I've never met anyone like you, and I'm not about to let you get away."

"You're not?" she giggled.

"I've never been more sure of anything in my entire life," Ty said, his voice steady but filled with emotion. His eyes searched hers, unguarded and vulnerable. "I'm falling for you, Julia Mariani."

Before she could respond, he leaned in, capturing her lips in a kiss that was both tender and passionate, the kind of kiss that carried every unspoken word he hadn't yet said. Without thinking, he swept her off her feet, twirling her effortlessly.

"Ty!" Julia gasped, laughter bubbling up despite the moment's intensity. "Okay, okay, put me down before Syd thinks I'm in trouble!"

He chuckled softly, his smile radiant under the glow of the torches. Gently, he lowered her back onto the ice, his hands lingering around her waist as though he couldn't bear to let go. Looking at her as if she were his entire world, he whispered, "I'm falling in love with you."

Julia's breath hitched, the weight of his words wrapping around her heart like a warm embrace. Her knees trembled beneath her, and for a moment, she thought she might crumble right there on the ice. Her chest tightened, and tears pricked the corners of her eyes as a lump formed in her throat.

Barely able to speak, she reached up to touch his face, her fingers tracing the faint stubble along his jaw. "I think I'm falling in love with you, too," she said nervously, her voice soft but certain.

Upon hearing those words, Ty's heart soared. He looked up at the night sky, where stars shimmered like scattered diamonds across an endless black canvas. His thoughts drifted to his Mom, and a wave of warmth and peace washed over him. Deep down, he felt her presence, as if she were there, smiling down and sharing in his joy.

Mom, he thought silently, his eyes glistening. *I hope you're seeing this.*

Julia tightened her grip on his hands, grounding him in the moment. As their foreheads touched, the world around them melted away, leaving just the two of them standing together on the ice, wrapped in a love that felt timeless and true.

December 23rd

Southbound

Over the next hour and a half, they skated the looping trail through the forest, their laughter and breath visible in the crisp night air. Ty stayed close to Julia, matching her pace and pointing out the frost-covered branches that sparkled under the moonlight. By the time they returned, their feet felt frozen and their legs exhausted.

Sydney and Bryce flopped onto a bench simultaneously as the park's speakers announced the thirty-minute warning before closing time.

Julia knelt beside Syd, helping her unlace her skates while Bryce worked on his.

Joining them, Ty did the same, his fingers stiff from the cold but his smile warm. Thankful not to be recognized that evening, he thought he could get used to the anonymity.

Once Bryce had his boots back on, he headed out to warm the truck.

Wincing at the chill in the air, Julia pulled on the cold boots while Ty helped Syd slip into hers. When they'd gathered their belongings, they walked back to the parking lot, ready to load up their gear.

After handing over the last of the skates, he gave Bryce a grateful pat on the back. "Thank you for your help today. I think it was a success. Don't you?" Ty said before climbing in beside Julia.

With a courteous nod, he closed the back hatch. "Indeed. You've made these ladies very happy."

The guy smiled. "I'm glad."

On that note, the two got in.

The vehicle's heated seats began to thaw their frozen limbs.

Exhausted, Sydney buckled herself into the middle row but quickly grew restless. Unclipping her seatbelt, she climbed into the front seat beside Bryce. Reclining the chair back, she buckled in, using her jacket as a makeshift pillow and her Mom's coat as a blanket. Within minutes, her soft breaths signaled she was fast asleep.

In the middle, now alone, Julia and Ty settled into their quiet moment.

Lifting his arm, she instinctively nestled against his side, drawing warmth from his embrace as the heat began to fill the cabin.

Bryce glanced over his shoulder and whispered, "Alright, ready to go?"

Julia nodded. "Yes, we're good."

"We should be at the Carling in about an hour, give or take," Bryce replied, easing the truck onto the road.

The vehicle hummed as it crossed the bridge and merged onto the southbound highway, the city lights fading into the darkness behind them.

The two talked softly for a while, their voices barely above a murmur. Before long, Julia's head dipped against his shoulder, her eyelids fluttering closed.

When he gazed down at her sleeping face, a soft smile tugged at his lips. Outside, the world rushed by in a blur, but in that moment, everything felt perfectly still.

45

December 23rd

A Promise Made

A while later, Julia woke to the sounds of Ty and Bryce whispering back and forth, trying not to wake Sydney and her.

"Can I be frank with you?" Bryce asked, his tone serious yet warm.

"Yes, absolutely. Shoot."

"I've known these ladies for almost ten years. I've been through the news of David and Ben's passing. I was there for their first Christmas the following year. Julia is like a daughter to me, and I think of Sydney as my granddaughter. I love them both with all my heart. They are my family. With Bev gone, I'm all alone now, so spending time with them is very important to me. Guess what I'm trying to say is, one, thank you for allowing me to accompany you today and share in the fun. I appreciate that very much, and two, I am going to say, you'd better not break their hearts because you know that with Julia comes Syd. If you're looking to join their family, in turn, you are joining mine. So, maybe I'm overreacting, but I must ask, man to man. What are your intentions with Julia? I feel it is my job to protect her since she does not have a father to do that for her."

Taking a deep breath, the weight of the moment settling over him, he met Bryce's gaze without hesitation, his voice steady and sincere. "I'll be honest. When I arrived at the Carling, I wanted to hide away and just make it through another holiday season unscathed. I could have never imagined meeting anyone. She came out of left field. Sorry for the baseball analogy - but it's true, she did. I could never hurt them. I've told Julia I've never met anyone like her. She is so giving and kind - a breath of fresh air for me. She reminds me of my Mother, too – everything she does makes me think of her. I don't know; I can't help but smile when she's around. I get this warm feeling. I know this year will be tough, and she understands that to a degree. I travel a lot, so that will be a challenge, but if we can make it to November and hopefully the World Series, I am retiring after the final game. Then, I will be free of it all. After that, I want to spend every waking moment caring for these two. Julia will be the center of my life, and I will protect and love Syd like she is my own. No exceptions."

The man nodded thoughtfully. "If you don't do all those things, you'll have to deal with me otherwise."

"Yes, Sir. Don't worry. That won't happen. I promise."

"A man's word means a lot around here," Bryce said firmly. "Do I have yours?"

"You have my word."

Julia's heart swelled as she pretended to stir awake, letting their heartfelt conversation settle in her mind. She shifted slightly, opening her eyes and glancing around. "Sorry, guys, I must've nodded off. What did I miss?"

"Not much," Ty said casually. "Bryce and I were just talking."

"Yes, deary," Bryce added with a smile, his eyes twinkling as he glanced at her in the rearview mirror. "We're about ten minutes out. Not far now."

The glowing lights of the Carling Hotel came into view as they turned onto the final stretch of road.

Leaning her head against Ty's shoulder, the warmth of his promise still echoed in Julia's heart as the magical holiday night drew closer to its next chapter.

46

December 23rd

The Deal

Driving up the winding resort road, they were the only vehicle there. The headlights illuminated the trees hanging with snow. Above them, through the panorama roof, Julia could see a universe of stars and thought about her boys. Closer and closer, they could see the lights of the hotel sparkling through the trees.

Julia said, "Every time I see this place, day or night, I love that it is deep in the woods. It is the area's best-kept secret, and we are lucky enough to know where to find it."

"I believe it's one of the nicest places I've ever visited," Ty smiled at her, knowing he thought that mainly because she was there.

Bryce drove under the covered entrance and shifted the truck into park. "And here we are. Back again. All safe and sound."

Getting out, Julia walked around to Sydney's side to wake her. Gently tapping her arm, she spoke to her calmly. "We are back, Sweetie pie," she said softly.

Ty looked on, recalling how his Mother would wake him for school when he was young. She used a similar tone. It was something he had almost forgotten.

Not sure how she would wake her sleeping beauty, she figured she would carry her upstairs.

"I can carry her if you need."

"Poor thing. She's so tired," Julia said, allowing Ty to scoop her into his arms.

"You go on upstairs, and I will bring up the bags," Bryce suggested as the tailgate lifted.

"Okay. Thank you, Bryce. I appreciate that." Not wanting to be empty-handed, Julia took what she could with her.

On the way to their suite, her little girl mumbled.

"Sometimes she talks in her sleep," Julia shared.

Ty was surprised by that.

"Once and a while, I can get her talking even though she is still dreaming. It can be entertaining."

"I'm sure," he chuckled.

Almost there, Julia jogged ahead to prop the door open for them while Ty carefully maneuvered Syd through the doorway. Taking off her daughter's boots, she set them on the mat and continued to her room.

Quickly pulling back the covers, she said, "Just put her there. I will change her into her pajamas later."

He did what she asked and returned to help Bryce with their bags. He could hear him shuffling about in the other room.

Taking everything off the trolly, Ty offered his hand to the older gentleman and said, "Thanks again for all your help today. I couldn't have pulled this off without you."

Staring at it, the older man suddenly moved it away and offered a manly pat on the back. "It's been a great experience for me too. Thank you for including me." Backing off, he whispered with a snicker, "Remember what I said earlier."

"Don't worry, Sir. I promise."

He shot him an eagle eye. "Make sure."

"Make sure, what?" Julia asked.

Creating a diversion to cover up their conversation, Bryce said, "I just told him to get some rest. It's been an action-packed day."

"Yes, I will do that," he replied, playing along. "For sure."

Julia followed Bryce out into the hallway and hugged him. "Thank you for everything. It was so nice spending time with you."

"You are very welcome, my dear, but you should thank that guy in there. It was his idea. I made a few suggestions, and he took care of the rest."

Julia knew he was right.

Pausing a second, Bryce opted to pry just a little. "Can I offer a word of advice?"

"Of course." She wondered what he'd say.

Reaching his arms out to her, he placed a hand on each arm. Before speaking a word, he leaned toward her right ear. "Don't let that man go," he whispered. "He is a good one. You have a chance to find happiness again. Don't let it slip away. I believe he truly cares for you - both of you. I can tell. I know this happened fast, but sometimes it's just meant to be."

Those were LeeAnn's exact words.

"Thank you. I'll keep that in mind. I love you too, you know."

"I know. I feel so lucky to have you and Sydney in my life. But, promise me you will give him a chance," he asked sincerely.

Parting ways, she promised, "I'll try my very best." Kissing him on the cheek, she said, "Goodnight. I love you. Drive home safely."

"I will. I love you both too. Good night, my dear. I will see you tomorrow." The white-haired man pushed the trolly down the hall. Waving to her, he soon disappeared into the elevator.

Walking back into the room, releasing the door from its fixed position, Julia saw Ty sitting on the sofa. The blanket boxes were on the floor beside him.

"Where would you like these?" he asked.

"Maybe we should place them under the tree."

Doing that, he set each box along the back wall while Julia hung up their coats and snow pants before spreading their hats and mitts out to dry.

"I guess I'd better get going. You should get some sleep. We have a super busy day tomorrow. What time do you need me here to help you?"

"Well, they usually deliver the turkey early in the morning."

"Early? Like how early?"

"Umm, they arrive between eight and nine o'clock."

"I'll make sure to be here by then."

Not having had help making the turkey dinner since David was alive, Julia felt that sinking feeling. "Let's make it nine. It should give us enough time to prep a few things before I get the turkey in the oven at eleven. The staff starts coming to eat between five and six."

"So, there is a whole schedule for the day?"

"Yes, pretty much," she confirmed. "It's hectic, but in the end, it's all worth the trouble. You'll see."

"Looking forward to it."

"Perfect," Julia replied with a smile that warmed his heart.

About to leave, Ty stood at the door with his boxed blanket beside him. He looked happy.

"What is it?" She lowered her head.

"I feel kind of proud that I was able to surprise the two of you today. I've never done that for anyone before." Ty reached out to her.

Julia watched their fingers intertwine. Inching closer, she placed her arms around his neck before he slipped his around her waist to pull her in tightly. "Thank you for a wonderful day."

"You're welcome. Thank you for joining me," Ty said, towering over her. Gently lifting her feet off the floor, their bodies dangerously close, he did not want to let go. "So, I guess I'll see you in the morning bright and early?"

"Yes, you certainly will."

Mindful not to move too fast, he leaned in and pressed his lips firmly against hers. Leaving them to linger, he respectfully backed away and said, "Goodnight."

"Goodnight," she whispered.

Still holding her hand, Ty opened the door and maneuvered his large shopping bag across the hall. Extending their arms as far as they could reach, he finally let go. Whispering goodnight one last time, not wanting to leave her, sadly, he knew he didn't have a choice. If he had any chance of building their relationship, he knew he had to be patient. As both doors fell shut, Julia bashfully smiled before she disappeared.

Now alone, he switched on the lights and noticed the gallery had delivered the packages he'd bought earlier. Remembering he'd left his cell phone behind, he checked it to see if he'd missed anything important. Surprised to find multiple missed phone calls and texts, he quickly scanned the list.

"Of course. The day I don't have it with me, all hell breaks loose."

Matt and Michael had tried to contact him several times in the last seven hours. He assumed they'd reached a deal while he was out. Concerned about what his agent would say with the lack of response, the phone suddenly rang in his hand. It was Michael. Not in the mood to talk business, he let it go to voice mail and waited for him to leave a message. Ignoring all the texts, he knew there was no point in reading them since, within minutes, this last message would say it all. Not caring as much about the life-altering decision as he once did, Ty hoped this whole thing wouldn't interrupt his Christmas with Julia and Syd, understanding all too well that when the Hot Stove starts heating up, things usually move along pretty fast.

Looking down at the screen, he saw Michael calling again. He was sure the guy was about to blow a gasket. Ty listened to the message he left.

Hey, Ty. Where are you? I've been trying to get a hold of you all day. The Sox have renewed your contract for another year in Boston. You get to play out your final season for the team you love. Congratulations, man. I got them up to nineteen mill with one-point-five in incentives. Now, all you need to do is come home and sign the contract tomorrow, and it's a done deal. Your itinerary is attached. Call me when you get this message.

Feeling like someone kicked him in the gut, those words knocked the wind out of him. "Tomorrow? He can't be serious?" Ty said out loud. "It's Christmas Eve."

47

December 24th

Two Against One

Not having the best sleep, tossing and turning throughout the night, and waking up often, Ty dreaded having to do the unthinkable. Deep in thought, staring at the ceiling, without warning, his alarm sounded, cutting through the silence like a knife. Darkness still blanketed the sky as he sat up and planted his feet firmly on the floor. His body felt weighed down. The guilt was almost unbearable. He kept thinking about how Julia would react. But, what worried him the most was disappointing Sydney. She had done nothing to deserve this. Neither of them did. Having to break the promise he'd made Bryce was even worse.

"What are you doing?" he whispered. "You shouldn't be going anywhere."

Aware of the importance of these signing announcements, Ty figured he had no choice but to leave. Struggling to drag himself out of bed, he recalled the special day he shared with Julia and Sydney yesterday. As he peered past the French doors, he spotted the beautiful packages sitting on the table. A terrible feeling hit him, knowing he wouldn't be there when they opened them later tonight.

Believing he was about to make the biggest mistake of his life, Ty's phone rang. Forcing himself to pick it up, hating to talk business so early in the morning, he quietly said, "Hello?"

"Ty. Why didn't you text me back last night? I probably left you like twenty messages. I worked for hours to get this deal done."

"I know. I think it was twenty-seven messages if I recall correctly. I was busy."

"What?" Michael paused. "Yeah, whatever... Hey, I'm going to conference in Matt. One second."

Waiting on the other line, not wanting to be ganged up on by the two advisors, Ty focused his gaze out the window while a hint of light started to grace the eastern sky.

"Is everyone on?" Michael asked, his voice sharp through the speakerphone.

"Yeah, it's Matt. I'm here. Congrats. That's awesome news."

Michael waited, but there was no response from the person who mattered most. "Ty? You there?"

A hesitant voice finally replied. "Yeah, yeah. I'm here."

"We locked in nineteen with one-point-five—more than you wanted. It's a done deal." Michael's tone carried the pride of a job well done.

"Congrats, man," Matt chimed in, genuinely happy for his best friend.

Still, Ty's silence lingered, his enthusiasm noticeably absent.

"Hey, Reynolds?" Michael pressed, a trace of irritation creeping into his voice.

"That's great, Mike. Thanks," the first baseman said, his tone distant.

Matt frowned and sensed something was off. "You okay?"

"I'm fine. Why wouldn't I be?" Ty deflected, but his distracted tone only raised more questions.

Not buying it, Matt stated, "You didn't answer any of our texts yesterday."

Michael cut in, his words laced with irritation. "You know, Ty, this isn't just for fun. I don't get paid for you to ghost us."

"And that's why I pay you a hefty commission." The athlete's tone cut like a knife.

"What were you doing last night anyway?" His agent was curious.

"Nothing important," Ty shot back, dodging. He had no intention of mentioning the night he'd spent with Julia. Pivoting the conversation, he asked, "What's next?"

Clearly frustrated, Michael sighed. "The deal needs to be signed and finalized before the live press conference and Q&A tonight at six."

"Wait…" Ty's chest tightened. "Tonight?"

"Yes. Is there a problem?" Michael's words were blunt, practically a challenge.

"It's Christmas Eve," Ty protested. "I can't leave."

"There is no negotiation here. You gotta return to Boston, sign this agreement, and finish the promo. It's that simple."

Waiting to hear anything coming from their client of sixteen years, the two men heard nothing but silence.

Angry, Michael lost his patience. "Reynolds!"

"What!" The baseball player thought his agent sounded more and more like his father with each passing day.

"Come back, do the promo, and sign the damn contract. After that, you can go back to wherever the hell you are. I don't give a…."

"Mike, stop!" Matt cut him off.

Impatient, Michael said bluntly, "Is it just me, or is something amiss here?"

"Hey, man, what's goin' on?" Matt asked sincerely.

Not about to tell them about Julia and Sydney, Ty divulged, "It's nothing. I'm having a rough day and wasn't expecting to travel anywhere on Christmas Eve. Couldn't this wait a couple of days?"

"I want this over and done with, so I can enjoy the holidays with my family. Did you ever think of that?" Michael sounded overly frustrated and stressed.

Interrupting him, Matt shouted, "Mike, hang up. I'll call you later."

Intent on having the last say, his agent rudely laid everything out on the table. "Look! I don't care what you do in the off-season. It's not my business – but this is. Your flight leaves Pearson at noon today. You'd better be on it. This is it, Ty. Your last lap." Hearing more silence on his client's end, he angrily ended their conversation. "I need to go! I'll meet you at the airport this afternoon when you land. We can go over your press announcement on the way to HQ."

On that note, hearing a click, Mike hung up without saying goodbye.

"Hey, Ty. You still there?"

"I'm here."

"I think you should have fired him years ago."

"He is good at what he does despite being rough around the edges. He gets stuff done," his boss complimented, understanding how his dad used to conduct business, too.

"Tell me the truth. What's really going on? I've been around you long enough to know when there's something wrong."

The great baseball player hesitated before confiding in his friend. "I met someone."

Glad to hear it was positive versus negative, Matt replied, "Well, I'm happy to hear that. I look forward to meeting her."

"Her name is Julia. She has a daughter named Sydney."

"A daughter?"

"It's a long story. Not what you think."

"Okay." Concerned, Matt flipped into business mode. "This contract has been a long time coming. It would be best if you did what they asked. Then, as Mike said, you can continue your time off. You know the drill. This is how it works. I realize this time of year is difficult for you. I get it, but it's only one day. That's all."

Knowing it was far more complicated than that, Ty dreaded disappointing and irreversibly hurting Julia and Syd.

"Yeah, sure. One day. Right. Look, I gotta go."

"Promise me you will be on that flight." His friend sounded desperate.

Looking out the window, Ty knew he would miss the Christmas Eve festivities.

"Fine. I'll call you when I'm on the road."

"Good. I'll wait to hear from you."

Hanging up, he looked at the Christmas tree in the corner of the room. Approaching it, he reached out to remove the handmade glass ornaments one by one and carefully placed each in the decorative box Julia had picked out to give to the women's shelter. Wrapping up the strands of lights, he packaged it neatly. The tree looked so bare when he'd finished. It made it even harder for him to leave.

"Well, it was nice while it lasted..." he said sadly, not knowing where things would stand after today. "Hopefully, she will understand."

48

December 24th

A Bitter Goodbye

With his suitcase resting on the end of the bed, Ty gathered his things from around the room. Slowly placing everything in piles beside the suitcase, his body felt numb. He hated himself for what he was about to do. The world suddenly seemed so cold and dark. It had lost all signs of life.

Securing the extra box of ornaments in the middle of his carry-on, he surrounded it with clothing to ensure nothing broke during his travels. Keeping an eye on the time, alarmed that it was after eight o'clock, the sound of someone in the hallway piqued his curiosity. Walking to the door, he realized Julia had just received her turkey delivery. Knowing she asked him to swing by between eight-thirty and nine to help her, Ty continued packing the last of his things. Rolling up the HBC blanket and stuffing it into his duffle bag, he knew his dream of watching movies with them tomorrow would never materialize.

About to leave, he double-checked that he had everything. With his chest caving, he didn't know how to face her.

"See, you're doing what she wanted to avoid disappointment and more hurt." He felt sick.

Opening his door, he quietly closed it behind him. Shifting the suit-case a few feet away from Julia's room and setting the duffle bag beside it, his heart raced while standing there with the Christmas gift bags in one hand and the ornament box in the other. Knocking gently on the door, he hoped not to wake Sydney.

Within seconds, Julia greeted him with a big smile. "Hey, you are right...on...time?" she said, slowly pausing mid-sentence, seeing him fully dressed, holding gift bags and the ornament box. "Wait? What is going on?"

"Julia, please. Let me explain." Ty stated with great sincerity.

"You're leaving, aren't you?"

"The deal went through. Management wants me in Boston tonight to sign the contract. They've arranged a press conference at six o'clock to announce the agreement and my retirement."

Staying silent, trying to process what he said, Julia looked at him and tried to put on a brave face. "Well, that's great news. You got what you were hoping for."

"Please don't be mad. I will be back as soon as I can. I promise."

"I'm not mad. Please don't think that. I'm disappointed, yes, but not mad," Julia replied as those words stabbed through him like a knife, provoking a flood of guilt. "You have responsibilities and need to go. It's okay, really," Julia reassured in a solemn tone. Swinging the lock to hold her door open, she walked into the hall.

Putting the gift bags down, he said, "I boxed up the ornaments just in case...."

"In case you don't come back?" She finished his sentence.

"No, in case they need the tree down before I get here."

"Ty, if you are not returning, please tell me. It's okay." Her eyes glistened, and tears quickly developed.

"I promise I will return as soon as I can."

Julia reached out and wrapped her arms around his waist. Grasping her so tightly, holding her head against his chest, Julia heard his heart pounding a mile a minute, knowing this was far from easy for him. Looking up into his eyes, she found a tear drifting down his cheek, which he swiftly wiped away.

"I'm sorry I'm going to miss Christmas Eve dinner."

"You can't help it." She tried her best to diffuse the situation. "Of course, I want you to be here, but I know there is nothing we can do."

Ty slid his fingers behind her ears. Drifting each thumb across her cheeks, he leaned in and kissed her lips. The emotions attached were immeasurable, and their connection was unexpectedly stronger.

"I'll miss you," she said.

"I'll miss you more." He handed her the ornament box. "I'm sorry. I have to get going. My plane leaves Pearson at noon. Here, I have a couple of Christmas gifts for you and Syd."

"You didn't have to do that..." she muttered tearfully.

Seeing her cry, all Ty could do was say, "I know. I wanted to." Dabbing away her tears with his fingertips, he said, "I will call you throughout the day and let you know what's happening."

"Alright," she said, holding the ornament box and gift bags.

Turning around, he grabbed his suitcase and placed the duffle bag strap on his shoulder. While moving further down the hallway, he glanced behind him a few times to wave goodbye before approaching the elevators. Upon reaching out to press the button, he felt every ounce of his being wanting to return to her. Julia blew him a kiss and waved. Raising a confident, steady hand, lowering it to cover his heart, he saw her smile, making it a little easier.

Pressing the lobby button, he mumbled, "Why are you leaving? Seriously, why? After so many years of sacrifice, this is how you want it to be. Really?"

The doors opened on the main floor shortly after. Ty hoped Bryce wasn't at the Concierge desk when he checked out. That would be the worst conversation ever.

Reaching the foyer, he noticed Nick was there. Thankfully, Bryce wasn't.

"Good morning, Mr. Reynolds?" Confused, Nick saw his suitcase and knew what was happening. "You're leaving us so soon?"

"Unfortunately. I have to head back to Boston to handle some business. I'm checking out. Can you print my statement?"

"Yes, I can do that, but Mr. Reynolds, it's Christmas Eve. Are you sure you can't stay?"

Sighing, knowing the answer, Ty replied, "I wish I could, but this can't wait."

"If I may. It seems like this is not the only thing that can't wait..." he mumbled under his breath, hoping the baseball player heard him.

"What was that?" Ty questioned.

"Sorry, Sir. It's none of my business."

"Look, Nick. I feel bad enough. It's my last year to play ball, then...."

"Then, indeed, Sir?"

Nick got his keys from the valet cupboard. He handed them over with the printed statement and said, "Good Luck, Mr. Reynolds. Safe travels. Merry Christmas."

"Yeah, Merry Christmas."

Knowing that Nick believed he was making a mistake, Ty still took the keys and walked out. Getting into his truck parked close to the banquet entrance, he got in on the driver's side and started the engine. Little did he know, someone was watching him.

49

December 24th

Heartbroken

Hovering by the window high above the entrance, Julia watched Ty walk out to the vehicle. The glass felt cold under her trembling fingers as if mirroring the chill settling in her chest. Every part of her begged for him to stop, to glance back, to reconsider. She envisioned him changing his mind - turning on a dime, running upstairs, and declaring he couldn't leave. But the SUV's engine rumbled to life. With praying hands resting upon her lips, almost breathless, she watched him slowly pull away and drive down the lane. Her chest heaved, and tears flowed the further he got. Losing sight of him when he passed a dense patch of trees, she placed her hand on the window, feeling her heart breaking into pieces. In disbelief, she stayed there for a moment, frozen in place, until the overwhelming ache forced her to move.

Careful not to wake Sydney, Julia slipped into the bathroom, locking the door behind her. Grabbing a thick white towel, she buried her face in its softness, her body shaking with sobs. The dam she had held back broke, releasing a torrent of emotions: anger, hurt, disappointment, and love—so much love. She let herself crumble until the echo of her crying became too much to bear.

"Get it together," she whispered harshly, forcing her breathing to steady. The sting of reality cut deep. No amount of tears could change what had happened, and the staff would be arriving in hours to celebrate. She dabbed her swollen eyes and inhaled deeply, summoning every ounce of strength she had.

"You'll be okay," she told herself, her voice shaky but firm. No stranger to being alone, she refocused and forcefully dried her tears before taking a deep breath. "There is so much to do," she said.

Back in the kitchen, the silence felt heavier than it had before. Julia pulled out her checklist and began methodically preparing the turkey stuffing, trying to focus on the small tasks at hand. Her mind, however, wandered to a version of today that would never come true.

Trying to force the thought away, it clung to her stubbornly and wouldn't let go. Amidst it all, the question remained - how would she break the news to Sydney? While the task loomed in her mind, her stomach twisted at the thought of her daughter's heartbreak. Julia glanced at her room door, hoping the little girl would sleep just a bit longer. She needed time to rehearse, to find the words that might soften the blow. Her hand paused mid-stir.

"Focus, Julia," she whispered to herself, her voice firmer this time. "You can do this."

With a checklist in hand, she moved through the motions, each task a delicate attempt to stitch together the fragments of her broken world. As the oven warmed and the scent of spices wrapped around her, the thought crept in—how different today might have been with him here, laughing, talking, and turning ordinary moments into cherished memories.

50

Christmas Eve

Change of Plans

Driving further and further away from the hotel, linking up with the main road, Ty believed, without a doubt, that his trip to Carling was probably the best thing that had ever happened to him. After living alone for so many years, he could, for once in his life, tangibly see a future with someone.

Everything a baseball analogy, he muttered, "How can you let this game slip away without taking your swing at bat? Especially when you've waited an eternity to find her?" He gripped the steering wheel so tightly that his knuckles turned white. His fist angrily slammed against the center console. With his mind reeling, Ty suddenly thought of a solution.

Calling Matt, he listened to it ring again and again. "Come on, man. Pick up the phone," he said, overly frustrated. About to hang up, he suddenly heard the guy's voice whispering on the other line.

"Hey, Ty? Is everything okay?"

"I'm sorry, but can you do me a favor? You know I wouldn't ask unless it was important."

The guy didn't hesitate. "Sure. Anything. What do you need?"

"Can you book me a flight from Boston to Toronto tonight? I want to get this thing done and make it back to the Carling as soon as possible."

"I'll do my best, but I can't guarantee it. It's Christmas Eve. It's the busiest travel day of the year."

"Please try. That's all I ask. I'm sure there has to be one seat on one flight somewhere."

"Give me a minute. I'll call you back," Matt confirmed.

"Thanks. Appreciate that."

Turning onto the main highway, continuing to beat himself up verbally, Ty held onto hope that he would be able to return before midnight. Realizing he'd never been great at relationships, mostly because he never fully committed to anyone - not even his family, now, for the first time, he felt differently on so many levels. It wasn't just guilt—it was a clarity that struck him like lightning. His priorities had shifted, and for once, he couldn't ignore it. The realization brought an unexpected smile to his face, but it vanished as quickly as it came when his phone rang, interrupting his thoughts.

Seeing Matt's name flash on the screen, he snatched it up, his voice tense. "Hey. Please tell me you have good news."

Matt hesitated, then sighed. "Sorry, man. Not a single seat is available until after Boxing Day. I checked every airline."

The weight of those words sank into Ty's chest, crushing the flicker of hope he'd been clinging to. He stayed silent for a beat, the frustration simmering under his skin. Finally, he exhaled sharply, forcing himself to keep his tone even.

"It's okay. You tried. I'm on the road. Gotta go. I'll call you later." He hung up before Matt could respond, tossing the phone onto the passenger seat in a burst of anger.

For a moment, the disappointment clawed at him. But Ty wasn't the kind of man to sit in defeat for long. An idea sparked, and without hesitation, he grabbed his phone again. This time, he dialed Michael, his notoriously difficult agent.

When the man picked up, Ty didn't wait for pleasantries. His voice was firm, almost commanding. "Mike, it's Ty. Listen to me carefully because I'm not in the mood to argue. This is what's gonna go down..."

His tone was sharp and unyielding, every word cutting through the line with authority. The frustration burning in his chest ignited something deeper—a relentless determination. Failure wasn't an option. Not tonight. Not when everything that mattered was on the line.

51

December 24th

Christmas Eve

With the turkey stuffed and ready for the oven, Julia heard Sydney stirring in her room. Knowing she had to tell her about Ty, she got a sinking feeling in her stomach. When the little girl's door opened, she still looked half asleep.

"Sorry, Sweetie. Did I wake you?"

"No. I woke up on my own. But I'm still tired."

"Well, we've had a few busy days. Maybe all the activity is catching up."

"Yeah, but it's been so much fun." Rounding the island in the kitchen, she walked over to get a morning hug before finding a seat on a bar stool. Looking around the room, she seemed confused. "Where is Ty? Wasn't he supposed to help this morning? Did he sleep in?"

Julia leaned across the countertop and offered her hands for Sydney to take hold. "Umm, I have to tell you something."

"What? What is it? Is something wrong?"

"Syd, he had to return to Boston. Work called last night and said he had to go home to sign some paperwork."

"Ty left without saying goodbye?" she mumbled, slumping down in the chair and lowering her gaze sorrowfully.

"It was quite early. You were still sleeping. We didn't want to wake you."

"He left us on Christmas Eve?" The disappointment on her face was heartbreaking.

"I know. Please don't be angry. He felt so bad."

Getting up from the chair, Sydney moped back to her room and did not say a word. Julia watched her door swing shut behind her.

Saddened by the little girl's reaction, she knew Ty would have stayed if he could. Beyond his control, a part of her wondered if he would return to them or if being in Boston meant they would be out of sight and out of mind.

Continuing with the list of things she needed to accomplish, Julia slipped her red apron over her head and tied the belt around her waist. She took a deep breath and said, "Okay, casserole time."

Amid side dishes two and three, Julia took a quick break to check her phone, wondering if he may have texted her even though she didn't hear any notifications. With nothing to report, she assumed he was probably battling chaotic holiday airport travelers, line-ups, and delays.

As she continued cooking, finishing everything she needed for their Christmas Eve feast that night, the smell of turkey, stuffing, and gravy invaded the hallway.

Once everything was almost ready, Sydney emerged to help her Mother mash the potatoes while Julia made the gravy. Pulling the green bean casserole, maple-glazed carrots, and freshly baked buns out of the oven, she felt exhausted. Happy with everything, they placed the food on warming plates provided by the hotel in a buffet-style line for the staff to come and help themselves.

Calling downstairs, running a bit late, Julia heard Nick pick up the phone. "Yes, Ms. Mariani. What can I do for you?"

"Dinner is ready for anyone wanting to join us," she confirmed with less excitement than in previous years.

"Thank you so much. I will pass that announcement along. This tradition of yours was a surprise to me. It's so very nice of you."

"I am so glad to hear that," she sighed.

"Is everything all right, Ma'am?" he asked, his tone laced with concern. The abrupt departure of their mystery guest told him otherwise.

"Uh, yes, everything is fine," she replied, her voice steady but unconvincing.

"Very well. I'll notify the staff. I'm sure they will start arriving shortly."

"Perfect. Thank you. See you soon."

Within a short time, she could hear voices coming down the hall. Julia tried not to think of the one person that was missing. Nine hours had passed, and he hadn't called or texted. Was she right? Were they now considered out of sight and out of mind?

Not wanting her sadness to distract her from spending time with those who mattered most, Julia fixed her current, less-than-happy smile before everyone arrived to dish out a plate. Each complimented her on how delicious everything looked. A majority decided to stay, eat, and socialize in Julia's suite. Hours before, some had discovered through the grapevine that Ty had left. Each of them knew she needed the company more than ever. Taking a seat to talk and reminisce about years past, everyone loved their tree decorations this year. But Julia and Sydney still kept their women's shelter donation a secret. They felt anonymously giving was always considered best.

Noticing Sydney plating her food, Julia watched her bypass everyone before returning to her room. The group could feel her sadness.

Worried, she knocked on her daughter's door. Finding Sydney sitting at her desk by the window, Julia whispered, "Why are you in here, Syd?"

"I don't know. I'm still tired."

"Sweetie, I want to apologize."

"For what?"

"Well, I let someone get too close to us. It's all my fault. I ruined our Christmas."

"No, you didn't, Mom. It's not your fault. I still can't believe he left. I didn't think he would." Exhaling, she added, "I guess it's not his fault either. It's a work thing. His job can't be easy."

"Yes, he has special responsibilities. So, I guess we have to be understanding. He's probably sad, too."

Moving her mashed potatoes around from left to right on the plate, Sydney said, "Go back to the party, Mom. I'll be there in a second."

"Okay. Remember, after dinner, we go downstairs to the big tree to hand out the ornaments. I believe there are a few things for you there also."

"Yes, I know."

Tapping her shoulder, hating that she was hurting, Julia kissed her forehead before leaving the room.

When her Mother had gone, Sydney looked out the window. There in front of her was a bright star trying to peek through the clouds moving in. Snow was beginning to fall, which they'd expected. Lake effect squalls were a frequent occurrence.

A knock came on her door. "Come in?" she said, seeing Nick peek inside. Remaining in the doorway, not crossing the threshold, he said, "Merry Christmas, Sydney."

"Merry Christmas, Nick."

"Everything okay?"

"Yeah..." she hesitated. "Actually, no, not really."

"What's wrong?"

"Well, you probably heard that Ty left early this morning. He didn't say goodbye."

"Yes, I know."

"You do?"

"I spoke to him. He felt terrible about leaving but believes he didn't have a choice."

"He felt bad?"

"Yes, he never wanted to hurt you and your Mom."

"Really?" A glimmer appeared on her face.

"Absolutely," Nick said with a comforting smile. Looking out the window, he pointed to that star shining brightly in the night sky. "Well, would you look at that? It's the Christmas wishing star."

"I'm too old to believe in wishes," Sydney mumbled.

"Well, I'm sorry to hear that. You know, it's worked for me in the past. Just saying." With his plate of food in hand, he mentioned, "I might not see you downstairs at the Christmas tree later. I've got a few things to do, so Merry Christmas, Sydney Mariani."

Turning around to answer him, she said, "Merry Christmas to you too..." but found he had already gone.

Seeing the star twinkling brightly, Sydney closed her eyes. Making a wish, she hoped it would come true with all her heart. That is when she realized something. Wheeling over the craft trolley, she turned on all the lights in her room and quickly got busy, hoping she had enough time to finish it all.

52

December 24th

Christmas Eve

While mingling with her guests, Julia found Bryce in the hallway. Having brought a baggage cart upstairs, he knew he could only stay a short time before heading out to see his sister Betty and spend Christmas Eve with her.

Offering him a hug, she said, "Come on in. Grab a plate."

She sneakily pointed into her bedroom at the many bags filled with gifts he was to take with him this year.

Bryce nodded, not saying a word. He kept the secret between them. Dishing out a small plate, he hoped to save room for his sister's meal later that evening. Joyfully joining the rest of the staff gathered around, the volume in the crowd went up a few octaves.

Catching Julia staring out the window, Bryce whispered, "I heard about Ty."

"Yes. I hope he got to Boston on time."

He didn't respond. Julia could tell he was somewhat annoyed by what the baseball player did.

"It's not his fault. He didn't have a choice," she said, almost reading his mind.

"Oh, he had a choice. He just made the wrong one."

"Don't be angry with him. It was a tough decision to make."

"Was it?"

"Bryce, don't."

The older gentleman sighed. "I'm just looking out for you two. That's all. I don't ever want to see you sad."

"I know." Julia reached her arms around his neck to hug him.

"It will be okay, dear."

"Yes. I think so, too. What is meant to be will be."

"Agreed."

After Bryce finished his food, Julia helped him load the bags onto the trolley. She then walked to Sydney's room to tell her he was leaving. Joining the two of them in the hallway, she hugged the man they loved so much.

"Say Merry Christmas to Betty for us," Julia mentioned. "We will stop by at the end of next week to drop off the ornament boxes."

"Will do," he replied, clinging to them tightly. "Thank you for dinner. Merry Christmas. I'll see you soon."

Watching the gifts roll down the hall to the elevator, Bryce waved while rounding the corner as they returned to the party. Wondering how Ty was doing, Julia checked her phone, but he had not sent any messages. Sighing, she gathered the casserole dishes and placed the empty ones in the sink for a quick soak before loading them in the dishwasher.

While nibbling on a bit of turkey, Lisa and Jun walked over to her.

"We heard what happened this morning," Lisa stated, unsure what more to say.

"You and everyone else," Julia muttered.

"Yes, I'm sorry." Jun stood tall with his arms crossed in front of him. A bit angry at the baseball player, he hoped Julia would be okay.

"It's fine. I mean, I only knew him for a few days. When I think about that now, it seems rather irresponsible of me. Doesn't it? I'm a Mom. My priority is my daughter. Maybe there isn't room for anyone else in my life."

Stepping forward to offer a group hug, Julia could feel tears developing. She also knew that her last sentence wasn't entirely correct. She thought he would do anything for them. *Guess I was wrong*, Julia silently pondered.

Releasing her from their hugs, her friends backed away while everyone started to disperse.

"We will leave you to say your goodbyes to the others," Jun suggested. Turning to Lisa, he had his eyes on the kitchen. "Want to help me tidy up a little?"

"Yes," Lisa said. "Lead the way."

Starting to gather dishes, cups, and cutlery, he watched Lisa fill the sink with water to hand wash what she could.

Seeing them fluttering around, Julia found LeeAnn.

"How are you holding up, my dear?" she said, quite concerned.

Tired of everyone asking how she was, she gravitated to her loving tone. "I know deep down it's not his fault."

She hugged her tightly. "I know. It's…"

"Complicated," they both said simultaneously.

Clarence watched the two of them from across the room. It angered him to see Julia hurting, and he could only imagine how Sydney was coping.

Suddenly feeling overwhelmed by their guests, her focus mainly fixated on Ty leaving, Julia noticed Lisa washing dishes. "It's okay," she said to her. "Don't worry about all that. There's not much left to do. I can tidy up later. Besides, I will need something to keep my mind occupied." Turning to LeeAnn and Jun, she added, "Why don't you guys go ahead downstairs."

"Are you sure?" LeeAnn asked, getting a strange vibe. She figured she needed a minute alone.

Clarence joined his wife.

"We don't mind staying to help," Jun said, not wanting to leave her a mess to clean up.

"It's fine, really." Julia put on a brave face. "Go ahead. Syd and I will be there shortly."

When everyone had left and the room was quiet, Julia snuck a peek at her phone. Still, there was nothing.

Should I text to see if he is okay? She wondered. Not wanting to add to his stress, she opted against it.

Deciding to leave things alone, she went to get Sydney and found her room exploding with craft supplies.

"Sweetie..." Julia said, scanning the cluttered space. "What on earth happened here?"

Not turning around, she continued working diligently with the glue gun. "Umm, Mom, I'll explain later. Give me one more minute."

"Everyone is going downstairs to the tree now."

"Yes, yes. Almost done."

"Alright. I am just going to go and change. We can leave after that."

"I'll be ready," the girl replied.

Julia passed through her bedroom doors and walked over to the window. Pulling back the drapes, she remembered when Ty left that morning. The same ache returned to her heart. With tears developing, she knew there were feelings she hadn't felt in a very long time. Wiping the droplets away, she quickly went to fix her face and change clothes.

Emerging fifteen minutes later, she walked to the front door and asked, "Syd, are you ready?"

Greeted with a smile, her daughter said, "Yep! I am. Let's go." She confidently strolled past her and went out the door.

With a ten-step gap between them, her Mother wondered why she was in such a hurry to get downstairs.

"So, what were you working on, Syd?"

"Just a few last-minute gifts."

"Oh? For who?"

"For Ty, of course."

Julia assumed she wholeheartedly believed he would return to them. Knowing that he had not contacted her all day, she didn't know what to do. The last thing she wanted was to discourage her or give her false hope.

Upon reaching the main level, the elevator doors slid open. The Carling family erupted in a round of applause to salute their Christmas Eve chef. Used to them doing this yearly, Julia and Syd graciously moved toward the tall, magical Christmas tree inside the Lakes lounge and offered their annual speech just before nine o'clock.

"We would like to humbly thank you for sharing your Christmas Eve with us when I'm sure some of you have other places to be. Five years ago, Sydney and I lost everything. But most of you were there for us during that time. You welcomed us into this tight-knit Carling Family, and we are forever grateful for everything you've done to make our Christmases special ever since. We started this Christmas dinner and your ornament gifts to create new traditions that would help us through the most difficult time of year. Thank you for allowing us to do that." Tearing up, Julia hugged Sydney tightly and felt the love from the crowd. "Thank you for giving us a place to come home to for Christmas." Pausing a second, Julia added, "On that note, Sydney has something for each of you."

The tween began handing out everyone's gift bags, accompanied by a hug and a smile. "So that you know, Ty helped me this year. He did a good job, too," she said, sounding quite positive.

The guests engulfed the Marianis, offering many heartfelt thank yous before the evening came to a close. With gift bags in hand, having read their personalized, handwritten notes thanking them for all their support, they could see how the words touched each soul in that room. Proud of what they accomplished, smiling at her daughter, Julia walked over to her.

"I see you are much happier now."

"Everything is going to be okay, Mom. As long as we are together, nothing else matters."

She hugged her little girl tightly. "You are so right. I love you, Sweetie."

"Love you too. Merry Christmas!" Sydney replied.

"Merry Christmas, baby girl."

Following tradition, Clarence and LeeAnn joyfully broke into song and led the caroling by singing *Silent Night*. One by one, the rest of the group soon joined in.

About partway through the chorus, they heard the beautiful sounds of the piano accompanying them.

"Who is playing? It sounds wonderful," Julia commented to Lisa.

"Maybe someone has a hidden talent we don't know about?" she speculated. "I'm going to go see who it is."

"We're almost done here. We'll join you in a minute."

Julia and Sydney continued talking to the staff, handing out cookies and their ornaments. Hearing the most joyful music from the library, some people waved the rest of the group over. While they gathered around, a few strong voices sang along with the music before everyone enthusiastically applauded.

With nothing left under the tree but the presents left for them after their gift exchange, *Have Yourself a Merry Little Christmas* echoed through the halls on the main floor.

"Let's go join them, Syd," she said, grabbing hold of her daughter's hand.

As they walked into the library, they found Clarence and LeeAnn lovingly embracing each other while singing along. The closer they got, Julia noticed every guest who turned to look at them wore an elated expression. It warmed her heart to be embraced by everyone. Parting like the Red Sea, the crowd created a pathway to the front row, where Julia noticed the person at the piano.

She was sure it was Nick playing—until she caught sight of a man swaying rhythmically with every push of the pedals. His head bent down, his focus entirely on his fingers dancing across the keys. Snow dusted his hat, and he wore a dark winter jacket. Then, as he lifted his head slightly, the soft glow of the Christmas lights illuminated his face.

"Mom, my wish! It came true!" Sydney's voice broke through Julia's reverie. When she looked over, her Mother's eyes widened as tears welled up, and her breath caught in her throat. There he was—Ty, smiling up at her with a look that spoke of longing and joy.

While he finished the song, his movements were dramatic and expressive. There wasn't a dry eye in the room. Everyone who was there felt that the Mariani's reaction was the ultimate Christmas gift of all time. The group swayed gracefully in unison, the music filling the spacious library with an unprecedented amount of Christmas spirit.

Ending on a softer note, he stood. His gaze did not leave Julia's as he made his way towards her through the applause and cheers. The excitement in his step matched the intensity of his smile—he could hardly wait to hold her tightly.

Continuing where the baseball player had left off, LeeAnn took his place at the piano and began playing *Oh Christmas Tree.* Her husband, Clarence, was by her side, encouraging everyone to join in.

Ty took Julia and Sydney aside.

"What are you doing here?" Julia asked, pulling him into a tight hug. "I thought you were in Boston?"

With a smirk that was part joy, part triumph, Ty met her gaze. "Well, let's just say I solved that problem because I needed to rush back here to celebrate Christmas Eve with my family."

The little girl's eyes sparkled with tears as she watched the reunion unfold. "I can't believe you're here. I hoped and wished you would be," she whispered, squeezing his hand tightly.

Julia's heart swelled with emotion as she looked between Ty and Sydney. "How....?" she asked, her voice trembling with happiness. "How did you manage it?"

His smile softened, and he brushed a tear from Julia's cheek. "It's a long story," he replied simply, his voice thick with emotion. "Let's just say there was a change of plans."

"Really?" Julia whispered with a gushing heart.

"Yes." Kneeling in front of Sydney, he said, "I'm so sorry I disappointed you." He looked up at Julia. "I disappointed the both of you. I promise that will never happen again. I hope to be someone you can count on and trust."

Syd reached out and hugged his neck, revealing with enthusiasm, "I knew you'd come back!"

"I'm so happy to hear you say that." Standing up, Ty found Julia wiping tears from her cheeks.

He took hold of her hands. Looking into the blue eyes that have captivated him for days, he quietly whispered, "I am so sorry. Please, forgive me." About to respond, he stopped her. "Wait... Before you answer, I need to say something." Pausing, he added, "While driving to the city today, I felt that losing the World Series did not remotely compare to the sadness and regret I suffered - knowing I'd probably lost you."

Julia's body trembled as she nodded and cried.

"Over the past week, everything you did reminded me of what is most important in life. I can't change what happened today, but I'm here to make it right."

"Oh?"

"It seems my schedule has changed a little bit."

"What do you mean?"

"What are you doing for New Year's Eve?" Ty asked, pulling her closer and wrapping his arms around her waist.

"Oh, Mr. Reynolds. Are you asking me on a date?" she teased, her voice tinged with affection.

"It seems I am," he replied with a warm smile, his eyes locking with hers.

Elated, Lisa watched them while Jun quickly plucked a sprig of mistletoe from the tree and held it above their heads.

Aware of the playful tradition, Ty's grin widened. "Merry Christmas, Julia Mariani," he whispered before leaning in and brushing her lips in a sweet, lingering kiss. The sound of clapping and cheering filled the room, making the two blush as they melted into each other's arms.

Wondering if Sydney saw them, Julia looked left, then right, but did not see her nearby. "Where did she go? Where is Sydney?"

"Don't worry," Jun said, "I'll find her."

The tall young man left the library to search for their smallest hotel guest. Unbeknownst to him, she had strolled into the lobby to thank Nick for the advice on the wishing star, realizing he was right about holding onto hope. Not finding him there, she searched the back offices.

Jun stood in the center of the main foyer. Prepared to head outside, suddenly, he saw the little girl emerge from the office, still frantically checking every nook and cranny.

He asked her, "Who are you looking for, Syd?"

"I'm looking for Nick. I need to thank him for something."

"Who's Nick?" Jun was confused. "Nobody by that name works here."

Sydney paused, her brow furrowing in thought. It all clicked into place. The man always appeared briefly, only to disappear again. He had a twinkle in his eye when he talked to her, and his cheeks were always rosy. Without another word, she bolted towards the front doors.

"Hey! Where are you going?" Jun called after her.

"I'll be right back! One minute!" The little girl shouted halfway outside.

Quickly running past the bonfire, she tilted her head back, gazing up at the night sky dotted with stars. A few snowflakes drifted down, melting on her nose. A smile tugged at her lips.

Syd knew where Nick was at this very moment, but he wasn't at the Carling Hotel. As a streak of light flashed across the horizon, her eyes widened in realization. "Thank you, Santa," she whispered, her voice trembling with excitement.

The moment felt magical. She couldn't have asked for a better gift. Her heart filled with joy, knowing that this night had turned out exactly as she had hoped. Unable to shake the thought that maybe her Dad and brother had secretly told Santa to bring Ty back to them, a warm feeling enveloped her—a mixture of love and gratitude. Standing there, she knew somehow that this Christmas miracle was their doing. "I miss you, Daddy. Benny. Merry Christmas."

53

December 24th

Christmas Eve

Returning inside, the young girl approached where everyone had gathered. Finding her Mother and Ty still wrapped in each other's arms, their group slowly started to disperse. Many needed to make their way to family and friends before midnight. Julia was grateful for the time they had.

Clarence and LeeAnn approached hand in hand. "Goodnight, you two," LeeAnn winked, her husband getting down on one knee. "Sweet dreams, Sydney."

She hugged him tightly. "I will. You too. Merry Christmas."

LeeAnn smiled, "Merry Christmas, Sweetie pie."

Wishing everyone safe travels and thanking them for a memorable evening, Julia, Sydney, and Ty were soon left alone.

About to go back upstairs, Julia recapped the makings of their day. "How did you make it back here so quickly?" she asked him.

Lowering his head, Ty admitted, "I called my agent and told him to arrange the signing and press announcement at TSN HQ in Toronto because I wasn't flying to Boston. Upper management agreed and quickly pulled together a video call earlier in the day. Didn't you see it on the news?"

"No, I didn't have the TV on."

"Well, I gave them four hours of my time and signed the contract. Then I got back in the truck and drove back here. Might have made it in time for dinner if the weather wasn't so bad."

"If you're hungry, there's plenty of leftovers, right Mom?" Sydney asked, assuming that would be the case.

"Yes, there's plenty left."

"I would love some. Lead the way." As they walked, he remembered he needed to check in again at the front desk. "Oh, wait, I need to get a key for my room. You go ahead. I'll be there shortly."

Approaching the main reception, Ty noticed an unfamiliar face behind the counter. The man's round gold glasses glinted as he looked up. "Good evening, Sir. What can I do for you?"

He read his name tag. "Yeah, good evening, David. My name's Ty Reynolds. I checked out of room 1445 this morning. I want to book that same room from now until January 3rd," Ty said, scanning the foyer and searching for any sign of Nick.

"Not a problem, Sir. Here's your access card. I can use the same information already on file. Enjoy your stay," David replied.

"Thanks." Before departing, he asked, "Hey, have you seen the front desk guy named Nick?"

"Sorry, Sir. I usually work the night shift. Just got back from visiting my Mother in the hospital. Not sure who they had to cover for me. I don't know of any relief staff named Nick, though."

Thinking that to be strange, Ty squinted before double-tapping his hand on the counter. "That's okay. Sorry to hear about your Mother. I hope she is doing well."

"Thank you. She is."

"Happy to hear." Leaving him, he walked towards the piano, where he had stashed his suitcase and duffle bag behind the pool table. As he strolled past the cathedral windows, the moon's bright light poured through, a sudden comfort in an unexpected place. It felt like home.

Waiting for the elevator, he could hardly wait to change clothes and spend what remained of Christmas Eve with Julia and Sydney.

54

December 24th

Christmas Eve

On his way down the hall, thankful to be back, Ty tapped his access card on the reader, unlocked his door, and rolled his suitcase inside. Tossing the duffle bag on the bed, he changed into more comfortable clothes versus staying in his dress shirt and jeans.

Walking straight across the hall in joggers and a long-sleeved Henley, he noticed Julia's door propped open.

"Hello?" he said on his way inside.

Julia was in the kitchen making him a plate. "So, on a scale of one to ten, how hungry are you? Ten would constitute - famished."

He laughed. "Definitely a ten. I have not had anything to eat all day, come to think of it."

She handed him the warm dinner right out of the microwave. Heaping with turkey, stuffing, mashed potatoes, and veggies, topped with gravy, she even sprinkled a bit of parsley on top for an added touch. Julia sat down across from him at the table.

"Wow, this is amazing. It's been a while since I've had a home-cooked turkey dinner. Thank you."

"You're welcome. I'm glad you like it." She watched as he admired the Christmas tree while he ate. "Were the Sox mad that you changed their plans?"

"In the beginning, they weren't happy. Eventually, we came to a mutual agreement. They got what they wanted, and so did I. A win-win situation."

"I'm glad things worked out." Pausing, she asked, "But, there's something I... umm...I need to know. Why didn't you message me?"

Ty looked up from across the table. "I'm so sorry. I know. It's not that I didn't think about it because I did. I figured you'd be busy hosting everyone and cooking on top of that. I didn't want to disrupt things here. In a way, I also wanted to surprise you both. I hope you understand."

She nodded. "I was worried about you."

"You were?"

"Then I thought you got busy, and Syd and I suddenly were out of sight and out of mind."

Met by a sad expression on her face, Ty reached his hand across the table and grasped hold of hers. "Don't ever think that. Since we met, you've been on my mind - day and night. All I wanted was to get the job done and return to you as fast as possible."

Happy to hear such sincerity in his voice; it helped ease Julia's mind.

When Ty got up from the table to wash off his plate and put it in the dishwasher, he asked, "Hey, where's Syd?"

"She's in her room working on a special project. She said not to disturb her."

He laughed. "Sounds serious."

"Apparently, so."

"Care to sit and watch a movie with me? I'm sure *It's a Wonderful Life* is on somewhere. Maybe even *Miracle on 34th Street*. It's usually on Christmas Eve and Christmas Day."

"Sure, I'd like that." Before moving to the sofa, she asked, "Wine?"

"Yes. It's been a stressful few hours. Want me to order a bottle from downstairs?"

"No, no. I have a few more here," she chuckled.

"You do?"

She nodded and giggled. "Don't think badly of me."

"I would never," he replied playfully.

"Red or white?" Julia pointed to the white chilling in the fridge versus the red on the counter.

"Doesn't matter to me."

She grabbed the Liberty School bottle. "Think I'm in the mood for red."

"Red it is. Do you need me to open it for you?"

Handing him the opener, Ty pulled the cork with a pop. After pouring the first glass, he passed it to Julia and poured another for himself. Raising it between them, he said, "To our Christmas in Carling. Coming here has changed my life." Lost in her eyes, he rephrased what he had just said, "*You* - have changed my life."

Unable to speak, almost spellbound by his words, she couldn't help but get emotional.

Setting her wine glass on the counter beside his, he took a napkin and dried her tears.

"I've waited a lifetime for you," he said.

Inching closer, placing both hands along the hollows of Julia's neck, he slipped them behind her ears. Cradling her face in his hands, he kissed her forehead sweetly before brushing his cheek alongside hers. The love he felt was immeasurable. He had found the missing piece to fill the void – something he never thought possible. But he knew she needed more time. As his lips touched hers, their hearts beat rapidly. Believing Julia may get overwhelmed, he paid attention to the signals she gave - not wanting to make her feel uncomfortable. But this time, he noticed she did not pull back.

"I missed you," he said quietly.

"I missed you too," she said, raising her arms to wrap them around his neck. Pulling him in close, Julia held on while they swayed back and forth.

Mindful of Sydney in the other room, happy to share a minute alone, no matter how long or short, Ty respectfully gave Julia a little space. The timing couldn't have been better since Sydney appeared at that very moment.

Shocked to see her, Julia tried to compose herself but felt flustered. "Hi, Syd. What would you like, Sweetie?"

"Do we have any more of those sugar cookies?"

"Yes, we certainly do. They're in the cookie box."

Lifting the lid off the container for her, Sydney grabbed a handful.

Her Mother stopped her and said, "Only three. It's almost bedtime."

"I have a couple of more things to finish. Make sure you don't come in. It's a secret project."

"A secret, huh?" Ty repeated. "Who is the project for?"

"You," she said point blank.

"Me? Really?" Taken aback, he paused. "Wow. Thank you. I look forward to seeing it."

Smiling, she said, "Well, break's over. Gotta get back to work." The girl instantly disappeared into her room and closed her door.

"We couldn't have timed that better," he laughed.

She giggled. "Yes. That may have made for an awkward moment."

Ty's face brightened.

"What?" she asked, seeing him look her way strangely.

"Where did you come from, Julia Mariani?"

With a smile to light the room, she said, "I've been right here waiting."

"And I finally found you."

"You certainly did." Looking up at him, she was happy to hear that.

"Want to watch a movie now?"

"Sure."

"Where are the HBC blankets we bought?" he searched the room.

She pointed. "Under the tree."

He carefully removed the items from their boxes, savoring the quiet moment he'd pictured many times in his mind. Joining her on the couch, he settled into the corner, drawing her close as she instinctively leaned against him. Her warmth and the steady rhythm of her breathing felt like the perfect antidote to the whirlwind of the day.

The movie they had hoped to watch was sadly halfway over.

She sighed softly, a touch of disappointment flickering across her face, but the moment felt too cozy, too right, to let it matter.

As the commercials came and went, their conversation deepened. Talks of the months ahead unfolded naturally, the rhythm of their words blending with the soft glow of the television. Together, they explored dreams and details, each word weaving a sense of togetherness, of building something solid and unshakable.

"During the off-season, I can fly to Toronto whenever I want. It's probably easier for me to visit you since Syd's in school and you've got work," he said thoughtfully.

"That would be best. But we're flexible on weekends," she replied, offering a reassuring smile.

He hesitated as his expression shifted slightly. "There's one thing I should mention... In the spring, I attend training camp. It's seven weeks with limited contact with family. That month and a half is pretty intense."

Her brow furrowed briefly, but she nodded. "We'll handle it. Seven weeks isn't forever."

He reached for her hand, his thumb tracing gentle circles against her skin. "Unfortunately, during the regular season, we can only visit during home games and, of course, when I play Toronto."

"Whatever happens," she said with quiet certainty, "We'll figure it out."

For a moment, his eyes dropped, and a solemn expression flashed across his face. "You know, I've never had any family in the stands. Not once."

Her heart ached at his admission. "Never?" she asked sensitively, her voice thick with emotion.

"Nope. All the guys have families who sit in the VIP box. I've never reserved that seating for anyone. When you visit, it will be the first time. Guess I'll have to inquire as to how it all works."

"Well, we'll be proud to watch you play."

He wrapped his arms around her tightly. "And I will be proud to say you both are there."

Throughout their conversation, Julia noticed Sydney had not come out of her room once. "Give me a second. I am going to check on her," she said, tapping his leg.

Leaving the sofa, Ty watched her walk to her daughter's door.

Opening it, Julia whispered, "Ty?"

He saw her waving at him. Getting up from the sofa, he went to see what was happening.

"Look." She pointed to Syd, who had fallen asleep at her desk.

Inching over quietly, careful not to make any noise, Julia got him to pick her up and put her in bed. Covering her, the little girl did not move at all. She was so tired.

"Night, sweetie pie," Julia whispered, removing a few strands of hair from Sydney's face. Turning off the light, they left the room.

"Well, on that note, I should probably leave you." Moving toward the door, he wished he could stay longer but knew it would be best to call it a night.

"We will see you in the morning," Julia said, hugging him casually.

"Yes." He looked into her eyes. "What time do you ladies usually wake up on Christmas morning?"

"Well, normally, we get up when our eyes open. It's the first day we sleep in."

"I like that idea. I don't do that often enough," he said, unable to stop staring into her blue eyes. Embracing her tightly, he tucked his chin against her neck.

"What is it?" she whispered.

He stayed silent. Longing for her, he contemplated things but knew it was too soon.

"Ty? Is everything okay?"

Leaning back, he found the look he'd always hoped to see from the one he'd spend the rest of his life with. Finally, after waiting for so long, she was standing right in front of him. He answered, "Everything is fine. Perfect, really."

Kissing her lovingly, he said, "How about you text me when you get up?"

"I will."

He pulled away quietly. "Have a good sleep."

"You too."

Holding her hand for as long as he could, Ty let go and walked across the hall. Opening his door, he waved. "Goodnight, Julia."

"Goodnight," she whispered before having to leave him.

Alone in his room, Ty got ready for bed. Slipping under the covers and repositioning his pillows, he couldn't help but think about the future and how the Marianis would fit into it. Suddenly, his life had meaning. Instead of dreading his retirement, he couldn't wait for it to begin. A new chapter was about to unfold. Now, he was more than just a baseball player. Today, he meant something to someone and would do whatever it took to build upon what they'd found.

55

December 25th

Christmas Day

Christmas morning, Ty woke to the wind blowing against the balcony door while ice crystals hit the window. Slowly opening his eyes, he was thankful to be waking up at the Carling Hotel versus the city of Boston. With the weather not being the greatest today, he figured it would be one to sit by the fireplace and get some rest. Thinking about his conversation with Julia last night, his life seemed surreal.

"I guess this is really happening." Ty sat up in bed and glanced out the window at the clouds drifting by. "Thank you for everything, Mom."

Despite being his last year playing ball, Ty felt okay with it. Settled. It helped knowing he now had something outside his career to focus all his energies on while transitioning out of the MLB. He thought about taking Julia and Sydney on incredible vacations, maybe even buying a place on the water in Carling to spend the summers on the lake. The possibilities were endless. Believing this year would be rough on them, he knew Julia and Sydney would do what they could to help him finish off his career on a high note. That meant everything. Finally, like his teammates, he would have someone to love waiting in the wings after the game. The newness of it all, somehow, seemed unfathomable. Ty remembered how they parted ways last night. Every ounce of him wanted to stay, but he knew this relationship was worth waiting for – no matter how long. He told himself to be patient.

Realizing that the ladies would be up soon, he slipped out of bed to complete thirty minutes of push-ups, sit-ups, planks, and squats before having a shower.

Unzipping his suitcase, he got dressed in the last of his clean clothes and wondered if they had laundry facilities onsite. Remembering he saw his gifts still under their tree, Ty realized they hadn't opened them yet. That sparked a heightened level of anticipation. He hoped they'd like what he bought them.

Amidst his thoughts, he heard his phone. It was Julia.

Good morning! Merry Christmas! How did you sleep? She texted.

He smiled before typing his reply. *I slept pretty well. Have been up for about an hour. Merry Christmas.*

Seeing her thinking bubbles on his screen gave him a feeling of warmth. When her reply popped up, he read it aloud. "I slept well, too, knowing you were across the hall." Those words pulled on his heart. "When are you coming over?" he read.

I'll be there in five minutes. He typed and pressed send.

Perfect. See you shortly.

Receiving a shy, blushy face in return, along with a pink heart, Ty took a deep breath. The sappy feeling was hard to describe. Somehow, her words just effortlessly melted his tough exterior. Funny enough, he was okay with it. In awe of these unfamiliar emotions, he noticed the snow squall had passed, and ribbons of morning light began cascading into the room. Pulling back the drapes, he found a picture-perfect postcard beautifully framed in front of him. The ice pellets had left behind a shimmering white blanket across the lakeside trail. In contrast, the open water looked cold and dark.

"I will never get tired of this view," he said before checking the time.

Five minutes had quickly dwindled. Ty grabbed his card key, ready to walk across the hall. Before going out the door, he glanced in the mirror and ran his hand through his damp hair, hoping it looked okay.

Happy with the reflection staring back, Ty believed the guy in the mirror seemed different. He lowered his head. Nervous about spending Christmas morning with someone special for the first time in his life, he opened the door and let it fall shut behind him. Standing outside Julia's suite, he gently knocked, wondering if Sydney was up too.

When the barrier between them swung open, Julia greeted him dressed in fleecy Christmas-themed pajamas. Walking in, it wasn't long before Sydney flew out of her room in a matching pair.

"Wow, twins. Love the PJs."

"Morning, Ty! Merry Christmas!" Sydney's giggle was almost infectious.

"Merry Christmas, Kiddo."

Turning to Julia, taken by her natural beauty, she had her blonde hair tied up in a messy bun, and the collar on her pajama shirt was standing on end to keep her neck warm.

"Good morning," Ty whispered while reaching out to her with open arms.

Willingly embracing him, she said, "Morning. Can I get you a cup of coffee?"

"I'd love one." He followed her to the kitchen.

Noticing they'd opened some gifts, Sydney quickly gathered a few packages from under the tree and set them on the coffee table.

"What are those?" he asked curiously, pointing to them.

Sydney laughed mischievously. "Oh, you'll see."

Handed a freshly brewed cup, Ty sat at one end of the sofa while Julia sat beside him.

Grabbing her blanket, the little girl cozied up in the armchair by the fireplace.

"So, did you have a restful night with the contract out of the way now?" Julia asked, wondering if the burden had lifted.

"Last night was the best sleep I've had in a while. Knowing my year is set in stone certainly helps."

"I bet. Can't imagine the stress you must have been under all this time."

"Yeah, it suffocates you until everything is said and done. Now, I can move forward and focus on the new year." Pausing a second, nervous about giving out his gifts, Ty glanced at Syd. "So... Is anyone interested in opening a present?"

"Who? Me?" Syd questioned, not expecting anything.

"Yeah, I got you something. First time I've shopped for a tween," Ty laughed, getting up from the sofa to grab the gift from under the tree.

Placing the heavy bag on the floor in front of her, the little girl turned to her Mom.

Julia nodded her head. "What do you say?"

"Thank you, Ty."

"You are very welcome. I hope you like it."

Surprised by its weight, she timidly sat on the edge of her chair. Piece by piece, she removed the tissue paper to discover what was inside. Lifting the gift out of the bag, wrapped in Christmas paper, Sydney carefully set it on the floor and began tearing it open. Finding a layer of bubble wrap underneath, she realized what it was.

Sydney shouted, "No! It's not. No way."

"What?" Julia asked, unable to see from the opposite side of the table.

Picking it up off the floor, Sydney said, "It's the tree sculpture from the gallery the other day."

"Oh, my goodness." Shocked, Julia watched Ty's reaction while her daughter gushed. It warmed her heart.

Running over to him with open arms, Sydney tearfully said, "Thank you. I will treasure it always."

"You're welcome. Merry Christmas, Kiddo. I knew you would love it, especially because it has sentimental meaning. That way, you can have a piece of Carling at home, too."

Staring at the sculpture, Sydney nodded, still in disbelief that it belonged to her.

He glanced her way with the biggest smile. "Okay, now for your Mom." Ty got up from the sofa and went over to the tree.

A little uncomfortable, unsure what to do or say, Julia watched Ty sit beside her. Fearfully taking the gift bag he'd presented, she said, "You didn't have to get me anything. When did you do all of this?"

"Well, truth be told, while you both were browsing the shops the other day, I took note of the few things you liked and had them delivered to the hotel while we were out."

Peering into the bag after removing the tissue paper, Julia saw a long box. Taking it out, unwrapping the paper, she lifted the lid to find a suede sachet bag. Pulling the drawstrings, tilting the opening into her hand, out slid the sparkling sterling silver necklace with the unique blue stone pendant. In awe of the beautiful piece of jewelry, Julia didn't know what to say. "Oh, Ty... It's beautiful. Thank you."

He inched closer and asked, "Do you want to put it on?"

"Yes, please." She reached up to lift her hair out of the way.

Opening the clasp, he secured it around her neck.

She placed her hand over the pendant before rolling her collar down to better display it. "How does it look?"

"Perfect," Ty replied.

"Looks great, Mom." The little girl beamed.

"Okay, two more." Ty grabbed the biggest box from under the tree.

Afraid of what could be inside, intimidated by its size, Syd and Julia glanced at each other and waited in anticipation.

"I suppose this is kind of for both of you," he said.

Sydney peeled the paper first, then Julia lifted the lid. Removing the tissue paper inside revealed the hand-crafted wooden salad bowl from the gallery.

About to cry, Julia leaned her head to one side and said, "Oh, my...."

Worried by Julia's hesitation, hoping it wasn't too much, he asked, "Did I get the wrong one?"

"No..." she whispered with glistening eyes. "I can't believe you did..."

He immediately interrupted, "I know. I wanted to."

With open arms, she reached out and hugged him tightly. "Thank you. You have given me something I've always wished for."

"What's in the last one?" Syd asked curiously.

"This is for you. I had a little help from Clarence," he hinted.

"Clarence?" Sydney was perplexed.

"Open it, Kiddo."

She pulled the tissue paper out of the bag. Peeking inside, she added to the suspense by scrunching her face with excitement. Reaching in, she pulled out a light grey leather Rawlings baseball glove with mint-colored accents and stitching.

"Wow, Syd! You're own ball glove." Julia was so excited for her.

"There's more," Ty said. He was thrilled by her reaction.

Dipping her hand in the bag, she pulled out three baseballs. "This is awesome!"

"Now, we can play catch."

Syd was awestruck. "Really? Truly?"

"Whenever you like."

She slipped the glove on her hand. "It's a perfect fit." Walking over to him, she hugged Ty. "Thank you ever so much." She took a seat between the two of them.

"Now, you will have to bring it to my games. Maybe you can catch a fly ball."

"I think I'll need to practice more before that." She sounded anxious.

"Don't worry. I'll help."

"Deal." Sydney stood up and handed him his first gift. "Okay, Okay. It's your turn now."

He took it from her and rested his back against the sofa beside Julia. Removing the tissue paper, he found a black leather braided bracelet with three beads.

"Wow. Did you make this for me?" he asked happily.

"Yes, I did. I know you travel a lot, so wherever you go, you have us with you." Pointing to the bracelet, she explained in great detail, "See. You are the dark blue bead, Mom is the pearl bead, and I am the pink bead. You can adjust it this way." She took hold of the bracelet and opened it enough for Ty to slip his hand through. Once on his wrist, she tightened it slightly. "Good. It fits." Proud of it, she said, "I made it last night after making my wish."

"What wish?" Ty hadn't heard what she'd done.

"Nick told me to make a wish on the Christmas star. I wished for you to return to Carling and spend the rest of the holidays with us. When I did that, I realized you would need something to open Christmas morning."

So touched by the gift, he said to Sydney, "I will wear it always - even when I play ball."

Excited to hear that, she turned to her Mom with bright eyes and whispered, "He likes it."

"Yes, he does. Great job, Syd."

Selecting another wrapped gift from the table, Sydney handed him another. "Okay. This one is breakable, so be careful."

Gently opening the wrapping paper, he found a glass ball ornament with snow inside and writing on the outside. He read the script. "Ty's 1st Christmas in Carling."

"Ornaments in our family often mark a place in time," Sydney explained. "Before we lost Dad and Ben, our tree used to tell a story of when my brother and I were young. It included all of our milestones in life – first steps, the first day of school, places we visited on every family vacation, special accomplishments - and stuff like that. So, over time, our tree got filled with precious memories, reminding us how thankful we are to be a family."

Julia wiped the tears from her face with her sleeve. Looking over at Ty, she nodded, agreeing with everything Sydney shared.

"I remembered you don't have the ornaments from your Mom, so I figured I would start a memory collection for you."

"This is amazing."

She handed him the next three. Ty opened one at a time. The first was an angel ornament made of white felt.

"It's an Angel on skis. I made this one as a reminder of how you saved me the other day. It was like you were my guardian angel."

Moved, Ty got up from the sofa and knelt to hug her while tears streamed down Julia's face.

"Thank you for being there for me."

"You're welcome. I would do it again in a heartbeat." Ty returned to his spot on the couch.

"Okay, two more," she said, thinking a moment. "One is a memory, and the other is more of a future ornament, but I'm sure it will be one of your best memories this year."

"Oh?" he replied. Wondering what it could be, he opened it to find a pair of skates and homemade tiki torches hanging together on a string. "Is this to remember our fire and ice excursion?"

"Yep." Sydney grasped her hands together and held them in front of her.

"Well, done. It's perfect. Thank you." Unwrapping the last gift, he found a gold trophy ornament. Looking at the plaque attached, Ty read the inscription, "Boston Red Sox, World Series Champions. Awesome! Do you think we'll win, Syd?"

"I know you will." She jumped up from her seat and raised her hands in the air. "You will also have your biggest fans cheering for you."

"Well, thank you both very, very much. I will treasure these always. Should we put them on your tree?"

"Yes, that's a great idea. Just let me find a place to put my sculpture in my room first. I'll be back. One minute." Sydney grunted while carefully lifting the heavy art piece off the coffee table.

When she left the room, Julia waited until she disappeared around the corner. Bringing her attention back to Ty, she smiled. "Umm..."

"I know what you are going to say. Please don't. Buying those gifts ignited this feeling inside me. The Christmas spirit, I suppose. Haven't felt that in a very long time."

Julia could see the sincerity all over his face. "Yes, but..."

"No, buts, remember." He looked at the necklace sitting proudly around her neck. "Do you like the necklace and bowl?"

"Yes. I love them." She placed her hand over the pendant and lowered her head. "I'm sorry I didn't buy you anything. I wasn't expecting this. I feel so bad."

"Julia... I don't think you fully understand what you've done for me. Being here with you and Sydney has given me the love of a family - something I never thought I'd experience in my lifetime. I hope you don't mind me saying that?"

"No, I'm happy to hear it." Glancing at Sydney's room, Julia soon refocused her sights on Ty. Wrapping her arms around his neck, feeling him encircling her waist, she hesitated before whispering, "There is one gift I can give you above all others."

Not sure what she meant, he stared into her blue eyes, almost afraid of what she might say.

"Ty Reynolds, I believe I have fully and completely fallen for you."

"You have?"

"Yes."

"That's good 'cause I fell hard for you the night we met," he quietly replied without skipping a beat.

Hearing Sydney rustling around in her room, the two parted before she walked over to the tree. "Okay, let's hang Ty's ornaments first, then it is pancake time."

"Pancakes?" Ty repeated.

"It's another one of our Christmas traditions. Homemade pancakes with Carling maple syrup."

"That sounds great. Can I help?"

Getting up from the sofa, Ty went with Sydney to hang the ornaments while Julia put on her red apron and got out the flour. Joining her in the kitchen, he put his finger in the mixing bowl and dabbed a bit of flour on Julia's nose.

"There," he said. "Perfect."

56 |

December 26th to 31st

Five Days of Fun

Over the week between Christmas and New Year's, the trio immersed themselves in Muskoka's snowy enchantment, crafting memories that felt like they were a world away from the hustle and bustle of everyday life. They filled their time with fun and exciting activities, each moment a shared adventure.

On Boxing Day, they went snowshoeing through the serene wooded trails. Safer than ski shoeing, the stillness enveloped them, broken only by the soft crunch of snow underfoot and the occasional laughter that carried on the crisp air. Every breath filled their lungs with the freshness of the season, bringing a rosy flush to their cheeks.

The landscape was a pristine blanket of snow, draping the trees in shimmering white and piling high in untouched drifts that glowed under the weak winter sunlight. The sight of deer meandering through the trees, undisturbed by their presence, only deepened the sense of peace and solitude.

Two days later, to add to their list of outdoor activities, Ty arranged a snowmobile adventure ride on the kilometers of uncrowded, groomed trails nearby. Meeting up with Sam Mask one afternoon, he gave them a guided tour through the forests around the Carling Hotel.

With Julia clinging to his waist, Ty drove their snowmobile while Sydney got to ride her own mini snowmachine. Staying close to their guide, Sam maintained a steady pace, making sure they all stayed safe, laughing and chatting as they drove through the winter wonderland.

Zipping along with a mix of determination and glee, they could hear Syd's voice carry above the hum of the engines. Constantly grinning from ear to ear, the girl maneuvered around every curve, feeling like a little adventurer in her own right.

"This is so cool!" she called out excitedly.

Ty and Julia watched with fond smiles.

When they returned to the Carling after two hours, Syd flipped up the shield on her helmet, full of energy.

"I want to do it again!" she declared. "Can we stay out longer?" Exchanging amused glances, Julia and Ty knew their outing was a hit, so they promised to arrange a second ride that week.

Bidding Sam goodbye, they each poured a hot chocolate from the fancy dispenser inside the foyer. Taking it up to their rooms, they planned to end the day with chili and buns delivered to Julia's suite after warming up and changing into cozy clothes for a more relaxing evening of board games, most sprawled across the coffee table, bringing out everyone's competitive spirit. Laughter flowed freely, lighting up the room and weaving their little trio even tighter together.

Once Sydney's energy waned, and she drifted off to sleep under a mountain of blankets, Ty gently lifted and carried her to bed. Julia followed, tucking Sydney in with a tender kiss on her forehead.

Finally, the two got some alone time, and the atmosphere shifted to a quieter intimacy. They sat by the fire, shoulders brushing, as they shared meaningful conversation and whispered to one another.

"So, where do you see us in a year?" Julia asked, her voice low and soft in the stillness of the room.

He believed her question had many working parts. "It's going to be a big one, I'm sure." Sounding contemplative, he drew a little closer to Julia. "But, honestly, I'm really enjoying this time with you here. I don't want to think too far ahead because that means I have to go back to my life in Boston." He paused, his eyes reflecting a level of sadness. "In January and February, I would like to make the most of the time we have before spring training starts. So, I figured I could maybe visit you in Toronto for a while, if that works for you?"

Julia's heart leaped. "I'd like that."

He smiled gently, reaching for her hand and squeezing it tenderly. "Looking further into the year, I want to finish my career on a high, hopefully winning the series in November. It's an experience I'd love to share with both of you." Tightening their embrace, he peered into the flames flickering in the fireplace. With careful consideration, he added, "This might be too soon, but I feel the need to put it out there..." Waiting a moment, hoping what he was about to say wouldn't scare her off, he blurted, "Once I retire, I'm yours if you want me."

Julia's eyes searched his. "I was hoping you'd say that."

Nodding firmly, he said, "There isn't a doubt in my mind. I want to be with you."

She heard a quiet certainty in his tone, a promise of a future that felt more real than ever before. Given no choice, she confessed, "I never thought I'd feel this again." Her voice was barely a whisper.

A smile tugged at his lips. "Well, you're not alone," he replied. "I never thought I'd be lucky enough to find someone like you, yet here you are, and you're everything I've been missing. All this time, I figured I'd be alone the rest of my life because I'd missed my chance to find someone special. But now, it feels like everything's falling into place."

Each of them longed for the other, a quiet ache growing deeper with every shared glance and unspoken word. But they took their time, not rushing, respecting the uncharted territory they were navigating. There was a mutual understanding that now was too soon; they needed more time to build upon their connection naturally. Until then, they found solace in the shared silence—a comfort of what was slowly unfolding.

As they chatted, Ty's tone lightened with enthusiasm as he began sharing stories about his teammates. "I can hardly wait for you to meet the guys."

She smiled.

"Xander is the health nut of the group. Before a big game, he swapped out all the coffee for a mushroom brand."

"Really?" she giggled. "Oh my."

"And then there's Eduardo. He's like a walking sports encyclopedia, but sometimes, when it comes to street sense, he's a little less knowledgeable," he snickered. "Ian's the practical joker—always pulling little pranks on and off the field. And then there's Mitch. He's the tech guru of the team, always up-to-date with the latest gadgets and apps, but if you talk to his wife, when it comes to fixing things around the house, he can only put together a shelf after consulting YouTube." Tightening his arms around her, giving Julia a loving squeeze, he knew they'd love her.

She tried to imagine the camaraderie Ty shared with these men, who were like a second family.

"Maybe you can visit me in Boston sometime. I live right downtown. Not far from Fenway. It's a nice building, but it doesn't feel like home. The only positive is the proximity to Boston Common, a beautiful park in the middle of the city. In the fall, the trees turn the most incredible colors, and in winter, the Frog Pond becomes an ice-skating rink. It's where I go to clear my head when I'm there. I usually jog early in the morning before the city wakes up. It's my favorite part of the day."

"I'm sure we can arrange that," Julia said, listening intently, picturing the life he'd built. A place she had yet to explore. His words painted a vivid image of the places and people that shaped him, drawing her into his world piece by piece. Their closeness grew with each shared detail, weaving another thread into the bond that was quickly becoming unbreakable.

As each evening came to an end, parting ways got harder. While wrapped in each other's arms, their kisses seemed to linger just a little longer.

Julia's heart ached as she watched him walk to his room across the hall. She knew she wanted more than the brief glimmers of connection they shared before saying goodnight. Yet, she was willing to wait and let the slow burn of anticipation continue to build between them.

She could see the same longing in his eyes, the same struggle to hold back, to savor every moment. They were both afraid of rushing and pushing too hard, too soon. The tension between them was a mix of desire and caution, of need and restraint. Having only known each other a short time easily warranted this slow progression.

When they woke the morning of December 30th, Julia and Sydney were excited to continue their week of fun activities. But today, they had a surprise for Ty. Something he would not expect.

Over breakfast at Cottages, Sydney couldn't keep the excitement from bubbling up as she revealed their plans.

Sitting around the small table in the cozy dining room, they each perused their menus, the morning light casting a soft glow through the windows. The space hummed with muted conversations and the clink of cutlery, noticing they no longer had the place to themselves since a handful of other guests had arrived with plans to ring in the New Year at the Carling Hotel. From the corner of her eye, she noticed the way he looked up, curiosity flickering across his face when she cleared her throat.

A smile tugged at her lips as she leaned forward, keeping her voice low, teasing. "So, we have a surprise for you today."

He glanced up from his menu. "A surprise?"

"Yep," she confirmed, smiling across the table at Sydney, who was still brimming with excitement. "A belated Christmas gift."

He tilted his head, eyes narrowing as he considered the possibilities. "What is it?"

Sydney's grin widened. "We're taking you dogsledding this afternoon. A real Muskoka winter experience."

His eyebrows shot up, clearly surprised. "Dogsledding?"

"Yep, something a little different from the usual," Julia said. "You seemed to be interested when we talked about it, so we thought it would be fun."

"That's awesome." Clearly touched by the gesture, he said sincerely, "Thank you."

Julia's hand found his across the table, fingers brushing in the dim light.

He looked down at them, a quiet contentment in his expression. "I'm really looking forward to it now."

Beaming, Syd had a hint of mischief in her eyes. "I bet your friends will be jealous when they hear about it."

His laugh was low, genuine. "Yeah, I can see the look on their faces now. Dogsledding in Muskoka. Definitely not what they'll expect."

Heading out later that day for their three-hour excursion was definitely the ultimate Canadian experience. Tackling the twenty-kilometer mushing journey took them through forested trails, guided by a team of American huskies.

Out of all the dogs, Sydney gravitated toward Presley and Elsa the most. They were lovely, high-energy pups with the kindest of eyes and their tails excitedly wagging as they harnessed up for the run.

As they set off, the crisp winter air stung their cheeks, but the thrill of the ride kept them warm.

Sydney and Julia sat in the sled while Ty took the helm. The dogs worked together in perfect harmony, pulling with a mix of strength and precision.

During a few breaks, Sydney lovingly petted the dogs and encouraged them while each playfully leaned into her touch with a happy whine as if thanking her for the attention.

The winter wonderland boasted snow-covered branches arched over the trail, casting dappled shadows in the soft light. The team of dogs led them into the dense wooded areas, where the only sounds were the crunch of snow beneath the sled and the excited barking of the huskies.

It was a peaceful, exhilarating experience, a reminder of how much joy one could find in nature.

By the time they finished the tour, Sydney was all smiles. "That was incredible," she said, still catching her breath. "Presley and Elsa were the best. I could have stayed out there all day."

Knowing this adventure had been the perfect cap to their week, Ty and Julia exchanged a look of shared amusement and happiness, feeling their connection growing stronger by the day.

As New Year's Eve approached, they couldn't shake the feeling of anticipation. The promise of a new year—a fresh start, a new baseball season, and a host of changes and challenges that were both thrilling and scary. It was a time of new beginnings, with the promise of dreams to chase and a life full of possibilities.

57

December 31st

New Year's Eve

The Carling Resort transformed into a hub of festive energy as New Year's Eve unfolded. Throughout the day, guests and locals alike continued to arrive in a flurry as they moved through the grand lobby adorned with sparkling garlands and twinkling lights. The warm hum of conversation, punctuated by bursts of laughter, filled the air while people checked in or gathered in small groups to marvel at the elegant decorations that seemed to capture the magic of the season.

Relaxing on the plush sofa in his suite, Ty let out a long breath and leaned back, staring at the frost-laced window. The crackling fire was a perfect contrast to the icy landscape beyond as he got caught up on the sports highlights.

Missing the girls, who had gone to the spa to indulge in a little pampering—he recalled Sydney being ecstatic about choosing her nail colors and Julia teasing him with a promise to return, looking even more stunning than usual.

Left with a quiet moment to himself, it gave him a chance to think. As much as he treasured this time together, the thought of leaving soon was bittersweet. His holiday escape had felt like a dream, but reality loomed closer with each passing hour. Ty hated the idea of returning to the relentless grind, where he'd be on the road more often than not. What weighed on him most was the thought of being away from Julia and Sydney for long stretches. He couldn't imagine missing Sydney's laughter echoing through the room or Julia's warmth beside him.

He leaned forward, elbows on his knees, and ran a hand through his hair. The year ahead would be tough—he knew that. Balancing his career and his growing bond with them would demand more than he'd ever given before. Yet, as daunting as it felt, there was no question in his mind that it was worth it.

The idea of their reunions brought a smile to his face. He pictured the little girl racing toward him at an airport, her eyes bright with excitement, and Julia following with that soft, knowing smile she always reserved just for him. Those moments would make every mile, every long night apart, bearable.

"Absence makes the heart grow fonder," he said, the old saying feeling unexpectedly true. While the thought of being apart tugged at his heart, it also deepened his resolve. He'd find a way to make it work—for Julia, for Sydney, and for the life he wanted to build with them.

Resting his eyes, believing tonight was the start of a year of new beginnings, he was determined to cherish every second left of this trip.

That night, as they prepared for the ball, Ty and the girls parted ways to get dressed. Putting on his suit and carefully adjusting his tie, he took a moment to glance at himself in the mirror. Excited and nervous—he could hardly wait to see Julia and Sydney all glammed up.

At six thirty, right on schedule, he crossed the hall and knocked on the door. Within seconds, it swung open, and there they stood— elegantly dressed and radiant, their smiles lighting up the evening before they even stepped out.

"Wow, you both look amazing," he said, his voice full of admiration. Grinning, Ty stepped back slightly to get a better view of Sydney. "Your dress is so pretty," he said warmly, his eyes lighting up as she twirled happily. "It really suits you."

Sydney blushed, her cheeks tinged with a soft pink as she spun gracefully in the midi platinum taffeta gown. "Thanks, Ty," she replied, a shy smile curling at the corners of her lips. "I love it, too."

His eyes then locked on Julia, wearing an elegant, floor-length gown in deep sapphire blue, its flowing fabric catching the light with every movement. Holding his hand out to her, he gave the woman a twirl as her eyes sparkled. Noticing his necklace adding to the ensemble, he slipped his hand around her waist to pull her in a little closer. Whispering in her ear, he said, "You look stunning."

Julia blushed slightly, a sweet smile crossing her lips. "Thank you. You look pretty handsome yourself," she replied with a playful nudge.

Glad he'd shipped in his tailored black suit from Boston that week, he couldn't take his eyes off the pretty woman.

Sydney joined their banter. "Can we go now?"

He chuckled and took Julia's hand. "Yes, we certainly can," he said, giving her a reassuring squeeze as she stood by his side, ready to join the party.

While walking through the lobby, crowds of people turned their way, their faces lighting up with pleasant smiles and a touch of envy in their eyes.

Upon entering the ballroom, the opulent space was meticulously arranged for the celebration, with round tables draped in crisp white linens, all topped with glittering centerpieces of silver and gold. It looked magical. Chandeliers cast a soft, warm light over the room, reflecting off the crystal glasses and polished silverware. A live band performed in one corner, their music a lively mix of jazz standards and modern hits, setting the perfect tone for the night.

Dressed to impress, the women in shimmering evening gowns and men in sharp tuxedos and tailored suits sparked a glamourous and joyful atmosphere. Friends and strangers alike mingled, sharing toasts and stories as waitstaff circulated with trays of champagne flutes and bite-sized hors d'oeuvres before the dinner service began.

Sydney quickly found her group of friends, who accompanied their families to this annual tradition. The children laughed and played in their own little world, their excitement contagious as they reveled in the special occasion.

Meanwhile, Julia and Ty blended effortlessly into the sophisticated crowd. His pride was evident in the way he reached for her hand or smiled at her with quiet affection. He was clearly delighted to have her on his arm.

Julia noticed his posture straightening just a little bit more than usual as the band began a slow waltz.

He looked at her with a playful grin. "May I have this dance?" he asked, his voice tinged with charm.

"Absolutely," she replied softly, ready to pull him in close.

Under the glow of the chandeliers, they moved together in perfect sync, her dress sweeping the floor as he guided her with steady confidence. The world around them seemed to blur, but their connection grew stronger with every step and every shared glance.

"This feels like something out of a dream," Julia murmured as Ty spun her gently, her cheeks flushed with happiness.

"The perfect start to a new year," he said.

The hours passed in a whirl of music, laughter, and delicious food from the gourmet buffet, which boasted everything from fresh seafood to decadent desserts.

Sydney popped in occasionally, bounding over to Julia and Ty with stories of the games she and her friends had played, only to be coaxed back to her little group for another round of fun.

As midnight approached, the excitement in the room grew. Everyone gathered together for the final countdown with champagne glasses filled and noisemakers in hand. Soon, the band struck up a lively tune to usher in the new year.

Julia and Ty stood close together, Sydney tucked between them, her eyes wide with anticipation when the countdown began, the guests shouting in unison: "Ten... nine... eight..."

Julia looked up at Ty, her heart full as the moment stretched out.

"Three... two... one... Happy New Year!"

The room erupted in cheers, confetti raining down as everyone clinked glasses and embraced. Covering Sydney's eyes, Ty turned to Julia, his gaze warm and intent as he kissed her softly. The world seemed to fall away in that brief but perfect moment.

Breaking free, peeking through his fingers, Syd found her Mother beaming.

Happy beyond words, the little girl jumped up and down beside them, giggling as she waved a noisemaker. Hugging and kissing her Mom, she declared, "Best New Year's ever!" Her enthusiasm lit up the room.

Lifting the girl in his arms, he exchanged a loving look with Julia. "I'd have to agree," he said, feeling them becoming a family.

Calling it a night, they left the ballroom, their feet sore from hours of dancing and standing. Having waited their turn for an empty elevator, they made their way upstairs as exhaustion slowly crept in.

"We are just going to change," Julia said upon reaching their door.

"I'll do the same." Hoping the night wasn't over, he asked, "Is it okay if I come by to say goodnight?"

Without hesitation, she nodded. "I'd like that."

"Okay, see you shortly."

Parting ways to change clothes and get ready for bed, Ty waited fifteen minutes before going across the hall. Knocking, Julia opened it.

Now wearing her Christmas pajamas, she said, "Come in. I'm just going to say goodnight to Syd."

Walking into her room, they found the young girl already tucked in bed, snoring with covers up to her neck.

Julia picked up her dress from the chair, carefully smoothing the fabric before placing it on its hanger. Taking it with her as they left the room, she walked to hers and hung it neatly in the closet. Returning to Ty, who was waiting on the sofa, she let out a contented sigh and collapsed beside him, cuddling into his warmth.

"Did you have fun?" he asked softly, wrapping his arm around her and pulling her closer.

"Yes," she murmured with a smile, her head resting against his chest. "And you?"

Kissing her temple, he replied, "I've never had a New Year's quite like this. It was a first for me."

"How so?" she asked, tilting her head and looking up at him, her curiosity piqued.

"Because I was with you," he said simply, his voice full of sincerity.

Heart swelling affectionately, she smiled upon hearing that.

Lost in her eyes, he traced his fingertip along her brow, brushing a stray strand of hair from her face. Thumb drifting across her cheekbone, his sights bouncing between her eyes and mouth, he slowly leaned in as their lips touched ever so gently. The warmth sent a shiver racing through her as their kisses intensified. Lying on the sofa, they clung to each other.

Pouring everything he felt into that single, timeless moment, Julia's hand found its way to his chest, her fingers curling lightly in the fabric of his shirt before she gently pushed him back.

Catching their breath, she whispered, "Please don't be mad. I just don't want her to wake up and see us."

Their foreheads touched briefly, and their breaths mingled as their eyes met again.

He nodded sincerely and said, "I understand." Believing it best to call it a night and remove the temptation, he hugged her "I should go and let you get some sleep."

"It's not that I..." she stopped mid-sentence.

"I know. Don't worry. We have time."

Getting up off the sofa, Julia followed him to the door.

He glanced toward Syd's room to ensure all was quiet before wrapping his arms securely around Julia's shoulders. "Good night," he said, leaning down to kiss her softly, savoring the moment before stepping back.

"Good night," she whispered, resting her head briefly against his chest, comforted by the steady rhythm of his heartbeat and the warmth of his chin resting atop her head.

"See you in the morning." His voice was low, reluctant to part. He opened the door, gave her a small wave, and crossed the hall.

She stood in the doorway, watching him until he disappeared into his room. Closing the door with a contented sigh, Julia smiled to herself, feeling as though the evening they'd shared was something out of a dream—one she hoped she'd never wake from.

58

January 1st

New Year's Day

Sleeping in until ten-thirty, Ty stretched and reluctantly pulled himself out of bed. Unable to sleep for hours, he'd finally drifted off sometime after four o'clock, his restless mind reeling before then. Between navigating a series of press engagements scheduled when he returned to Boston and figuring out when he could return to Toronto, he had spent the early hours ironing out a number of details in his head.

Grabbing his phone, Ty sent Julia a quick text, knowing she might wonder what happened to him. Her response arrived almost immediately. They, too, had indulged in a rare, lazy morning. Relieved to hear he hadn't kept them waiting, he smiled to himself and replied with a suggestion to meet in an hour.

When the time came, Ty walked across the hall, knocking lightly on the door. Julia answered, greeting him with a warm smile. Her casual yet cozy outfit looked super relaxed as the heavenly aroma of something delicious wafted past her.

"What's cooking?" he asked curiously.

"Hors d'oeuvres," Julia replied, waving him toward the kitchen. "We have a few New Year's traditions, and these little bites are always part of it. Want to help?"

"Sure," he said, following her into the kitchen. "Tell me what I need to do." He watched as she moved efficiently around the small space, pulling trays from the oven and setting them on the trivets. "You've got my stomach growling already."

Julia laughed. "After all the big meals we've been having, sometimes it's nice just to munch. We stuck to the classics—mini quiches, stuffed mushroom caps, spring rolls, coconut shrimp, and sausage-in-a-blanket. Not the healthiest, perhaps, but always a hit." She pointed to the fridge. "Can you grab the veggie and cheese platters? Oh, and the spinach dip."

He did as she asked. Passed a box of crackers, he assumed she wanted it alongside the sliced cheese bites. Washing his hands and drying them, he placed a few on the plate.

As they chatted, Ty noticed Julia emptying the cupboards and packing things into structured grocery boxes neatly placed on the floor by the door.

"Getting a head start?" he asked.

"I suppose," she said with a shrug. "Just clearing out the extras we didn't use. I try and pack up in stages, so it's not so overwhelming."

When the food was ready, the three of them gathered on the sofa with plates in hand and spent the next three hours watching a movie, laughing, munching, and reminiscing over their holiday adventures.

Sydney animatedly divulged her favorite part. "Out of everything we did, I loved the ice skating through the forest, the restaurant we visited that night, and, of course, snowmobiling!" Her voice went up an octave when she said it.

"Well, I can't choose. I think it was all great," he said sincerely. "Probably the best vacation I've ever had." He locked eyes with Julia.

She knew why.

Out of the blue, Sydney found the s'mores kit in the grocery box. "Hey, can we head to the cauldron to roast some marshmallows, Mom?"

Turning to Ty, she asked, "Up for it?"

He got up off the sofa. "Sure am."

Grabbing their coats and slipping on hats and boots, they ventured outside to the cauldron fire, hoping to find golden flames flickering in the chilly winter air to roast their marshmallows.

Setting up the graham wafers, chocolate bars, and marshmallows on their tray, Sydney giggled as her first try at roasting only ended in flames, making her frantically blow it out. After that, she watched how Ty expertly browned them for her.

Julia sat back and observed the two building the decadent sandwiches. She couldn't help but marvel at how different this trip had been versus other years – how her opinion of him had changed so much since the night they first met. Thinking about the quiet moments they shared alone by the fire - each filled with joy, warmth, and connection, she knew she had strong feelings for him. But was it possible? After only two weeks, could she be in love?

"Definitely a holiday to remember," she muttered, almost to herself.

Ty glanced over, catching her words. "It certainly has," he said softly, his gaze steady.

Later that night, upon returning inside, Julia started packing the room while Ty and Sydney took the ornaments off the tree.

Separating the ones she made for him, she packed them well with tissue paper and placed them in a handled bag before she wrapped the others from Clarence and LeeAnn's store in the special box to deliver to Betty the following day.

When the tree was bare, Syd stood back. Ty heard her thank the little tree for such a wonderful Christmas. He was amazed by the young girl's sentiments. It pulled on his heartstrings.

Cleaning her room and packing while her Mom did the same as she talked with Ty, Sydney walked over and collapsed on the bed.

"I'm beat," she said. "Think I'm gonna shower and get some sleep."

"Okay, sweetie pie. I am almost done here."

When she left, she closed her door. They could hear the water running.

"I know I've said this before, but you did an amazing job raising her."

Bashfully lowering her head, she said, "Thank you. When Ben and David passed, it was just she and I. All we had was each other."

Taking a break and sitting on the bed, Julia didn't feel pulled in two directions for the first time. She thought about her love for David and knew what they had would never be forgotten - but thinking about the love she was developing for Ty made her smile.

Noticing, he asked, "What is it?"

She sat quietly, fidgeting with the sleeve of her sweater before folding it and placing it in her suitcase. "Umm, nothing. I'm just thinking."

"Penny for your thoughts?"

Julia didn't know if she should share this with him.

"Please tell me. What is it? What's wrong?" His voice was deep and sounded so confident and protective.

"Nothing is wrong. It's the exact opposite, actually."

"Oh, it's good then?"

"Yes."

He hoped to hear more.

Looking at him with a tilt of her head, she said, "You make me happy."

"I do?"

"Yes, you do."

He lovingly walked over and pretended to tackle her before gently kissing her forehead. "On another note," he asked, "How is the internal battle of feelings going?"

"Slowly subsiding, I believe."

"I want you to know I don't think of this as a competition between David and me. Please talk about him and Ben freely with Sydney. You never have to hide that part of your life. Think of it this way. We are just adding another chapter. That's all. They will always be part of you, and I have no reservations about that. None."

Amazed by what he said, she couldn't respond.

He knew how hard it was for her. It reminded him to take things in stride and slowly build upon what they had, inch by inch. Despite it being complicated, he hoped to heal her heart and get her to the point where she was content in her new life with him. In return, he would do everything he could to keep David and Ben's spirits alive.

Not wanting to leave her tonight, Ty asked, "Do you want me to stay?"

Julia sat up nervously.

"No, umm." Ty diffused her worry. "I'm just happy to fall asleep beside you tonight. That's all."

She timidly looked his way and hesitated a second before nodding.

Saying goodnight to Sydney when she emerged, they waited for her to go to sleep before Julia locked their door. Lying down along the back of the sofa, resting his head on the pillow, he raised his arm to allow her to snuggle alongside him. Pulling the HBC blanket over them, he covered her up before tightening their embrace.

"Are you comfortable?" His voice had a hint of uncertainty.

"Yes," she said softly, feeling the warmth of his body against hers. It had been so long since someone had been so close. Conflicted, she thought about what it would be like to love him but knew she couldn't. It was too soon.

"Goodnight, Julia."

She whispered, "Goodnight."

Following his heart, he said with absolute certainty, "I love you."

Julia froze for a moment, her breath catching at Ty's unexpected words. She looked into his eyes, seeing nothing but sincerity and warmth, the kind that melted the walls she hadn't realized she was still holding up.

"I—" She trailed off, searching for the words.

"You don't have to say it back," he interjected gently, his tone steady and reassuring. "I just wanted you to know. That's how I feel. No pressure. I'll wait for as long as you need."

"No. You shouldn't have to wait..." Julia's gaze dropped to their intertwined hands, her fingers trembling as they gripped his. "I love you, too."

Ty's eyes didn't waver as her words hit him. Instead, they burned with intensity, the kind that sent a shiver down her spine. A slow, confident smile curved his lips. He didn't hesitate. Wrapping his arms around her, he pulled her flush against him, his grip firm but careful, like he was holding something precious.

She let out a breath she hadn't realized she was holding as he leaned back slightly to look her in the eyes, his hands still on her waist.

Reaching up, brushing his thumb across her cheek, he kissed her—not rushed, not hesitant, but sure. His lips claimed hers with a tenderness that spoke of patience and trust.

When they parted, Ty rested his forehead against hers, his voice dropping to a near growl. "You have no idea what you mean to me. But I'm going to spend every day making sure you do."

In his arms, Julia felt safe and cherished. Ty wasn't just a man who loved her; he was a man who would stand by her no matter what came their way.

As the north wind whistled outside, they drifted off to sleep, wrapped in each other's warmth. Despite their Christmas in Carling coming to an end, they both dreamed of a future where, each day together held the promise of a love that could stand the test of time.

59

January 2

The Departure

In the morning, Julia woke to the sounds of a family of children dashing down the hallway, yelling and screaming. An orangey glow came from the windows. She was sure the sunrise was beautiful on the lake-facing side. Realizing where she was and who was still there, Julia panicked and listened to see if Sydney was up yet. Not hearing anything from her little girl's room, she knew she had to get Ty out the door.

Sitting up, she hoped her movement would help wake him, but sadly, he did not move a muscle. Captivated by the sleeping giant, she watched him a moment longer, hating the thought of leaving him today. Amidst it all, Ty opened one eye.

Disoriented, he stretched and smiled at Julia before realizing where he was. Startled, he looked toward Sydney's door. "Is she up yet?" He asked quietly.

"No, but..."

"Yeah, I need to go." Ty rubbed his hands across his face to help him focus. "Okay..." Making his way over to the door, he carefully opened the locks, trying not to make a sound. "I will text you later."

When he kissed her, Julia found his eyes fearfully affixed to Sydney's room door, hoping they wouldn't get caught. Slipping out into the hallway, Julia smiled and waved before closing it behind him. Now safe, she rounded the corner into her bathroom to have a shower. The whole time, she kept thinking about Ty leaving. Every so often, it caused her to stop what she was doing and take a deep breath.

While she put on her makeup, she heard Sydney rummaging around across the suite. Determined to be a happy day despite the sadness looming, Julia went to greet her good morning.

She already had her suitcase on the end of the bed and was packing the craft supplies from her desk.

"Morning, Syd. How did you sleep?"

She looked over while securing the craft trolley drawers with tape. "I don't want to go home."

"I know, Sweetie. Me either. But aren't you excited for a new year to begin?"

"I suppose." She seemed so sad. "I'm gonna miss everyone."

Julia hugged her tightly. "We will be back next year. Or maybe we should take a trip here in the summer? Would you like that?"

"Oh, yes. Then we can see Grandpa Bryce."

"Yes, we could."

"I think I would battle the summer crowds for that."

"Me too." Scanning the room, she said, "Have you got everything? There is nothing in the drawers or closet?"

"Everything I have is on the bed beside my suitcase." She thought for a second. "Oh? How should I pack my sculpture? I still have the bubble wrap. Maybe I should use that so it doesn't get broken."

"Yes, that would be a good idea. Need any help?" her Mother asked.

"Nope. I've got it." Sydney kept packing while Julia returned to her side of the room.

Hearing a knock at the door, she walked over and found Ty with baggage in tow.

"Hey. Thought I'd come over and see if you ladies need a hand."

"Thank you. I'd appreciate that. I was just about to go and grab a luggage cart from the foyer."

"No worries. I'll go and get that for you."

"Are you sure?"

"Absolutely." He opened the door and said, "I'll be back in a minute."

"Thank you."

"Sure thing."

When he left, Julia moved all the bags by the door. Accounting for everything, perusing her room and the kitchen for anything left behind, she double-checked the closets.

Sydney emerged with her sculpture nicely packaged and placed it back in the gift bag from the gallery. "There. I think that is everything."

"Good job, hun."

"Are we having breakfast here?"

Julia replied, "Yes. Believe we should."

"Is Ty going to eat with us?"

"I think so. He just went to get us a luggage cart."

Meanwhile, downstairs, Ty exited the elevator to a foyer bustling with people. It was unusual to see, given that things were so quiet the week before. While rounding the corner, he spotted Bryce behind the concierge desk. Stopping in his tracks, he knew he would have to address the elephant in the room since Bryce had avoided them all week. He had every right to be angry at him for abandoning Julia and Sydney on Christmas Eve, not to mention that he'd broken his promise. Ty felt it was time for him to man up and clear the air.

Bryce caught sight of him and did not look happy.

He knew their conversation would not be pretty. Approaching, he smiled and said, "Good morning, Bryce," hoping to make amends.

"Mr. Reynolds," the older gentleman replied in a stern tone.

To address the situation head-on, Ty said, "Look, I know what you're going to say. I disappointed you on many levels, and I'm sorry. Leaving them was the worst mistake of my life."

"Yes, it was." He couldn't look him in the eye.

"At the time, the pressure from everyone got to me, but I fought for them. Thankfully, everything worked out in the end."

"I suppose so."

He didn't know what to say to change Bryce's tone. With a long pause, he finally blurted out, "I told her I loved her. I plan to marry her one day. Hell, I'd marry her tomorrow if she'd let me."

Bryce glanced up from his paperwork, surprised by the comment. "Really?"

"Yes, and I promise I will spend the rest of my life proving that love to both of them daily. No exceptions."

Hesitating, Bryce continued organizing a few slips of paper behind the desk. Suddenly, he offered an olive branch and looked Ty in the eye. "I will hold you to that."

He shook his hand. "I know," he said, thankful to have his blessing.

"You go and help our ladies with their bags. When you are ready to go, I'll help you load up."

"Sounds good, Sir," he said, glad to have mended fences with the other man in the girl's life.

Commandeering a free trolley, Ty wheeled it through the foyer to the elevators.

Returning upstairs, he found Julia's door propped open. Upon seeing Ty arrive, Julia opened it fully so he could thread the trolley inside.

"Oh, good. You were able to get one. I didn't know if you would. I'm sure it's busy," Julia said, taking their things from Syd's bathroom.

One by one, he started loading the bags. "Yes, it's busy downstairs." Hooking a few totes over the hanger posts, he said, "I saw Bryce."

Julia stopped dead in her tracks. "How did that go?"

"Not well initially, but I apologized right out of the gate."

"Oh?"

"We are good now. We have an understanding."

She wanted to hear more about their conversation but thought it should be left between them. "I'm glad."

"Me too."

"I think that's all of it." Julia loaded the last bag on the cart.

"Where's Syd?"

Not seeing her in the living room, she said, "Sydney?"

"Yeah, Mom," a little voice called out from the bedroom.

Julia and Ty walked over and found her on her bed with tears streaming down her cheeks. "What's wrong, Sweetie?"

Wiping her face, she said, "I don't want to go home. This Christmas has been the best ever. Do we have to go?"

"I know, honey, but think about all the fun things that lie ahead this year."

Ty intervened. "I'm excited for you to visit me in Boston, and when the team plays against Toronto, I will fly here to visit you for a couple of days. How does that sound?"

Sydney sat up. "You promise?"

"Yes, I promise."

Ty put his arm around Julia, and the two hugged the little girl.

"How about we head down for breakfast now?" Julia brushed the hair from Sydney's face.

"Okay. I'm pretty hungry."

"Yeah, I'm pretty hungry, too," Ty said, smiling while they moved toward the door. "What are you going to order? I think I'm going to have...."

"Let me guess." Sydney put up her hand to stop him from revealing the answer. "Eggs Benny, again."

Julia and Ty laughed.

"What's wrong with that?" her Mother chuckled.

"Well, I am going to switch it up today," the great baseball player said.

Sydney's eyebrows raised. "Really?"

"Yes. I think I'm going with the blueberry pancakes and syrup."

Holding up her hand for a high five, Ty obliged.

"Yes, finally! You won't be disappointed," she said with excitement dancing in her eyes.

60

January 2nd

Saying Goodbye

The hotel had a solemn feel when it was time to bid their Carling Family farewell for another year. They were thankful to have spent the holidays with those who mattered most and couldn't have been happier to meet the new staff, who were now considered part of the family.

After breakfast, Julia, Sydney, and Ty returned to their room. Julia did a final sweep before Ty maneuvered the luggage cart out the door.

"Mom?" Sydney said, lugging her gift from Ty.

The woman's sights gravitated to her.

"Can you carry my sculpture? It's heavy, and I don't want to drop it."

Julia carefully took it from her.

Dramatically wiggling her freed arms, she said, "Thank you." Not wanting to be empty-handed, intent on helping, she slipped on her backpack and volunteered to drag Ty's suitcase along.

Bryce had their trucks warming up outside the doors. Assisting Ty when he took the cart outside, he helped him pack Julia's things while she looked on, strategically placing some bags in the middle seats beside the ornament boxes.

Minutes later, it was time. Julia walked over to Bryce with open arms and clung to him tightly, making sure not to break him. Seeing him smiling with rosy cheeks from being out in the cold, she said, "Bye, Bryce. We will call daily to check in on you, alright?"

Nodding his head, lost for words, he muttered, "Yes. I'm looking forward to it already."

"Remember, if you have a day off, you are always welcome to visit whenever you like."

"Thank you. I will probably take you up on that, especially if it includes a baseball game?" His eyebrows raised when he glanced over at Ty.

"Would love to have you in the stands." Reaching out, Ty shook Bryce's hand.

The man pulled the baseball player in for a manly hug. "I'd really like that."

Joining her Mother, Sydney waited her turn.

Seeing the little girl standing there so patiently, Bryce knelt in front of her. "Bye, my sweet girl. Be good for your Mom."

"I will. Bye, Grandpa Bryce. Thank you for skating with me. Love you," she said, saddened to leave him.

His eyes welled upon receiving the hug from her. "I'm going to miss you, little one."

"I'll miss you too. But from what Mom says, we will see you soon. You're gonna come to our house and visit, right?" Sydney stated quite firmly.

"I will try my very best."

"Maybe we can Zoom?"

"What's Zoom, again?" Bryce had no clue what she was talking about.

"It's a video phone call. Don't worry. I'll arrange that with Lisa or Bruno. Then you can join in. Sound good?"

Bryce laughed. "I guess so."

She waved to him before walking out the door to the truck. "Bye."

"Bye, Sweetie Pie." The white-haired man waved back.

Ty stepped forward before departing and said, "Well, Bryce, thanks again. It's been a pleasure getting to know you."

"Yes, it has. Remember what I said. Take care of my girls."

Giving the nod, Ty smiled. "I promise. Don't worry."

"Best of luck this season. I will be watching."

"I was hoping you would. Thanks for that."

Joining Julia, the two exited the front door, waving to their Carling family. "Bye, everyone!"

"Bye! See you soon!" Rebecca shouted from the Lakes podium, waving frantically.

Bruno raised a steady hand while serving a guest their drink.

"Did I miss them? Hurry, Lisa, they are going!" Jun yelled to his colleague while rounding the corner. Seeing Julia and Ty leaving, he shouted, "Bye! Safe travels!"

Lisa was right behind him. "We will see you soon!"

Blowing them a kiss, Julia waved.

"Am I following you?" Ty asked, unsure of the plan.

About to jump in the driver's seat, Julia replied, "Yes, but we have one stop to make. Hope that's alright."

"Sure, no problem. Just lead the way," he said while walking toward his truck.

Tearfully walking out the door, leaving their Christmas home behind for another year, Bryce stood idly by while they left. Raising a steady hand, he bowed his head and went back inside.

"I'm going to miss him, Mom."

"I know. Me too. We will make sure he spends lots of time with us this year. Would you like that?"

"Very much." Sydney grabbed her blanket from the back seat and rolled it into a ball. Hugging it, they drove down the laneway with Ty right behind them.

"Are we going to Betty's now?"

"Yes, we are."

The girls deviated from their usual route and made a slight detour.

Turning onto a narrow, deserted road, Ty followed. He watched as they pulled up to what looked like a large estate home. While she spoke to someone on the speaker, the wrought iron gates parted. Driving through, they climbed a hill to find a grey-stone manor on the other side. A woman stood at the front door, seemingly waiting. Parking their vehicles, Julia and Sydney got out and found the ornament boxes in the middle seats. Waving Ty over, he joined them.

"So, this is the women's shelter?" he asked. "I assume that lady is Betty?"

"Yes, this is the place we told you about. Nobody knows it's here."

Sydney ran up to the pretty white-haired woman and hugged her when she opened the security door. "Hello, Betty! Merry Christmas and Happy New Year."

"And to you, my dear. How are my favorite girls?"

"We are good," Syd replied.

"Yes, we had a wonderful holiday at the Carling."

"So nice to hear." Betty spotted Ty hovering behind Julia and Sydney. "Who's your friend?"

"I hope you don't mind. This is Ty. He has a Christmas box for you, too."

"Oh, you're the baseball player?"

"Word gets around fast," Ty laughed. With an outstretched hand, he said, "Pleased to meet you, Ma'am."

"Oh, please call me Betty, deary."

"I've heard so much about you from Bryce," she stated. "Please. Come in. It's cold."

Not allowed to go any further than the vestibule, seeing another electronically secured set of doors in front of them, Ty watched Sydney hand over their ornament boxes.

"I am so thankful for these two. Aren't they amazing?" Betty stated lovingly.

"Yes, they certainly are," Ty agreed.

Pulling her phone from her pocket, the elderly woman showed them pictures of the Christmas trees decorated by the families staying with her this holiday. Remembering each theme, not seeing anyone in the photos, Julia and Syd described each one to Ty.

"Thank you for the gifts also. The children and mothers loved them. You thought of everything."

"I'm so glad," Julia hugged her.

Hearing this, Ty was amazed. He had no idea what they'd done.

"Bless you, child."

"He has. That's why we pay it forward." Julia saw Betty was so thankful.

"I wish I could spend more time with you, but duty calls. It's lunchtime."

"No worries. We need to get on the road. We're just happy to see you."

Julia and Sydney hugged her one last time while Ty raised his hand to bid her farewell.

"Travel safely! Happy New Year. See you soon."

Before she disappeared inside, Ty walked over. "Hey, Betty. Wait."

The woman turned around as Ty presented her with an envelope.

"What's this?" she asked curiously.

"Well, I was going to give this to Julia to pass along to you later, but since we are here...umm, this is just a little something to help the shelter," Ty replied.

Opening the seal, Betty pulled out a piece of paper and quickly covered her mouth in shock. Unable to say a word, she burst into tears. Seemingly holding her breath, she reached out her arms to Ty and hugged him tightly.

"What is it, Betty?" Sydney wondered what he had given her.

Shaking her head, still unable to speak, Betty showed her the formal cheque.

"Mom, it's a cheque for three hundred thousand dollars!"

Julia was stunned.

"Look, it's not a big deal. I just wanted to help. This should be enough to keep things afloat here for a little while."

"Oh, my goodness. You are an Angel. Thank you. Thank you so much!" Betty whispered, still shaking from the surprise.

"Bryce told me who to make it out to, so I'm sure it's correct. My agent couriered it to me this past week. It's a certified cheque, so you shouldn't have any problems cashing it."

Double-checking to see who he made it out to, Betty nodded. "Yes, that is correct." Still in disbelief, she said, "You will be in my daily prayers. God bless you." She held out her arms and insisted on a group hug before they went on their way.

Waving goodbye, the woman soon disappeared behind the security doors.

Since Sydney was cold, she jumped into the truck to warm up while Julia talked with Ty.

"That was an incredible surprise. I don't know what more to say. She's been struggling to pay the bills to keep the place open. Sadly, this year, she had to turn a few families away because she barely had enough to keep those staying here fed. What you did...." Sobbing, unable to comprehend his generosity, Julia added with a whimper, "What you did is an absolute miracle for her right now. You have no idea."

He humbly lowered his head. "I'm happy to hear that she'll put it to good use. The way you spoke of her and everything she does for these families made me want to do something special. She deserves it."

Julia hugged him tightly. "I love you." Parting, she wiped the tears from her face.

"I love you more," he said, making her smile.

Checking the time, she jumped. "Oh, I guess we should get moving. You have a flight to catch."

"Yes, sadly, I do."

Julia set the GPS for Pearson Airport. When they pulled away from Betty's, it wasn't long until they joined the main highway heading south toward the city. Thankfully, the roads were clear. But the closer they got to the city limits, Julia's heart started to ache while she tried to stop thinking about what they had to do next. How would she ever say goodbye to the man she's grown to love?

| 322 |

61

January 2nd

Pearson

After battling southbound holiday traffic for over two hours, they finally arrived at the bustling Pearson International.

Julia and Sydney went straight to the visitor parking, hoping to find a spot, while Ty went to return the rental. Waiting inside the terminal for him, they found the place filled with travelers who had spent Christmas and New Year's in the city. Julia wondered what their families were like and what festivities they enjoyed, anything to sway her from thinking about Ty leaving.

"There he is, Mom." Sydney pointed to the handsome man walking into the terminal. He stood out among the rest. When he smiled at them, her heart melted.

"We made it," he said, getting closer.

Julia nodded. "Yes, we arrived safe and sound."

"It wasn't a bad drive compared to my trips back and forth in the storms. At least I got to see more of the scenery this time."

A silence fell upon them.

"I guess I should check in. One minute." Ty walked over to the counter.

Before long, the woman returned his documents with his boarding pass tucked inside his passport. Repositioning his duffle bag strap on his shoulder, the three walked towards the security entrance while other passengers followed them in a hurry. Setting the bag on the floor, Ty reached out with open arms to hug them both.

"When I land, I'll try and get things squared away so I can fly back next week."

Julia's heart was breaking. She tried to hold back her tears so that it would be easy for him to leave.

"I'll send you the details when I know more," he said.

"We will be here waiting for you."

The flight was boarding in fifty minutes. Ty reluctantly let go and checked the time, knowing he still had to get through security and to his gate.

Glancing over at Julia, then Sydney, Ty said, "Sydney, hide your eyes."

"What?" the little girl questioned, scrunching her face in confusion.

He snickered and signaled for her to turn around. Giggling despite herself, she did as he asked.

Stepping closer to Julia, he kissed her softly, hoping the warmth of her lips would stay with him until he could return.

"Can I look now?" Sydney asked, her voice impatient.

"One more minute," Ty replied, stealing one last kiss from Julia. "I love you. I'll call you when I get there."

Julia nodded, her eyes shimmering with emotion.

"It's okay now, Syd." Ty crouched to hug her tightly. But instead of her usual bounce, Sydney clung to him, her small arms trembling.

"Do you *really* have to go?" she asked, her voice wobbly. Her big, tear-filled eyes stared into his.

It sent his heart twisting. "Hey, hey," he soothed, brushing a tear from her cheek. "It's not forever. I promise I'll be back before you know it. You just have to take care of your Mom for me, okay?"

Sniffling, Sydney nodded but didn't let go.

"I'll miss you so much," she whispered, her voice barely audible.

"I'll miss you too, Kiddo," Ty said, holding her close. He pressed a kiss to her forehead and gently pulled away, giving her a brave smile.

Behind them, Julia wiped at her own eyes, struggling to stay strong as she watched.

"Make sure you hurry back," Sydney added, her lower lip trembling.

"I'll try my best," Ty promised. Standing, he took Julia's hand, squeezing it tightly before letting go at the last second. "Drive home safe, you two."

"We will," Julia replied, her voice thick with emotion as she wrapped her arm around Sydney's small shoulders.

"Bye, Ty," Sydney called after him, her voice still shaky.

"Bye. Love you both," he said, raising a steady hand and then lowering it to rest over his heart.

"Love you too," Julia murmured, her voice soft as she and Sydney stood together, watching him go.

Ty disappeared behind the frosted glass panels, leading to security. As he placed his bag on the conveyor belt, he stole one last glance at them, already feeling their absence.

Stoic, Julia stayed with her arm wrapped protectively around Sydney, the little girl still clinging to her side, her face pressed into her Mother's coat.

His chest ached at the sight, the distance already stretching between them. What he would give to have one more day—to wake up to Julia's soft smile, to hear Sydney's giggles echo through the room. Just one more day to hold them, to remind them how much they meant to him.

Taking a deep breath, he turned away, blinking back the sting in his eyes. He had to go, but leaving was far from easy. Once again, he felt alone.

A Year of New Beginnings

62

January 15 - February 15

Off-Season

Over the next week, the first baseman attended the interviews and promo requested by upper management. While he was away, Julia and Sydney had settled into their everyday life since school and work resumed on Monday. Planning for his return, Julia got the spare room freshened up for his arrival and contemplated the dynamics of everything happening between them. She didn't know if she was ready for any next steps. Their relationship was new despite feeling like she'd known him forever. Thinking about being near him made her feel flustered.

Meanwhile, in Boston, the day before his scheduled flight, Ty finished his contractual obligations and packed everything he would need for spring training, figuring when it came time, he'd leave Toronto and fly straight to Florida. Thankfully, he still had a month left in the off-season to spend with Julia and Sydney.

That Saturday morning, bright and early, he left the New England state bound for Toronto, thankful it was only an hour and a half flight. High above Lake Ontario, he thought about the direction his life was taking. Everything had fallen into place like it was supposed to, it seemed. Still in disbelief that he'd met the love of his life, he smiled uncontrollably at the thought of seeing her in a couple of hours. Aware of what lay ahead, Ty knew it would be a challenging year for them. The life of a baseball player was not the easiest. Despite being amongst many people, it was a lonely existence. Confiding in his teammates that week, Ty listened to them express how difficult it was to leave their families behind for six weeks at the start of every season. It was something Ty knew he'd also come to dread. After all this time, he understood why the men were always quiet during the first couple of days of training camp. Determined to make the most of his time with Julia and Sydney, he told himself to stay in the moment and not overthink it; otherwise, it would ruin their visit.

Landing at Pearson, Ty wanted to be the first off the plane. Shuffling through customs, pulling the brim of his hat slightly lower over his face, he finally made it to the baggage area. Grabbing a luggage cart, he waited off to the side, hoping nobody would recognize him. The last thing he wanted was to deal with selfies and autographs when he was so close to seeing his girls. Receiving a text from Julia, he was happy to know they'd arrived and were waiting for him. He glanced over at the arrival doors, knowing they were just beyond it. Finally, the conveyor belt started spitting out suitcases. He grabbed his bags and set them on the cart one by one.

With everything accounted for, he hurried along. Grouped with a few other people, waiting his turn to exit, he walked out the doors to a crowd waiting for their loved ones. It didn't take long to find Julia and Sydney. Near the back, amongst so many unfamiliar faces, there was a big bristol board sign. It read *We love Ty.* Sydney had drawn a massive heart in the middle to signify the love. She even had a pair of red socks in the bottom left corner.

"Ty! Over here!" Syd shouted, waving the sign back and forth.

He waved to them and maneuvered down the ramp, not leaving Julia's gaze for a second. Met by the biggest smiles, he walked over with open arms. Unable to wait, he kissed Julia again and again. "I missed you," he whispered.

"Missed you too."

"Oh, you guys. Warn me first," Syd rolled her eyes.

"Hello, Miss Sydney. How are you?" Ty asked, kneeling in front of her.

"I'm good," she said, hugging his neck tightly. "Did you have a good trip?"

"Yes, I did." He stood up. "Okay, let's get out of here."

While walking out of the terminal, the couple couldn't stop stealing glances at one another. Each time their eyes met, a warm smile passed between them, as if neither could quite believe he was finally there. Their hands brushed as they walked, fingers intertwining until Ty eventually pulled her closer, wrapping his arm around her shoulders. He leaned down, pressing a kiss to her temple.

Julia smiled up at him, her eyes soft and full of love.

Reaching her truck in the parking garage, they loaded his luggage into the back, thankful it all fit. Lowering the tailgate closed, he glanced over to see Sydney already climbing into the back seat, her excitement bubbling over as she chattered about the drive home.

As Ty moved toward the passenger side, Julia hesitated. "Hey," she called, catching his attention. "Want to drive?"

Ty's brow lifted, and a grin spread across his face. "Are you sure? Do you trust me?"

She laughed and tossed him the keys. "Yes, of course. Why wouldn't I?"

Catching them easily, Ty shook his head with a chuckle and walked over. "That's good to hear. Always wondered what it would be like to drive the two of you around. Guess I'll soon find out." He slid into the driver's seat, looking over at Julia as she settled beside him, her expression a perfect mix of joy and relief. "I'm going to need some directions."

"No problem," Sydney interjected. "We will tell you where you need to turn."

Within forty minutes, they were pulling up to the Mariani's.

Parking in the driveway, Ty got out and marveled at the quaint townhouse before opening the tailgate to unload. "Wow, it's really nice."

"Thank you," Julia replied as a few neighbors looked on curiously, wondering who he was. The sight of them made her anxious. She didn't know most of them but could only imagine what they were thinking, seeing this man seemingly moving in with them.

Ty brought all his bags into the foyer. There was barely any room to walk.

About to lug one bag up the stairs, Syd groaned, struggling. "This way," she said. "We have your room ready."

Grabbing another bag, he went to help the young girl. Picking up the duffle she'd left partway up the stairs, he found her already at the top. Following Syd around the corner and down the hall, she showed him his room. Looking around, Ty noticed it was bright and spacious. Painted light grey with platinum accents, he set the two bags near the closet.

"What do you think?" Syd asked with her hands on her hips.

"I think it's great." He noticed Julia peeking inside the doorway.

"Hey, Syd, how about you set out the sandwiches and iced tea we made."

"Okay," she said excitedly.

Left alone, Julia approached and said, "I hope this is okay."

"Yes. It's perfect." Ty could feel that Julia was nervous. "I know what you are thinking."

"You do?"

Inching closer, wrapping his arms around her waist, he said, "Please don't think about that. We have time."

She nodded, feeling ever closer to him.

Holding her head lovingly against his chest, he reassured her, "It's all good. I'm just happy to be here with you."

Julia relaxed a little.

"The sandwiches are ready!" Syd shouted up the staircase.

Both of them looked toward the door.

"Okay. We are coming!" Julia replied. "Are you hungry?"

"Yes, always," Ty laughed.

"Great. We got a sandwich wrap platter from Village. Our grocery store. They are amazing. Nushee made them fresh this morning."

"Who is that?"

"Wait until you meet her. We've been friends for years, and she always sports a welcoming smile and loves to chat." Julia walked out of the room while Ty followed her hand in hand. "Then, there's John, Gary, David, Ben, Mike, and Mario. Oh, and Olivia and Jeanette. Wait until you meet Rita. She wants me to bring you shopping so she can meet you in person."

"Oh? Is she a baseball fan?"

"No. She just wants to see how handsome you are." Julia stopped in the hallway.

"Oh, really... Where did she get that idea?"

"I don't know. I think a little birdie told her."

63

February 14

Valentine's Day

After spending an incredible month with Julia and Sydney, spring training was fast approaching. Ty tried not to think about it and never brought it up in conversation. Over the last five days, it was the elephant in the room. Tomorrow, he'd be heading to Fort Myers for six weeks, and the season would be in full swing after that, taking him away from them for months on end. He kept reminding himself it was just one more year. Then, he'd be free to live the life he always wanted.

Thinking back on the last month, Ty recalled everything they'd done together. The one thing that stood out in his mind was taking the girls downhill skiing at a resort outside the city limits called Lakeridge. It was a modest hill but was perfect for beginners. He was surprised at how fast the girls caught on. Especially Sydney. She had no fear.

On the other hand, Julia knew she had more to lose if she got hurt. Skiing cautiously at first, she eventually kept up with Sydney and him. He looked forward to those Saturdays on the hill. It reminded him of Wyoming from time to time, but on a much smaller scale. Thinking of Jackson, he thought he might take Julia and Syd there someday and share that part of his life with them.

During the week, he started to drive Syd to school and picked her up at the end of the day. It helped Julia be more productive at work without interruptions. That way, they could spend quality time together in the evenings as a family.

He even joined the girls on trips to the grocery store to buy ingredients for their rather adventurous meals. Ty met everyone at Village and settled in quite nicely. He was amazed once again by how Julia treated everyone with an equal level of respect. She talked to them like they were family. As with the Carling staff, he soon discovered she had a Village family, too. Surrounded by those who cared for them, these strangers had become more than friends. It made the thought of leaving them a little less difficult - but challenging nonetheless. At least she would have people to lean on.

Thankful to celebrate Valentine's Day together, Julia and Ty cooked a fantastic dinner and had some time to themselves while Sydney went to finish some homework. Even though for most, it was a day of celebration, for Julia, there was a sadness looming. They could no longer count their time together in days. It had now reduced to hours, minutes, and seconds.

Having to take a work call, Julia stepped away.

Ty went to help Syd read a few chapters from the novel assigned in English class.

After discussing and answering the questions, she was happy to be done.

Leaving her to it, he returned to his room to fold some laundry while she cleaned her desk and got ready for bed. Within minutes, he heard Sydney call for him again.

Returning to tuck her in, he said, "Night, Kiddo. Have a good sleep."

Sydney knew he was leaving the next day. She'd overheard him talking with her Mother. "So, do you have to go?"

"Yes, unfortunately so. But don't worry. I promise I'll see both of you as much as I can."

She nodded.

When he got up to turn off the light, Ty stayed in the doorway. "Sweet dreams."

"Night. Sweet dreams, Kiddo."

He left the door open a crack and went downstairs to help Julia in the kitchen. He could hear her loading the dishwasher. Upon rounding the corner at the stairs, he entered the room and found her with tears streaming down her face. Seeing him, she quickly dried her eyes.

He walked over and held on tightly. "It's going to be okay." Rubbing her arms, he tried to offer whatever comfort he could. "I know. I'm sorry."

She covered her mouth, trying to stop the sobs from overtaking her.

Reaching for a tissue, he dried her face as her body trembled. "I don't want you to be sad."

"It's just hard." Julia tried to be brave but found herself failing miserably. "What am I going to do when you're gone?"

Intent on lightening the mood, he replied, "Watch a lot of baseball?"

Saying that made her laugh a bit through the tears.

"Don't cry. I need you to be strong. If you are strong, that will help me survive the next few months."

She looked up at him. Nodding, she said, "I'll try my best."

"That's the spirit. We are a team now - you, me, and Syd."

"Yes. We are."

He moved a few loose strands of hair away from her face and tucked them behind her ear. Tracing her hairline with his finger, he tilted her chin upwards. Staring into the eyes that had captivated him for two months, he softly kissed her lips. Step by step, inching closer and closer, he lifted Julia onto the counter. Now at equal height, he felt her legs wrap around him.

Caressing his face, studying every feature, she grazed her cheek alongside his. Ty could sense something was different.

"I will forever love you," he said quietly, knowing she needed to hear it.

Her heart skipped a beat and brought about a sense of urgency. It was their last night. Her last chance. Sliding off the countertop, she endearingly grazed her body against his and allowed her feet to float to the floor.

Only holding her for a moment, she slowly broke away. Walking hand in hand, turning off the lights in every room, he followed her through the darkness and up the stairs.

Checking on Sydney, Julia found her fast asleep. Turning Ty around, she guided him toward her room. Every piece of her shivered - her breathing, uneven as she quietly closed the door, careful not to make a sound. Alone with the man she loved in the calmness of night, his silhouette mere inches away, she reached out to him.

Confidently grasping hold, he placed her hands on his chest, making Julia rise on her tiptoes to wrap them around his neck. Leaning forward, he intermittently hugged her tighter and tighter to get rid of every millimeter of space between them. Longing for the woman who stole his heart, he suddenly stopped, understanding the gravity of what was about to happen. "We don't have to?" he whispered, almost short of breath. Seeing her look away, feeling rejected, he brought her sights back to his. "I want you to be sure because, afterward, my heart will be entirely yours."

She gently caressed her hand along his cheek. "And mine yours," she whispered back.

Reassured, he lifted her in his arms and lightly set her down amidst a pile of pillows.

Slipping between the covers, she inched backward, unable to veer from his loving stare. As his arms encircled her, soon, she felt their alluring warmth. Legs intertwined, the tension escalated with every precious kiss granted.

Ty took his time and stayed mindful.

Without reservation, she sweetly tugged on his shirt and drew it upward. While her hand glided across his chest, her touch sent chills down his spine, making him pause. Drifting over to his heart, she left it there a minute, lovingly appreciating its rhythm. His hand soon covered hers. An innocence unexpectedly washed over her. To him, she was so pure, almost angelic. The feeling prompted a need to keep her safe and protected - treasured and loved with the utmost care and tenderness, no matter the cost. Time diminished to a blur. Neither of them said a word. Gently peeling his shirt from his body, leaving him vulnerable and exposed, Julia embraced him willingly. As he brushed his hand along the curve of her waist, there was no turning back.

64

February 15

Spring Training

Julia's alarm went off a half hour before it usually does on a school day. The house was still quiet for a Thursday morning. Reaching for her phone, she opened her eyes to find Ty lovingly watching her sleep.

"Good morning," he whispered.

Her face erupted into a smitten smile. Blushing, she said, "Good morning."

Kissing her forehead, then her lips, he shuffled closer and wrapped his arm around her. Aware of Sydney's usual routine, he said, "I guess we should get moving."

Julia held him tightly. "One more minute."

While cuddling her, he knew he would have to leave in a few short hours. He could feel her tears silently pooling on his chest. In hopes of cheering her up, he said, "You know, a lot of the guys have their families visit at March Break. Is that something you would consider?"

"We can do that?"

"Yes, of course. I'll check and see what the team usually does and will let you know." Ty started to get antsy. With his eyes and ears peeled, he kissed Julia lovingly and said, "We'd better get a move on, just in case she wakes up. Meet you downstairs in fifteen? I'll make breakfast."

She knew he was right, no matter how badly she wanted to linger in bed.

Quietly leaving Julia's room, he slipped into his and closed the door. Turning on the faucet, he waited for the water to warm up. Standing in front of the mirror and resting his palms on the vanity, he lowered his head. "How am I ever going to leave her?" A flood of emotion hit him as his heart ached. Remembering their night together, he said, "One more season. One more. Then that's it. You will never leave again."

Julia checked on her daughter. Letting her sleep a little longer, she tied the belt on her robe around her waist. Ten minutes later, after freshening up, she returned and sat on the edge of her bed.

"Is it morning already?" Sydney said.

"Yes. Did you have a good sleep?"

"Not really." She seemed sad.

"Is it because Ty is leaving today?"

The little girl nodded.

"I know it will be hard, but we must be strong. Remember, he has to win the World Series this year."

She sat up and put on her game face. "Yes, he does!"

"Are you with me?" Her mother asked, hoping to rally the troops.

"For sure!"

"Okay, let's get moving. He is making breakfast."

Little did they know, the baseball player had listened to them the entire time. Sneaking back to his room, he needed a minute. Clutching his hands into fists, he rested them on the wall and leaned his head against them. "Come on, Reynolds. You're getting soft. Pull yourself together." Breaking from his mindset, he hit his fist into his palm. "Come on... Gotta make breakfast."

Arriving downstairs, Julia started making scrambled eggs, bacon, and toast. She heard Ty walk up behind her.

Resting his hands on her shoulders, he said, "You beat me to it."

"Don't worry. I've got this covered." She handed him a cup of coffee.

He said, "Thank you," but noticed she was distant. Afraid to ask if she was okay, he needed to know what was wrong. "Julia?"

Unable to look at him, she said, "No. No, don't do it."

"Do what?"

"Don't ask because it will make me cry again."

Setting his cup on the counter, Ty wrapped his arms around her waist from behind and snuggled his head next to hers. Immediately leaning back into him, she rested her hand along his cheek.

"I know how hard it will be, but I need you to be strong."

She turned around upon hearing the words she had just relayed to Sydney. "Were you listening to us?"

"Most incredible pep talk I've ever heard."

Julia nodded.

"It's just one season, and I know it's a huge sacrifice, but afterward, I'm all yours. I promise you." He held her tightly against him.

"Next year, at this time, I will make you breakfast and brew your coffee every morning. I will make Syd's lunch and take her to school whenever you want me to. We will make dinner together and go grocery shopping. We will do normal things. Normal couple things - agreed?"

She silently nodded. Hearing Sydney bound down the stairs, Julia quickly dried her tears so her daughter would not see her upset.

"What's for breakfast? It smells so good."

"Well, Miss Sydney, we made scrambled eggs, bacon, and toast. Interested?"

"Yes, please."

"Oh, and we have blackberries on the side."

"Awesome. Thank you."

They laughed and talked while eating together. Sadly, Ty kept an eye on the time.

Carefully rinsing the dishes and placing them in the dishwasher, he and Julia remained quiet.

Resting his hand along the small of her back, he said, "I should go and finish packing."

"That's fine. Don't worry. I'll take Syd to school."

Upon hearing that, he felt left out. "I have a better idea. Why don't we both go? I still have time."

She smiled. "That would be great."

While Ty made Syd's lunch, Julia raced upstairs to get dressed.

Meeting in the foyer, with winter coats and hats on to greet the cold, Ty started the SUV and got it warmed up. Julia and Sydney piled in shortly after.

On the drive to school, Ty wanted to say a proper goodbye to the little girl. Not sure where to start, he looked in the rearview mirror and said, "So, I've gotta head to spring training in Florida, Kiddo."

She flashed a sad expression. "Yeah, I know."

"But it won't be long before we see each other again. I promise."

Julia tried holding in her emotions.

Moving slowly through the conga line of traffic, Syd reached in front of her and clung to Ty's neck. "Make sure you practice hard. You've got a World Series to win."

"I will try my best. You make sure you take good care of your Mom for me."

"Don't worry. I got this," she said courageously.

"That's my girl."

Ty pulled into the school's kiss and ride. Syd slid over behind her Mom.

"Bye, Sydie. Have a good day. I'll be here to pick you up. Love you," her Mom said.

"Have a good day, too. Bye, Ty." She hugged him one last time.

"Bye," he waved as she walked towards the front doors and disappeared inside.

Moving with the traffic and back out onto the street. Ty reached over and took hold of Julia's hand, kissing the back of it.

Once they returned to the house, he walked upstairs to his room. Julia followed and sat on a small portion of the bed. Hugging a pillow, seeing the entire space filled with the clothes he'd washed the day before and folded neatly in piles, she watched him take each stack and place them in the suitcase. Brushing his teeth, he gathered everything before packing it in his shaving kit.

"I guess you've done a ton of packing over the years."

"You're not kidding. I am pretty much on the road every other day. We are never in one place for more than three days unless we have back-to-back home games. Speaking of that, I will send you the schedule. Can you visit me in Boston when we play there?"

"Hopefully so."

"At least I'll see you when I'm in Toronto."

"Yes. We would love that."

"And who knows, if we make it to the end, I would love for you to be at those games."

"I wouldn't miss that for the world."

Ty zipped his suitcase closed and stood it up before extending the handle. With open arms, he said, "Well, my ride will be here shortly. I need to get this stuff downstairs."

Julia got up from the bed and solemnly soaked up every last second with him. Kissing her, she hoped the warmth it gave would fuel him for the next month.

One by one, he brought everything down to the foyer.

Noticing the airline SUV pull into the driveway, she felt her stomach in knots.

Standing with her arms crossed in front of her, holding back tears, Ty put on his shoes and Featherlite down jacket. Seeing her level of emotion, he also wiped away a few tears. Towering above her, he held her head against his chest. His heart was pounding. "See you soon." Smothering her with kisses, he hugged her tightly. "I love you."

"I love you too," she whispered as he let go.

"I will call, text, and facetime whenever I can. We will talk every night."

Julia just nodded as the tears fell. Her chest began heaving with every breath.

Not saying another word, he grabbed his bags. Walking down the path, he greeted his driver and returned for the rest. Hugging her again, he said, "Be strong - for me."

"I'll try."

Placing his hand over his heart, he smiled. "I'll call you when I get there."

Julia couldn't mutter a word. She tried to keep a brave face, but as soon as he waved and drove away, Julia closed the front door, went into the powder room, and cried. She wished they had more time. After being a family of two for so long, she felt a family rhythm had returned to the house. Finally, it felt like home. The feelings of abandonment and loss returned. Once again, the world had ripped the happiness from her instantly. Just like the accident did many years before.

65

April

First Home Game

March Break had passed too quickly, but the memories lingered. Julia often thought back to their days in Fort Myers—the warmth of the sun, the Gulf Coast views, and Sydney's giggles as she steered the boat under Ty's watchful eye. The sheer joy on her daughter's face during her birthday dinner was priceless. Seeing Ty play under the stadium lights at JetBlue Park had been the highlight of their trip, a glimpse into his world that made the distance between them feel a little smaller.

The break had been just what they needed, a reminder of the love tying them together despite the miles. But as March faded into April, the separation resumed, and the ache of missing him crept back into their daily lives.

Ty had promised to see them soon, and true to his word, plans came together quickly.

On the fifth of April, he flew Julia, Sydney, and Bryce to Boston, determined to share another piece of his life with them.

The girls were thrilled about the trip, Sydney especially. She spent the flight buzzing with excitement, her chatter shifting between seeing Fenway Park and spending more time with Ty. Even Bryce, usually the reserved one, couldn't hide his anticipation.

When they landed, Manager Matt greeted them. Not wasting any time, they headed straight to Fenway, maneuvering the historic streets of Boston. It felt surreal. Julia couldn't help but glance at the many landmarks she'd seen only in movies.

Arriving at the Stadium, the private driver dropped them off while they followed Matt to meet security near the players' entrance.

Sydney's face lit up as she clutched her new baseball cap, hopeful she'd get a chance to see him before the game. "Is he here?" she asked, her eyes darting around the bustling crowd.

Julia crouched to adjust Sydney's jacket. "He's already on the field, Sweetie. He had to prepare for the game."

Sydney's face fell for a moment, but she quickly brightened. "That's okay! We'll see him after, right?"

"Definitely," Julia assured her with a smile.

Bryce gave Julia a nudge. "This is pretty amazing. Not every day you get VIP treatment at Fenway."

She grinned at his attempt to play it cool but felt nervous herself.

Ushered to the player's box by two fairly large men, Julia noticed that she and Sydney were less than half the size of them.

Concerned about mingling with the other players' families, they stood outside the room for a minute so Julia could gather the courage to go inside. Taking a deep breath, she opened the door, thankful to have Bryce waiting in the wings. All eyes were on them. It made Sydney feel uncomfortable. Following behind her Mother, she didn't like being the center of attention. Unsure if everyone would accept them into the tight-knit group, suddenly, one by one, the player's wives and kids approached to introduce themselves. They'd heard so much about them through their husbands and had been rooting for Ty silently since they heard about his romantic Christmas in Carling. Finally, after all this time, they met the girl who stole Ty Reynolds' heart.

Julia and Syd made the rounds and got acquainted with everyone. Bryce exchanged happy banter with some of the players' parents, too.

Thankful to be welcomed with open arms, they quickly developed connections with the other families.

Very proud to see them in the family box that day, the first baseman thought it was especially nice to glance up and find them laughing with the others and cheering on the team. Something he never thought would ever happen in his lifetime.

Tired after their win against Tampa Bay, the team got showered and dressed to depart. Ty had texted Julia to meet with the other families in the player's hallway.

When he emerged from the locker room, looking smart in business casual, Julia's heart fluttered. Arms out, he hugged his girls tightly. "Hello, how is everybody? Did you enjoy the game?"

"It was awesome!" Sydney exclaimed.

Greeting Bryce, Ty gave him a manly handshake and pat on the back before Sydney said, "It was a close one. I hoped and prayed you would win."

"Thank you, Syd. It worked."

Looking over at Julia longingly, he whispered, "Hi…" as the word trailed off. "I've missed you." Before embracing her and kissing her lips, he had Syd hide her eyes. Bryce humorously assisted and turned Syd around. "Everybody ready to go?" Met by smiles and nods, he was happy to head home and go out for dinner.

Not having seen his place in the city, Julia wondered what it would be like.

Meeting his driver, they piled into the SUV and drove from Fenway into the downtown core.

When the man stopped in front of a big building, Ty announced, "Here we are. Home Sweet Home."

"Is this where we are staying," Bryce asked Julia, seeing many valets hovering about.

"I suppose so," she said.

Ty got out and went to open the tailgate.

"The guys will unpack your luggage here and will bring everything upstairs." The baseball player shot Bryce a look and snickered. "Remember, you are on vacation, my friend. Don't do anything. You're my guest. You need a break."

"Okay, okay. I'll try." Bryce got out and looked up at the tall building. Amazed by his surroundings, he felt a little uneasy amidst the concrete jungle.

The ball player could see it. "Come on, let's go inside and get you settled in."

Everyone walked into the luxurious foyer. The valet followed with their baggage. Welcomed by light colors with beige marble slabs beneath their feet, Julia could no longer hear the sounds of the city.

Going up the elevators, they soon arrived at Ty's residence on the thirty-seventh floor. When he swung open the door, Julia wasn't sure what to expect. The foyer had a simple table and a mirror above it. It was sparsely decorated but opulent. To their right was the living room, and directly in front was the dining area. On either side were two long hallways.

"Here. Let me take your coats," he said, grabbing one hanger at a time from the closet.

Julia could hear a pin drop. It was so quiet.

Just then, the valet arrived at the door with their luggage. Wheeling everything inside, Ty pulled a few bills from his pocket and passed them to the gentleman. "Thanks, man. Appreciate it."

"Thank you, Mr. Reynolds," he said before departing.

"So, where were we? Oh yes, down this hallway are three bedrooms. The staff got them ready for me. I think you will like the decor," he said, helping Julia and Syd with their suitcases. "I thought this one would be good for you, Syd, and this one is for you, Bryce. Each of them has a private bath."

Both walked into their rooms to scout the space, leaving Ty with Julia.

To his right, he opened another door. "This one was designed for you. I had it painted in slate blue, your favorite color." Ty shut the door quietly to have a moment alone. He framed her face with his hands and kissed her. "I'm so glad you're here," he whispered.

"Me too," she held him tightly.

"Look, umm, I'll leave the decision up to you. Whatever you decide, I understand."

She didn't know what to say. "We'll see..." she winked.

He knew what she was implying.

Taking hold of her hand, he asked, "Do you want to see the rest of the place?"

"Yes, please."

Leaving the room, they walked down the hall to the kitchen. The views of Boston Common, the river, and the city were amazing. Ty opened the doors that led to a large balcony with a teak outdoor dining set and corner sectional. Julia could see for miles from that spot.

"Feels like you are on top of the world here," she said, gazing out over the landscape.

"When I first saw this place, the sights got me. I liked that it was spacious too. After a while, I thought it was too big for one person. But now, this works quite well, don't you think?"

"Yes. It's perfect."

Moving inside, hearing Bryce and Syd calling for them, Ty left the doors open to allow the spring breeze to flow through. Julia peeked into his living room. Dressed in hues of grey, it had a masculine vibe but looked comfortable. His office was neat and tidy, something he knew she'd appreciate.

"So, shall we head downstairs for dinner?" He asked, feeling famished, needing to always eat after a game.

Agreeing wholeheartedly, one by one, they stepped into the elevator to be on their way.

Ty led his guests out the main doors of his residence and down Washington Street. He held Julia's hand while Bryce held onto Sydney's.

Having never been in any city other than Toronto, Bryce was concerned about the crowds meandering through the theatre district. It was a bit overwhelming for him. Thankfully, the Sox player swung open the restaurant door, which allowed them to escape the mayhem. There, the frequent VIP customer found his friend at the host podium. Julia assumed as much since he greeted him with a manly grab of the hand and pat on his back.

"Reynolds, my man. How are you? Long time no see." The guy looked over at Julia and Syd, then Bryce. "How was the game today?"

"Won by a run."

"Oh, close one, then? Sorry, I missed it. Duty calls."

"No problem. It wasn't that exciting."

"So, glad to see you brought some company finally. It's about time," he laughed. "This guy spends too much time alone."

"Okay. Okay, say what you will." Turning to everyone, Ty introduced, "Jake, meet Bryce, Sydney, and my Julia."

"Oh, wow." Shocked, Jake was noticeably taken aback. "This is *the* Julia?"

"Yes," he confirmed proudly.

"She does exist." Jake chuckled. "Sorry, how he described you made me think you were imaginary."

Ty shot his friend a look.

"Sorry, my man. All in good fun. Anyway, it is so nice to meet all of you. First time in Boston?"

"Yes. First time for all of us," Julia stated, a little out of her element.

"Well, welcome. Follow me. I'll get you seated." Jake led the way through the restaurant with menus in hand. The place had black ceilings and walls, accented by honeywood and dark brown leather chairs. The almost monochromatic pallet worked very well together.

"Here we go?" Jake presented them with a booth in the corner of the room beside a large picture window. He knew Ty preferred being a little further away from the other patrons. "Hope this works for you."

"Yes, it's great. Thanks, man."

"No problem. I'll have someone over to grab your drink orders in a minute."

"Appreciate that."

Over the next hour and a half, Ty caught up with everyone. Intently listening to them share their news, they enjoyed bountiful laughter and delicious food.

Only asked for two autographs while they were there, he was thankful it happened near the end of the night. Otherwise, it could have started a flurry of fans.

About to pay the bill with Jake looking on, the baseball player got approached by two teenage brothers who knew exactly who he was. Sharing what league they played in, Ty signed their napkins and took selfies with them before giving the boys noteworthy advice.

Listening to what he had to say, Julia felt proud of the man he was.

The boys soaked up his every word of wisdom and thanked him for taking the time to talk to them.

Holding Julia's hand, he wished the guys the best of luck in their upcoming season and bid Jake good night on the way out.

Leaving the restaurant, they turned left and walked back to the Ritz residence. Bryce and Syd led the way through the crowd. Strangely, Ty never got recognized once amidst all those people.

Almost there, Julia could tell Bryce was exhausted. "I've noticed a change in him recently," she said. "I'm not sure what is going on, but he seems more tired these days. Maybe it's because he was worked up about this trip. It was the first time he'd ever been on a plane."

"You're kidding?" Ty flashed a surprised look. "No wonder he's exhausted." Thinking a second, he added, "I'm sure he will perk up tomorrow at the game. He seemed pretty alright today while he was there."

"I'm sure he will. It was the happiest I'd seen him in a very long time. Thank you for inviting him, too."

"Of course," Ty replied sincerely. "He's a member of the family. I knew he'd love it."

66

April to October

Regular / Post-Season

Returning to Toronto that Sunday night, having enjoyed watching Ty's first home game in Boston, the memories replayed in Julia's mind as their life quickly returned to its usual rhythm.

With the Sox's hectic travel schedule, Julia and Sydney relied on televised games to feel close to him when they couldn't be there in person. Each time the team played Toronto, Bryce made the two-hour drive to join them. His visits brought a lively energy to the house, and Julia noticed how much younger Bryce seemed during those early summer months. Cutting back his hours at the Carling had left him with more time on his hands, and their game nights gave him a sense of belonging he cherished deeply.

When Ty invited them to spend a few weeks in Boston during July and August, Julia was thrilled, but Bryce politely declined. He waved off the offer, mentioning the hassle of travel and his preference for staying close to home. Julia didn't push, knowing his independence was important to him.

"You all go have fun," Bryce had told her with a smile. "The first trip was enough for me—I'll treasure that memory forever."

Instead, Julia and Sydney turned their focus to making the most of their time with Bryce closer to home. True to her word, they spent five days with him at the Carling that summer. Though Ty couldn't join them, his frequent FaceTime calls kept him close in spirit.

During their visit, filling their days with laughter and delicious home-cooked meals, Julia made sure to leave Bryce's freezer stocked with portions for easy dinners he could warm at his leisure. Between catching up and exploring the many swimming pools, the girls discovered a number of fun water sports centered around Lake Rosseau. Immersing in the time together, they created new memories that Bryce quietly treasured.

By September, the season was nearing its end, and Ty's grueling schedule was taking a toll. While playing the Braves in Atlanta, Sydney excitedly pointed out the bracelet she'd made for him, tucked neatly into his glove.

"He's missing us," she whispered to her Mother with a knowing smile.

Julia's heart swelled, knowing his small gestures—gifts, flowers, and daily calls—helped bridge the gap during their long separations.

After a grueling stretch in Houston, Ty's team traveled north to face the Blue Jays in Toronto. Julia and Sydney eagerly awaited him after the game, determined to make the most of their limited time together.

When Ty finally emerged from the locker room inside the Rogers Centre, his tired eyes lit up at the sight of them, and Sydney ran straight into his arms. Julia couldn't help but smile as he scooped the little girl up, holding her tightly as if to make up for all the moments he had missed.

Though visibly drained, Ty tried his best to remain upbeat, asking about their drive downtown and what they had been up to since their last call. Julia noticed the stiffness in his movements—reminders of how demanding the season had become. The team was only halfway through their ten-game road trip, and the toll of constant travel was apparent. Still, he squeezed her hand and smiled in that familiar way that made her heart ache with love.

Over the next couple of days, they cherished the few hours they could spend together. Whether sharing a quiet meal, taking a stroll through a nearby park, or simply sitting in his hotel room talking, they made each moment count and learned to adjust their expectations, knowing how much Ty needed rest to stay at his peak performance.

In the evenings, he'd reluctantly returned to the team's hotel, needing to recover from the physical demands placed upon him. Julia and Sydney understood, even if it hurt to let him go so soon.

"Take care of yourself," Julia whispered one night as she hugged him goodbye. "We love you." Her words, simple but sincere, stayed with him long after he said, "Love you, too, before having to close the door behind him.

When their visits together ended, as hard as it was, Julia found comfort in the little gestures that spoke volumes. The way he kissed Sydney's forehead or how he embraced Julia each time made them feel just as important as the game he loved.

As the regular season wound down, a bittersweet anticipation filled the air, carrying a sense of both achievement and loss. The finish line was in sight, a stark reminder that Ty's career was drawing to a close. Every game brought him closer to saying goodbye to a lifetime of hard work, dedication, and dreams fulfilled. This year, it wasn't just the pursuit of a championship. It was a farewell to the sport he loved, the teammates who became family, and the life he had built around the game. Julia could sense the mixed emotions he carried—pride for all he had accomplished and the weight of leaving behind something he loved so much. Yet, his focus never wavered.

Surviving a grueling week, the Sox had clinched a spot in the AL Division Series, and with it, Ty threw himself into preparing for their match-up against the Yankees. The girls cheered him on from afar and offered what support they could as those games unfolded, one by one.

When the Sox triumphed, defeating the Yankees three games to one in the best-of-five, the celebration was short-lived. The pace quickly increased, leaving no time to rest. They were already shifting their focus to the Houston Astros in the ALCS—a new challenge that promised even more intensity and pressure. Every game from here on out was crucial, a chance for redemption and a step closer to a championship that seemed just within their reach.

For Ty, it was the final push. Knowing that the end was drawing near, he focused on every victory that brought them closer to the ultimate goal. The tension was profound as they prepared for the next series, knowing it could be their last.

67

October 18th

Game Five of the American League Championship Series

The weekend after Canadian Thanksgiving, the Boston Red Sox prepared to play Game 5 of the ALCS. Ahead three to one in the series, they hoped to end it on the road in Houston. Julia and Sydney had hoped Bryce would join them to watch the game, but he had other commitments and couldn't make the trip. They understood but missed having him there to share in the excitement.

Instead, it was just the two of them in the living room, wearing their Sox jerseys and surrounded by snacks. Sydney clutched a foam finger as they settled in to cheer Ty on, their hopes pinned on a decisive victory that could send his team to the World Series.

The game was a nail-biter from the start. By the end of the third inning, Boston was ahead 1–0, and Sydney kept glancing nervously at her Mother, hoping the Astros wouldn't tie it up. As the innings progressed, the tension in the room grew.

Finally, in the top of the sixth, Boston brought in three runs, extending their lead to 4–0.

Bryce called during the game, his voice full of excitement as he cheered over the phone. "This might be it! They've got it in the bag!" he exclaimed.

Julia smiled at his enthusiasm but remained cautiously optimistic. "It's not over until it's over," she replied, not wanting to jinx anything.

The little girl's energy matched Bryce's. "We've got this, Mom! I can feel it!"

"Let's hope you're right, kiddo." She softly ruffled Sydney's hair.

The three of them stayed on edge, watching the game unfold and hoping Ty's team could hold on to their lead and secure the win.

Sydney happened to catch a close-up of Ty.

"Look, Mom. He's wearing my bracelet again," she said excitedly. "Maybe it will bring them more good luck."

"Maybe so." With eyes peeled, Julia waited patiently to catch a glimpse of him whenever she could.

The past few weeks had been a rollercoaster ride. They didn't get to see each other much. Many of his teammates' wives often remarked that being married to a baseball player meant embracing a life of independence—spending time alone and managing everything at home while their husbands were on the road. Sadly, the only one-on-one time was during the off-season—nothing else.

Given how close the team was to the end, Julia tried her best to soldier through. It was a marathon, and the finish line was close at hand. She was glad he was retiring, but a piece of her wondered if he would play one more year if they didn't win the World Series.

How would I ever survive another season being apart? She thought. Not getting ahead of herself, she put it out of her mind.

At the bottom of the seventh, the Astros brought in a run to make it 4 - 1. Julia and Sydney watched to the bitter end, hoping their team could hang onto the lead through the last two innings. Neither side ended up crossing home plate.

"That's game!" Julia shouted, falling backward onto the sofa.

"What does this mean?" Syd asked.

Julia covered her face with her hands, her voice breaking with emotion as tears streamed down her cheeks. "They did it! They just won the American League Championship and clinched a spot in the World Series!"

"Yeeaahh!" Syd cheered. "So, now they have to play another team to win that?"

"Yes."

While the Sox celebrated on the field, they watched Ty place his hand over his heart when he looked straight into the camera and pointed. They knew that was for them.

As the girls came down off the high of the big win, the house gradually grew quiet, the earlier cheers fading into a contented stillness. Julia found herself glancing at her phone, hoping Ty would call so she could hear his voice and share in his excitement, even if only for a moment.

After tucking Sydney in bed, Julia checked the time. It was almost midnight as she got under the covers. Despite the game only ending twenty minutes ago, with the time difference and the late start, she wondered how he was doing and figured the team might be celebrating their win.

Suddenly, her phone rang. Grabbing it off her side table, she desperately said, "Hello?"

"What are you still doing up?" He asked humorously.

"I was waiting for you."

"Sorry to be calling so late. There were a few interviews and photo ops tonight. We're headed to the hotel now."

Julia could hear he was riding in a vehicle. "I'm so proud of you. Congratulations."

"Thank you. The chances of winning the series are getting closer and closer by the day."

"Yes. Almost there."

"We got our schedule. The first two games against the Dodgers will be at home - October 23rd and 24th. Can you and Sydney make it to the one on the 24th? Maybe ask Bryce if he wants to join you. I think he'd love that."

"I will try my best." Checking the dates on the calendar, she noticed they landed mid-week. "Guess I will take Syd out of school for a couple of days - see if work is okay with me going."

"After that, we head to LA. If I make all the arrangements, could you be there?" Ty went quiet. "I'd love for you both to be in the stands. But understand if you can't."

She didn't have to think twice. These were the final games of his career—moments that mattered. "Yes," she said simply. "We wouldn't miss it."

"Thank you for all the support. It's meant the world to me," he replied, his voice quiet and worn.

"You don't have to thank me," Julia said softly. "We're in this together, every step of the way." She paused, her voice warm with reassurance. "I'm so proud of you, Ty." Knowing he was exhausted, she said quietly, "You go and get some sleep."

"I will," he murmured. Then, after a beat, he added, "I miss you."

"I miss you too," she said, her tone steady but warm. "Rest up, and we'll talk tomorrow."

"Will do. Looking forward to it. I love you," he said, the words soft but genuine.

"I love you too. Goodnight. Sweet dreams."

"I'm hoping you'll be in them."

Ending the call, Julia smiled while setting the phone on the nightstand. Rolling over in bed, she hoped to dream of him, too.

October 24th

Game Two of the World Series in Boston

Landing in Boston after the Sox had won their first home game the night before, Julia and Sydney stepped off the plane into the crisp autumn air. Their driver was already waiting at the curb, but the trip felt incomplete without Bryce. He had decided to stay home, saying he'd cheer them on from afar, and though Julia understood, she couldn't help but miss his presence.

By the time they arrived at Ty's residence, he was already at Fenway, deep into pregame preparations. True to his meticulous nature, he had left instructions with the concierge to let them in, ensuring they could freshen up and get ready before heading to the ballpark.

Now accustomed to the fast pace of Ty's world, Julia took it all in stride. She helped Sydney get moving, and before long, they were back downstairs to meet their driver. As they made their way to Fenway, Julia reminded herself that this whirlwind wouldn't last forever—just one more week, and Ty would be with them full-time. The thought gave her a small surge of relief.

At the ballpark, they got ushered to the family box. Julia exchanged warm greetings with the players' wives while Sydney immediately gravitated toward a couple of the daughters she'd bonded with over the past few months. Settling into her seat, Julia allowed herself a moment to breathe, the hum of Fenway's pregame energy buzzing around her.

That night, the game lacked the electric energy of previous matchups, the kind that had fans gripping their seats in suspense. Still, it was a solid showing for the Sox. The crowd remained lively, cheering at every solid hit and pitch. Boston had established a steady lead at 4–2, and the atmosphere grew more relaxed as fans anticipated a win.

Julia watched intently, clapping and smiling at each play, while Sydney, sitting beside her, alternated between cheering and asking questions about the game. The Sox's defense held strong through the final innings, shutting down the Astros' attempts to rally. When the final out was called, the crowd erupted, filling the stadium with a wave of triumphant cheers.

Though it wasn't the most dramatic victory, it was a meaningful one. With the win, the Sox inched closer to their ultimate goal, and the team's focus and determination were clear. They had their sights on winning the World Series.

Swept up in the collective pride and optimism of the fans around her, Julia already found herself thinking about what the games in LA might bring.

Following the families down to the players' hall, the Marianis waited for Ty to come out of the locker room. Even though the team won, they noticed the players still had their game faces on. They could not celebrate yet. Ahead two to nothing in the series going into game three, the men seemed all business.

Bubbling over, Sydney tugged on her Mom's arm. "There he is!"

Julia caught Ty's eye immediately as he walked toward them with purpose. A wide grin spread across his face, his exhaustion momentarily forgotten.

As Ty reached them, he swept Sydney up into his arms, twirling her around as she squealed with delight. "How's my favorite kiddo doing?" he asked, his voice warm. Setting her back on her feet, he ruffled her hair playfully, his love for her evident in every gesture.

Then he turned to Julia, and for a moment, the bustling hallway faded away. Pulling her into a firm embrace, he held her tightly, burying his face in her hair as if drawing strength from her presence. "I missed you," he murmured, his voice low but full of emotion.

"I missed you too," she replied, her hands lingering on his arms as if to anchor him.

Ty pulled back just enough to meet her eyes, his beaming smile turning heads among the other families. Without hesitation, he leaned in, kissing her softly, a gesture that left no doubt about his feelings.

The other wives exchanged knowing glances, some smiling at the display of affection enviously.

Realizing Sydney was still watching, Ty quickly covered her eyes with one hand, making her giggle. "Alright, alright, no need to see all that," he joked before crouching to her level.

"So, did you like the game?" he asked, his tone lightening as he focused on her.

"It was awesome!" Her face lit up. "But I like it better when you get more home runs."

Ty chuckled, the sound, rich and genuine. "Fair enough. I'll let the guys know we need to work on that just for you."

Syd gave him an enthusiastic thumbs up, her confidence in his ability unwavering.

As the first baseman glanced back at Julia, his eyes softened, the weight of the long season momentarily lifting. Being with them, even for a short while, was enough to recharge his spirit.

"Come on, you two. Let's go home." Taking hold of Julia's hand, they walked out of Fenway and got into the SUV waiting. While driving to the Ritz residences, Ty said, "We are flying out tomorrow late morning. I guess Bryce doesn't want to head to LA?"

"I think it's too much for him. When he came with us to Boston, it took him a few days to recover. It wasn't bad when you were playing in Toronto. He didn't mind going back and forth. But this is a five-hour flight, give or take."

"Alright, I'll make arrangements for the two of you then. Do you want to head home and pack? Maybe leave on the 26th? That first game is going to be intense. So, I'll need to stay focused. It's best if you are there for the games on the 27th and 28th. Hopefully, the series won't go back to Boston."

"It will be hectic, but we will make it work."

"Perfect." Ty texted the team's family services people and let them know what he would like done. Putting his phone away, he said, "Okay. When they get everything squared away, I'll forward you the itinerary."

"That sounds good."

Ty texted his building concierge and ordered food from the restaurant downstairs for delivery to his residence within a half hour. Pulling in front of the building, he proudly walked in with his ladies and headed to the elevator. Julia could tell he was tired.

Arriving on his floor, he held the door open for them as they walked inside.

While helping them hang their coats, he said, "Give me a few minutes. I'm just going to change. If you hear a knock at the door, it will probably be the concierge with the food. Do you mind answering it in case I don't hear it?"

"Sure. No problem." Julia watched him slowly move down the hallway to his room. She knew he was hurting.

When he returned, dressed in joggers and a t-shirt, he went straight for the freezer to grab a few ice packs before finding his slippers in the living room beside the couch. As he put them on, a knock came at the door. Ty went to open it and grabbed their food order.

"Thanks, man," he said to the guy who seemed starstruck by the famous baseball player. After passing along a tip, the door closed behind him. Bringing everything to the kitchen, he added, "Sorry, I don't have much here. I've rarely been home."

"That's fine. We will manage." Julia gave Sydney her dinner. She had already set up her laptop on the kitchen counter to chat with friends.

Seeing Ty moving rigidly toward the sofa with his food container in hand, he sat down slowly and packed the ice around his ankle and knee.

"Are you okay? Stiffening up?"

He turned to her when she sat beside him. "Yeah, I might head down to the Club for a steam later, if that's alright."

"Yes. Just do what you have to do. Don't worry about us."

While Ty started eating, he was overly quiet. It seemed he had something on his mind. "Umm, I was thinking about when this is all over. I mean, the series. I'm looking forward to doing whatever I want—living wherever I want. I'm thinking of selling this place. Don't think I'd have any reason to come back here. What do you think?"

She was surprised to be included in that decision. "That depends. Do you want to still live in Boston if you're no longer playing?"

"No, I think my heart wants to live somewhere else." He reached his hand to her and gave it a few gentle squeezes.

Julia was happy to hear that.

"I'll call the agent for the building this week and get it listed."

She nodded.

He took a bite of pasta. "So, I was thinking about moving to Toronto. What are your thoughts on that?" He glanced her way out of the corner of his eye.

"Toronto, huh?"

"Yeah. I want to look at a few places in your area."

"Well, we would love to have you in the neighborhood," she giggled.

He smiled from ear to ear.

Sydney walked into the room, balancing her laptop in both hands, showing her friends a live view of the apartment and the city lights from the windows. "I finished my dinner, Mom. I'm going to my room to play games for a bit with my friends."

"Okay, Syd. But just for an hour, then it's time for bed. We are traveling back home tomorrow."

"Okay," she replied, half listening.

Julia turned to find Ty's eyes drifting shut. "I think you should probably head to bed."

Half awake, he said, "Umm yeah."

"Don't worry. I will turn off the lights and put things away. You go ahead."

"Are you sure?" He could barely string a sentence together.

"Yes. You go."

Getting up, Ty made his way down the hall to his room.

Julia walked down the opposite hallway to remind Sydney to keep her voice down. Her daughter's enthusiasm for online games often came with loud, uncontainable outbursts lately, and the last thing Julia wanted was for her to wake Ty.

She peeked in the doorway. "Please keep it quiet. Ty's trying to get some rest," she said gently but firmly.

Sydney nodded, her eyes still glued to the screen.

Back in the kitchen, Julia tidied up, disposing of the garbage and wiping down the counters. The condo felt peaceful in the dim light, the earlier excitement of the game settling into a calming stillness. After finishing, she turned off the remaining lights and made her way to check on him.

When she entered his room, she found him sprawled across the bed, still in his clothes, sound asleep. He hadn't even bothered to pull the covers over himself. Julia's heart softened. Quietly slipping back to her room, she grabbed a soft throw blanket. Returning to him, she gently draped it over his broad shoulders, tucking it around him with care. For a moment, she lingered, contemplating whether to crawl in beside him. The idea of being close, even just for a little while, was tempting, but she decided against it. He needed rest more than anything, and she didn't want to risk disturbing him. With a soft sigh, Julia left again, her footsteps light as she walked back down the hall. She poked her head into Sydney's room, finding her already turning off her game. "Bedtime, Sweetie," she said softly.

"I know. I am," Sydney replied, yawning as she set her controller aside.

In minutes, Julia got into her bed, the place now entirely quiet. As her head hit the pillow, she thought of Ty down the hall, thankful just to be near him.

69

October 25th

Travel Day

Very early the following morning, Julia heard Ty's alarm echo down the hallway. The sun had barely breached the horizon. Like clockwork, he got up and started moving around. Tossing some clothes into the washer, she heard him press the button before the water started pouring.

Wrapped in her robe, tying the belt around her waist, she walked down the hall. Peeking in, she found him folding his clothes in piles. Organized with his suits, shirts, and ties for the next three games, all hanging in the doorway of his closet, he drifted here and there, gathering what he needed.

Finding Julia watching him, he turned, smiled, and said, "Good morning."

"Morning." Taking the blanket off the bed, he said with a smitten smile, "I believe this is yours."

"While you were sleeping, I covered you up." She took hold of it as he passed it over, all neatly folded. "Didn't want you to get cold."

"Thank you for that." Strolling over, he placed his hands on her hips. "Did you sleep well?"

"Yes, you?" she asked, her voice soft.

"Suppose so. Sorry, I wasn't much company last night."

"It's okay," she reassured him. "I know you were exhausted. You needed to rest and prepare for today."

He pulled her into a tight hug, his warmth seeping into her. "Feels like I missed out on more than just a good conversation," he muttered, his voice laced with a teasing edge.

She caught the meaning behind his words, her cheeks instantly warming.

"There's still time," he added, his tone lighter now but still suggestive.

Julia glanced over his shoulder, spotting the bed cluttered with clothes he had yet to pack. "I don't think there's room for anything else," she said, giggling at the mess.

Turning to follow her gaze, Ty chuckled. "True. But, you know, I can think of one place that's not overcrowded," he quipped, raising an eyebrow.

Her heart raced at his playful suggestion, and with a quick glance down the hall, she slipped her hand into his. Together, they quietly made their way to her room.

The door closed behind them with a soft click, the sound amplified in the stillness of the early morning. Locking it, they found the first rays of dawn filtering through the edges of the drapes, casting a warm glow that made the space feel intimate.

As she turned to face him, Julia's eyes met his with a quiet intensity that spoke of all the moments they'd missed and the love that had remained constant through it all.

Staying quiet, mindful of Sydney still sleeping in the room down the hall, Ty reached for Julia's hands, their fingers intertwining as if by instinct. He pulled her closer, his movements unhurried, his gaze never leaving hers. "Soon," he whispered, brushing his lips against her temple, "We can do this every morning."

Her heart fluttered at the promise in his words.

He kissed her then, slow and unguarded, the kind of kiss that made her feel adored and cherished. Her free hand found its way to his chest, feeling the steady rhythm of his heartbeat beneath her fingertips.

Hands cradling her face, his thumbs brushed her cheeks in a tender caress. He said, his voice low and full of emotion. "Even when I'm on the road, I feel you're with me."

She leaned into him, their foreheads touching as they shared a quiet moment of connection. "And you with me," she replied, her voice steady despite the lump in her throat. "No matter where you are, I always think of you."

His lips found hers again, this time with more urgency, a reflection of all the time they had spent apart.

Slipping her arms sensuously around his neck, she melted into him.

As he moved her toward the bed, their steps were in sync as if drawn by an invisible pull. Ty eased her down onto the soft mattress, his hands carefully guiding her. He hovered a moment, his eyes searching hers as if to memorize every detail. "I love you," he said simply, his voice full of conviction.

"I love you too," she whispered, her hand cupping his cheek.

What followed was a meeting of souls, not just bodies—a quiet celebration of their love and their bond that had weathered distance and challenges. Ty's touch was gentle, his hands exploring her as if rediscovering a map he knew by heart.

With equal tenderness, her fingertips traced the contours of his shoulders and back, grounding herself in his presence.

Sharing a hint of quiet laughter when they got tangled awkwardly, he whispered loving words when their emotions were about to overwhelm them. Breaths mingling, their foreheads rested against one another in the aftermath. They remained immersed in the peacefulness they'd longed for for so long.

Julia tried to soak up what little time they had. She clung to him, thankful to share a loving moment, knowing she'd have to say good-bye soon.

"I wish I could stay here with you all day. How nice would it be just to let the world go by?"

She smiled and looked up from his chest. "Yes, it would, but you have a series to win."

"Yes, I do." Reminded of the time, he hugged her tightly. "Don't hate me, but I've got to finish packing. I'm supposed to be at the airport in less than three hours."

"I understand. I know you have to get moving."

He gently kissed her. "I'm sorry. I love you."

Leaving the room, making sure Sydney was nowhere in sight, he checked on his laundry and threw it in the dryer. Understanding his routine, she stayed out of the way. Going to sit with him as he packed, he said, "I just ordered breakfast. It should be here shortly."

With his bags at the front door, he enjoyed the last few minutes before having to depart. Happy to eat together, Ty said, "You can leave whenever you like. There is no need to rush."

Knowing their flight was late afternoon, she said, "Maybe we'll try and catch an earlier plane home. That way, we will return sooner and can get organized for the trip to LA."

"That would be a good idea." He hated the thought of leaving them behind. Suddenly, his phone vibrated. "I just got your itinerary from family HQ. I'm forwarding it to you now."

Julia made sure she got it. "Yes, I see it. Thank you."

Checking on the time, he said, "I've gotta run."

Getting dressed, he returned and met Julia and Sydney at the front door, looking dapper in jeans, a white shirt, and a sports jacket.

"I'll see you in LA, then? Travel safe." Hugging Julia and kissing her goodbye, he turned to Syd. "See you soon, Kiddo."

"It seems we are always saying goodbye." The young girl looked so sad.

"I know. Not for much longer. Soon, I won't be traveling anywhere unless it's on vacation with the two of you." That comment made her face light up. "If you could go anywhere in the world, where would it be?"

It got Sydney thinking.

"Do some research and tell me your plan when you get to LA. Deal?"

"Deal!" she exclaimed.

"Awesome."

Wrapping his arms around Julia again, he kissed her one last time and whispered, "Bye. Love you both," before wheeling his luggage out the door.

Julia stayed strong. She knew if he saw her that way, it would mean he wouldn't worry about them. Waving as he got in the elevator, Ty soon disappeared.

"Well, Syd, we should get packed up and be on our way. Ready to head home?"

"Yep." Her daughter walked towards her room.

"Hopefully, we will land in Toronto before dinner."

70

October 27th

West Coast Bound

Only home for two days, Julia and Sydney moved quickly to prepare for their upcoming trip to LA, where they would attend games four and five of the World Series at Dodger Stadium. The excitement of being part of such a monumental event buzzed through their home as they packed their bags. Julia meticulously double-checked their tickets and travel plans while Sydney eagerly chose her favorite outfits, already imagining the thrill of cheering for Ty in a ballpark packed with fans.

By evening, their suitcases were lined neatly by the front door, ready for their early morning departure. The anticipation of seeing Ty on baseball's biggest stage kept Julia's thoughts racing.

After making sure Sydney got tucked in for the night, she climbed into bed but couldn't sleep just yet. She turned on the television to watch Game Three as the opening pitch echoed through her room, allowing herself a quiet moment to soak in the enormity of it all—the culmination of Ty's career and the memories they were about to share.

That night, the teams battled for eighteen innings - a marathon that lasted a grueling seven hours and twenty minutes. Sadly, the Sox came out one run short. At a score of three to two, the Dodgers took the first win at home. Upon seeing their opponent's winning run and getting a glimpse of Ty's disappointment, she turned off the television.

Rolling over at three-thirty, desperate to fall asleep, she didn't expect him to call.

Dragging herself out of bed a couple of hours later, Julia turned off her alarm at five o'clock. Exhausted beyond words, she walked to Sydney's room in a zombie-like state to wake her. Gently shaking her daughter's shoulder and whispering that it was time to get up, the young girl stirred.

"Are we leaving today?" she asked curiously.

"Yes, we are. Are you excited?"

Syd perked up. "Very much! I hope they win."

"Me too, Sweetie." On the way out her door, she said, "Make sure you get ready, okay? We need to leave in an hour."

"Don't worry. I will," she said, jumping out of bed with a bounce in her step.

Walking back to her room to change into comfortable travel clothes, Julia moved through the morning routine on autopilot, checking and double-checking that they had everything they needed.

After printing their boarding passes online to save time, she grabbed the luggage tags and looped them over each suitcase handle. Satisfied that they were all set, she gave the house one last look to ensure nothing was left behind.

Seeing their airline SUV pull up in front of the house and back into the driveway, she opened the door and met the gentleman ready to load their luggage.

"Good morning, Ma'am," he said cordially.

"Good morning," she replied, desperately trying to shake off her grogginess.

Sydney threw her backpack on her shoulder and headed out while Julia locked up. Taking her mobile office with her, she settled in beside Sydney.

It was a quiet ride to Pearson.

Arriving just after six-thirty, they checked their bags and got through security unscathed. Able to grab breakfast, Julia could see last night's crazy World Series game was making headlines.

Her daughter listened in while they ate a breakfast sandwich at their gate.

"Wow, that game was long. Did you watch the whole thing?"

"Yes, unfortunately so. If you see me falling asleep on the plane, don't be alarmed," her Mom yawned.

"No problem."

Julia checked their tickets to see where they were seated. At the top of the boarding pass, it said signature class. She was in row A5, and Sydney was in D5. Afraid to be separated, Julia said, "Give me a second, Syd. I am going to go and ask the lady something."

Walking to the check-in desk to speak to the woman on duty, the kind lady explained that their seats were pods and reassured that her daughter would be directly adjacent to her. Returning to Syd, her little girl asked, "Is there something wrong?"

Intent on leaving the seating a surprise, she said, "Nothing. Everything is fine."

By twenty after seven, the boarding announcement echoed through the airport. Slowly getting up to gather their things, Julia made sure nothing got left behind.

About to board the plane, she watched for Syd's reaction to their seating arrangements.

The stewardess greeted Sydney first. "Well, hello there. Good morning." She checked her name on the boarding pass. "Welcome aboard, Miss Sydney." Taking Julia's as well, she said, "Your seats are right here." Escorting them, the woman opened the privacy drapes. These are seats A5 and D5."

Sydney turned to her Mother. "What is this?"

The stewardess smiled. "Well, it's Signature Class, dear. Go ahead. Take your seat. I'll be back to check on you shortly."

Timidly looking around, she asked, "Did Ty do this for us?"

"Yes, I believe so. It's a long flight. Guess he wanted us to be comfortable."

The little girl snuggled up in the luxurious chair. "I could get used to this."

Offering a gentle smile and a short snicker, she said, "Oh, no, you don't, young lady. We won't be making a habit of it. He did it because it was a special occasion. That's all."

Settled in, ready for the long journey ahead, in minutes, they departed from the gate on time and taxied out onto the runway.

Feeling the plane move, Sydney grabbed hold of her armrests with an excited look on her face. "Here we go!"

As the engines roared, soon, they took off and soared into the blue skies above, bound for the West Coast.

Successfully on their way, the tween got out her headphones and started scrolling through the list of movies available.

Taking in a breath, hoping to relax, Julia thought about Ty's teammates and their extended friends and family always around to cheer them on. She felt sad for him because he had nobody in the stands all these years. It got her thinking of his sister.

Taking out her phone, she racked her brain, trying to remember the name of Jenna's husband. "Dan and Jenna? Dan..." she said, hoping that repeating the name would trigger her memory. "Dan... Oh, what was his last name." Pulling up Facebook, she said, "Jenna and Dan...Ducane. That's it." Julia started a search for anyone named Jenna Reynolds, Jenna Reynolds-Ducane, or Jenna Ducane. Surprisingly, Jenna Reynolds came up. In her profile, she read she was from Texas and married to Dan Ducane.

"That wasn't so hard. Perfect." She touched the button. "Send a friend request," she whispered, hoping it wouldn't take Jenna long to respond. Julia wondered whether or not his sister had watched him play against the Astros when he was in town. "How nice would that have been?" she said. Barely able to keep her eyes open, she motioned to Syd to get her attention.

"Yeah," her little girl said, slipping one headphone off her ear.

"I'm going to try and get some sleep. Do you need me for anything?"

"Nope, I'm good. If I do, though, I'll ask that nice lady."

"That's fine. Don't go anywhere. If you need to go to the bathroom, please wake me up. Do not go alone, understand."

"Yes. Okay."

Julia reclined the chair and got comfortable. It wasn't long before she fell asleep.

Sometime later, in a muffled state, Julia heard her name and felt someone tapping her arm. Opening one eye, she found Sydney's excited face mere inches away.

"The pilot said we are beginning our descent into LAX. Want to see out my window? There are mountains down there, Mom."

Moving to sit in Sydney's seat, the little girl plopped herself down on her lap and peered out at the view.

"Look! There's the beach and the ocean. Guess we are flying over Ty's head right now."

"Yes, I suppose we are," Julia replied, not entirely coherent. Seeing the fasten seatbelt sign illuminate, she realized she needed to buckle up. "Sadly, I need to return to my seat. We will be landing shortly. Make sure you fasten your seatbelt." Julia stepped across the aisle.

Sydney did as she said.

Before the wifi got turned off, she checked her phone and found nothing from Ty yet, and Jenna had not responded. About to land, she gathered all of her things in her pod and made sure her daughter did the same.

When the wheels hit the ground within minutes, it prompted everyone on board to applaud the landing.

Knowing Ty would still be sleeping, she refrained from texting him, hoping to let him rest.

At exactly 10:22 Pacific, the plane stopped at the gate, and the door opened. Julia and Sydney disembarked and headed through customs before picking up their bags. Happy it didn't take long, they were then on their way out the arrival doors. Scanning the crowd, assuming there would be a driver holding a sign with their name on it, Julia noticed a tall man with a baseball cap standing in the back corner near the exit. She thought of Ty. Getting a closer look, she realized why the man was smiling.

Sydney picked up on it right away. "He's here!"

Running to him, jumping into his arms, he hugged her. "Hey, Kiddo."

Hurrying to catch up to her daughter, Julia soon approached, surprised. "What are you doing here?"

"What do you mean? I came to meet my girls at the airport." Hugging Julia, he kissed her lovingly. "How was your flight?" he asked, looking like death warmed over.

"Uneventful." Julia felt bad.

"Well, that's good to hear." Afraid to deal with any disgruntled fans, he put his head down and said, "Let's get going. I have a driver waiting outside."

Wheeling the girls' luggage out the doors, he approached the SUV as the driver got out to load their bags in the back. Getting into the middle row, each found a seat.

Ty wrapped his arm around Julia. Resting his opposite elbow on the door, he held his head in the palm of his hand and closed his eyes.

"What time is the game today?"

"It starts just after five. The team has to be there at three. That gives me a little more time to sleep when we get back to the hotel."

"You should have stayed and got some more rest."

He lovingly turned to her. "And miss seeing you before the big game. Never."

The vehicle pulled up in front of the Ritz Carlton on West Olympic. Stopping outside the entrance, Ty got out and held the door for the girls to join him while the driver got their luggage.

"I've already checked you in. So, here is your key. The room is on the twenty-second floor - room 2218. It's written on the card right here," Ty pointed on their way inside.

Heading toward the elevators, they got in and he pressed the button for their floor. "The team and I are on the twenty-third floor. My room is 2320." He leaned against the wall. "I can't stay. We are running on a tight schedule today. You may want to order room service and have something to eat. At 4:00 pm, or just before then, you will get a call from the security team I hired to escort you to Dodgers Stadium."

"Security? Why?"

"A lot is going on there. Never know how fans will react to the outcome of the game. Just wanna make sure you are both safe."

Julia was surprised to hear that, but it made sense.

"Don't worry. The guys will bring you up to the family box. You don't have to worry about anything. They'll stick with you the entire time."

"Alright," she said while the doors opened on the twenty-second floor. Exiting, they turned left. Their room was a few doors down.

Julia touched their card key to the reader. It opened the Club room suite. In awe of how beautiful the room was, she marveled at the light, airy colors, with two queen-sized beds, benches at the foot end, and a seating area to the left. Peeking into the bathroom, Julia found a double vanity and a wet room with a shower and tub.

Ty rolled their suitcases inside.

"This is stunning."

"I thought you would like it. A nice home away from home." He walked back toward the door. "Well, I've got to go, but I'll see you soon. Follow the other families to the locker room hallway after the game. I'll text you if anything changes. And, oh, by the way, your welcome basket has your passes in it. Going over to check, he pulled out the official VIP tickets attached to MLB lanyards. Handing them to Julia, he said, "Here, put these with the bag you're taking to the game. You must have them visible at all times."

"Alright." Julia noticed the vase of red roses on the table. "Did you do this?' she asked with a smile.

Hugging her tightly, he said, "Of course. I am so happy you're both here. I love you," he said, hearing the alarm on his phone inside his pocket. He took it out. "I'm sorry. I gotta go. I'll see you later."

"Good luck."

"Thanks. Say a few prayers. We need a win."

When he went out the door, Julia locked it behind him. Her mind was reeling as she sat on the bed. There was too much going on, and she was exhausted. "I hope I remember everything he said."

"Don't worry. I got it all. The security people will be here at four o'clock," Sydney reminded.

Needing to snap out of it, Julia clapped her hands together, hoping to rally herself to get moving. "Okay. First things first, let's order some food, and then once we are done, we will get changed and wait for the security to arrive. How does that sound?"

She gave a thumbs up. "Perfect!"

71

October 27th

Game Four of the World Series in Los Angeles

As anticipated, the security team called Julia's room and instructed her to meet them at the concierge desk in the lobby.

Hanging up, she said, "Okay, here we go, Syd. Are you excited?"

"Yes! Are you kidding?" She bounced nervously. "This is awesome."

Slipping their passes around their neck, the two went out the door. The sound of it closing reminded her of their room at the Carling. So much has happened since then. With their Boston swag tucked in their backpack, Julia knew they were in enemy territory and didn't want to attract negative attention.

While descending to the main lobby, they found the concierge and the two fairly big guys dressed all in black. Both had earpieces hanging to one side.

Seeing them approach, the one man turned and said, "You must be Julia and Sydney?"

"Yes, that's right," Julia replied.

"My name is Aaron, and this is Derek. We will be escorting you to Dodgers Stadium today. Happy to see you have your passes. Right this way, the SUV is just outside."

Aaron opened the door for the ladies while Derek got behind the wheel. "We are about eleven minutes out. It won't take long," the burly man said, getting into the front.

Merging onto the 110, they drove along in silence.

Julia was nervous after last night's loss. Needing conversation, she asked, "So, did you watch the game last night?"

"Sure did! It was a marathon, but we won." Aaron said excitedly before backtracking upon seeing Julia pull out their Boston sweaters and hats. "Oh, sorry..."

"It's fine. Don't worry. Our team plans to dominate tonight," she chuckled, hoping to egg them on.

"Ohhh. Sounds like a challenge, Aaron." Derek said, turning to his counterpart.

"We'll see." Aaron was skeptical.

Merging off the highway onto the Dodger Stadium exit, they climbed the hill and rounded the corner to see the stadium lights straight ahead.

Derek pulled up in front of the building while Aaron got out and opened the door for them.

"This way. Ladies. Follow me." He put his credentials around his neck and said, "I believe the Sox reserved three boxes for the visiting families." Approaching the security check-in, Aaron said, "Hello, these lovely ladies are going to Red Sox 222."

The man scanned their passes and double-checked their names on the register before allowing them to proceed.

Granted permission to enter the gates, Aaron led them to the elevator and pressed the button. When it arrived, he got the girls in and held others back to avoid anyone riding with them. Upon exiting, they walked down the hallway. Aaron opened the door when they arrived at their destination. Thankfully, Julia saw a couple of familiar faces. Taking a breather, she said hello to everyone and made the rounds. Upon hearing a few whispers and noticing the odd, peculiar expression, she didn't know what to make of it. No matter how she tried, even though everyone was welcoming, she didn't feel like she was one of them. Realizing it was her insecurity and nothing else, she went to sit out on the balcony and have a quiet moment while Sydney spoke with friends.

Soon, the game was underway after the warm-up and the national anthem. Packed with mostly Dodgers fans, the jumbotron picked out some Red Sox jerseys embedded in the stands. Julia stayed in her seat outside, where she could see Ty the best. Her stomach was once again in knots.

Scoreless until the bottom of the sixth, the Dodgers brought in a whopping four runs to make it a 4 - 0 game.

"Are the Sox going to lose, Mom?" Syd asked, having heard another kid say that.

Julia motioned for her daughter to come and sit with her. "I hope not. A lot can happen still."

The Christmas wishing star crossed Syd's mind. Scanning the skies above her head, she hoped to find it so she could make a wish. But the stadium lights drowned out the stars.

Seeing this, Julia asked, "What are you looking for?"

"The wishing star. It worked last time. Maybe it will help me again."

"I have a better idea. How about we pray for Ty and the team to give them the strength to win? Maybe even get a home run."

"Yes, that's a great idea."

At the top of the seventh, Julia and Sydney closed their eyes and quietly bowed their heads to pray together. The second they said "Amen," the Sox player who was up to bat cleared the bases and scored three runs, making the score 4 - 3.

"Wow, Mom! It worked." She was so excited. "Woohoo! Thank you, God. Go, Sox!"

"Okay, they need one run to tie the game."

Ty stepped up to bat. Julia's heart pounded out of her chest. She was so nervous. Both she and Syd raised their praying hands to their chins and waited as he completed his batting ritual. Closing their eyes just before the pitch, they suddenly heard the crack of the bat. Quickly opening them to see what had happened, they saw the ball flying into center field.

Syd raised her hands in the air and shouted, "Yeah! Homerun!"

The roar of the crowd filled the stadium as Ty sprinted toward first base, his strides long and confident. His cleats kicked up the red dirt, and the excitement in the air was electric. As he rounded second, he glanced toward the stands, searching for the familiar faces cheering him on. Spotting Syd and Julia, he grinned.

Slowing his pace around third, Ty raised his hand to his chest, pressing it over his heart as he turned his gaze upward toward them. With a loving point in their direction, his expression softened, a mix of pride and affection lighting up his features. Julia, catching the moment, stood up and blew him a kiss, her smile wide and radiant. Dashing the final steps to home plate, his teammates greeted him with high-fives and cheers.

The announcer said the game was now tied at four at the top of the eighth.

The hits continued after that, with a single to center bringing in one run. Then, at the top of the ninth, Ty was up again. Hitting the ball deep right-center field, he brought in three and made it to second base. The Red Sox maintained their lead with a score of 8 - 4.

Their team's pitcher hit a nice homer to the left, bringing Ty home and adding to the board.

"Reynolds comes in to score. What a night for the veteran first baseman on the verge of retirement. What a great week to end a career," the announcer said enthusiastically.

When he spotted the girls waving to him on the way to the dugout, he placed his hand over his heart. Julia blew him a kiss while Syd gave him two thumbs up.

Sydney was losing her mind. "This is so exciting!"

"Remember, it isn't exciting for everyone," Julia said, seeing the Dodger's team looking so frustrated. "As much as it is great to be in the lead, it is bittersweet."

"Yes, so true."

Finally, at the bottom of the ninth, the Dodgers brought in two runs to end the game. But the Sox were victorious, winning 9 - 6. Like clockwork, the crowds began clearing out, and a white noise blanketed the stadium.

Receiving a text from Ty, Julia passed along the message to Aaron, who was still standing at the door.

Seeing them, he asked, "Ready to go?"

"Yes, but there is a team meeting, so he told us to go to the hotel. It might take a while, so he didn't want us waiting for him. He said to drop us off and return to pick him up."

Aaron radioed Derek and updated him on their change of plans. "Okay, this way, ladies. Back the way we came. Stick tight to me. It's going to be crowded, and just FYI, you should probably pack the Boston swag - if you know what I mean. We don't want to rile the locals."

Julia and Sydney removed their Boston sweatshirts and hats and put them in their backpack.

Ready to leave, Julia reached out for Syd. "Hold my hand. Do not let go and stick close to me."

Her daughter got anxious and took a deep breath. "Okay, Momma."

Swiftly ascending to the main level, Aaron guided them through the crowd with ease and over to where Derek was waiting. Soon, they were sitting in the truck, safe and sound. Derek pulled away. Sitting in traffic, they slowly inched toward the highway and, not long after, pulled into the Ritz. Escorted to their suite, the girls said goodnight to Aaron.

"Night, Ladies. I guess we will see you tomorrow."

"Yes, goodnight," Julia said before closing the door.

Changing into comfy clothes, she checked on her emails for work and got caught up on the project updates she'd missed.

Lazily lingering on her bed watching YouTube, Syd seemed wiped from their hectic day.

Within half an hour, Ty texted to say he was on his way to the hotel and had ordered room service. He expected it would be delivered to them in a few minutes.

Hearing a knock at the door, Julia greeted the gentleman who wheeled the trolley into their room with their orders stacked and covered. Spreading a tablecloth across the coffee table, he set up everything nicely in the seating area. Before departing, Julia thanked the man and passed him a tip before allowing the door to fall closed behind her automatically.

Ty arrived not long after. Already changed into joggers and a t-shirt, outright exhausted, he said, "Hi. How is everyone?"

"The game was awesome. You did great!" Syd was so happy.

"Thank you for cheering for me."

"We are so proud of you," Julia said, realizing he was shutting down.

"Appreciate that," he said, barely able to get the words out. "I'm sorry, ladies. I'm just tired."

"Well, hopefully, you can go to sleep after you eat. Maybe get a good solid eight hours, if not more."

"Hopefully so."

"The food is here. Are you hungry?" Julia asked.

"That's an understatement."

Taking the container and cutlery, he sat down on the bed and put a rolled blanket under his knees and pillows behind his back. Able to finish his food, he went to the bathroom to brush his teeth with the complimentary toothbrush before returning to the same spot. Sydney was watching A Wrinkle in Time. The tone of the actors' voices made him quickly drift off. Within minutes, he was snoring.

"Is he staying here with us tonight, Mom?"

"I guess so. I don't have the heart to wake him."

"Yeah, me either."

"Come on, let's get ready for bed. Tomorrow is going to be a busy day. We need to get some sleep too. Guess you are sharing a bed with me."

The girls quietly brushed their teeth and washed their faces before tip-toeing into the room to call it a night.

72

October 28th

Final Game of the World Series

The sound of a phone alarm filled the room with its intrusive noise. Julia woke up to find Ty still in the other bed. He had taken his device from his pocket and turned it off without even opening his eyes. She watched him slowly sit up and stretch a bit. Rising on two feet with his hands on his hips, Ty waited before bending from side to side. She heard his back crack more than once. When he turned around, he saw Julia watching his every move. Giving a silent wave and a smile, he walked over and sat beside her on the edge of the bed.

"Good morning," he whispered. "Sorry, I fell asleep so fast last night."

"Don't apologize. You could hardly talk."

He placed his hand over the top of hers. "Well, this is it. This could be my last game..."

"Are you ready?"

"Yes, because it means I get to spend every waking moment with the two of you. After today, a new phase of life begins. So, the real question is, Ms. Julia Mariani, are *YOU* ready?"

"I'll love having you around more often."

"You're sure?" He leaned over and kissed her.

"Yes. One hundred percent."

"Good to know." He paused with his eyes locked to hers. "Sadly, on that note, I need to get going."

Julia sat up and hugged him. "Be safe."

"I will."

"Good luck."

"Thanks." Ty held onto her tightly. "Remember, Aaron and Derek are picking you up again at around four o'clock."

"We will be ready."

"Today, depending on what happens, I should be able to drive back with you guys. I'll meet you in the player's hallway."

"Alright."

"See you soon," he whispered.

Kissing her again, he stood up and walked out of the room. Julia went to lock the door behind him. Luckily, they had the luxury of sleeping a little while longer.

Later that afternoon, under a cloudy sky, crowds made their way to Dodger Stadium for possibly the year's final game. Julia and Sydney met up with Aaron and Derek downstairs in the lobby. While driving over, the guys were excited and made bets on the outcome based on stats.

Listening in, Julia was able to throw in her two cents and bet the Sox would win it all today. Being Dodger fans, they begged to differ, but the client was always right, so they reluctantly conceded to her claims.

It didn't take long to get to the Red Sox family box. Now, they knew the shortest route to take to get there. Once safely inside, with the same familiar faces, Julia said hello to most of the wives but felt sick for Ty. Keeping to herself, she sat with Sydney in the bottom row of the seats on the balcony and got ready for the game.

Grandpa Bryce texted and said everyone was watching from the Lakes Bar inside the Carling Hotel. Jun, Rebecca, Lisa, and Bruno were all there with him. Even David took an interest.

After the national anthem, the game moved into the top of the 1st, and Ty was third at bat. Surrounded by nervous energy, Julia held onto

Sydney's hand as he took a few practice swings. Ready for the pitch, he stared down the man on the mound.

Getting a hit over center field, they watched it fly toward the back wall.

"Home run!" Syd shouted, "Woohoo!'

The announcer's voice echoed through the stadium box. "There will be no zero in the score tonight! It's 2 - 0 Boston with Reynolds bringing in Holt from first."

Over the next three innings, the crowd got restless. A low hum blanketed the stands. The bright white stadium lights blazed down onto the diamond, illuminating the iconic palm trees swaying gently beyond the outfield walls of Dodger Stadium.

Ty crouched at first base, hearing the buzz of over fifty thousand fans.

The crack of the bat sent a grounder zipping toward the shortstop. The Dodgers' runner took off down the baseline, digging hard as the shortstop scooped the ball, pivoted, and fired it toward first. Ty planted his cleat firmly on the bag, his glove stretched wide. The ball smacked into the leather just as the runner lunged for the base.

"Out!" the umpire shouted, cutting through the noise.

A groan rippled through the Dodgers' faithful while a smattering of Red Sox fans cheered in the stands behind the visitors' dugout.

Ty stayed cool, tossing the ball back to the pitcher with a subtle nod, his eyes already shifting to the next batter.

The play came fast. The new batter chopped the ball sharply toward third base, where the infielder charged forward, scooped it on the run, and whipped it across the diamond, making Ty stretch to his right, the toes of his cleats barely clinging to the bag as the throw rocketed into his glove just ahead of the runner.

"Out!" The call rang out again, this time drawing louder groans and scattered boos from the home crowd.

The first baseman straightened, keeping his focus as the tension in the stadium rose. Behind him, the Dodger fans clapped rhythmically, trying to will their team back into the game.

The faint hum of "Let's go, Dodgers!" echoed from the bleachers, but the scoreboard told the real story: the Red Sox were closing in on victory.

Price stood tall, his signature six-foot-six, lanky frame silhouetted against the backdrop of the pitcher's mound. He toed the rubber with precision, his left hand dangling at his side like a coiled spring, ready to explode.

Ty shifted at first, glove resting casually at his hip, his confidence in his teammate's arm unwavering.

The first pitch—a slicing slider—swept across the plate and left the Dodgers' batter flinching as it thudded into the catcher's mitt.

"Strike!" the umpire shouted.

The crowd groaned, and Price faintly smirked as he received the ball back. His next pitch, a blistering 97-mph fastball, roared past the batter's swing.

"Strike!"

Ty kept his focus, standing ready in case of a stray grounder, but he could feel the certainty of what was coming.

Price's final pitch—a devastating changeup—dropped into the strike zone at the last second, leaving the batter frozen.

"Strike three!" the umpire bellowed, punching the air emphatically. The Dodgers' batter slumped back toward the dugout, his head shaking in disbelief.

The infielders jogged in and patted Ty's back.

Under the bright lights of Dodger Stadium, Julia noticed how unfazed he was by the noise around him. Tonight, he was all business.

Not one run got scored until the sixth, seventh, and eighth when Boston hit three home runs to bring the game to a score of 5 - 1. At this point, the Sox families were already celebrating.

Julia could see the Dodger's box across from them. The families were more solemn, with many sitting stoically in their chairs.

Searching for the game on ESPN, Julia put in her earbuds. She wanted to hear the sports commentary in the final inning. Recording her screen to keep it as a memento for Ty, she listened in.

"It's the bottom of the ninth, in game five of the World Series between the Boston Red Sox and the LA Dodgers. Boston is ahead three games to one in this series. The team is currently leading 5 - 1 here tonight," the announcer updated.

At the same time, Julia watched Ty keep his eyes on Price as he set up for the pitch and the likelihood of a ground ball coming his way.

"Price is sitting at three balls, two strikes on Taylor. Here's the pitch."

Taylor let it go and walked to first.

"That lead-off walk breaks the string of fourteen consecutive outs that Price retired. Has he ever stepped up for this team tonight? Wow."

"Yes, he certainly has."

With his eye on the game, another commentator stated, "Boston just called a time-out."

"Looks like they are making a change." Watching the coach make his way to the mound, everyone could see Price bow his head. He knew that was the end.

"What an emotional moment. He's done an amazing job, and he knows it. The crowd's appreciation is evident—everybody agrees. Sale is coming in to replace him," the second announcer commented.

As Price walked off, the field fell into a momentary hush, followed by a burst of applause from the crowd and his teammates.

The catcher headed out to meet Chris Sale to discuss the strategy and confirm the game plan for handling the incoming batters.

The infield and outfield players adjusted their positions to align with Sale's pitching style. The crowd watched the player warm up with a few practice pitches, waiting to see how he would perform in this critical moment. It was a high-tension transition where every detail mattered as the game hung in the balance.

Julia's hands shook.

The crowd chanted, "Let's go, Dodgers," and clapped rhythmically.

She stopped paying attention to what was happening on the field and said a prayer for Ty. When she finished, the commentator said, "There's the pitch—chased one off against Hernandez. Machado is on deck. Hernandez now has two balls and two strikes as he steps away from the plate to adjust his gloves and refocus."

"Let's talk about Reynolds for a moment," the commentator said, "It is a bittersweet day for the long-standing first baseman, set to retire this year. The veteran has three home runs in two games. What a career he's had. Everyone here wishes him the very best."

"Sales is setting up. Again, two balls, two strikes."

"Here comes the pitch!"

"Breaking ball. Struck him out! The Red Sox are one out away. Machado is on his way to the plate. He will try and extend the game, but he's O and three tonight. Tremendous pressure on him right now. A weight that only he can carry."

"Machado is ready. Sale sets up for the pitch. Swing and a miss! Strike one!"

Another commentator chimed in. "Here we go. O and one pitch. Strike two on Machado!"

Julia peeked over the barrier to watch the game. She found Sydney's eyes affixed to what was happening but covering her ears. Putting her arm around her, she said, "This is it, Syd."

"This Boston organization has been run well for a long time. From the top down, it's been amazing," the sportscaster complimented. "Sale is trying to end it here. Ready, it's O and two..."

In slow motion, the ball crossed the plate. Hearing it land force-fully in the catcher's mitt, the stadium erupted, knowing Machado had swung at the ball and missed. Surrounded by screaming and clapping, Ty and his teammates swarmed the mound to celebrate.

"Red Sox win the World Series! Five to one, the final tonight. And the best team in baseball wins it all!"

Decked out in Red Sox apparel from head to toe, Sydney hugged her Mother as she cried. "They did it, Mom! I knew they would!"

The two stood up and applauded their championship team, keeping their eyes on him.

Seeing Ty look up into the stands, he placed his hand over his heart and pointed to them. Julia and Syd did the same.

Bryce texted and used every celebratory emoji known to man. Julia called him. He was so emotional.

"I knew he could do it," he said. "That's our boy!"

Amidst the celebrations, the girls watched the press snap picture after picture to commemorate the moment as it happened. The team gathered for a group photo as the crowd slowly trickled out of the stadium. Julia and Syd found Aaron and Derek at the door.

"So, I believe I was right." Julia snickered while both men accepted defeat.

"Congrats, Ma'am. It was a game well played," Aaron said with a smile. "I assume we are heading down to the locker room hallway?" He wanted confirmation on that.

"Yes, that is where Ty said to go afterward."

Aaron parted the crowd while Derek followed behind them.

After all the interviews and festivities had finished, the families had gathered around happily waiting for their Champions.

Watching for Ty to emerge from the locker room, Sydney and Julia kept their eyes peeled for him amongst the players exiting one by one.

Suddenly, he walked through the doors. Handsomely dressed in his tailored suit, his face immediately lit up when he spotted them. Approaching with open arms, he hugged the two tightly while the other families looked on.

"We are so proud of you!" Julia said with great enthusiasm.

"Thank you," he humbly divulged. "Every minute has made this last year all worth it."

Picking up Sydney, she joyfully said, "I knew you could do it. I told you!"

"Yes, you did, kiddo. Thank you for cheering for me today."

"You're welcome. It was so much fun."

Firmly holding Julia's hand, he asked, "So, would you ladies care to join me on my last walk about the field?"

"We would love to." Julia knew this would be an emotional moment for him. Purposefully dodging the reporter's hallway, they walked through a few long corridors with Derek and Aaron shadowing them.

Sydney led the way, listening to Ty's instructions. "Can we really go out there?"

"Sure can. Turn here, Syd."

Upon reaching the gate, they followed the path onto the turf. Each took a minute to enjoy the staggering view from that vantage point. Ty turned to face the stands. Mother and daughter imagined what it must have been like to see so many people watching him play.

"Come with me," he said. Proceeding to his position on first base, Ty stopped and looked around. He placed one foot on the bag.

"Are you sad to be leaving?" Sydney asked.

"I have mixed feelings right now." He smiled at her. "But that's okay."

Julia looked at him, a bit confused. "How come? Are you having second thoughts?"

"No, no. Not at all. It's time. I finished my career in this very spot today, and where one phase of life ends, a new one will begin right where I left off."

"I don't follow?" Julia expressed.

Pulling a small box from his pocket, kneeling one knee on the base, a look of shock overwhelmed Julia, and her hands began to tremble.

Holding out his hand to her, she slowly walked towards him. Ty lowered his head, composed himself, and then looked into the eyes of the woman he loved. "Julia Mariani, I have waited a lifetime to find you, and I am not prepared to wait another day. You and Sydney are my future now, and I can hardly wait for all of it to begin. Would you please do me the great honor of becoming my wife?"

Opening the box, revealing a sparkling diamond ring inside, Julia could barely breathe as joyful tears flooded her cheeks.

Seeing her Mother speechless, Sydney grabbed her arm and said, "Mom? Are you going to answer?"

Her daughter's ecstatic expression helped Julia nervously offer a reply. "Yes," she whimpered as cheers and whistles broke out from his teammates and their families watching from inside the dugout.

Sliding the ring on her finger, rising from his knee, Ty cupped Julia's cheeks and happily kissed the love of his life, taking his time. "I love you."

"I love you too," she said, still shaking uncontrollably.

Turning to his team, he raised one arm in the air and shouted, "She said Yes!" before picking Julia up and swinging her around. Noticing Sydney watching everything unfold from a distance, he walked over. Giving her his full attention, he knelt and sweetly confirmed, "You are the family I've prayed, dreamed, and wished for all these years. I hope to be there for you through good times and bad. I want you to feel comfortable coming to me if you are sad or troubled. I will be there to help you whenever you need me."

Sydney reached out to him and hugged his neck. "I love you, Ty."

"Love you too, Kiddo." Ty thought he should lighten the mood. "How about a piggyback ride around the bases?"

Clapping excitedly, she climbed aboard.

"Hold on!" he said before galloping to second, third, and then home base, where Julia was waiting for them with open arms.

Hearing the team applauding and whistling, Ty smiled. "I never thought my life could get any better until I met the both of you."

73

November 22nd

Home Sweet Home

Sadly, Ty had to fly back to Boston for a few weeks to tie up loose ends while Sydney and Julia returned home to Toronto to finalize plans for a special Christmas in Carling. This year would be unlike any other, as the couple had decided to marry over the holidays, not wanting to wait another moment to begin their lives together.

The weeks apart were a whirlwind of activity. With the help of her trusted friends, Lisa and Rebecca, Julia managed to find a stunning designer wedding gown despite the tight timeline, its elegant lines and intricate details capturing the romance of the season.

For Sydney, the decision was far simpler. She had always dreamed of wearing her Mother's Nicole Miller navy taffeta, high-low hem gown. The moment she tried it on, it fit perfectly, and Julia couldn't argue. Sydney looked radiant in the classic dress, its deep hue adding a touch of timeless sophistication to their winter wedding.

By the time Ty's flight back to Toronto was due, the preparations were nearly complete. With the flowers ordered and their Carling family invited, Julia had one last task—arranging a special surprise wedding gift for her husband-to-be. Carefully planning every detail, she could barely contain her excitement at the thought of his reaction.

On the crisp morning of November 22nd, Julia and Sydney stood eagerly at the arrivals gate, scanning the crowd for Ty. The moment he emerged, Sydney let out an excited squeal and sprinted toward him. Ready to catch her as she jumped into his arms, he bent slightly and laughed. For a moment, he held her tightly. But it wasn't long before his eyes shifted to the love of his life, and a soft expression crept across his face. Putting her down, they walked hand in hand. Eyes locked on Julia, he wrapped his arm around her and pulled her in close.

"Hi," he whispered, kissing her lovingly. "Missed you."

"I missed you, too."

Happy to finally be together, the three of them briefly immersed in their reunion.

Making their way to the car, Ty held out his hand for the keys with a playful grin. "I'll drive," he said, leaving no room for argument.

While they left the airport and joined the main highway, lively chatter and laughter filled the vehicle. But it wasn't long before Julia noticed something unusual about their route. Her brows furrowed as she glanced out the window.

"Where are we going?" she asked, curiosity lacing her voice as Ty passed their usual turn.

"Humor me," he said with a sly smile, leaving Julia and Sydney to exchange curious glances as they settled in for the unexpected detour.

Adhering to the GPS on his phone, Ty watched their reaction while they pulled into a newly built, gated home on one acre. Seeing a lady waiting in her vehicle, with the engine still running, he parked beside her in the courtyard.

"Why are we here?" Julia was confused. "You didn't tell me we were visiting someone?"

Ty got out and walked around to their side to open their doors. Grinning from ear to ear, he took Julia's hand and extended the other to Sydney while the woman got out of the car. "This is Doris Clayson. My real estate agent," he said, introducing them to the woman he had been conversing with for the past couple of weeks.

"Hello," she said, "You must be Julia and Sydney."

Both girls nodded and said, "Yes."

"Ty, what's going on? What's happening?" Holding his hand, she got nervous.

"I know we haven't had time to talk about it, but I've had Doris send me listings for the past while. This one just came on the market, and she thought it was a must-see. So here we are. What do you think?"

From the outside, Julia stepped back and humbly replied, "It is certainly a large house."

"I know. Keep an open mind. Let's check out the inside," Ty said, following Doris to the front door.

The three walked into the grand foyer and respectfully took off their shoes. While entering the beautifully decorated home, impeccably designed with custom moldings and furniture throughout, twelve-foot ceilings, and every possible upgrade imaginable, Ty kept a close eye on Julia's reaction. Loving the well-appointed kitchen with two islands, Julia brushed her hand along the smooth quartz countertops. She could see herself cooking and baking there. Looking at the living room's coffered ceiling and bright, spacious dining room, Doris showed her to the office enclosed in mahogany panels and cathedral windows with a view of the gardens.

"Think this would be a good office for you?" Ty stated.

Nodding her head, knowing how creative she could be in a space like that, she whispered, "Yes, but this house must be so expensive."

"Do you like it, though?"

"Of course, yes, it is stunning. It is perfect in every way."

Following Doris upstairs to see the master and the other bedrooms, Sydney quickly staked a claim on the one she liked.

"The furniture all flows so nicely." Julia instantly fell in love with the place.

Glancing over at Doris and nodding, Ty escorted Julia downstairs to the family room.

Taken by the cathedral stone fireplace, she spotted a large frame without a picture in it. "Isn't that odd? Why do they have a frame hanging empty like that?" Upon moving her sights to the picture, flanking the opposite side, Julia stopped.

Feeling Sydney's hand glide into hers, gently taking hold, she said, "I hope it's okay. Ty thought this place would feel more like a home with Daddy and Ben here. He asked me for our old family portrait a little while ago."

Ty went to stand beside Julia.

She whispered tearfully, "I love it…" Inching closer, she focused on the painting. It was like David and Ben were right there with them.

"I figured, once we settle in, maybe we can have a portrait done too. It would balance it out." Ty hoped she caught on to what he had said.

"Wait? Settle in?" Julia repeated.

At that moment, Doris lifted the keys from her pocket and handed them to Ty.

"Yeah, I was pretty sure you'd love this place. I immediately knew it was for us. It is minutes from Sydney's school and has multiple parks we can visit. Even a baseball diamond down the street. The backyard is a blank canvas. That way, you can put your personal touch on it. I hope you don't mind, but I had her team furnish the rooms. The house is ours and everything in it. We can move in anytime."

Overwhelmed, Julia turned to find Doris with tears in her eyes.

"Welcome home," the woman said, so happy to witness such a beautiful moment.

74

December 21st

Second Christmas in Carling

Over the next two weeks, life became a whirlwind of transition as they slowly settled into their new home. Ty had his belongings shipped from Boston, and Doris took charge of putting Julia's townhouse on the market. Ever efficient, she even arranged for a company to pack everything, making the process seamless so Julia wouldn't have to lift a finger.

Despite the ease of the move, Julia often found herself wandering the large halls within the new house in quiet amazement, still adjusting to the idea that this was where they would now be building their life together. Though the changes came quickly, they took everything in stride, creating a sense of home within the sprawling space.

With only a few days to enjoy their new surroundings, they found themselves packing suitcases again, this time for their second Christmas in Carling. The excitement of their upcoming wedding added an extra spark to their preparations, knowing their hotel family would soon gather to celebrate with them.

On the frosty morning of December 21st, Ty locked the door and remotely closed the garage, a quiet sense of satisfaction on his face. As the wrought iron gates parted, he guided their SUV down the driveway and onto the snow-dusted road. With Sydney and Julia chatting, he settled in behind the wheel for the scenic two-hour drive to Cottage Country, where their holiday celebration—and the next chapter of their lives—awaited.

Bottom of Form

"So, ladies? Are you sure we have everything?" he asked halfway down the street.

"Oh, no, please don't say that. I'm stressed out enough as it is," Julia said, double-checking her lists inside her notebook. "Flowers, check. Rings, check. Dresses for Syd and me, check. Shoes, check and check. Tux, check..." Scanning the rest, she hoped they'd accounted for everything. "I think we are ready."

Ty reached across and took hold of her hand. "It's okay. As long as Sydney and I are beside you, nothing else matters."

Smiling, with a tilt of her head, wanting everything to be perfect, Julia could hardly wait to arrive at the hotel and give Ty his gift. It was something she had been working on for a while. It took a lot but was well worth it.

About half an hour away from Carling, Julia checked her phone and sent a text. Driving past the inlet, she saw the hotel on the hill shining brightly and received a message in return. It made her heart pound a mile a minute.

When Ty turned right, they were on the home stretch. Following the winding driveway, they soon pulled up under the covered entrance.

Turning off the engine, Ty said, "Well, here we are. Back to where it all began."

"I'll go and check us in." Julia hastened inside and disappeared, leaving Ty and Sydney behind, wondering why she was in such a hurry.

"Maybe she has to go to the bathroom," Syd laughed while gathering her things from the middle seat before getting out to see what was wrong with her.

Unbeknownst to them, Julia walked through the doors and immediately found Bryce. "Is the surprise ready?"

With great excitement, he confirmed, "Yep. All good."

Hugging him, she then crossed her fingers.

"You go ahead; I'll keep him busy." Bryce pointed towards the giant Christmas tree inside the Lakes Lounge and quickly headed outside to Ty standing at the rear tailgate of their SUV. He had already started unloading their bags onto a trolley.

Greeting the champion baseball player with a handshake and a manly hug, he said, "Hello! Welcome back. Congratulations on the series. I watched the entire game. What an amazing night for you."

"Thank you so much, Bryce. Appreciate it. I'm looking forward to some well-earned time off," he responded while setting a suitcase on the trolley.

"I'm so excited about the wedding. Been looking forward to it since I heard the news." Looking back inside the doors, seeing Julia waving and giving him the signal, Bryce added, "Oh, Ty. I believe Julia needs you inside for a second."

"Okay. I'll be back to help you," Ty replied.

He didn't notice Bryce close the tailgate. Sneakily bringing the trolley inside behind him, there was no way he was going miss a minute of what was about to happen.

Upon entering the lobby, he saw Julia and Sydney standing near the big tree in the middle of the Lakes Lounge.

Ty went over to see what Julia needed. "What's going on, hun?"

As he got closer, Julia reached out both hands to him. Taking hold, bouncing his eyes between his bride-to-be and Sydney, he didn't know why they were acting so strange.

"In the past few weeks, I have been planning a surprise for you. Now, this is not just any surprise. This is my wedding gift to you."

Confused, looking her way with considerable uncertainty, he tracked Julia's line of sight when it veered to the right. A group of people walked into the room. The girls kept their eyes on Ty to see his reaction.

Slowly recognizing their faces, he glanced at Julia. "No? No way." Lost for words, he slowly walked towards his sister with open arms and shared an emotional embrace. "Jenna…"

Nodding with tearful smiles, she could not respond. Choked up, she hugged her brother so tightly.

When he saw her husband Dan and his nephews, Alex and Brayden, he said, "Wow. I can't believe you're here..." Finding Julia and Sydney witnessing the reunion from afar, he said to Jenna, "But how?"

Still unable to say a word, Dan held his wife to comfort her. She explained, "About two months ago, I got a Facebook friend request from a woman named Julia Mariani. Not knowing her, I initially ignored it. Then, we saw the tabloid pictures of your World Series engagement to the woman of the same name. I accepted her request, and Julia messaged me right away. We've been talking ever since. When she invited us to the wedding, no questions asked, there wasn't a doubt in my mind. So here we are."

"Really?" Ty exclaimed with a wealth of excitement. "I can't believe it."

"Me too," Jenna exclaimed tearfully. "I've missed you, Ty. So, so much. Congratulations, and Merry Christmas. I'm so happy for you both."

Still in shock, he remembered how he had hurt his sister years before. Hugging her, he said, "Jenna, I'm sorry."

She lovingly looked up at him and placed her hand along his cheek. "I know. I know. It's okay. Let's keep the past in the past and start fresh."

"Thank you for making the trip. I know this couldn't have been easy for you."

Jenna revealed, "Well, Julia arranged everything for us. All we had to do was get on a plane."

"You know what I mean," he added, knowing there was far more that needed to be said.

"I understand. We can talk later. For now, let's enjoy getting acquainted again."

Sitting in the lounge, they watched Sydney and Jenna's boys connect and start sharing favorite Reels and YouTubers they followed.

Needing a minute, Ty excused himself from the reunion and took Julia aside. He looked into her eyes and said, "I can't believe you did this for me." Eyes welling, he slipped his arms around her.

"Are you surprised?"

"Yes, are you kidding? Beyond." He was speechless. Tightening their embrace, he said, "This is the most incredible gift I have ever received. Thank you."

Among the few remaining hotel guests on their way out the door, Ty and Julia returned to his family. The past seemed to have washed away, leaving a clean slate for the future.

Jenna kept staring at Ty. "We watched the series, you know. Cheered for you during the ALCS game in Houston and every game against the Dodgers. Mom and Dad would be so proud."

"Thank you..." he replied humbly. "Thank you for coming all this way."

"We would not miss this wedding for the world," she replied. "Now, you both need to get down to business. We'll leave you to get settled and will catch up with you later at dinner. How does that sound?"

"Perfect. We will see you then," he said.

Walking out to the truck with Julia, he stopped partway and pulled her close again. He couldn't say a word.

"I'm so happy you were surprised."

"I love you so much," he said.

"Okay, break it up, you two," Syd said on the way past, ready to help unpack.

Noticing that Bryce had witnessed everything, he offered Ty a manly pat on the shoulder. "You good?" he asked his famous friend.

With the biggest smile on his face, he replied, "Couldn't be better."

75

December 21st

Settling in

The lobby of the Carling Resort sparkled with holiday charm, the grand Christmas tree twinkling with white lights and ornaments while soft carols played in the background. Julia and Ty stepped up to the check-in desk, where the ever-friendly concierge greeted them with an enthusiastic smile.

"Welcome back, you two!" David said, his voice warm with genuine excitement. "I hear congratulations are in order. We're all thrilled about your upcoming nuptials—it's the talk of the hotel."

Julia exchanged a warm look with Ty, her cheeks flushing as she smiled. "Thank you, David. We're happy to be back."

Sliding their room cards across the counter, he said, "Here we are. Rooms 1444 and 1445 are ready for you—just as you requested."

"Appreciate that, Sir," Ty replied respectfully. Turning to Julia, he said, "Shall we go and settle in?"

"Absolutely." Carefully carrying her wedding gown and Sydney's dress, Julia followed Ty toward the elevators, her nervousness growing with every step. "Your family is staying with us on the same floor," she shared as they walked.

"You've thought of everything," he replied, his smile softening as he guided the luggage cart alongside her.

When Ty pressed the elevator button, David gave them a final wave. "See you soon—and if you need anything at all, you know where to find me."

The baseball player raised a steady hand. "Sounds good!" then gestured for Julia to step inside when the doors opened, ever mindful of the delicate dresses. He positioned their trolley securely on the left as Sydney and Bryce arrived to wait for the next lift with the second luggage cart.

As the elevator began its ascent, Ty stepped close to Julia, wrapping his arms gently around her waist. She softly laughed as he leaned in, his voice a low murmur only she could hear. "I can't wait to marry you," he said, pressing a kiss to her cheek. The moment felt like a pause in time, a quiet promise of all the joy and love yet to come. "I don't know how you did it." He was so sincere in his words. "You never cease to amaze me. You know that."

Elated by his reaction, Julia felt she could now relax and focus on their wedding.

Heading down the hallway, Ty pushed the trolley while Julia juggled the dresses. The two of them laughed and talked the entire way.

"It feels like I walked into the foyer for the first time only yesterday, seeing you looking all cute that night. I'm pretty sure you were annoyed at me for being in the room across the hall."

"Truth be told, I was. But when you shared the story about your Mom, things changed for me."

"Is that right?"

"You know, some professional athletes have a reputation." She shot him a disappointed look.

"Hold on..." Ty prepared to defend himself.

Julia quickly interrupted. "But you are not at all like them. I misjudged you and should have gotten to know you first."

"Exactly. And I'm glad you did."

Arriving at their suites, Julia and Ty propped open each door. Following her into her room, he helped with the dresses while Julia hung them on the hooks. Taking her hand, he pulled her in close.

Giggling, she said, "Hey, what are you doing? Sydney and Bryce will be here any minute."

Towering above her, standing so straight and tall, he said, "Love you."

Her arms found a home around his neck. "I love you too."

Hearing happy banter coming down the hall, knowing Sydney and Bryce were close, Ty said, "I guess we should keep unloading the bags."

"Yes, we should."

Ty and Bryce threaded the second trolley through the doorway into Julia's room.

In an instant, she started barking orders, turning from his sweet fiancé to a woman on a mission. It didn't take long to put everything in its place. Taking a deep breath, she couldn't believe this year had come around full circle, and this was really happening.

An hour later, Julia called Jenna's room, asking if they wanted to join them. Excited to get to know her sister-in-law-to-be, she propped open their door. In minutes they heard the nephews running down the hall and their Mother telling them to slow down and act accordingly.

Knocking on the door frame, Julia and Ty both said, "Come in!" at the same time while standing in the kitchen, opening a bottle of wine, and putting out a few snacks and drinks for the kids. Seeing his sister with a large box in hand, wrapped in wedding paper, she set it down on the coffee table in the living room. Jenna gave Ty another hug before Dan shook his hand.

"I still can't believe it."

"Well, we wanted to be here for you," she said.

"It's definitely colder than we thought it would be," Dan laughed humorously in a Texan accent.

Walking around the other side of the island, Jenna revealed, "I always wanted a sister – no offense, Ty."

"I don't blame you," her brother said.

"Now, my dream is about to come true. I'm so excited."

Directing her comment to him before moving her sights to Julia, Jenna solidly revealed, "Thank you for finding the best sister-in-law ever."

"You're welcome," he laughed, taking full credit.

Offering a toast, they raised their glasses. Ty lowered his head and then made eye contact with everyone around him. "To the presence of family. Let us always celebrate together. Thank you for traveling all this way, Jenna, Dan, Alex, and Brayden. Our wedding now feels complete. Thank you to my beautiful wife and daughter-to-be. I can hardly wait to marry you, Julia, and become a family."

"Cheers!" Everyone said, clinking their glasses together joyfully.

"Shall we sit down?" Julia asked, offering them a seat.

"Hey, Mom. I'm gonna show the boys around the hotel." Syd was already halfway out the door.

"Please behave," her Mother stated. "Mind your manners."

Her daughter gave her a thumbs up.

"Boys, you do the same," Jenna said sternly.

"Don't worry. We will," the twins replied.

When the door closed behind them, Jenna lifted the box from the table onto her lap and announced, "So, I never thought I'd be blessed to pass this along to you. I am sure you will love and cherish it as much as I have."

Not knowing what it could be, Jenna handed it to Ty. Moving closer to Julia, he rested the box on both their laps. Opening the beautifully wrapped package, Ty lifted the lid to find many tissue-paper-wrapped presents inside. Unraveling one, Ty stopped. "Umm, are these...."

Nodding, Jenna replied, "Yes. Every last one of them. Mom kept them all these years and instructed me to hold onto them for safekeeping. Just in case she wasn't here when you found someone to love. It is her wedding gift to you both."

Julia unwrapped a few of the packages. There were bells with ribbon, iron-crafted sleighs, styrofoam snowmen, and more – each made by his Mother's hands.

Not knowing what to say, Ty immediately stood and hugged his sister and Dan. "Thank you so much. This means the world to us. You know, last year at this time, Julia and Sydney were making ornaments for the Carling Staff. Mom's came up in our conversation."

"Speaking of Christmas ornaments, I think these may need a tree," Julia suggested.

"A tree?" Jenna sounded intrigued.

Glancing over at Julia, Ty knew what she was thinking precisely. "It seems you have plans with us tomorrow," he said with a grin.

Julia's smile widened. "We're going to visit the tree farm."

Excitement bubbling over, Jenna clapped her hands together. "Oh, that sounds amazing! I've always wanted to do something like that. It's so festive!"

"We've never done anything like that before. It should be fun. The boys will love it—they've never picked out a real tree." Dan seemed excited.

"Great! We'll make a day of it," Julia beamed at their reactions. "Hot chocolate, fresh air, and finding the perfect tree—it'll be a Christmas memory to remember."

"Count us in," Jenna said with a grin, already imagining the adventure.

After so many years apart, they found themselves catching up on each other's lives, the conversation flowing easily. Julia noticed Jenna stealing fond glances at her and Ty, her expression soft and full of emotion.

"I still can't believe you two are getting married," Jenna said, her voice trembling slightly. "And that we're here to witness it. There was a time I thought we'd never get this chance." Her eyes glistened with tears.

Ty reached over to gently place his hand on hers. "But you're here now," he said warmly. "That's what matters. And I'm so grateful for that."

Smiling, her eyes locked with her brother's in a moment of unspoken understanding.

Suddenly, there was a rapid knock at the door, followed by the muffled sound of children's laughter. Julia stood and crossed the room, a smile tugging at her lips. When she opened the door, a chorus of excited voices spilled in, filling the space with energy and warmth.

"Looks like the party's arrived," Julia said while stepping aside, her heart full as she watched the joyful reunion continue to unfold.

Moving the evening's festivities downstairs with dinner at Tecca, a cozy Italian Bistro inside the hotel, the warm glow of candles flickered on their table as they indulged in rich pasta dishes, freshly baked bread, and tiramisu that melted in their mouths. Laughter filled the air as stories were shared, Jenna recounting old memories while Julia and Ty shared their plans for the future.

Ready to head upstairs, Sydney's energy was finally waning. Stepping onto the elevator, the girl yawned and leaned against Ty, her eyes growing heavy.

Saying goodnight with hugs all around, they waved to Jenna and her family as they parted ways outside the elevator.

About to make their way down the hall, Syd asked, "Can I get a piggyback ride, Ty?"

Knowing moments like this were already few and far between, he didn't hesitate. "Sure, Kiddo. Climb aboard," he said, kneeling on one knee.

With her arms wrapped around his neck, he carried the exhausted little girl to their room.

When Julia opened the door, Ty went inside and dropped her off in her bed. Leaving the ladies to do their thing, he stepped out and went to tidy up the kitchen.

It wasn't long before Syd was cozily under the covers.

Kissing her forehead, Julia said, "Ty?"

"Yeah, I'm coming." Rounding the corner, he approached. "Sweet dreams, Kiddo," he whispered, smoothing her hair as she mumbled a soft reply.

"Night, night."

The two exited the room and left the door open a crack. Julia collapsed on the couch in the living area. The quiet hum of the hotel mirrored the peacefulness between them. With legs curled beneath her, she leaned against Ty, her hand brushing his. "What a day," she murmured, her voice barely above a whisper.

He looked down, a soft smile spreading across his face. "I still can't believe you located my sister and got her to come for the wedding," he said, his voice filled with awe, prompting him to kiss her lovingly. "How can I ever thank you? It's like the problems between her and me never existed."

Head tilting to meet his gaze, Julia's face brightened. "A small Christmas miracle?" she offered playfully, her eyes sparkling.

Quietly chuckling, he pulled her closer. "The best one I could've asked for," he replied, his voice thick with gratitude.

Julia yawned and closed her eyes.

"I suppose I should go and let you get some sleep." Ty's heart ached at the thought of leaving her for the night, even if it was just to cross the hall. "Soon, I'll never have to do this again," he promised, his voice thick with emotion. "We'll always be together."

Julia smiled, her gaze lingering on him as she placed her hand along his cheek. "I can't wait."

The moment hung between them, warm and intimate, as if time itself had paused to give them this space to breathe.

Finally, with a reluctant sigh, Ty stood and kissed her on the forehead before heading to the door.

She followed, holding his hand.

Hugging her tightly, he said, "Goodnight."

"Night," she whispered. "Sweet dreams."

"You too." He glanced back once more before stepping into the hall, waving with a steady hand.

Julia lingered a moment, her heart warmed by his quiet strength.

When the door closed, he walked over and sat on the edge of the bed. Looking up, he smiled as a deep sense of peace washed over him. He could almost feel his Mother's presence, certain she was smiling too, knowing her children were finally back where they belonged—in each other's lives.

December 22nd

Oh, Christmas Tree

Bright and early the next morning, the resort was alive with the cheerful hum of activity as Julia, Sydney, and Ty made their way to the cozy Cottages dining room. The scent of freshly brewed coffee and warm pastries greeted them as they stepped inside, where Jenna and her family were already waiting with welcoming smiles.

"Good morning!" Julia said, her voice bright as she hugged Jenna. She then introduced her to Rebecca, Jun, and Lisa, who had joined them.

After the introductions, they all settled around the table, the sparkling lake view through the panoramic windows providing a breathtaking backdrop to their breakfast.

As plates of fluffy pancakes, crisp bacon, and fresh fruit got passed around, laughter and easy conversation filled the room. Midway through, Bruno stopped by, beaming with pride as he showed off pictures of his baby girl, Adriana.

"She's as cute as a button!" Julia exclaimed, leaning closer to admire the photos. Sydney and Jenna chimed in with heartfelt compliments, their enthusiasm making Bruno's proud smile grow even wider.

As the plates got cleared and coffee cups refilled, the conversation naturally shifted to the day's plans.

"Are you excited to go with us today?" Julia asked as Ty added with a grin, "And join the fierce debate over which tree is *the one*."

"Definitely!" Jenna nodded eagerly. "It sounds like a lot of fun. We are looking forward to it. Hopefully, it won't be too cold."

Sydney joined in, her eyes lighting up as her new cousins looked on. "You gotta dress warm. I can't stress that enough."

Clearly excited about the idea, Alex confirmed, "We are going too, right?"

"Of course," Sydney replied with a smile. "The more, the merrier!"

Leaning against her husband Dan, Jenna smiled. "I can't wait!"

The group left breakfast in high spirits. The morning unfolded with warmth and camaraderie, the perfect start to a day as the countdown to Julia and Ty's wedding continued.

Within the hour, Jenna had ripped the tags off of all the new winter clothes they'd bought in town the day they arrived. Meeting in the foyer, dressed in all their winter gear, they prepared for their first family outing together.

Eyes peeled, Sydney was disappointed not to see Nick back for another season. She remembered he'd driven them to the Christmas tree farm last year.

Finding Bryce with his jacket on, Julia said, "Hey, Bryce! Where are you going?"

"I am heading home, my dear. My shift is over."

"We were hoping you could join us. We are heading to the tree farm."

He inhaled deeply, tempted by her offer. "As much as I would like to join you, I am tired after the mass exodus yesterday and wanted to catch up on some sleep. Please don't be disappointed."

"That's okay. Don't worry. You rest." She hugged him.

"Besides, if I recall correctly, I need to walk a certain young lady down the aisle soon."

Her eyes sparkled. "Yes, you do."

"On that note, enjoy your afternoon. I will see you tomorrow."

As he walked out, Julia watched him moving slowly.

"Is Grandpa Bryce not coming with us?" Syd asked her Mom.

"No, Sweetie Pie. He's tired. It's been a very busy couple of days for him. He went home to rest." She paused as Ty overheard her. "We will check on him later."

Swaying from tradition, instead of having a Carling escort, they took their SUV and had Dan, Jenna, and the boys follow them into the countryside.

Anticipation buzzed through the air when they arrived. The scent of pine and the sight of glittering snow-dusted trees stretched into the horizon.

When Jenna saw the building, she immediately got out of the vehicle. "This looks just like..." she said to Ty.

"Jackson Town Square?"

"Yes! Oh my goodness! They even have the red sleigh. Remember that? Everyone would always take their family Christmas pictures there."

"I remember us having to do that once or twice." Ty was never a fan of photos.

In true Sydney fashion, she gathered everyone at the shuttle platform. After explaining what would happen, their group boarded the spacious hayride sleigh instead of the small traditional red one they took last year.

While dashing through the thick tree plantation, Syd explained the reasoning behind their choice of Christmas tree and shared their family's secret ornament donation.

Jenna clutched her chest as her heart melted. "Oh my God, that is the most beautiful thing I've ever heard."

"So, now that you know our family secret, are you in, or are you out?" Syd asked all business.

"Definitely, in, right boys?" Dan, Alex, and Brayden agreed with their Mom.

Picking out their trees, the greeter wrapped them up while the driver took them on a sleigh ride through the forest. Not having seen woodlands like this in Texas, Jenna's sons were in awe.

"This is like another world," Alex said to his brother.

Brayden answered, "Yeah, it's like we are the only people left on earth. There's nobody around. It's just us."

Sydney smiled, happy to hear they appreciated it as much as she did.

Returning to the main building, Jenna couldn't get enough of the homemade decorations sold inside. She must have bought at least twenty. The owner was pleased to see her approach the cash with a full basket.

It wasn't long before they were on their way to Clarence and LeeAnn's store. Upon pulling in, Julia noticed LeeAnn's car was already there. She knew they were excited to see them.

Before Ty shifted the vehicle into park, Sydney was already out the door and racing inside.

Rushing to greet her, LeeAnn was all smiles.

"There's my sweet girl!" LeeAnn shouted with open arms. Kissing her cheek, she said, "I've missed you!"

"We've missed you too."

Clarence waited his turn patiently.

"Hi, Clarence," Syd said, her head tilted in such a way that it melted his heart.

He got down on his knee and hugged her at her level. "Missed you, Munchkin." When he stood up, he said, "Wait. Something is different?"

"What?" she said, seeing her Mom, Ty, and Jenna walking through the door.

"I don't think I can call you Munchkin anymore. You're getting too big now."

With arms open, LeeAnn walked over to Julia and Ty. "Hello, my dears!" Tightly hugging the two of them, she squished her cheeks against theirs.

"LeeAnn and Clarence. Meet Ty's sister, Jenna, her husband, Dan, and their two sons, Alex and Brayden."

"Welcome! I'm so happy to meet all of you! I assume you are here to shop for decorations with these three."

"Yes, we are. It's so heartwarming to hear what they do." Jenna clutched her chest.

Not surprised that Julia let them in on their little secret, LeeAnn backed away and stared at the engaged couple. "So, I guess I was right. You can say it," she winked with a chuckle. Julia looked confused for a second, but then she understood what the wise woman was implying.

"Yes, you were." Julia nodded. "One hundred percent."

"Right about what?" Ty asked, bouncing his sights between the both of them.

"Last year, when we were here, LeeAnn said you were the one for me."

"You're kidding?" He looked to the woman for confirmation.

"I knew you would make our Julia happy when we met you." She had tears in her eyes. "And I was right." Wiping away the droplets falling across her cheeks, she added, "And, oh, before we forget! Congratulations to our World Series Champion."

"Yes, so proud of you. I watched every game." Clarence's face lit up.

"Thanks. I appreciate that."

Shaking Ty's hand, Clarence said, "LeeAnn even watched with me."

"Oh, it was so exciting. There were a few nail-biters that I had a hard time with. My heart couldn't take it," she giggled. "But you won. That is the main thing."

Noticing the boys getting restless, Syd grabbed a cart from the front. "May I have your attention, please?" she said as everyone gravitated to her. "Show of hands! Who is ready to shop?" Met by a unanimous vote, she smiled. "Perfect! Let's create some beautiful trees!"

Both boys passed along their hats to their Mother before unzipping their jackets and following the girl down the aisle with a flurry of questions.

Impressed, Jenna turned to her husband, then to Julia. "Can we take her home?"

Ty laughed.

Knowing Syd had captivated the boys, the adults watched as she expertly helped them choose décor that would be suitable for the shelter.

"Now, keep in mind. You are not buying this for you. This is going to a family next year. They are who you are buying for. Think of them, not yourself."

The two listened intently to her. Their parents stood back, astonished that the boys started working together, and asked Syd for her opinion.

Once they finalized their themes and found lights, ornaments, Christmas bobbles, and a star for the top, Syd maneuvered their full cart into the box aisle.

"So, on January 2nd, we visit this nice lady named Betty, and we deliver these Christmas boxes, all wrapped nicely, for the families who stay with her.

"Will we get to meet, Betty?" Alex questioned.

"Perhaps. You've gotta be good, so you're Mom lets you."

Everyone chuckled upon hearing that.

The boys, in turn, made a pact.

"Dude, we gotta stay outta trouble, or else Mom won't let us go," Brayden stated firmly.

"Don't worry. I got this."

The two shook on it as their parents looked on in amazement.

Once they had everything, the children wheeled the cart to the cash register. A kind lady rang everything through as Sydney grouped the items to make it easier for her to scan them in bulk. In record time, Ty took out his card and paid for everything.

That evening, after sharing their special afternoon, they went for dinner before returning upstairs to hop from room to room to decorate their trees.

Syd kept the twins in check while the adults sat and chatted with endless laughter, tears, and joyful conversation. Admiring what the children had created, Syd turned out the lights with each one. It was the perfect way to end the day.

While the kids went to play ping pong in the gaming room and Dan and Ty went to play a game of pool in the library, Julia and Jenna sat in front of the large fieldstone fireplace.

Holding up her head with her hand, she said, "This has been the most memorable lead-up to Christmas we have ever had. Thank you for including us in your traditions. It's been a wonderful day."

"You're welcome. Are Dan's parents going to be missing you this year? What will they do if you are not home?" Julia asked.

"I wouldn't know."

She was confused. "Ty mentioned that you have your in-laws at your place for Christmas Eve dinner."

"Yes, that's the way it used to be. Then, they asked Dan to take over the company. When he turned it down to continue building his law practice, they lost interest, I guess."

"So what does that mean? You don't even see them?"

"Sadly, no. So when you invited us here, Dan was pleased since last Christmas was a tough one for him."

"Well, maybe this could become a new Reynolds, Ducane tradition?"

Jenna reached across and took hold of Julia's hand. "We would love that."

December 23rd

Morning of the Wedding

Awake by nine, Julia sent a quick text to Jenna around ten while Sydney got dressed. Inviting her to join them while they checked on the decorating underway in the banquet room, Julia couldn't wait to see if what they created matched her vision.

Meeting at the elevators, the three made their way downstairs.

"This is it," Jenna said as they stepped out and walked across the foyer. "Your wedding day. Excited?" Jenna paused for a moment, her smile softening as Syd looked up at her. Knowing the woman had been married once before, she wished she'd chosen her words more carefully.

"I'm more excited for him," Julia said gently. "But I can hardly wait for us to be a family. It's been a year of constant separation, so to have him with us full-time will be wonderful. Right, Syd?"

The young girl nodded happily.

As they walked through the banquet room doors, the sight that greeted them took their breath away. The evergreen forest was already aglow with white mini-lights, the tables adorned with crisp white linens, and fresh pine bows dusted with frost, nestled amongst white pillar candles of varying sizes. The aisle leading to the festive wedding arch was lined with birch trees every five feet—each one sparkling with mini lights and dangling crystals.

Trying to soak it all in, Julia raised her praying hands to her lips. "Oh, it's so beautiful."

The decorator, Nancy, was elated to see Julia's reaction. "I assume we created what you envisioned?" she asked.

"Oh, yes. Beyond my expectations," she said, choking up as her daughter walked around in awe.

Jenna wrapped her arms around her. "It's just stunning." She could tell Julia was overwhelmed. "Are you okay?"

At that moment, Julia was thinking of her husband. Believing that he and Ben may have had a hand in bringing Ty into her life, she was so thankful. Unbeknownst to most, David was a Red Sox fan, so Julia thought of it as a possible sign. "Yes, I'm fine. I'm still waiting for someone to pinch me. It's like I'm living in a dream right now."

Leaving the banquet area, they returned upstairs briefly before meeting up again to head to the Spa for some pampering, makeup, and hair - a much-needed break before the big event.

After two hours, with hair swirled in updos, sporting French manicures, and makeup dusting their cheeks, they left the tranquil space and stopped by the banquet hall one last time, double-checking with the caterer that everything was on schedule.

About to walk back toward the elevators, Jenna spotted the men and her sons entering the front doors. Unexpectedly, she swung Julia around and hid the bride from sight.

Understanding what was happening, Sydney shouted, "Ty! Close your eyes! It's bad luck to see the bride before the wedding!"

Startled, he did just that and immediately turned his head, not having seen a thing.

Escorting her soon-to-be sister-in-law away, Jenna questioned, "What have they been doing all morning?"

"Oh, Ty said he'd planned to take Bryce and the guys ski-shoeing today."

Sydney looked over at her Mother with a less-than-enthusiastic expression.

Julia chuckled and said, "I know, Syd. That's not funny."

"What's not funny?" Jenna knew there was a story behind it.

"Aunty Jenna? Can I call you that?" Syd inquired maturely.

"Yes, I would love it if you would."

"Well, let's just say it's a memory I would rather forget. One day, I will share the details with you. It's still too fresh. If you know what I mean?"

Laughing at her response, Jenna said, "Okay, then. I look forward to hearing all about it one day. No hints?"

"Nope." Sydney did not have a fond look on her face.

With her interest piqued, Jenna noted to get more information from Julia on that later.

Swiftly returning to their room, knowing the boys wouldn't be far behind, she checked the time. "We should probably get dressed. The photographer should be here within the hour."

The girls rushed around the room, getting each other ready. Finished with Sydney first, it was then time for Julia and Jenna to get dressed, too.

Stepping toward the full-length mirror behind the main closet door, Julia saw her reflection. Proudly standing in her wedding gown with intricate beading, lace accents, and ruching, Jenna fastened the long line of buttons on the back. Placing the crystal belt around Julia's waist, she took hold of the ends and tied a perfect bow before Julia pinned Ty's blue stone pendant inside the neckline.

"I hope it's okay, but I have your something old and something borrowed since I see you already have your something blue." Jenna pulled a box from a small gift bag beside her purse. "This was my Mother's Aquamarine stick pin. She wore it at her wedding, and I did at mine. She would have loved for you to wear it too. I placed it on the strap of my dress."

Staring at the beautiful diamond halo aquamarine pin, Julia felt so touched by the sentiment. "Oh, thank you. Can you pin it on?" She pointed to her neckline on the right-hand side near her shoulder. "That way, Ty will see it."

Placing the pin where she wanted, Jenna stepped back. "There. Is that okay?"

"Yes. It's beautiful."

"Now for your something borrowed, I brought you my diamond tennis bracelet."

Grateful to Jenna for being so kind, Julia got emotional. "Thank you. It's stunning. I'm so excited to share this day with you. I don't have any family, so Sydney, Ty, all of you, and our Carling family, you're all I have. Thank you for traveling here to be with us." Hugging Jenna tightly, Julia saw Sydney looking on. She'd brought them a box of Kleenex.

"As I said to Ty. We wouldn't miss it for the world," Jenna said, blotting the tears with a tissue, hoping not to ruin their makeup. "Now, let's get you married to my brother."

Laughing, all three girls gathered in the living room. Within minutes, the photographer knocked on the door.

78

December 23rd

The Wedding

As the day went on, nervous energy settled over everyone, growing stronger as the ceremony drew closer. Despite having taken their pre-wedding photos, the bride and groom had yet to see each other.

Minutes before walking down the aisle, the ladies gathered in the holding room adjacent to the banquet hall. Julia stood while Jenna adjusted her veil and smoothed out the fabric of her dress as she glanced at her reflection one last time. Each of them wore matching smiles, their eyes reflecting a shared joy and the weight of the moment.

"This is it, Sydney," Julia's voice cracked with emotion as she turned to her daughter, who was watching her with wide, sparkling eyes. "Are you happy?"

She nodded vigorously. "Yes, Mom. Beyond happy." Her voice trembled with the emotion of the day, her smile breaking into a full grin. "I can't believe it's finally happening. You and Ty—together forever." She reached out and took Julia's hand, squeezing it tightly. "And I'm so glad you found him. It feels like everything's just right."

Her Mother pulled her in for a hug. Tears slipping down her cheeks, they heard a knock at the door. It was Bryce.

When he walked into the room, he froze when he saw Julia for the first time. His eyes welled up, and he covered his mouth with his hand, trying to hold back the wave of emotions.

She couldn't help but sob. "Hi," she squeaked out as the word trailed off while she wrapped her arms around him.

"You look so beautiful, my dear," his voice crackled as he stepped forward to embrace the bride.

"Thank you," she managed to say. "Ready to walk me down the aisle?" Her heart ached at the gravity of what they were about to share.

"I am. More than ready," Bryce replied, his voice shaking as he tried to steady his nerves. To distract himself, he turned to Sydney, who was standing there in her pretty dress. "Wow, Sweetie pie, you look so grown up," he said, his voice brimming with pride.

"Thank you, Grandpa Bryce," she replied, flashing him a bright smile. "You look pretty handsome in your tux, too."

Bryce's heart swelled with love. Never having had the chance to walk anyone down the aisle before, he knew it was a moment he would cherish for a lifetime.

The officiant knocked on the door and gave Jenna a two-minute warning. "Everybody ready?" she asked.

Julia nodded. So did Sydney and Bryce.

Meanwhile, Ty was pacing with Dan and the boys in a separate room, his heart pounding out of his chest. He could hardly wait to see Julia, to stand at the altar and promise himself to her for the rest of their lives. The guys joked to lighten the mood, but Ty wasn't listening. It was game time, and he was focused, imagining her walking down the aisle toward him.

As the minutes ticked by, the officiant arrived and shook his hand.

"We are ready to begin. Follow me," the man said as they entered the large room, where their guests were already seated.

Walking down the aisle with Dan, his best man, and Alex and Brayden, his groomsmen, Ty turned and stood at the wedding arch to wait for Julia to arrive. Pretty music added to the magical theme.

Outside the hall, Julia joined Bryce in the corridor. When she heard the wedding music start to play, she gave him the biggest hug. "Are you doing okay?" she asked as he looked on and nodded. "Thank you for giving me away."

"There is nowhere else I'd rather be than right here beside you, my dear." Getting emotional, he paused and cleared his throat. "You deserve so much happiness, and I can see that you are wholeheartedly in love with Ty."

She nodded tearfully.

"Then, that makes me happy too." Offering his arm to her, Jenna and Sydney led the way down the aisle ahead of them. Bryce glanced over and said, "Here we go..."

She smiled while he led her through the archway.

That night, with the lights twinkling like a magical winter forest, Julia emerged at the end of the aisle, her smile wide and tears glistening in her eyes. As she walked toward Ty, his emotions were noticeably running high.

Keeping it together as best he could, he watched her inch closer.

Dan patted his shoulder, offering a reassuring presence as the groom anxiously shifted his weight.

Shaking Bryce's hand, the man took it with a tremble, his own eyes brimming with emotion.

Reaching out, Julia grasped hold of her groom.

Immediately, he noticed the familiar shimmer of his Mother's pin on her dress. The symbol of family and love that transcended generations. In that moment, the past seemed to blur away, leaving only the two of them together at last.

In the blink of an eye, the pastor pronounced them husband and wife after the exchanging of vows and the giving of rings in front of an emotional room.

Without hesitation, he kissed Julia, whispering, "I love you, Mrs. Reynolds."

She replied softly, her voice thick with emotion, "I love you too, Mr. Reynolds," just as a wave of applause erupted to celebrate their union.

Radiating with joy, they walked down the aisle arm and arm.

Surrounded by family and friends, the happy couple accepted congratulatory hugs and best wishes before sitting down for dinner. From corner to corner, they could feel the place was alive with warmth and laughter.

Nearing the end of the meal, Ty stood up to give his speech.

Being in the public eye for so long made speaking easy for him, but tonight was different. Stepping toward the podium with his paper in hand, he said to the crowd, "Good evening, everyone. As you may have guessed, I am playing the groom's position today, not first base."

Everyone chuckled.

He turned to Julia with a gentle smile. "I was asked to pass along an abundance of congratulations from the team. Unfortunately, they couldn't be here today as they're spending Christmas with their families, but every single one of them said they're with us in spirit, cheering us on."

Julia acknowledged the news happily.

"Most of you know me as last year's mystery guest. Before I arrived, people were under the impression I was trying to avoid the holidays at all costs. And if you thought that, then I would say you would have been right. But upon arrival, I spotted the most beautiful woman I'd ever seen. Dressed in tights, a t-shirt, and a chunky knit sweater, I watched her shuffle along in her slippers before she ran straight into a Christmas tree. Making an excellent play, she saved the tree from falling over and smashing the ornaments, but in the process, that pretty woman with black-rimmed glasses and her blonde hair in a messy bun stole my heart. After that, she helped me find my room – which was, to her dismay, conveniently located – right   across – the – hall from her."

Their guests laughed at how Ty paused for dramatic effect.

"Now, some would say our meeting was a coincidence, while others believed Nick from the front desk was playing matchmaker."

The staff nodded in agreement.

"But, personally," Ty stated, "I think Sydney was quite instrumental in hindsight."

The little girl grinned from ear to ear.

"Nonetheless, I intentionally invaded the Mariani's resort activities that week and the rest is history," Ty confessed. "To date, we've had a year of new beginnings. While I enter retirement, I know my biggest accomplishment wasn't playing for the Braves or the Sox or winning the World Series. Having the honor of being introduced as Julia's loving and devoted husband and Sydney's supportive and caring Dad will far outweigh all of that. So, please raise a glass to toast my lovely wife, Julia, and daughter Sydney. I love you both always and forever. I can hardly wait to see what this new season of life has in store for us. Cheers."

The room celebrated Ty's toast with the clinking of glasses. When he walked back to Julia, everyone urged them to kiss.

"We can't break tradition," he said humorously. Sauntering up to her, he gently cupped her cheeks and looked lovingly into her eyes before kissing her sweetly. All the women in the room melted.

Sydney hid her eyes, not wanting to see the mushy part.

Upon letting go of Julia, Ty tapped Syd's shoulder as she snuck a peek, wondering if the coast was clear. Kneeling with open arms, he hugged her tightly and said, "Love you, too, Syd."

"Love you, Ty."

Tearfully realizing it was her turn, Julia walked to the podium. She was extremely nervous.

"As I look around the room tonight, I feel like the luckiest girl in the world. I feel loved, and that is all because of each one of you. Thank you to our Carling Family for all your caring support throughout the years. You always make us feel at home. Thank you to my new sister-in-law and her family for traveling so far to share our special day. I look forward to many more holidays spent together in the future." Sights lowering, her thoughts made her hesitate. "Many of you were there on that fateful day. I don't want to bring sadness into this, but most of you don't realize grief is what drew me to Ty the week we met. If it wasn't for mutually losing someone special around Christmastime, I don't know if we would have stood together before you today. The night Sydney and I were baking our cookies, Syd felt sorry for *the lonely guy across the hall,*" she giggled. "Yes, that is what she'd dubbed him."

Ty laughed, shook his head, and agreed wholeheartedly.

"So, in true Sydney fashion, she knocked on his door with three shortbread cookies. He was pretty happy about them, but it wasn't long before he timidly dropped by in search of the gingerbread I was baking, too. That night, I learned he'd lost his Mom and Dad over the holidays a couple of years before. My heart went out to him because I knew the feeling. Syd will attest to this, but I never discuss David and Ben with strangers. But for some reason, his grief caused me to share our story with him. Maybe fate brought us together, or that guy named Nick, but from that moment on, we had a bond. And it wasn't morbid or sad - somehow, our stories became tales of survival and the strength to live despite the loss. That is how I met Ty Reynolds. Not the Red Sox baseball player, but the Ty who wears his heart on his sleeve. The man who saved my Sydney and shared in our many holiday traditions. The patient, kind, and giving man who taught me how to love again." Julia raised her glass and looked at her husband. "Ty, I will love you always and forever."

There was not a dry eye in the room when he walked over to embrace his wife.

"Now, I have a few special mentions, first, to my daughter Sydney. I thank God for you every day. You are such a strong, confident young woman, and I am so proud of who you have become. Your Dad and brother would be proud, too. And to our Grandpa Bryce. Thank you for creating a safe haven for us so many years ago. You protected us, prayed for us, and supported us through thick and thin like every loving father would do. So, with that said, I was hoping you'd do me the greatest honor of a father-daughter dance?"

Everyone applauded.

Bryce beamed. "The honor is mine."

Meeting Julia on the dance floor, the music reminded him of dancing with his wife Bev many moons ago. Never having children of their own, he knew Julia and Sydney had fulfilled a lifelong dream of having a daughter and granddaughter. Now, with a son-in-law and extended family introduced to the mix, he felt his life was complete.

The wedding celebration ended in the early morning hours.

Ready to head upstairs, they walked with Jenna and her family and rode the elevator together. The soft hum of conversation filled the air as they discussed the wedding and how perfect the day had been. Fondly recalling the magical evening, Julia took a deep breath, happy everything went as planned.

When they reached the fourth floor, they bid Jenna and her family goodnight, exchanging heartfelt hugs and parting words. As the families went their separate ways, Ty reached for Julia's hand, his other arm securely cradling Sydney, who was fast asleep on his shoulder.

Julia glanced up at him, her heart swelling at the sight of her husband effortlessly balancing strength and tenderness.

He caught her gaze and smiled softly. "She's out cold," he whispered, shifting Sydney slightly to keep her comfortable.

"It's been a busy day."

"Yes, it has," Ty said, giving Julia's hand a gentle squeeze. They walked slowly down the quiet hallway, savoring the peace and the joy that the night had brought.

Going into their suite, he walked to Syd's bedroom and gently rested the little girl's head on the bed, leaving Julia to change her into pajamas.

Waiting for his wife, he watched as she exited the room and left Syd's door open slightly. Extending his hand to her, Ty stopped and scooped her into his arms before effortlessly carrying her across the threshold. Her eyes sparkled with joy as she looked up at him, clearly enchanted.

"Well, I guess from now on, you're stuck with me."

Her smile widened as she wrapped her arms around his neck, pulling him closer. "I could very easily get used to this."

Capturing her lips in a soft, lingering kiss, he suggested, "Shall we get some sleep?"

With a playful twinkle in her eye, she replied, "Not just yet."

Ty smiled and hugged her even tighter. "If you insist," he teased, his voice soft with affection. "We have all the time in the world now." Those words held a deeper meaning—no more goodbyes, no more short visits. His eyes met hers with a soft, contented gaze as if he was savoring the moment and everything it represented.

"I love you, Mr. Reynolds," she said again.

"I will forever love you more." Taking a moment, wondering how to phrase what he needed to say, he took a deep breath. "For Sydney's sake, I think you should keep your name and use Mrs. Mariani-Reynolds."

Understanding what he meant, she nodded, touched by the sentiment.

As they stood together, Ty's heart swelled with gratitude. Finally, having a family of his own, he knew his Mother would be watching over them, guiding them with a quiet, loving presence. This wasn't just a night of celebration; it was the start of a new chapter—one filled with hope, love, and a lifetime commitment to one another. With Julia by his side and Sydney nestled in their hearts, Ty felt complete. Straightening his posture, he whispered to Julia, "Thank you for loving me."

79

December 21st

One Year Later

A year had passed since their lives had taken a turn none of them could have predicted. After a year of transition, full of firsts, the new house, once filled with the chaos of everyday life, now carried a quieter kind of warmth—steady, comforting, like the glow of the fireplace crackling in the nearby living room.

Outside, a light snow was falling, dusting the neighborhood in a pristine white blanket. It clung to the branches of the evergreen trees lining the driveway and softened the sharp edges.

In the foyer, Sydney and Ty were working hard, putting the finishing touches on their towering Christmas tree. At twelve feet tall, it soared toward the cathedral ceiling, its star nearly brushing the second-floor railing. From top to bottom, Ty used a step ladder to hang his Mother's cherished ornaments amongst the bobbles and bows. Admiring the intricate glass angels that seemed to sparkle with an inner light to the faded wooden snowflakes she had painted herself decades ago, each piece told a story.

Sydney reached out, adjusting a small silver bell near the middle of the tree. The chime was soft and sweet as she let it settle into place.

"This one was her favorite," he murmured, his voice filled with a nostalgic kind of joy.

Etching that to memory, Sydney nodded, happy to hear this.

Standing back, he looked up at the star perched at the very top of the tree. "She always said Christmas was the one time of year where everything felt right, no matter what," he said, his voice steady but laden with emotion. "She would've loved all of this."

The two lingered in the moment, the silence filled with unspoken words and shared memories. It wasn't just the tree or the ornaments—it was the way the light caught each one and the faint scent of pine mingling with the scented cinnamon sticks Sydney dispersed through it a little while beforehand.

The house felt alive, not just decorated, and carried with it the essence of those they all missed.

And as they stood there, side by side, Ty asked, "So, Syd. What do you think? Are we done?"

She rubbed her chin between her fingers. "I think so. Just in time, too." Peering out the window at the snow falling, she said, "They should be here by now." Worried, she went to sit on the floor in the dining room.

"They said they'd be here shortly," Ty acknowledged while checking his phone. "The weather probably slowed them down."

The girl gasped as headlights glimmered down the street. "Hey! Is that them?"

Ty moved to the security panel and remotely opened the wrought-iron gate. "Looks like it."

The SUV's tires crunched over the snowy driveway as Sydney flung the front door open, the icy air rushing in. "Mom, Aunty Jenna is here!"

"I'm coming. I'm coming!" Her Mother called from her office.

When the SUV stopped, the door swung open, and Jenna stepped out, bundled in a thick coat and scarf. Her face lit up as she was the first to enter the house.

"Hello, Ms. Sydney! Merry Christmas, dolly," she said joyfully, hugging her tightly.

"Merry Christmas, Aunty Jenna!" Sydney beamed, wrapping her arms around her tightly.

Once she let go of her niece, Ty stopped for a hug, too.

"I can't believe we made it. Merry Christmas, Ty."

"Merry Christmas to you, too," he replied, his voice filled with relief. "It's snowing pretty hard. Glad you made it safe and sound. I'm going to help the guys with the bags."

Jenna spotted Julia rounding the corner. "Hello, my sister," she said excitedly.

With open arms, Julia exclaimed, "I'm so happy to see you."

"Oh, you look wonderful." Jenna placed her hands on Julia's growing belly. "This is amazing—only four more days to go. Don't worry. We are here now, so there is nothing to fear. I'll take care of whatever you need. You will not have to lift a finger. Oh, I can hardly wait! There is nothing like holding a newborn baby."

"Ty will need all the help he can get. He is super nervous." Her hand instinctively rested on her bump.

"Don't worry. He'll be a great Dad," Jenna confirmed sincerely. Wanting to lighten the mood, she added, "Athletes always man up in the thick of the game."

Julia laughed. "I hope you're right." She had experience with this, but it was unfamiliar territory for him. No matter how she tried to reassure her husband, he was worried about everything. She hoped Jenna could help keep him calm and level-headed through it all.

Reaching over, the woman gave her arm a reassuring squeeze. "He loves you and Sydney. Trust me, when it's time, he'll know what to do."

The conversation seamlessly shifted to lighter topics. The sisters-in-law shared laughs and stories, catching each other up on milestones that had happened since their summer visit to the new lake house.

Through it all, Julia's heart held onto Jenna's words. Seeing Ty come through the doorway, bags in hand, she believed he would be fine and knew everything would fall into place.

CHRISTMAS DAY

In the early hours of Christmas Morning, Julia and Ty welcomed their son,

Parker Bryce Reynolds, into the world at 4:34 AM.

His middle name honored the wonderful man closest to Julia's heart. Although saddened that Bryce did not get a chance to meet their little boy, she knew he and Bev were watching them from above and smiling.

NEW YEAR'S EVE

Returning home from the hospital, they slowly settled into life as a family of four.

The living room buzzed with warmth and laughter as the family gathered around the large dining table.

Raising his glass of champagne, Ty offered a toast. "Even though we didn't get to spend the holidays north of the city this year, having our little man makes it all worthwhile." He turned toward the small bundle cradled in Julia's arms and smiled. "Welcome to the family, Parker. You've already brought more joy into our lives than I ever thought possible." Pausing a second, he turned to his sister and her family, "Thank you for your support and for coming to celebrate the holidays in Toronto. It means the world to us. And finally, to Julia and Sydney. You've given me something I never thought I'd ever have in this lifetime – the love of family," he said, holding back his emotions. "I'm looking forward to another year of exciting firsts. Here's to continuing our traditional Christmas in Carling holiday together next year."

"To Christmas in Carling!" Sydney exclaimed.

The group raised their glasses, "Cheers to that!"

The End